1-13-97 Mys Guild 10.00

Father Dowling #13

DEMCO

❧ THE ❧
TEARS OF
THINGS

A Father Dowling Mystery

Ralph McInerny

St. Martin's Press
New York

ISBN 0–312–14746–5

For Dan and Amy

Sunt hic etiam sua praemia laudi;
sunt lacrimae rerum et mentem mortalia tangunt.

Aeneid I, 461–2

❧ THE ❧
TEARS OF THINGS

Ponader's Motors occupied a prime corner in downtown Fox River, once the site of a building reminiscent of the Sullivan School of Architecture that had fallen as a casualty to "urban renewal." After its subsidized razing had taken place, no immediate plans for the use of the location emerged, and Ponader's was given a lease that had been renewed annually over a ten-year period.

Perhaps this contributed to the temporary look of the place. The first time Winegar saw the lot he seemed to recognize it. It looked like the dozen other used car lots in which he had worked over the years. The sales manager recognized him as a brother under the skin, and he was told to call in the next day; there might be an opening. But he had meant it, and soon Winegar had his own desk in the mobile home mounted on a platform that housed Ponader's Motors. One came out of the office onto the platform and could look out over the rows of automobiles, the flapping pennants, the placards in the windshields enticing potential buyers. Secondhand cars, a secondhand life. Winegar was off the sauce now and had been clean since August and was in stage two. Stage one was deep depression, stage two began with a sense of physical well-being, almost euphoria, but that eventually gave way to a philosophical phase in which the futility of his life seemed inescapable. If he didn't watch out, he would soon be making the argument that he had nothing to lose by getting drunk just one more time.

"Why Fox River?" Blake the sales manager had wanted to know when Winegar did in fact call him the following day.

"Why not?"

"Don't get me started."

"I used to live here."

"No kidding."

"Before your time."

Blake gave him the fish eye. "I've been here over twenty years."

"Where'd you come from?"

Blake's curiosity gave way to a chance to talk about himself, or at least to tell a story of which he was the principal character, if not hero. It was a story Winegar could have told himself. All the accidents and enemies that had thwarted his life, the big chance missed by a whisker, the promotion lost to a relative of the owner. In a well-ordered universe—this was the moral—Blake would be at the top of the heap and appreciated for what he was.

The first day on the job the lot was open until nine, and afterward Blake suggested dinner, and Winegar answered that he'd better wait until his first paycheck.

"You can pay me back."

They went to a steak house where the bar was busier than the restaurant. The drinks were served in glasses the size of bowls.

"I said it was on me," Blake said when Winegar ordered a Coke.

"I'm on the wagon."

"Never trust a man who doesn't drink," Blake said, but it was just something to say. He wasn't going to let Winegar's Coke interfere with his enjoyment of his triple scotch.

"What's the happy hour like here?"

"This is it. It never stops." Every third drink was free. At the bar patrons sat with three drinks in front of them, saving money.

Winegar was still in phase two, and the smell of booze and smoke, the din of the bar, gave him a pleasant sense of being above and beyond all that. Once he too had swilled it down the way Blake was doing, talking more, and louder, as he did. He had enough experience on the wagon to know not to try to talk when a drinker was talking.

"Who's Ponader?"

"He's dead."

"So who owns the business?"

"The widow." He added, as if reading Winegar's thoughts, "She's built like a Sherman tank."

What did Blake know of Sherman tanks? Everyone has his surprises. Blake lived with a handicapped wife—"Being married to me is only one of her handicaps"—was a devoted husband, even if he drank too much, and was a World War II buff. He had four shelves full of it and spoke with the authority of a veteran of every battle. He had been born the year of Pearl Harbor.

* * *

Mrs. Ponader was not built like a Sherman tank; there was a lot of her, but it was proportioned and compensated for by an extremely pretty face. By his second week at the lot, Winegar had the use of a car, and he reacquainted himself with Fox River. He drove by the address given for Mrs. Ponader in the book. It was only a block away from Nancy's house.

Mrs. Ponader's day seemed the definition of dullness. Three days a week she went shopping, an endless browsing through malls and boutiques and department stores, always buying an item or two. Winegar knew he was entering phase three when he asked himself if his life was any more futile than hers. She often had lunch at Dayton's Tearoom, and it was there that Winegar accidentally made her acquaintance, turning to ask if he might borrow the sugar from her table. It was the first chance he'd had when she didn't have another widow along with her.

"I haven't seen you here before," he said.

"But I come here often."

"You're Marjorie White, aren't you?"

Marjorie White was a woman with whom Winegar had seen Clara Ponader on other occasions.

"Do you know her?"

Soon he had joined her and gotten the conversation away from who he knew and did not know. He had already decided that he would not tell her he worked for her. He doubted she had any idea who worked at the used car lot, let alone at the massive Honda franchise her husband had also left her. He told her he was a broker and that afternoon turned in his notice to Blake.

"What the hell?"

"Sorry, Jimbo. Something has turned up."

"In Fox River?"

He punched his arm. "I'll keep in touch."

"You owe me a dinner."

"Tonight?"

Blake said no. It was his bowling night. Winegar had known that. He figured he had enough money for a week, but Mrs. Ponader was going to be his way to meet Nancy on an equal basis.

He applied for unemployment and then drove to St. Hilary's Parish to register.

3

2

Marie Murkin watched television furtively during the day, never wanting to admit to herself that a person in her position, housekeeper of St. Hilary's Rectory, could stuff her head with the nonsense that filled the screen from morning to night. If nothing else the practice had taught her how to lip-read because she kept the volume down very low, not wanting to be teased by Father Dowling about her addiction to the soaps. The programs were like a window into a world Marie found incredible: women leading loose lives as if there were nothing odd about it, people falling into bed with one another at a moment's notice. The only redeeming thing about it was how miserable they all were. It seemed a backhanded endorsement of the moral law.

If there was a confessable fault associated with watching television it was the resentment she felt when the doorbell rang at an inopportune time. But, like a good soldier, she stomped immediately down the hall, doing her duty, not wanting the pastor to get there before her.

"Mrs. Murkin?"

He was a handsome man of obvious charm, the kind of man a woman instinctively distrusts and is helpless with. Marie smiled vaguely, embarrassed that she did not recognize the man.

"Of course you won't remember me. Not after all these years."

It might have been a scene in one of her television dramas. For a mad moment Marie imagined that sometime long ago she and this very good-looking man had, well, never mind.

"Is Father Pachomius still the pastor?"

Marie actually fell back a step. She could count the people in the parish who still remembered Packy, the mad friar who had all but ruined the parish during a three-year appointment.

"That was nearly twenty years ago."

4

"Twenty-one."

"So you do remember."

And then she realized that she was talking to him through the screen door, that he was still standing on the doorstep and must think she was about to slam the door on him. She unhooked the screen door and pushed it open.

"Father Dowling's the pastor now."

"Another friar?"

"No, thank God." It was out before she could stop it, and she clamped a hand over her mouth, but the man's eyes twinkled with delight at the revelation. Out of the friar pan into the fire, that had been Marie's view during her first years here when the archbishop turned the parish over to the order. The first pastor they sent was good, too good for this earth. He died six months after being appointed. Marie had seen four friars in all before the cardinal recognized his mistake and took the parish back. That was when Father Dowling had been named pastor, and it had marked a turning point.

"I would have strangled him if he weren't a priest," the man said. Somehow he had taken her hand in his. "My name is Winegar. Father Pachomius advised a girl not to marry me."

She took him into a parlor where he could sit while she called the pastor, but he went on talking for all the world as if he had come to see her. Marie sat in a chair near the door, not getting comfortable, just getting off her feet, and listened to Mr. Winegar tell her about the girl he had wanted to marry and would have too if it hadn't been for the interfering pastor of St. Hilary's.

"Why did he stop it?"

"Who knows? I never got to have a proper talk with him."

"I don't remember it. Not that Packy told me much. He thought he could come in here and run things without relying on advice or experience or anybody else."

Winegar shook his head, as if he found this an old, and all-too-familiar story. And then his expression changed as he looked toward the door. Father Dowling was standing there.

"This is Mr. Winegar," Marie said, scrambling to her feet. "He belonged to the parish ages ago."

"No, no. I wasn't a parishioner. The girl was."

"The pastor then advised her not to marry."

Father Dowling managed to respond to these various bits of information in a receptive way, but he said nothing.

5

"But I came to join the parish now," Winegar said. "How do I go about it?"

"Why don't we go into my study." He turned away but then stopped and looked back. "You've finished with him, haven't you, Marie?"

Oh, she could murder him when he said things like that, particularly in front of someone as nice as Mr. Winegar. But the caller laughed as if it were a great joke, and he and Father Dowling went down the hall to his study. Marie stayed in the front parlor for a moment, waiting to see if Father Dowling would close the door of his study, but he didn't. A moment later she drifted silently down the hall, through the dining room, and into the kitchen, where she moved a chair to keep the door ajar. The flickering television distracted her, and she turned it off. She had a premonition that Mr. Winegar promised a real-life story far more interesting than the contrived melodramas of daytime television.

But a moment later there was the sound of the study door closing. Miffed, Marie moved the chair again, let the door swing shut, and turned on the television.

She was surprised to find, forty-five minutes later, that Mr. Winegar had left without her hearing him go. She had looked out several times to see if the study door was still closed. Then, having turned off the television for good, she went up the hall to the front door, just to check and make sure that it was tightly closed, and as she came quietly back, cocked her ear for the sound of voices. Nothing. She stopped and tapped at the study door.

"Come in."

Inside, wreathed in pipe smoke, engrossed in a book, was Father Dowling.

"You're alone."

"Not when I have a good book."

"I didn't hear him leave."

He pretended not to understand, and she had to make it a direct question. "Mr. Winegar. When did he leave?"

The pastor shrugged. "I don't log them in and out, Marie. When did he come?"

Well, she should have known he would bring that up. "He detained me in the parlor."

"Did he?"

She shut her eyes. This was her penance for the mild imagining she had done before she let Mr. Winegar in.

"Supper's in ten minutes."

"Detained you about what?"

6

"He remembered another pastor. Father Pachomius. He thought he was still here."

"Ah."

"Did he join the parish?"

"The card is on my desk, if you want to check it. And I gave him a box of envelopes for the collection, although I gather he's between jobs."

Marie's eye was drawn to the card on the desk that would contain basic information about the visitor, but she was darned if she would give in to her curiosity. She would look it up tomorrow when Father Dowling was away.

"A very romantic story."

"Oh." She put the back of a hand to her forehead and looked distractedly about.

"But I won't bother you with it."

"About Father Pachomius telling a girl not to marry him?"

"That's right. You'd already gotten that out of him."

"Supper," she repeated, the soul of patience. She would not let him get to her. "Supper is in ten minutes."

Her passage down the hall was regal. She went through the dining room with head held high, but in the kitchen she clenched her fists and vowed that she would never never again give the pastor an excuse to treat her as if she were prying into matters that were not her concern.

Clara Ponader believed her friends when they told her how lucky she was, the way Don had left everything to her, free and clear, joint property before he was even ill, so that when he died there was no fuss about inheriting or taxes or anything like that. It was all hers.

"You'll never have another worry in your life," Marjorie White assured her.

Marjorie had to fight the state and her children for the sliver she got from what Chet had left, which hadn't been that much in the first place. That was why Clara always picked up the check unobtrusively when she and Marjorie had lunch together; she did not want her generosity resented. Once she would have joked about widows getting together to shop and have lunch and waste the day together, but she really did not know what she would do without Marjorie. Marjorie might not get along with her kids, but at least she had kids to fight with. Don had left a childless Clara well-fixed and the owner of a prosperous auto dealership. On business matters she didn't know what she would do without their attorney, Jason. Like Marjorie, he went back to when Don was still alive.

Don had trusted him completely. It was Jason who had insisted that everything be in both their names, saving her all that money and trouble. And it was Jason whom she asked to keep an eye on the dealership.

"I'm just a lawyer, Clara."

"Is there someone else you would recommend?"

That she could trust the way she trusted him? Not likely. So he was the one the managers of the new and used dealerships reported to. With his skeptical eye watching the books, and the bookkeeper, there was no likelihood that anyone would take advantage of the Widow Ponader.

"I wish you wouldn't call me that."

"It's a title of honor, meant in respect."

"Even so."

"And affection."

Jason, for all his reliability as a lawyer, was a bit of a roué. Oh, nothing scandalous, but he just couldn't abide dining out without a lovely lady across the table from him. It was only natural that Clara half expected, half hoped, that she would become one of his numerous companions, the terrible regiment of women she and Marjorie had once joked about. Maybe Marjorie had hopes as well. But it seemed Jason didn't think of either of them that way, if he thought of Marjorie at all.

While Don was still alive, there were times when she'd been mad at him and imagined how nice life would be without him after he went, as all the actuarial tables insisted he would, before her, but that was just a mood, nothing she really wanted. And she had no idea then how lonely it was to be alone. Men could always go out and find another woman, some young thing who could put on an act for the old dog, willing to endure a few years of servitude in order to get it all when he died. Maybe even women like that came to see how lonely it was. Get beyond a certain age, and men might be nice to you and polite, but that was all. Not even Jason, it seemed, wanted her as a date.

"We never see you at the parish center," Marie Murkin, the busybody housekeeper, said to Clara one day.

"Isn't that for senior citizens?"

There was no way Marie could answer that without insulting her, so she hadn't answered. But Clara did get a call from Edna Hospers, who directed the center, wondering if she would be interested in volunteer work.

"Volunteer work?"

"Nothing burdensome, a little help around the office, help in organizing things for the old people."

"Is Marie Murkin involved?"

"Good Lord, no."

So Clara had gone to the school one day and been shown around by Edna, looking for a sign that this was all a ruse to get her to admit that she was the age of most of the people who showed up every day for cards and shuffleboard or to just sip coffee and talk. The truth was, Clara found it attractive, but she honestly did not see herself as ready for that. Except as a volunteer, and Edna obviously had meant just that.

"Why did you ask about Marie Murkin?"

"She more or less suggested I should join the old people."

"Marie works in the parish house; I run things here."

Clara discovered that she was good at organizing things, and Edna gave her a free hand. Still, she kept it a secret from Marjorie, not willing to risk her old friend's interpretation of her involvement at St. Hilary's Parish Center. But then she hadn't told Marjorie about going to the noon mass most weekdays either.

Don's death, the wake, the funeral, had opened her eyes, and she realized how little she and Don had ever talked about the fact that, after all, life did come to an end eventually and what did that mean? Of course they were Catholics, but they didn't make a big thing out of it, mass on Sunday except for the rare miss, practicing but not fanatic, they had, she supposed, thought they were good Catholics. Good enough, anyway. Now she felt a duty to pray for Don even as she gave more attention to the condition of her own soul. Father Dowling had been so wonderful during her ordeal, and his sermon at the funeral mass, the words he had said over Don's grave, went straight to Clara's heart. The parish bulletin told her the pastor said mass every day at noon, and one day she went. After that, her lunches with Marjorie were always scheduled at one o'clock.

It was at a noon mass that Marie Murkin had mentioned the parish center, and it nearly decided Clara to stop going. The last thing she wanted to do was turn into what Jason called a sacristy mouse.

"What is a sacristy mouse?" He had been talking about one of his girl-friends.

"She hangs around the church all day, fixing flowers, lighting candles, pestering the priests."

"Is she a widow?"

"Of course she's a widow."

All Jason's girlfriends were widows. He had known their husbands in most cases, the way he had known Don.

"I suppose she's lonely."

"I told her to go sit in a bar."

"Jason!"

Clara too had felt the urge to get religion in a showy way. Thank God she just went to the noon mass and helped out in the parish center and managed to get through her days more or less on her own.

"It is you," a male voice said behind her, and she turned to see the man who had spoken to her in Dayton's Tearoom. Seeing him on the steps of St. Hilary's did much to remove the wariness she had felt talking to him in the tearoom. "Just a gigolo" was the phrase that had banged around in her head on that occasion, from the song with the same words.

"I don't remember your name."

"Winegar. Jerome Winegar."

The name sounded familiar, so he must have told it to her before. What a handsome man he was, much more handsome than he had seemed in the tearoom, where the lighting had a pastel effect more favorable to women than to men, but how many men ever ate there?

"Let me buy you lunch."

"I don't have much time."

"Then we won't have much lunch. Do you have a car?"

Didn't he?

"Mine's in for repairs."

They actually went to a McDonald's when he said he bet she had never been in one.

"I haven't!"

"They're one of the entrepreneurial glories of the nation." He spoke as if he were handing out awards for achievement. What did he do? He certainly wasn't retired; she guessed him to be five years younger than she, perhaps more. He dressed casually, in the kind of clothes that make it im-possible to tell the economic status of the wearer. Some kind of wash pants, a denim shirt, loafers. He might have been a college boy, except for the gray hair and the telltale lines in his face that she began to notice over

10

their meal. Everything was in plastic and Styrofoam and paper, greasy and oily and impossible to eat without making a mess. He laughed when she tried to cut her burger in two with a plastic knife.

"You have to wallow in it. It's the only way."

He showed her how and she followed his example and soon it was the most fun she had had in so long, laughing, and sharing private jokes with him. He had cast her in the role of the pampered woman who had no idea how most people lived. Well, maybe he was right. Walking through malls, she often felt that she was an observer of the others there rather than a shopper herself.

"I will be your guide into darkest America."

She dropped him off back at St. Hilary's at his request.

"Isn't your car in for repairs?"

"I thought I'd drop in on Father Dowling."

"Don't you just love that man?"

He smiled. "I wouldn't put it just that way."

"He's just the way I think a priest should be."

"I'll tell him you said so."

"Don't you dare!"

She watched him walk off in the direction of the parish house, turning twice to wave before she drove away. She went around to the far side of the school and parked there, feeling that she was deceiving Jerome Winegar by not wanting him to know she was a volunteer at St. Hilary's Parish Center. She was late and Edna was aloof and Clara could see she didn't like it.

Marie Murkin said nothing when she heard that Clara Ponader was helping Edna out at the center. She wanted to think that her remark to Clara had borne fruit, but she didn't want to make a point of the little things she did around the parish to make things run smoothly. Priests were necessary, of course, and you would never catch Marie Murkin talking about women getting ordained; besides, she had all she could handle with the Women's Altar Society, a bunch of biddies that made pests of themselves once a week. But a parish did need the woman's touch; there were times when only a woman's voice could speak to another's heart, and now that there weren't any nuns left, nuns like there used to be, Marie felt an expansion in her own role. Like speaking to Clara. But she would not toot her own horn; that would undo all the good doing good did for her. But it did give a sense of satisfaction to see the effect of a chance word of kindness.

"I see Clara Ponader at mass regularly."

"You taking roll, Marie?" Phil Keegan asked, sitting at the dining room table and eating more than his share of the lunch she had prepared for Father Dowling.

"I just notice. The way I notice you there."

The pastor looked as if he was about to say something, then didn't.

"How long's Don been dead?" Phil asked.

"Oh, I think it's been a decent interval, Phil."

"What's that supposed to mean?"

"I think they'd make a nice couple, don't you, Marie?"

"Oh, I do, I do." She just loved it when he turned his teasing on someone else, and Phil Keegan was a fair target, a widower himself and lonely as can be, spending as much time at the parish house as he did. Not that Marie objected. It was good for the two men to have someone to talk sports with, go to games with, commiserate about Chicago teams.

" 'I do, I do,' " Phil chirped, mimicking her. "You sound like you're getting married again yourself."

"Well, if I ever do, you'll be the last to know."

"Less than a year," Father Dowling said, and Marie and Phil turned to stare at him. "Since Don Ponader died."

"I bought at least three cars from that man," Phil said. "Personally. He showed me the car, he talked deal with me, he signed the papers. And not just me. He did that with a lot of people. That's why he prospered."

"Is there money in cars?"

Phil pushed back his chair and stared at the pastor. "Do you know the markup a dealer as successful as Ponader gets on a car?"

"No."

Phil Keegan seemed to have only a vague idea himself, except that he was sure it was a pile. He began to calculate how many cars a dealer like Ponader sold each month, times his cut, less his overhead.

"Are you saying Clara is rich?" Marie asked.

"Why else would Phil want to marry her?" Father Dowling asked.

"Well, he better hurry up," Marie said.

"What do you mean?"

"Oh, never you mind," and she sailed away into the kitchen.

Marie had seen Clara drive off with that nice Mr. Winegar who had come by the rectory, feeling a little pang when she did. A pang of what? Not jealousy, but it devalued the coin to think that he treated every woman as nicely as he had her. Of course, Clara Ponader was not every woman. She was large, Marie told herself, and pretty as her face was, that was simply a fact. Now she had to cope with the thought that Clara had lots of money too. Would she have felt as oddly as she did about seeing Winegar and Clara together if Phil Keegan hadn't mentioned her money? She shook the thought away; it was uncharitable to think that such a good-looking man had to have something in mind when he paid a little attention to a woman who was, after all, considerably older than he was. And it was Clara's car they had gone off in.

She saw them return, saw him get out of the car and start right toward the rectory. Marie stepped back from the window, feeling a sudden excitement. He waved at Clara several times before she finally drove away, and then he kept coming along the walk that would bring him to her kitchen door.

But he veered off and went toward the side door of the church and then along the wall of the church to the street where he got into a car and a moment later drove away. Marie slumped at her kitchen table, feeling almost jilted. What nonsense. She glanced at the clock, then sprang to her feet and turned on the television set.

5

Father Dowling had raised his brows when Edna Hospers mentioned that Clara Ponader was giving her a hand at the parish center.

"Is this Marie's doing?"

"Now, why would you ask that?"

"It isn't?"

"No, it is not, for heaven's sake. I noticed her at mass and thought she looked kind of lost, unoccupied, so I called and asked her to come help out."

"Fine." Edna was pretty insistent on it, and he wished he hadn't mentioned Marie.

"The funny thing is, Clara asked me the same question."

He eased them away from the subject, though he had wanted to talk to Edna a bit about Clara. He found it reassuring that she was pitching in at the parish center. She was nearly as old as the seniors who found the sort of things Edna set up for them to be just what they wanted.

"Mitch Striker has been after me again."

"What is it now?"

"He thinks there should be more for the mind here. That's the way he put it. A discussion group."

"Who would lead it?"

"Guess."

"Did he have any topics in mind?"

"Investments."

"Maybe a certain number would find that interesting."

"Not if Mitch did the talking—as he would."

"He was a broker, Edna. That's how he made his money."

"How can such a bore have such a wonderful daughter?"

"Doesn't he have two?"

"I mean Nancy Walsh. Sometimes she comes early for him and stops by the office. She's apologetic that she can't help. She says it does her father so much good."

"There's your reward."

"Are you saying I should let him start a discussion group?"

"Why don't we just schedule a talk on investments and see how it goes."

"A one-shot?"

"That sounds ominous. Yes, just one."

Mitch arrived at the rectory fifteen minutes after Father Dowling returned. He had olive skin and white hair and black eyes and dressed in a dapper way, but what came through was that Mitch Striker was a fussbudget.

"I can't possibly cover all angles in one talk, Father."

"Of course you can't."

Mitch brightened. "I'll need four at the very least."

"Four would do it?"

"Well, I'd like more, but four could be enough."

"Fine. Just work up a talk with four parts."

"I'm afraid you don't understand how complicated a thing it is to invest money wisely, Father."

"More complicated than Christianity?"

"I don't understand the question."

"I'll tell you what a wise old priest once said to me. He said that when I was a priest people would come and want me to tell them about the church. Now, sometimes they will come for instructions, and you have many meetings and can cover things in some detail. At other times there are fewer meetings. And, Mitch, sometimes you have only a few minutes, someone may be dying, and you have to get it all into the time you have. Now, if Christianity can be condensed into a few minutes . . ."

"I get your point, Father Dowling."

"I thought you would."

"I won't use it in my talk, though."

"Why not?"

"They might misunderstand the analogy and think I am talking to them on their deathbeds."

"How is Nancy?"

"Patient, Father. Patient. They put up with me and I know I am a trial, but whenever I suggest a solution, they won't hear of it. It would be ungrateful of me to tell them that it's not always a treat for Grandpa to be living in the same house as his grandchildren."

"Pretty boisterous?"

"Oh, I don't mean they misbehave."

Mitch seemed to have a series of talks on living with grandchildren too.

"How is your younger daughter?"

"Kate is a young lady, a junior in college."

"How many grandchildren are there?"

"Three boys."

Mitch had been looking around the study. "How this room has changed since the friars ran the parish."

"Were you close to them?"

"Close!" Mitch found the question unintelligible. "No. Well, I went toe to toe with one, I can tell you that, and in this room. Father Pachomius."

"About investments?"

"Father, I don't like to think about it even today, after all these years, but this room brought it back." He got to his feet, using the arm of the chair as a lever. He seemed to crank into an erect posture. "I hope you'll come to my lecture, Father."

"I wouldn't miss it, Mitch."

Edna Hospers had been asked to set up and direct a parish center in the St. Hilary school at a moment in her life when work was a necessity both financially and psychologically. Her husband Earl, desperate, had run afoul of the law and been sent off to Joliet for longer than either of them could begin to imagine, leaving Edna with the three kids. It had been the need for money that had caused Earl to go off the rails, so there was nothing on which Edna could rely: If she didn't earn it, they didn't have it. And of course there had been the shame. She had thought of packing up the kids and just going off somewhere they wouldn't be known and living an anonymous life. Father Dowling had saved her from all that.

"I don't know anything about running a parish center."

"We'll work it out."

"Father, I don't want charity."

"That's why I will expect a lot of work from you."

He made it easy, in that way he had, and the job reestablished her in the parish; she and the kids held their heads high. And the work turned out to be far more interesting than she would have expected. And she was good at it, as Father Dowling had assured her she would be.

As long as you thought of the elderly people who came to what had once been the parish school when the city's demographics had been such that young families made up a good portion of the parish, it really wasn't a job. Think of them as relatives, as your own parents, and somehow you knew what to do.

The great danger was to treat them as children, much as they invited it sometimes. What Edna never got over were the crushes and romances that bloomed and faded among these people in the twilight of life. Sometimes she wondered if life wasn't a big circle and people come back to what they were as kids. Arthritic old women would simper like debutantes, and silver-haired men would push out their chests and strut among the women. Sometimes the friendships formed were so tender, they brought tears to the eyes. And sometimes there were cases like Barbara Rooney and Mitch Striker. Poor Barbara followed him around with a rapt mooning look, but if Mitch even noticed her, he gave no sign.

"Ask him about investments," Edna had suggested.

"Investments!" Barbara just stared at her. "I don't know anything about investments."

"Mr. Striker does."

The rouged lips formed a comprehending O, and Barbara went off to address the male pride of Mitch Striker. With mixed results. Out of it had come the persistent suggestion, from him, that he lecture everyone as a group on the science and art of financial investment. Father Dowling's solution was worthy of King Solomon, maybe, but they still had to listen to the dapper old bore pontificate.

Barbara made it clear to everyone that it was her suggestion that lay behind the lecture, a claim that gained her equivocal responses. Gerry Major was furious.

"Getting him not to talk, now that would be an accomplishment."

"You could do worse than listen to him, Gerald," Barbara said primly.

"I could do better too."

"You're just jealous."

Gerry glared at her, then spun on his heel and marched off, bumping into an approaching Mitch Striker and sending him reeling. It is in the nature of the relations between the sexes that a woman is attracted not to the man who wants her but to the man who does not. So perhaps it was inevitable that Barbara did not see the merits in Gerry, who clearly wanted to know her better, and hankered after Mitch, who saw in her only the means whereby he would at last be able to talk investment common sense to this group of people.

Winegar, when he came by one day for Clara, saw the announcement of the lecture and made a face.

"Do you know him?" Edna asked.

"I know the type."

Edna laughed. "How can you, from just the notice of a talk?"

"I've never liked people who make a religion of money."

It was a surprising leap; so far as Edna knew, Winegar had never so much as laid eyes on Mitch Striker. It turned out that Clara had urged him to come hear the talk.

"I know Mitch is good. He has always been a great help to me."

The remark suggested a very different world from the one in which Edna lived. That the problem with money might be where to invest it rather than having enough in the first place was foreign to her. Oddly, though, it made her like Clara even more. Edna wondered if she would be so generous with her time if like Clara, apparently, she could do anything she wanted, go anywhere. The thought was dizzying.

"Do you travel much?"

"Florida in the winter."

"Have you been outside the country?"

Clara wrinkled her nose. She and her husband had been to Europe several times, and to the Far East.

"I was always so glad to get home. Of course, everyone speaks English everywhere now, but it is so different."

"Foreign?"

"Now, don't tease. I suppose you're good at languages."

"Computer languages."

18

But then she had the advantage there of her son Carl. Edna liked to browse through travel programs on Prodigy, seeing what trips to far-off places would cost. Not that she ever thought she would actually go.

Edna dreamed that when the family was all together again, Earl back with them, they would go to exotic places and try to make up for the years they had lost. What exotic places had to do with this daydream would be difficult to say; perhaps they only emphasized the unlikelihood of the family ever being the same as it had been before Earl had destroyed it all with several terrible deeds. Edna did not believe that if he had gone unapprehended their life could have gone on unaffected by what he had done.

"Will you introduce Mitch, Father?"

"You're in charge, Edna. I won't interfere."

"I hope you intend to be there."

"Investment opportunities are not high on my list of things to learn about, Edna."

"Father, I need someone who can bring the evening to a close. You know how Mitch is. I am afraid that no one will be able to pry him away from that podium once he has a grip on it."

"I'll be there."

He didn't really want to leave his comfortable study and walk over to the school and listen to a boring talk. But who did? Apart from Clara and Barbara . . . Oh, be fair, Edna chided herself. For all I know, most people are looking forward to the talk.

On the afternoon of the day the talk was scheduled, when the old people began to leave for the day, Mitch was out on the front walk as if he too had wondered how many of them would come back in order to hear him speak. Edna had tried in vain to get him to schedule it for the end of the regular day, at four-thirty. Mitch shook his head.

"No, Edna. I want them fresh. Have you ever looked at this bunch at that time of today? Let them go home, take a nap, freshen up, have a little supper. Then they'll be more receptive."

He was handing out a photocopied page on which a bar graph showed how swiftly and surely money would grow for one who followed the investment advice of Mitch Striker. Edna had studied it in disbelief. Mitch's chart showed what an investment of twenty thousand dollars would look like by the time one reached sixty-five. But the old people to whom he aspired to talk were over sixty-five. Mitch's chart could only make them resent not knowing when they were young what the chart told them now.

Edna went back to her office with the mordant certainty that Mitch Striker would be lucky if he drew an audience of half a dozen.

Disaster was avoided by the fact that Barbara brought three guests who had never before visited the center but whom she had persuaded that this was the chance of a lifetime. Gerry Major was there, slumped in a chair, one of the photocopied bar graphs crumpled in his hand, brooding as once Napoleon had brooded on Elba. The Dailey twins were there, bald, beaming, deaf, but then they always seemed loath to leave in the afternoon and were among the first to arrive each morning. Edna had no illusions about the center and wondered how lonely a life must be for one to look forward so eagerly to being there. It wasn't that the Dailey twins were escaping each other; they were inseparable during the day. But here they were, the souls of expectation, occupying seats in the front row.

The podium had been moved several times by Barbara, first to the left, then to the center, then back to the left. She took the opportunity, as long as she was on her feet, to look about to see if Mitch had arrived. She smiled vacantly at Edna, then drifted toward her.

"Is Father Dowling coming?"

"He may be a little late."

"I haven't seen Mr. Striker yet."

"I don't think he will miss it."

"Oh, I'm sure he won't," Barbara said, beyond irony. "I suggest that we give everyone plenty of time to get back. There really isn't that much time to go home, do whatever, and come back."

"That is what I told Mitch, but he didn't want to speak earlier."

"He is experienced in these matters, Edna."

So popular he never speaks twice in the same place? Edna went to the door that opened onto the parking lot, but there did not appear to be any more cars than before. Even as she watched, Clara's vehicle pulled in. Edna waited long enough to see if Clara had brought Winegar along. But she was alone. So Edna had lost a bet with herself.

Edna had been following what seemed to her to be a growing friendship between Clara and the handsome newcomer to Fox River.

"Not entirely new, Edna," Clara corrected. "He lived here years ago."

"What does he do?"

Clara leaned toward Edna and whispered, "Don't tell Mitch Striker. He is a broker."

Was it loyalty to an old friend that had brought Clara out on a night like this? The sky was darkening to the west, and the trees lining the lot were moving in a freshening wind. She held the door open, and Clara almost literally blew in.

"It's going to rain."

That seemed a good excuse to get the evening going on time and moving right along. Edna glanced toward the rectory, its lights looking cheerful and bright in the gloaming, and she wished Father Dowling were here to present Mitch to his handful of listeners. But the speaker had not yet arrived.

"I wish he would come," Edna said when once more Barbara drifted from her friends to stand beside her.

"Oh, he's here."

"Good. I think we should start right on the dot. The weather is looking worse all the time."

This was doubtful doctrine in Barbara's book, but she apparently decided not to contest it. "When he comes in."

"I thought he was here."

"I see his car in the lot. I suppose he's gathering his thoughts before coming in."

Ye gods. If Mitch developed stage fright after pressing so hard for this evening lecture, Edna would personally brain him.

"Which car is his?"

"The yellow one. There in the corner, near the walkway to the rectory."

"I don't see anyone in it."

"Can you actually see that far?"

The first drops of rain hit the window as she looked through it toward the yellow car. Beyond, the walk to the rectory was empty. It seemed a shame to expect the pastor to come through what was going to be a heavy rainfall by the look of the clouds just to make sure Mitch Striker did not overstrain his audience's patience. This group was too small to bother with anyway. Edna hurried down the hall to her office and called the rectory, closing her eyes and voiding her mind of thought as she listened to Marie Murkin's officious voice.

"St. Hilary's Rectory. Marie Murkin speaking. How may we help you?"

"Marie, this is Edna. Has Father left yet?"

"Are you expecting him?"

"Edna?" It was the voice of Father Dowling on the line. "Thanks, Marie." He waited and soon there was the sound of Marie's receiver being put down.

"Father, I'm calling to tell you not to bother to come over."

"Didn't anyone come?"

"Oh, there's a handful. I meant the weather. It is going to rain, and there's no need for you to come."

"Nonsense. I'll be there. How is Mitch behaving so far?"

"He's still out in his car."

"No."

"You can probably see it from there. The yellow one?"

A pause and then, "There's no one in it."

"Maybe he's here and we haven't noticed."

"That's hard to believe."

"It is, isn't it? Father, don't bother to come."

"A deal's a deal, Edna. I'll be there."

After he hung up, Father Dowling peered out his window again. The rain was coming down heavily now, and he could see it bouncing off the roof of the yellow car whose windows were so obscured by the falling rain that he was no longer certain the car was empty. Mitch was likely to wait for a lull in the rain before making a dash for the school. If he kept people waiting long who had come out on a night like this, the pastor would have words with him. Several times since Edna brought the matter to him he had regretted his proposed solution. At the moment one talk had seemed as nothing compared to the series Mitch yearned to give. Now, on the actual night, Father Dowling felt guilty for having anything to do with bringing people out in weather like this.

He himself was very reluctant to go out into the rain, though he would not let Edna down. She must have stayed on through dinnertime for this. He should get over there right away and give her the chance to get home to her family.

He put on his raincoat as he went down the hallway to the front door, where he drew a large umbrella from the stand. He turned to call out to Marie, but she was standing in the dining room doorway.

"Aren't you ready, Marie?"

"Ready! Ready for what?"

He pulled back his sleeve and looked at his watch. "We're going to be late."

"Late for what?!"

"This is the night of Mitchell Striker's lecture on investments."

Marie threw up her arms. "I'm not going to that."

"You're not?"

"I never planned to."

"Oh, very well. Look after things here while I'm gone."

He stepped outside and pulled the door shut on Marie's consternation. Shame on me, he said, but teasing Marie was such a habit now that she would probably complain at least as much if he stopped.

He felt half soaked before he got the umbrella opened over his head and started down the walkway, avoiding the puddles that had already formed. What a downpour. As he neared the yellow car, he saw no sign that anyone was in it, waiting for the rain to stop or anything else. But he did notice the exhaust, which rose in wreathlike whiteness from the rear of the car to be almost immediately absorbed into the rain as smoke was absorbed by the ashtray Marie had given him for Christmas. Had the car been running when he first looked out his study window?

He went along the driver's side and stooped to peer in, but as he bent over, his umbrella hit the top of the car and he had to tip it back. He put a hand on the window so the rainwater would run around it and provide him with a glimpse within.

Through the wet wavering window he saw Mitch Striker slumped on his side, lying across the seat. Father Dowling grabbed the handle of the car and pulled, but it was locked. Locked! He stood, looked first at the school, and then hurried back up the walk to the rectory.

Inside, he banged his feet and called to Marie. She came dashing out of the dining room, her expression still the annoyed one he had left her with.

"Call Phil Keegan and tell him to come immediately."

"What is it?"

"I think we have a dead body on our hands."

He continued into the study, where he rang Edna's office and then waited and waited before she breathlessly answered.

"Keep them amused until I get there, Edna. Mitch won't be coming, but don't tell them that."

"Is something wrong?"

"I think he's dead."

8

The rain drummed down on the yellow vehicle, lit up now by the spotlights of patrol cars that formed an arc around it, bracketing the ME's mobile unit. Phil Keegan had come outside again, after getting Cy Horvath and Agnes Lamb started on interviewing the old people inside the school, who were getting restless. Phil stepped under Father Dowling's umbrella.

"Any clue on the cause of death?"

"I don't think it was a heart attack or anything like that."

"Was he dead when you got to him?"

Roger Dowling nodded. That was probably the source of the priest's somber demeanor. The last blessing Roger had traced over Mitchell Striker was probably given after his soul had fled. Rain ran from the rim of the umbrella, adding to the puddle the priest was standing in.

"Why don't you go inside, Roger. Cy and Agnes will proceed as quickly as they can, but your parishioners are running out of patience."

"Good idea. Are you staying around?"

"I'll see you later."

He'd stay around. People would misunderstand if he said it out loud, but Phil was almost grateful to be called out at night, even in this kind of weather, away from the loneliness that enveloped him whenever he went home to his apartment. His wife was gone, the loss still a painful memory, and his children and their families lived hundreds of miles away. He would be truly lost without his work and his friendship with Roger Dowling, which took him back to his youth when he too had aspired to the priesthood, ineligible finally because he just could not get the hang of Latin. Or of any language other than English, for that matter. So he had left and gone into the service and served as an MP and joined the Fox River police force when he got out. He had been there ever since, was now captain of detectives, and reacted to the word "retirement" as to an obscenity.

He was filled with buoyancy to be out here in the parking lot, getting drenched, waiting for Lubins the medical examiner and his slowpoke crew to give a preliminary report that might be of some help in determining what had happened and how.

A figure backed out of the car and scampered to the shelter of the mobile unit. Lubins. Keegan followed him in and was there when the body was carried in from the car. Phil looked down at the dead man. In his seventies, the final equivocal expression almost one of surprise, his clothes dry as a bone. Whatever had happened had happened before the rain. The soles of the shoes were also dry.

"Well?" Phil said, looking at Lubins.

"You'd think heart attack, wouldn't you? Motor still running, the driver just keeled over onto the passenger seat, no obvious signs of foul play. A very professional job."

"Murder?"

"Death was not brought about by natural causes," Lubins said carefully.

"What was the unnatural cause?"

Dr. Pippen stepped inside, a raincoat pulled over her golden hair, filling the vehicle with her musky perfume. Her lower lip was puffed out as she blew upward.

"A good night for a murder," she said cheerfully, just glancing at the body. Lubins did not welcome his assistant, but then her glance at the body might have been interpreted as making sure nothing had been screwed up yet. "Isn't this your bridge night?" she said to Lubins.

"I was on duty."

"I can relieve you."

Lubins frowned as if he did not welcome the chance to dump the work onto Pippen's willing shoulders. Why a lovely woman would go through medical school, intern at Cook County, and then take a job with the Fox River medical examiner baffled Keegan.

"Smell anything funny?" Lubins asked Keegan.

"Sorry about the perfume," Pippen said, not sorry at all.

"I meant the chloroform."

Keegan leaned over Striker's body, and sure enough there was the smell of chloroform. Lubins was telling Pippen that he hadn't picked it up right away in the car, what with the rain-washed air rushing in and all.

"Then there's this."

Lubins put his hand behind Striker's right ear and flapped it forward. There was an almost invisible mark in the flesh behind the ear.

"Good work," Pippen said, meaning it, apparently not finding it strange that she should commend her boss. But then she had so few chances to do it.

"Did you check the backseat?" Pippen was asking as Phil went outside.

Now that the ME had finished with it, the car was in the hands of the lab, and investigators were going over it carefully, taking stills and videos, getting ready to haul it off downtown. Phil felt like a spectator and didn't like that at all. He struck off through the rain for the parish center.

Two bald old men who looked like twins stepped aside when Phil came in. They looked at him as if he would prevent their going.

"Has anyone questioned you yet?"

"The black lady." They spoke in unison, two pairs of eyes reading his lips.

"She tell you you could go?"

"Yes."

"It's wet out there."

"Oh, we came prepared."

They took raincoats out of little plastic packs, donned those and rain hats, and produced matching umbrellas that sprang into bloom at the touch of a button. And into the night they went.

Edna Hospers stood with folded arms, talking with Father Dowling and two women, one of whom was crying disconsolately. Was she Mrs. Striker? Edna came toward Phil and shook her head when he put the question to her.

"That's Barbara Rooney. She had a crush on Mitch Striker."

"Who's the one with the pretty face?"

"Clara Ponader."

"I thought I recognized her. She a regular here?"

"She's a volunteer. She helps me out."

"I knew her husband."

"None of these people know anything. What's the point of questioning them?"

"Routine." Meaning he had no better answer. Edna was probably right. Striker was killed in his car in the parking lot while these people waited for him to show up.

But most of them enjoyed being interviewed once it began, and Cy and Agnes took notes like crazy, writing down all kinds of things that would turn out to have nothing at all to do with their effort to find out what had happened in the parking lot. Still, you never knew. It was a way of getting familiar with the setting in which the victim had lived.

"Striker was a regular?" Phil asked Edna.

"Like clockwork."

"Why the lecture?"

"He volunteered."

"Why at night?"

"He insisted."

"Making you come back as well?"

"Oh, I stayed here."

"When did you notice Striker's car out in the lot?"

"I didn't. Barbara did. She pointed it out to me, and I mentioned it to Father Dowling when I phoned and told him not to bother coming over."

"But he came anyway."

"Because of the car. Barbara had thought Mitch was out there, and Father Dowling couldn't see anyone in the car."

Thank God it was Father Dowling who had discovered the body. After he had Marie call Phil, the priest had gone back to the car. And that is where he was, standing in the rain outside it, when the police arrived. He would have blessed the keeled-over Striker through that rain-washed window as he waited.

"Was it a heart attack?"

"Apparently not," Phil said.

Edna waited, but he decided to let it go at that. He told her he was waiting for a preliminary report from the lab, which was true enough. The ME's on-the-spot judgment was enough for him, however. But abruptly Phil changed his mind.

"He was killed."

"No!"

"Probably by someone who was in the backseat."

"How?" She formed the word with her mouth, but it came forth almost inaudible.

"Painlessly. An injection."

"My God."

"Any ideas?"

"About what?"

"Who might have done it?"

"Of course not."

Phil supposed she was remembering the role he had played in the arrest and conviction of her husband. She would never forget that, of course, but why blame him? If she did. She could resent him without blaming him.

"I don't know if I'll be here in the morning, Mrs. Hospers," a man said, going past them. He glared at Keegan, as if daring him to ask just one more question. But then he glared at Edna too.

"We may not be open, Gerry."

"It was a great lecture."

"Gerry, Mitch is dead."

"Too bad."

He slouched out the door, slowing as he went by Father Dowling and the women, and then speeding up.

"Gerry who?" Phil asked.

"Gerry Major," said Edna.

"Cheerful guy."

"He has a crush on Barbara."

"Who had a crush on Striker?"

"Whose only thought was of investments."

"And Gerry hated his guts?"

"Well, he was jealous."

"When did he get here tonight?"

"He was one of the first."

"Did he get here before Barbara noticed Striker's yellow car parked out there?"

"Long before."

"And stayed inside?"

She was about to say yes but then didn't, and he didn't press her. She just wasn't sure, that's all. But he wanted to find out what Gerry Major had said when he was questioned.

Father Dowling came toward them, escorting two women whom he introduced to Keegan. Barbara nodded through her sobs, but Clara Ponader put out her hand and looked him right in the eye. Phil liked that. Her face was even prettier up close.

Phil said he would stop by the rectory later, and Father Dowling left him with Barbara and Clara and escorted Edna out to her car.

"I told Gerry we might not open in the morning."

"Take the day off. I'll put a sign on the doors."

"I hate to do that."

"We'll think of it as a commemoration of Mitch Striker."

"I find myself wishing I didn't resent him so much."

"Somebody else must have resented him a good deal more."

"And right here in the parking lot," Edna said. "I suppose that does make it look as if it had some connection with the center. But who could it be?"

"That is only one of the questions I am going to leave in the competent hands of the Fox River police," replied Father Dowling.

"I told Captain Keegan about Gerry and Barbara. Gerry stopped by and growled at Keegan, and I wanted to give him some explanation for his behavior."

"And Phil asked if Gerry might have done it?"

"He asked where he was after the yellow car pulled in."

"What's the answer?"

"I don't know. I think he was just sitting there with the others, but I couldn't prove it."

"You probably couldn't prove what you yourself were doing."

"Am I suspected too?"

Outside, the rain had slowed to a steady whisper. Father Dowling handed Edna into her car.

Marie, wearing robe and slippers and some sort of plastic thing over her head to hide her curlers, called from the dining room, where she had been sitting at the table in the dark.

"What happened?"

"Something bad, Marie."

"What was in that car?"

He told her what he knew; she would never go upstairs to her apartment if he didn't.

"Mitchell Striker," she keened. "The poor man."

"In what sense? I understand he was quite wealthy."

"Money isn't happiness, Father Dowling."

"Indeed it isn't. Phil Keegan is going to drop by."

"Tonight?"

The thought of being seen by Phil Keegan in her present getup sent Marie hurrying through the kitchen to the back stairs that led to her apartment.

"Well, that was a waste of time," Phil said, when he settled down with the beer Roger Dowling had handed him. "Cy is talking to Striker's daughter now. It's more likely we'll get some idea of what happened there. Those old folks were just waiting around for a boring lecture that didn't happen."

"Because someone killed the lecturer."

"A preventive strike?"

"Is boredom ever the cause of murder?"

"Only between spouses. Jealousy is more likely."

"Gerry Major?"

"What do you know about him?"

"Nothing sinister."

"He was sweet on Barbara, Edna tells me."

"Not enough to kill for her."

"You're sure of that."

"What did Major do before he retired?"

"He was a pharmacist, I think."

"Hmmm."

"Give your mind a rest."

"What's on ESPN?"

Phil stayed through a replay of a hockey game. They did not discuss further what had happened that night, but a routine game whose score had already been decided was not sufficient to distract Roger Dowling from what had happened only hours ago a hundred yards from where they sat.

The method used to kill Mitch Striker was certainly not that of someone who had acted on the spur of the moment. It seemed clearly calculated and, Phil had suggested, professional. If that were true, if it had been professional, Phil's job was going to be complicated, since the one who did the deed would not be the one who had the motive to kill Mitch Striker.

Father Dowling let what he knew of Mitch Striker slide through his mind, though the man's insistence that he be allowed to lecture the others who came to St. Hilary's tended to overshadow things he had known of Striker before. His emergence as the bore of the parish center obscured the highly successful career he had had. While his wife had been alive, he had continued to live in St. Hilary's, but then he had moved to his daughter's house, where an apartment over the garage had been prepared for him. He had gravitated back to the parish in which he had lived for so many years in order to spend his day with others his age who found at the parish center just what they wanted—companionship, an easy atmosphere, not too heavily organized. Too bad he had an ungovernable impulse to instruct the others.

The daughter's married name was Walsh. Nancy Walsh. Father Dowling had been introduced to her once by Edna Hospers. He wondered if Phil was right in thinking that Cy Horvath would learn something from Nancy Walsh that would cast light on her father's death.

If anyone could bring such tragic news in a way that would diminish its terrible impact it was Cy Horvath. Phil's right-hand man had the unstudied knack of gaining the confidence of others. Father Dowling had no doubt that Nancy Walsh would trust Cy with anything she knew that might explain what had happened to her father. If Mitch had been the target of a professional killer, it was likely that some old score was being settled and that the clue would be found in Striker's business dealings.

"I suppose the method could be professional without a professional employing it," he said.

"What do you mean?"

"Nowadays all kinds of people have been taught the art of murder on TV, movies, books. I suppose Lubins will be able to tell the difference."

"Maybe Pippen will."

"I thought Lubins was doing the medical examination."

"Pippen came too. It will probably become her case. So stand by."

Dr. Pippen brought imagination and a need for drama to a job that provided little. It wasn't simply that one dead body was pretty much like another, but that the vast majority of deaths that come to the medical examiner's attention did not involve anything out of the way in the way of violence. Pippen was loath to accept this and had a tendency, deplored by Phil, to magnify the slightest anomaly into something deeply mysterious and suggestive of sinister forces at work.

"I don't suppose that even she will be able to turn Mitch Striker's death into a Greek tragedy."

"Don't underestimate her."

"I don't. But I underestimate you and your sure but slogging methods less."

"I'll have to think about that."

"Not here. I'm going to bed," said Father Dowling.

Jason asked her who she had been with at Lorenzo's, so he *had* seen them there. As soon as she and Winegar had entered the restaurant, Clara knew it was a mistake. People she had known for ages were bound to be here, and coming in with a good-looking man like Jerome Winegar would have the look of an announcement. They hadn't been inside two minutes before she saw her mistake, took his arm, and spun him toward the door.

"Let's go somewhere fun. This is the dullest place in the world."

"Didn't you make a reservation?"

"Oh, that doesn't matter."

Rex, the maître d', listened to this dispassionately. And they were on their way out the door. But that little look-in had been enough for Jason.

"Who were you with?" she asked him.

It almost worked. He liked nothing better than to develop his persona as aging Don Giovanni. But he put a finger to his lips and shook his head.

"So he *is* a secret, Clara."

"Don't be silly."

"Don't surprise me. Please."

He was serious. And just like that she realized that it was a serious matter for her to have fallen into the habit of letting Winegar be her escort. And that is the way it seemed to be. She the grande dame, he the obsequious courtier, just sufficiently mocking in manner to let her know this was a charade. His subservience, that is. That he was a man and she was a woman was the essential element.

Clara honestly did not know how she felt about this. Her marriage had not been a grand passion, simply the most satisfying and profound friendship she ever expected to enjoy, with the romance recurring at intervals, usually on trips. Their way of life had been even and without major fireworks. She realized that her marriage had developed to conform to her deepest wishes. She did not want to be buffeted by emotion, to live passionately, to careen from tears to laughter and back again. Marjorie's marriage had been like that, and she had an embarrassing way of saying how much she missed it all. A glass of white wine, and Marjorie would grow sultry with nostalgia for what she only half kiddingly referred to as the Marriage Bed.

Jerome was a stranger, unconnected with her past life, not quite real, so that to talk with him and to go places with him somehow didn't count, not really. But now Jason knew about him and of course Marjorie did too and Edna and . . . How absurd it was to think of Winegar as some secret. She wished she had told Jason all she knew of him. She didn't want secrets from her friends, particularly not from Jason, who was more than a friend. So she decided to ask Winegar to go with her to Mitch Striker's talk, just as an experiment, to see what it would be like to have people she knew at least to some degree see her with him.

"A lecture? Please."

"Oh, this is quite practical. On investments."

"All my money is tied up in currency."

He was full of little quips like that, all new to her, of course, but she sensed they were part of his standard repertoire.

"The speaker is an old friend of mine, Mitch Striker."

He looked at her for some moments. "When is it?"

"Wednesday night."

"Where?"

His smile became sardonic when she told him. "Clara, you are the soul of charity, helping out there, and I admire you for it, but they're no more your kind of people than they are mine."

"But they are my people. At least some of them. Mitch is. I've known him since I was a girl. We were both members of St. Hilary's then."

"Before Father Dowling?"

"Oh, long before."

"It's hard to imagine this place without him—and Marie Murkin."

"She's been here forever. She was here before Father Dowling came."

She found herself telling him about the parish in those days, of the period during which the pastors were friars. She and Don lived here and Mitch Striker and his wife and family.

"Family."

"He has a daughter Nancy. Actually two. They adopted another. He lives with the older daughter now."

Why was she telling him these things? He was a good listener, at least most of the time, but now he was encouraging her in order to keep her away from the suggestion that he come with her to Mitch's lecture. In the end she let it go. It seemed a first step to draw back from whatever it was she was getting involved in with Jerome Winegar.

She was flattered by his attention, of course she was, and she would have enjoyed being seen with him, starting a little gossip, as long as it was not serious. She could not read his manner. It was as easy to think that the attention he paid her was simply a little game the two of them had agreed to play as it was to think that he was interested in far more than their semiserious interchange. And then Jason changed all that.

"I didn't realize he was an employee, Clara."

"What are you talking about?"

"Winegar. I should say, former employee. He worked at the downtown lot for less than a month."

"At the lot? Doing what?"

"Salesman."

She felt her heart sink within her. Jason, thank God, made it easy for her, trusting her to put two and two together and realize that she had been very nearly led down the garden path by a used car salesman at a lot she herself owned. Had he heard of her, the eligible widow and owner, and undertaken a campaign? She thought of the first unlikely meeting, in Dayton's Tearoom. In retrospect she saw him as a good-looking opportunist, using a line in order to join her. More painful was thinking of her own reaction. How accessible to his flattery she had been. What contempt he must hold her in—the spoiled and bored widow, whiling away her time in tearooms at the mall, willing to respond to his obvious overture. Had he followed her and learned her schedule? Her day must have seemed to him the picture of a pointless existence. She would have seemed ripe for his advances, and so she had proved to be.

"I didn't know."

Jason nodded. "I was sure you didn't."

"How did you find out?"

"I made inquiries."

She wanted to feel indignant, but what she felt was gratitude. He was, after all, her protector as well as her friend; Don had chosen well to designate Jason as her adviser. He would simply have been doing what he took to be his duty toward his old friend Don Ponader.

"What else did you find?"

"Not much. He came to town only a few days before he applied for a job at the lot."

"Did he quit?"

"Yes."

"To do what?"

"That's unclear."

Was he one of the predators she had read about, good-looking ruthless men who make a career out of separating widows from their money after first having won their foolish hearts? Oh yes, she could see Jerome in that light. The past weeks were all too clear to her now. Jason's suspicions had been aroused, others would have seen what she had not, what she had been unwilling to see. Had she really thought such a good-looking young man was interested in her for herself alone? Her annual effort to bring her weight down to what she liked to think was its natural level was always followed by the steady regaining of what she had lost, and maybe a little more. Her body simply would not conform to her idea of what it should be. So she would surrender and settle for the face that resembled that of Elizabeth Taylor. The parallel was not pleasing. The actress's most recent ex-husband was a man years younger.

"I could continue the inquiries."

"No! No, please don't, Jason." She wanted to confess her folly to him, admit that she had been a caricature of a lonely widow. She wanted to promise him that she would never see Jerome Winegar or anyone like him ever again. But of course she said nothing.

"What are you doing tonight?"

"Mitch Striker is giving a lecture at St. Hilary's and I said I'd go."

"Good Lord, why?"

"Just as a favor."

"You're too good, Clara. I was going to suggest dinner."

"Not tonight."

"Another time?"

"Of course. I'd love it."

It was an odd thought that her susceptibility to Winegar had wakened an interest in Jason. That almost seemed a justification of her folly.

When Cy went to the Walsh home to talk to Striker's daughter, her husband came to the door and was visibly abashed to see a stranger on his doorstep at that hour of the night.

"Mr. Walsh?"

"Dr. Walsh. Is this about the theft?"

"Theft?"

"At my office . . ." He stopped.

"I am Lieutenant Horvath. Something has happened to your father-in-law."

"Happened?"

"He's dead."

Cy had thought he could say it to the husband and enlist his help in passing it on to the daughter, but Walsh went pale and staggered backward at the news. Cy took his arm and eased him into a chair.

"It is shocking news." His disapproval of Walsh's unmanly behavior was not conveyed by his tone any more than it was by his expression.

"What was it?"

Cy decided that the direct approach was inadvisable. "He was to give a lecture at the St. Hilary center."

"I know, I know. He talked of nothing else. How did it go?"

"He never gave it. He was found in his car in the parking lot."

Walsh screwed up his face as if to imagine the scene. "He died in the car?"

"Yes. He had fallen over onto the passenger seat."

"He took things too seriously. He was obsessed with giving that talk; he actually gave it here several times, the whole thing. He was a nervous wreck. He had built up a tremendous pressure on himself."

"Is your wife here?"

"Yes." And then, "You'll want to tell her. Wait, I'll get her."

Cy could see that he now represented a welcome intermediary who could give the bad news to Mrs. Walsh. She was a relief. She came down in a robe, her hair swept back, emphasizing the classical perfection of her face.

"Something happened to Dad," she said.

"Yes."

"Is it serious?"

Obviously Walsh had told her nothing. "He's dead."

She sat down, her eyes on him as she did so, as she absorbed what he had said.

"I knew it must be bad. You're a policeman?"

"He was found in his car in the parking lot of the parish center at St. Hilary's. We were called in."

"Was it a stroke?"

"It's still under investigation."

"Investigation!"

"The medical examiner is not satisfied that death was due to natural causes."

Walsh yelped at this, but Nancy Walsh remained calm. Cy liked the way she made him look her in the eye when he told her these things.

"The medical examiner thinks he was killed." He paused. "I know that sounds unlikely."

She remained silent. But her husband said it was not only unlikely, it was absurd.

"He was an old man, seventy-five years old. He was no harm to anyone."

"Was he robbed?" Nancy Walsh asked.

"We will have to have a better idea of what he had with him in order to say. The car was locked and the motor was running."

"Really? That sounds more like a heart attack, doesn't it?" She re-gripped her hands. "Perhaps it was meant to."

"Is it absurd to think that someone would have wanted to kill your father?"

"If he has been killed and someone did it, they must have had a reason. It doesn't sound like an unmotivated act of violence, does it?"

For the first time her eyes left Cy's, lifting to the mantel and to the photographs arrayed there. Her eyes grew moist. Cy turned and saw that one of the photographs was what looked to be a studio portrait of Mitchell Striker.

"Could I have a recent photograph of your father?"

She rose and went to the mantel and took the picture he had been looking at.

"This was taken only a few weeks ago." She looked down at it. "It is exactly like him." Her voice broke, but she retained control of herself.

"I understand he lived here with you."

"We had an apartment made, over the garage."

"Could I see it?"

"Now?"

"Yes."

"Would you show it to him, Jim."

"Can't this wait until morning? This is a dreadful shock, your coming here with news like this." His tone seemed to blame Cy for not first telling him how his father-in-law had died.

"What's the point of waiting, Jim? We're not going to get much sleep tonight." And then the thought struck her. "Where is his body?"

"The medical examiner hasn't released it yet."

"My God." She sat down abruptly. Obviously she could withstand a lot of shocks, but she was beginning to show the strain of her stoicism.

Walsh led him through the house to a stairway that rose from the dining room. At the top of the stairs, he turned the knob and pushed open the door.

"You won't need me, will you?"

"No. Thanks."

Walsh hesitated. "I didn't realize you meant he had been killed."

"When I came you mentioned a theft."

Walsh waved it away. "At my office. Some medicines, odds and ends."

"Did you report it?"

"I assume my secretary did." He expelled air. "It's not easy to absorb news like this. I better get back to Nancy."

The apartment was located over a three-stall garage, and the space was used ingeniously, providing a bath, a kitchenette, a bedroom, and a large comfortable-looking area lined with bookshelves; there was a television at one end and a desk at the other. The computer on the desk looked like the last word in technology. It was on. No surprise there; many people preferred to leave their computers on rather than subject them to frequent cooling and warming. Cy tapped the space bar, and a menu appeared on the screen. That would be the work of technicians.

He picked up the phone awkwardly, not touching it where a user normally would, and heard Nancy Walsh's voice.

"I'm on," she said. "Who's that?"

"Lieutenant Horvath."

"There's a phone on the fax machine, lieutenant, which is a different line."

He thanked her. He used the fax phone as he had the one on the desk, calling downtown for a crew to come to the Walsh house and go over the apartment of the deceased. Before telling the Walshes they would be having more visitors that night, he stood in the middle of Mitchell Striker's living room, trying to get a sense of the man whose body had been found in a parked car with rain drumming down on it.

The interviews at St. Hilary's Parish Center had produced all sorts of what was very likely irrelevant information. The picture of Striker's life in retirement that began to emerge was not of a man who was acquiring new enemies. Walsh was probably right in thinking that a seventy-five-year-old man would not have enemies wanting to kill him—unless he had made them long ago. But what could he have done long ago that would explain this delayed-action result? Someone would have had to keep a grudge a long time.

Cy stopped himself. It was Phil Keegan's rule, if not his practice, to avoid imaginative speculation about what had happened. That was right too; Cy knew it from experience. The more you learned, the more possibilities of what had happened presented themselves. What had actually happened was only one of innumerable things that might have occurred at the time, but it had the undeniable advantage of being what had happened. Stick with that: That was the point of Keegan's rule. Cy stopped imagining a past for Striker out of which his killer might have emerged.

He left the apartment, closing the door behind him, and went downstairs where he found Walsh in the kitchen, holding a large glass.

"Can I offer you anything, Lieutenant?"

"No, thanks. I called the lab."

"Yes?"

"They're on their way. I want them to go over the apartment for whatever it might turn up that will be of help."

"They're going to do that tonight?"

"Why put it off?"

Walsh took a long sip from his drink before saying, "I suppose you're right."

"Jim," Nancy Walsh said. "I have to telephone Kate."

12

The offices of Tuttle & Tuttle were not likely to fill a prospective client with the fear that he would be asked to pay for a lot of expensive overhead if he engaged the services of Tuttle. There was only Tuttle at Tuttle & Tuttle, the silent partner being the lawyer's deceased father, who had continued to support his son's ambition to become a lawyer despite the long and oft-duplicated route he had taken to that goal. Eventually he received his degree and in a half a dozen more years succeeded in passing the bar exam. By that time his father was dead, but it was as a tribute to him that he instructed the sign painter to put Tuttle & Tuttle on his door.

The lawyer sat in his inner office—the outer was presently unoccupied since he relied now on part-time secretarial help, not wishing to take on the burden of both salary and fringe benefits. It was, he assured himself, a slack time. The one remunerative task in recent weeks had been the request of Jason Broderick for background on Jerome Winegar.

The morning news about the death of Mitchell Striker had fascinated Tuttle, in a professional way. Distinguished retired financier found dead in his automobile just minutes before he was to address a group of senior citizens on the art of investing for short- and long-term profit. The mention of both Lubins and Pippen on the scene might or might not have significance. The newspaper story gave no indication of the whereabouts of the body. Tuttle called McDivitt to congratulate the undertaker on being chosen for the Striker funeral.

"Who is this?"

"I suppose the obituary will say when the hours of viewing will be?"

"Is this Tuttle?"

"I'm flattered that you remember my voice, Mr. McDivitt."

"What's this about Mitchell Striker?"

"Then you're not doing the funeral."

"The medical examiner hasn't released the body yet."

"Aha."

"Apparently there was no violence. But, even if there were . . ."

McDivitt's voice swelled with professional pride. But Tuttle had learned what he wanted to know. He ended the call to McDivitt and put in a call to Peanuts Pianone, his contact on the police force.

"How about a little Chinese, Peanuts."

"You buying?"

"If you pick it up and bring it with you."

"Oh no, you don't. You have it delivered and pay when it comes."

"I like a man who's careful with a dollar."

"How much Chinese you going to get for a dollar?"

"I won't try to find out."

Peanuts and the fried rice arrived at the same time, but the rumpled policeman held back until Tuttle had paid for the order. In a few minutes all was peaceful, the little office quiet except for the sounds of serious multicultural feasting.

"You working on the Striker case, Peanuts?"

Peanuts looked at him, chewing methodically, not giving a clue.

"The man found dead in his car in the St. Hilary parking lot."

Peanuts shrugged. He hadn't heard of it. The papers were full of it, it was on television and radio, it had to be a topic of discussion at headquarters, and Peanuts hadn't heard of it. Peanuts was the beneficiary of his family's clout, which had gotten him the job on the force that, even though the family had ceased being powerful, was still his for life—or at least until he put in twenty years and was eligible for a pension.

"I suppose they assigned Agnes Lamb to it."

Peanuts stopped chewing. Something like a growl began deep in his throat, and he stirred in his chair. Peanuts had convinced himself that Officer Lamb had unfairly filled the role that he was destined to play. He would not have put it that way. It was doubtful that he could have articulated it at all.

"I'll go downtown with you," Tuttle said. "After we've eaten."

Peanuts nodded and resumed chewing. After he swallowed, he shook his head slowly. "Tomorrow. I'll talk to you tomorrow."

Tuttle had never understood what led up to decisions on the part of his friend, but he did know that it was impossible to budge Peanuts once he had decided. It was clear that he was unwilling to take Tuttle into police headquarters until he had found out what new injustice had been done to him in the name of fairness to Agnes Lamb.

Thus, at least for the nonce that avenue to possible legal business was closed, and Tuttle was able to resolve his ethical dilemma in the Winegar matter.

"Is there some specific sort of thing you have in mind, Mr. Broderick?" Tuttle had asked Jason. Here was a boon indeed. Jason was a figure of both social and professional prestige in Fox River, and Tuttle permitted himself to think that his fortunes were about to take a turn, that a whole new level of clientele would come knocking on his door. He had apologized to Jason for his secretary's absence.

"It is one thing to be ill, but to call in when it is impossible to get a replacement is quite another." The statement was true enough, though its application to the present circumstances was nil. Tuttle had brought to his profession, rather than learned from it, the vagaries of the truth. He prided himself on always speaking the truth, a better device for misleading others never having been discovered. A lawyer misleads by not telling all he knows, and that is by way of being a professional obligation.

Like most professionals, Tuttle enjoyed thinking about the ethics of his occupation. After Peanuts left, he sat contemplating his ethical problem. Jason's coming had not been the dawn of a new day. One swallow does not make a spring, and it was still winter in the offices of Tuttle & Tuttle. His ethical problem was whether or not he could expand what he had done for Jason into further income.

What he had found out about Winegar had satisfied Jason but only whetted Tuttle's appetite. The man had dropped into Fox River a month before, antecedents unknown. What he had done since arriving had been easily enough learned. When he went to Ponader's Motors on a tip from a landlord, Tuttle had come with a sack from McDonald's. It was midday. There wasn't much going on beneath the flapping pennants at the used car lot.

"Know a guy named Winegar?" he asked the manager. The aroma from the bag of burgers began to fill the room.

"What about the bastard?"

That promising response led to Tuttle's offer of a Big Mac, and soon they were wallowing in junk food while Blake talked about Winegar.

"The thing is the guy is a natural salesman. He could have sold *me* a car. And no sooner is he settled in than he walks out."

"Why?"

"A better opportunity," he said.

"Another job?"

"Not with a dealer. I checked."

"He must have needed money if he took a job here."

Blake didn't like the implication of that remark, so Tuttle amended it. "I mean, why stop and work in Fox River rather than go on to where he was going."

"Oh, he meant to be here. He was coming back." ·

"From where?"

"You know, I never found out for sure. He had been everywhere. Even if you discount fifty percent as bullshit, he had been around. But where he had been last I don't know."

"Mysterious guy."

"Why you asking about him?"

"For a client." Tuttle removed his tweed hat and produced a plasticized business card and showed it to Blake. "I can't let you have that. I'm waiting for more from the printer."

Blake handed back the card without reluctance. "You in business with your brother?"

"My father."

Blake liked that. "Winegar done something wrong?"

"Well, he left a great job here."

Blake twirled in his chair, the better to survey his terrain. "I run a tight ship here but I'm fair. I know Winegar didn't leave here because of the way I treated him."

"You buy the lot from Ponader?"

A lie trembled on his lips but he overcame temptation. "I just manage it."

"Ponader's dead, isn't he?"

"A year ago."

"Who owns the dealership?"

"His widow." Blake laughed. "I remember having almost this exact conversation with Winegar. I liked that. A man ought to know who he's working for."

Tuttle had tracked Winegar down. He was living in a hotel of sorts, weekly rates, and it was pretty clear he wasn't working. He was drawing unemployment. As a self-employed professional Tuttle often groused about the ease with which people received money from the government when they were out of work. Where was the risk and adventure in life if you got paid whether you worked or not? This line of thought reminded Tuttle that the wolf was very near his door. Necessity had often in the past provided the solution to an ethical problem. He decided that he would approach Winegar and see whether the man thought information about people checking up on him had any value.

A delicate matter if he had not acquainted himself with Winegar's habits. He found him at what had seemed a regular stop, the cool bar of the Excelsior, whose windows looked out over a small courtyard richly green now after the rain.

Winegar half stood, half sat at the bar, a half-assed claim on a stool, his body turned so that he could see and be seen by anyone entering the bar. Not a flicker of recognition or curiosity crossed his face when Tuttle came in.

"Red wine and ginger ale."

"What?"

"Three ounces of Chianti, an equal amount of ginger ale."

"What the hell's that called?"

"I haven't named it yet."

"I don't have any Chianti."

"Gimme a diet Coke."

"Straight?" The bartender glanced at Winegar, but he was now smiling benevolently at Tuttle.

"That would taste awful," Winegar said to Tuttle.

"You never tried it?"

"I never even heard of it before."

Well, neither had Tuttle. He was glad he had thought of Chianti. If he'd just left it at red wine, the guy might have come up with something and he would have had to drink the concoction. But the order had served its purpose. He and Winegar were talking. The bartender put a Coke in front of Tuttle and went down the bar to watch the television. A local talk show host was discussing the finding of the body of Mitchell Striker. The police had announced that the death had been classified as murder, but they had not said how the old man was killed, an omission that infuriated the host and his callers.

Winegar ignored the set. Tuttle did too.

"Is that Irish tweed?"

Tuttle took off his hat, as if he hadn't realized he was wearing it. "The best they make."

"I didn't know you could twee the Irish."

Tuttle looked at him. Winegar had the look of a man expecting a laugh. Twee? Tweed? What the hell? Tuttle laughed politely and put his hat back on his head.

44

"I never wear a hat. Know why?"

Tuttle was about to say because you don't want to muss up your hair, but he didn't. "Why?"

" 'Cause Kennedy didn't."

"Yeah?"

"He knocked the hell out of the hat business because he didn't wear a hat and for a while he was the most popular man in the country."

"You remember him?"

"Don't you?"

"Know why I wear a hat?"

"Why?"

"To cover my head."

Winegar just looked at him. Tuttle was sorry he had laughed at tweeing the Irish. There was a commercial on, and the bartender joined them.

"What do you think of that? The guy's found in a locked car with the motor running, and they say he was killed."

"Carbon monoxide," Winegar said.

"You think so?"

"Or a laser beam that goes through glass without a trace."

The bartender looked at Winegar with admiring eyes. "You ought to write stories."

"Can a laser do that?" Tuttle asked.

"I don't know."

"You know who Striker was, don't you?"

"I'm new in town," Winegar said.

Technically true, maybe, but he was settled in enough to draw unemployment. That's my tax money paying for his drink, Tuttle thought.

"Want another Coke?"

"Thanks." It was like getting a refund.

Winegar settled himself on the stool, as if someone he had been waiting for had arrived. Tuttle was beginning to doubt there was any way he could profit from telling Winegar that a prominent citizen had spent good money to find out about him. Winegar couldn't pay for the information, and besides, nothing Tuttle had turned up really amounted to much. Anything interesting about Winegar must have happened before he came to Fox River. Talking with him, Tuttle could see why a man with little more than the clothes on his back managed to have dates with one of the richest widows in town.

13

After the body of Mitch Striker was released to McDivitt, Father Dowling accompanied James Walsh to the funeral home.

"What I keep thinking, Father, is that if I had gone with Mitch to the lecture, he'd still be alive."

"You meant to go?"

"I had an emergency and had to go to my clinic at the last moment."

"I didn't realize dentists had emergencies."

"You'd be surprised, Father."

McDivitt, with his cotton white hair and pinkish eyes, feigned delight at seeing the pastor of St. Hilary's accompanying the aggrieved son-in-law. This was a time when sadness, regret, maybe even remorse, if subtly invoked, could lead to lavish compensatory and expensive funeral arrangements. But it was not Walsh's vulnerability that explained Father Dowling's presence. He wanted to see the body before McDivitt and his staff had worked their wonders on it. He drew McDivitt aside to make this request.

"Of course, Father. Meanwhile, I will talk with Mr. Walsh."

Father Dowling did not encourage the interpretation that this was a quid pro quo. Hanson, a merry overweight mortician, came at McDivitt's summons and led Father Dowling down into the depths of the building. Strange odors rose to greet them, and a wave of dizziness passed through the priest's head, but then he recovered. Hanson emitted a sibilant sound as he descended, a kind of muted whistle, a tune Father Dowling could not quite make out.

"Have you started work on Mr. Striker?"

"He's next in line," Hanson said brightly, then resumed whistling.

The ceiling was low, the lighting unreal, the air glacial. The body of Mitch Striker lay on a wheeled table pushed against the wall, wrapped in a shroud. A nude bluish body lay face up on the table in the center of the room, illumined by sunken neon lighting in the ceiling above.

"Mind if I look?"

"Don't wake him up."

Father Dowling turned back the rough-textured cloth while behind him a machine started. He did not dare to look around to see what Hanson was doing to the bluish corpse. Mitch looked much as he had when Father Dowling peered through the window of the parked yellow car and saw him toppled onto the passenger seat. The body was no longer rigid, and he was able to turn the head and look behind the ear. A slight discoloration of the skin showed where the needle had pricked him, but the mark of its entry had all but disappeared.

Lab reports had turned up indications that someone had been in the backseat of the car.

"What kind of indications?" he had asked Phil when the reports came in.

"Wet footprints."

"Ah."

This suggested that Mitch had pulled into the parking lot and stopped. Had he turned off the motor? In any case, he did not get out, since his clothes had been perfectly dry. Someone opened the back door and slipped in. It might have been the work of a moment. A man Mitch's age could not have offered much resistance; besides, surprise would have immobilized him. In leaving the car, the assailant could lock the doors and turn on the motor if Mitch had turned it off.

"Any prints?"

"Sure. But none unaccounted for."

There was an expression of grudging admiration on Phil Keegan's face. Murder seldom presented a puzzle: It was usually clear what the motive was and who had done it, and Phil's task came down to supplying the prosecutor with enough evidence to make a legal case of what everyone already assumed. Whoever had killed Mitch Striker had performed a grisly work of art.

Why?

The main complaint anyone had against Mitch Striker was that he was an enthusiastic exponent of a method of investment that had made both himself and his clients wealthy. It apparently annoyed him that the world did not beat a path to his door even in retirement. But he was in all other respects an admired, even beloved, figure, a welcome addition to his daughter's family.

"Maybe a disgruntled client," Phil said.

"Were there any?"

"There hadn't been any clients, not really, since he retired."

"When was that?"

"He sold his business when he turned seventy."

His son-in-law, James Walsh, was a successful dental surgeon whose specialty was root canals, patients being referred to him on a scale that had turned his office into a model of efficiency, if that is the word. Experience had taught him that three operating rooms were the optimum number, enabling him in effect to deal with three patients simultaneously. He moved from room to room during the various stages of the procedure, as often as not talking on the phone that he had clamped on his head. Walsh was not interested in taking over his father-in-law's business.

The point of the invitation had been Nancy Walsh's request that her father be buried from St. Hilary's.

"It hasn't been our parish for years, not since we moved here, but that's where his heart was. He loved going to the center and, after all, that is where . . ."

Her voice trailed off, and her lips became a straight line. Father Dowling said that of course the funeral would be at St. Hilary's.

"I don't want to hurt Father Panzica's feelings."

"I'll talk to him."

"Does it really matter?" Kate, the younger sister, asked.

"To Father Panzica?"

"To Dad."

"I think it would, Kate. You don't remember St. Hilary's. It's the parish in which I was raised." The last was spoken to Father Dowling rather than to her sister.

Father Dowling was glad that so many people retained good memories of the parish despite the condition it had fallen into by the time he was sent there. His disgrace had seemed complete when he was sent to a parish not only remote from the center of things but also one that not even the friars wanted anymore. Whatever shape it was in when they took over, it was moribund when he arrived. The debt was astronomical, the school was a pointless drain on finances, and parishioners were moving to more desirable neighborhoods at a rate that threatened the extinction of the parish within a few years. Looking around on his arrival, Father

Dowling had the oddly exhilarating feeling that he had hit absolute bottom. It could never be worse than this. But his exile had been his homecoming to the priesthood, for failure in the careerist sense had brought back the scale of values that had been obscured in the days of his ascendancy. Like everyone else, he had tacitly assumed that he was on the clerical escalator that would soon lead to ordination as an auxiliary bishop, then on to a diocese of his own, and after that, well, the sky if not heaven was the limit. The stress and anguish of serving on the marriage tribunal, something for which his degree in canon law had prepared him, proved too much. Social drinking evolved into a private necessity, and the day came when he had to withdraw to an institution in Wisconsin that specialized in treating clerics with drinking problems. Elbow disease, as it was euphemistically referred to. His descent had been precipitous and it seemed complete. Now he saw all that as a necessary purgation before his true priesthood began, as pastor of St. Hilary's. The Strikers were part of that parish prehistory that he had pieced together from the somewhat chaotic records and from the authoritative source, Marie Murkin.

Mrs. Walsh suggested they have coffee, and Kate took Father Dowling into the sunroom.

"You're in school," he said to Kate, as they were waiting for Nancy Walsh to bring in the coffee. Such rituals at such times are often necessities for the hostess.

"I'm a junior."

"What's your major?"

"I don't really have one. I am in a special program, interdisciplinary. The aim is a liberal education."

"Ah."

"Last summer I worked at Jude Thaddeus House."

"How did you like it?"

"I think I'll do it again this summer."

He had the impression that she found the discussion of where her father's funeral would be held unimportant.

"You were close to your father?"

Her large dark eyes studied him for a moment. "He really wasn't my father, you know."

"I don't understand."

"I'm adopted."

"I didn't know."

And would never have guessed. Her manner when she brought this up told him that this was no offhand remark. The death of her father had clearly brought home to her her special status in the family so far as bloodlines were concerned.

When they were having coffee, Nancy Walsh handed Father Dowling a slip of paper.

"Dad wanted that on his tombstone. Do you know what it means?"

Father Dowling read the phrase. *Exegi monumentum aere perennius.* " 'I have raised a monument more enduring than bronze.' It's a line from Horace."

"Latin."

"Yes."

"You know Latin," Kate said, almost surprised, and her sister laughed.

"Sweetheart, he's a priest."

But of course Kate would have no memory of the Latin rite; for her the liturgy had always been conducted in sometimes dubious English and by priests fewer and fewer of whom knew the language that had characterized the liturgy from time immemorial. The switch to the vernacular after Vatican II had been both abrupt and complete. Once training for the priesthood had involved a classical education, years of both Latin and Greek.

"Horace has always served as a kind of secular breviary for many," he said. "Obviously, your father was a Latinist."

"He went to a Jesuit prep school in Wisconsin. He kept the books he used there. They're in his apartment." Nancy sighed. "What are we going to do with all his things?"

"Can't we just leave everything as it is," Kate said.

Nancy nodded. "For now, certainly."

Father Dowling was struck by the similarity of mannerism and posture in Nancy Walsh and her adopted sister. How many family traits are learned rather than inherited? There was a Modigliani serenity in the two of them. They sat forward, on the edge of chair or cushion, back erect, hands in lap, their heads tipped on stemlike throats. Theirs was a patrician air, and Father Dowling wondered how Kate had fit in at Jude Thaddeus House, an establishment that had operated in the Chicago slums long before concern for the homeless became widespread, almost fashionable. Maud Weaver, the founder, was dead now, and the house was in the hands of a new generation, but the spirit was the same: politically radical, theologically orthodox. Roger Dowling himself had spent a summer there after his first year at St. Mary's Seminary in Mundelein.

Now at McDivitt's he looked down at the face of the late Mitchell Striker who had not, Nancy had told him, approved of his adopted daughter's involvement with Jude Thaddeus House.

"In theory he preferred the direct approach to government welfare, but not when his family was involved."

Hanson, still whistling, had turned off the dreadful-sounding machine that suggested all kinds of grotesque functions. Father Dowling covered the face of Mitchell Striker, thanked Hanson, and started for the stairs. That was when he recognized the tune Hanson whistled, the song of the seven dwarfs.

The record of Mitchell Striker's civic involvement was a thing to behold, and Phil Keegan read it with awe. For some forty years Striker had been a public-spirited citizen of Fox River, involved in so many good causes, it was difficult to know when he had had time to do so well by himself and others. He had always kept the number of his clients below twenty-five, he accepted no one with an initial investment of less than a quarter of a million dollars, and he enriched them all while at the same time instilling in them a sense of their duty to the less fortunate. It was on Roger Dowling's advice that Phil called on Amos Cadbury.

Cadbury, the lawyer, had been a classmate of Striker's at Notre Dame. "There was nothing special about him as a student, so far as I or anyone else could see. And if the spirit of the place impressed him, he gave few signs of it. But once we graduated he became a fervent alumnus."

Striker had been president of the Notre Dame Club of Chicago, but then he had been an officer at one time or another in most of the organizations to which he belonged. He had given Maud Weaver money to start Jude Thaddeus, but there had been no personal involvement with it. He reserved his greatest enthusiasm for St. Peter's.

"The orphanage?"

Amos smiled. "We haven't called it that in years."

Well, it never had looked like an orphanage for that matter. Rather like a prep school. But then in many cases, the boys at St. Peter's had one parent living, and there was more than just fiction in the suggestion that they just happened to be away at school. The first headmaster, Father John Gorman, had held that post for almost a quarter of a century and had put his indelible stamp on the school, its curriculum, its determination to prepare its graduates for prominence and success in the world. The number of graduates who went on to good universities was a phenomenon, and the alumni were almost as loyal as those of Notre Dame. Of course there were some who in later life did not wish to draw attention to the fact that they had spent years of their boyhood in what "we no longer call an orphanage." Mitchell Striker had served on the board of the school for decades and had been the custodian of the school's portfolio. As a result of that, and the generosity of many, not least its alumni, St. Peter's was an extremely sound institution when Striker stepped down as member of the board and chief financial adviser.

"He sounds like a man without enemies."

Amos Cadbury looked thoughtful. "Captain, have you ever heard it said that there are people who can never forgive a kindness done them?"

Cadbury had the look of a man in the grip of a theory. He certainly had more to say on the subject, and there might have been an autobiographical tinge to his remarks. Keegan happened to know that Cadbury's children were spoiled ingrates. The eldest son, when arrested in possession of drugs, seemed eager to be interviewed and explain to the world that his father's tyrannical upbringing was responsible for his troubles. And then Cadbury made clear what he meant. Perhaps he considered a policeman someone in whom he could confide, given his son's arrest.

"I should have put him in St. Peter's," Cadbury said fervently. "My so-called tyranny was actually an inexcusable leniency. What the boy needed—what he needs—is discipline. Self-discipline."

"Could he have gone to St. Peter's?"

"Not at the time. Conditions of admission have changed in recent years. The school was founded to give orphaned children a first-class education. The curriculum, the whole academic tradition of the school, is a marvel. Many schools seem to have lost their rudders, but not St. Peter's. Except financially. I suppose that lies behind opening it to nonorphans.

The fees are astronomical, of course; there is no intention to open the flood-gates. Mitch was opposed to all this. The only reason for the change was what had happened to the school's endowment."

"Can you lose an endowment?" Phil asked.

Amos Cadbury rattled off an explanation of what the headmaster had been persuaded to do by Robert Frankman, the member of the board who had replaced Striker. Fortunes were to be made on foreign exchanges; methods were now available that promised profits beyond the dreams of avarice. The scheme, like all such schemes, collapsed, and St. Peter's had been a less newsworthy victim than Orange County and the Singapore representative of a venerable London brokerage.

"Needless to say, the headmaster didn't enjoy Mitch's saying I told you so."

The headmaster, a redhead named Cottage, had a degree in classics and had written a book on Virgil's *Eclogues* that, to the astonishment of the publishing world, had become a commercial best-seller. It was that rare book that pleased both the expert and the general reader. Cottage had become that even rarer entity, the scholar celebrity. When he was hired to replace the retiring Father Gorman, there was general agreement that the school had scored a coup. Who would have guessed that St. Peter's, because of the influence of Robert Frankman, was about to adopt an investment program that all but destroyed the endowment that Striker had built up over the years.

"Of course, Father Gorman has remained silent."

"Is he still alive?"

Cadbury laughed. "He will outlive us all."

"Of course I do," Roger Dowling answered when Phil asked him later if he knew the longtime headmaster of St. Peter's. "When I was a young priest, I helped out there one semester, teaching third-year Latin. Virgil."

"Didn't the new headmaster, Cottage, write a book on Virgil?"

"I'm amazed that you would know that. Yes, he did. This is it." And Roger took a book from the shelf, looked at it affectionately, then passed it on to Phil. "I can take no credit for this. Cottage was not on the scene when I taught the *Aeneid.*"

"Do you know him?"

"No I don't."

"How about Robert Frankman?"

"Why do you ask about him?"

"He seems to get the blame for putting the school in a financial hole."

"Yes. The dreams of avarice. He was a classmate of mine."

"He's a priest?"

"He was. He left a few years after ordination."

"And became a financial wizard?"

"Do wizards lose?"

"I don't suppose any of this had anything to do with the death of Mitchell Striker, Roger, but there is almost nothing to go on. The family had no inkling his life was in danger; he himself expressed no fear or concern. The whole thing had come out of the blue as far as they're concerned. They want to think of it as just mindless violence, a stranger killing a stranger. I suppose they're welcome to do that. God knows we have no better theory, even if what we do know suggests a planned and motivated killing."

"And out of the past?"

"Yeah."

"Hence the interest in St. Peter's. But that's the present too, Phil. The bone of contention is the endowment. Striker publicly criticized both Cottage and Frankman."

"I don't remember that."

"I suppose only people connected with the school, or its longtime headmaster, would have noticed it, or remembered it. But it was pretty sharp criticism. It wasn't that he thought they had committed a crime. 'Unless stupidity is a crime,' he had added."

"It sounds like I better talk to Cottage and Frankman."

Father Dowling neither agreed nor disagreed. Well, it was more a statement than a question, so what did he expect?

"You've made me feel guilty about how long it's been since I've visited Father Gorman. I intend to do that as soon as I can."

"I wish you'd talk to Frankman, Roger."

"I never interfere in police business."

And Father Dowling kept a straight face when he said this.

Aged priests, like old soldiers, fade away, but now provision is made for the new longevity. Once a priest stayed on in the parish of which he was pastor even when he was effectively replaced by his first assistant. The rectory had become the old man's home, and he would stay in it until and unless he had to be taken to the hospital. Things had changed. Bishops now retired and so did pastors, and homes had been built to accommodate this cadre of decommissioned clerical officers. Father Gorman was housed in a lovely place overlooking the lake, north of the city, almost to the Wisconsin border.

Being of the old school, Gorman would have expected to live out his days in the institution he had administered for so many years. But he had bowed to the suggestion from the cardinal and to the decision of his board and taken the heart of his library to the apartment awaiting him at Guardian Angels. Any sorrow or resentment he felt on being displaced and relocated in a building so new the smell of plaster clung to it was kept hidden. Nor would he discuss the present state of St. Peter's. But the past was another thing.

"You would have made a good classics teacher," Gorman said, recalling the term Roger Dowling had filled in at the school.

"That sounds pretty subjunctive."

"Latin lacks the optative."

To visit Gorman was to visit another world, the one Roger Dowling had entered as a young boy when he began his studies for the priesthood and was introduced to the classics, to an ideal of education become rarer and rarer in a world enamored of technology and innovation. The old priest's thin white hair was a halo, his black eyebrows shadowed alert, mischievous eyes, and the high forehead seemed to await the hand that usually came to rest upon it. Once every learned person's head was filled with the lore that filled Gorman's. It seemed ironic that, because of him, it had taken root in an orphanage.

"I am sure you heard of Mitch Striker's death."

"I said a mass for him," Gorman replied, his sadness genuine but also that of a man who had seen most of his friends die before him.

"It was a shock to have it happen in the parking lot of St. Hilary's. I actually discovered the body."

"He was already dead?"

"I gave him conditional absolution."

"Good."

"The death is classified as a murder."

"I didn't know that."

There was no television in the room, only a large old phonograph. Gorman no longer read the newspapers, ostensibly because the type was too small, but also in relief that he no longer had any duty at all to keep up on the follies of the world.

"There seem to be no clues as to who might have done it."

"There were days when I felt like it, Roger. He had an annoying habit of always being right. I must tell you that I was for a long time opposed to the idea of investing any portion of what little money we had. Mitchell assured me that there was no risk, that he would personally cover any loss incurred, not that he expected any. He wore me down. Thank God. He was a veritable Midas with money."

"Amos Cadbury suggested to Captain Keegan that the killer might be an unforgiving beneficiary of Striker's generosity."

"Ha." Gorman wheeled to a sideboard and brought forth a bottle of sherry and grinned elfishly. "A dollop?"

"Go ahead, Father, but I won't."

"Oh, you must."

"I never do."

"For heaven's sake."

"Exactly."

It was quite possible that Gorman did not know the story of his troubles, or if he had heard it, simply let it slip from his mind. It began to seem unlikely that he would remember anything at St. Peter's that might be the beginning of an explanation of Striker's murder. Besides, he wanted to talk of the family.

"I wonder how Nancy is."

Father Dowling told the old priest about the funeral. He was very interested to hear about the Walsh family, the husband, the children, the apartment over the garage.

"It sounds like a good life."

"I think it is, Father. I don't mean financially."

"Neither did I." He sipped his sherry with such relish that Father Dowling almost regretted his own total abstinence. "Sometimes early trouble is the making of a person, Father Dowling. That was a truth I saw exemplified again and again as headmaster. Give me a boy who has learned his capacity for foolishness, for sin, and I will show you someone ready to acquire moral maturity."

"You must hear from a lot of the old boys."

"Oh yes. The invitations, Father, the invitations. I suppose they remember me as I was and assume I can travel. But I have reached that stage in which I go where I do not wish to go and . . . But you know the passage in John." He closed his eyes and murmured pedantically, "Twenty-one: eighteen."

Father Dowling called up the eerily relevant passage. "But when thou art old thou wilt stretch forth thy hands, and another will gird thee, and lead thee where thou wouldst not."

He stayed with the old priest until he had finished his sherry. When he passed through the common room on his way out, several voices called to him like souls on an upper level of purgatory, and he stopped and gave them news of the world they had left behind.

In his car he sat for a moment, looking at the building. You might end up there yourself, he told himself.

If you're lucky, his self answered.

Robert Frankman's thick black hair was worn long and combed back straight over his head, a discipline it resisted by forming into waves as the time from his morning shower lengthened. If he had been a classmate of

Roger Dowling's, life had taken less of a toll on him than it had the pastor of St. Hilary's, not that Phil Keegan would tell his old friend that. Besides, before his interview with Frankman was fifteen minutes old, Keegan could see that much of the other man's youthfulness was of art rather than nature. The black hair was too black, the wrinkles remained after the professional smile had been turned off. And several times Frankman adjusted a small cushion that provided support for the small of his back.

"Sciatica," he winced the third time he moved the cushion.

"We're investigating the death of Mitchell Striker."

"Terrible thing."

"We haven't a clue as to what happened."

"I thought I read that it was murder."

"We're sure of that."

Frankman waited. His manner suggested that this was uncharted territory for him and he was willing to be guided through it by Phil Keegan.

"He doesn't seem to have had any enemies."

"Lucky man."

"He did annoy a lot of people."

"How so?"

"He wanted to lecture them on investments."

"Well, he was certainly an authority on that."

"I understand you took over from him at St. Peter's."

Frankman studied Keegan, saying nothing.

"Isn't that true?"

"Our tenures did not overlap, Captain. We were never members of the board at the same time. I am trying to remember if I ever met Mr. Striker. I don't think I did. It was his reputation of which I was aware."

"And I suppose vice versa."

"Say it, Captain."

"Say what?"

"My investment strategy for the St. Peter's endowment has suffered a severe setback. But I am confident in the future. Mitchell Striker criticized what I had done, and that is fair enough. I am sure he would have applauded if things had worked out as I had every expectation that they would. I am capable of taking criticism, Captain. I wouldn't want you to think I have been brooding over what Striker said to the papers, wondering how I could get even with him. I am far more interested in restoring the endowment of St. Peter's to its former vigor."

"You were a classmate of Roger Dowling, I understand."

"Do you know him?"

"I count him a dear friend."

"Say hello to him for me. It would be good to see him again, after all these years. Where is he stationed?"

"St. Hilary's."

"Never heard of it."

"In Fox River."

"Fox River? Well, well. In any case, give him my regards."

Philip Cottage, the headmaster of St. Peter's, affectionately known as the Big Cheese, looked old for his years. He had the stoop of the scholar and the squint of the nearsighted. The tweed jacket and knit tie and corduroy trousers completed the academic persona. He had an unlit pipe in his mouth.

"We will have a memorial service in the school chapel for Mr. Striker. I just this moment got off the phone with my predecessor, Father Gorman. He doesn't feel up to saying the mass but intends to be here for the event. He suggested that I ask a Father Dowling."

"Good suggestion."

"Do you know him?"

Keegan nodded. "Roger Dowling actually taught a course here at one time."

"So Gorman told me. Virgil. I intend to invite him."

"You know why I'm here."

Cottage blinked at him, the corners of his mouth dimpling in incomprehension.

"Mitchell Striker was murdered."

"Murdered. Is it as bad as that?"

"I'm afraid so."

"I hope having a memorial service is a wise thing."

Did he imagine that the Chicago media would descend on the school and turn the memorial service into the news of the day? Given the headmaster's apparent belief that St. Peter's was at or near the navel of the universe, it was perhaps no surprise that he reacted with near alarm to Keegan's reference to possible motives for the killing in Striker's past, perhaps connected with St. Peter's.

"But the man was a hero in the school. He gave us financial independence." The narrow face clouded. "And now we have fallen on evil days."

"I had a talk with Mr. Frankman."

"What about?"

"He says he knew Mr. Striker only by reputation."

"He said that?"

"If I understood him correctly."

"Oh, you couldn't have. When Mr. Frankman was invited onto the board and when he proposed himself as financial adviser—he had a good deal of support on the board, I hasten to add—it was agreed that he should consult with Mr. Striker. As a courtesy, but professionally as well. I am sure they met several times."

"Would he have told Mr. Striker of the new investment strategy?"

"I have always wanted to ask Robert that. It would be a comfort to know that the misfortune could have occurred under my predecessor and his financial adviser."

"But you haven't asked Frankman?"

"No." He drew air through the pipe. "I suppose because I fear the answer would be no."

"If Striker had approved it, he wouldn't have publicly criticized it."

"One would think so."

He left Cottage with pipe smoke hovering over him like the cloud of unknowing.

Twice Kate had said in a voice whose tone sent chills through Nancy that of course Father hadn't really been her father.

"Don't say that, sweetheart."

"But it's true."

Nancy waited for the dreaded words but they were not spoken. Nevertheless, it was as if she heard Kate say them, heart speaking to heart: *And you're not my real sister.* Her father's dreadful death brought back an old argument, one she had lost to her parents.

"Of course you shouldn't tell her," Nancy had insisted. "You have no obligation to. What difference does it make now anyway?"

"We'll regret it if we don't," her father said, and he had on his side the seemingly daily instances of young men and women turning on their adoptive parents as if they had done them some terrible injustice by taking them in and giving them a home, a name, and a love that was in many cases keener than any their natural parents might have given them. Nancy supposed the adoptive parents, if they thought of it in a calculating way, which never seemed to be part of such stories, would have said they had done a good thing by adopting the now estranged child. It seemed a bitter reward for having gone through the gamut of government and social and other tests and appraisals, and then waiting, waiting, waiting. If God required such qualities of natural parents, no one would get born. Kate's remark about her father filled Nancy with fear as to what would come next in her sister's odd distancing of herself from this family tragedy.

"I'll miss him so much," Nancy said, her voice trembling, and then she felt Kate's arms about her.

"Oh, Nan, Nan."

And they wept in each other's arms. If tears could solve anything, that might have been the end of it, but Kate returned to it again, more tenderly, but her words still held the same bitter message.

"I don't mean that I don't miss him and that I didn't love him, Nan. That isn't it. You know it isn't."

"And, darling, he loved you."

"I know . . ."

"Better than the boys," she burst out, wanting to say it, having to say it. It was true and she felt she owed it to her father to say so. That was one of her reasons for not wanting Kate told that she had been adopted.

"You know what it will sound like. Are you going to tell her every secret we have?"

It was the ultimate trump, but she had lost the argument anyway. The pain in her father's eyes sent Nan rushing into his arms. His stoic silence had always provided a haven for her. It was the dread she felt then that she wanted to spare Kate. But her father felt an obligation to tell Kate. The revelation was followed by the insistence that he loved her more rather than less, and a bewildered Kate had accepted this, apparently absorbed it, been seemingly untroubled by this radical change in her status. But then her father's tenderness toward Kate had increased, and the event slid into the past and with it the dread her father's action had stirred up in Nancy. Her father, thank God, did not feel obliged to divulge all their secrets.

After the funeral, after Kate returned to campus and her own boys were back in school, routine reestablished, Nancy sat in her father's apartment and pondered the agonizing line of her life. She knew that others thought her blessed, and she was, she was, but they were certain she had never known sorrow. Marjorie White had actually said that, with respect to her father's death. "It is your first real sadness, isn't it?" Dear God. Now that her father was dead, there was no one else to whom she could turn who would remember that time years ago when she had realized she was pregnant. How had they managed to keep it a secret? There had been no question whether or not she would carry the baby. Any other course would have been unthinkable. Nancy had been swept into a whole series of consequences of her weakness, her sin, her fall. It was her father, without condemning, showing nothing but love and kindness and support, who had taken her in charge. Her mother was almost mute with disbelief, and Nancy had found it impossible to talk to her about it. Before long it would be as if it had not happened, but there was a rupture between her and her mother that was never healed. And she drew closer to her father.

Out of town she had gone, to a clinic in Minnesota, discreet, a bower of kindness and understanding. Her time came, she went into labor, and when it was over her baby was gone. For her it had been as bad as an abortion, perhaps worse. She had carried her child, felt life within her, had communed with it in the silence of her shared body, her whole system ordered to the moment of birth. That moment came, and her child was taken away by those who had also waited and were ready to give it a home. When Nancy came back to Fox River, it was as if no time had passed, and a lifetime. She finished college on a different campus, made new friends who could not ask any painful questions while her old ones were never seen again, the better to confirm the story that she had not liked her school and wanted to be somewhere else.

The apartment that had been her father's was filled with photographs: They hung on the wall; they stood on the bookcases that lined two walls; they were on the mantel. Pictures of her family, of the children, of her father with them, many of him with Kate. He had loved her best, the way fathers and grandfathers seem to prefer daughters and granddaughters, loved her as if he meant to erase from her mind the knowledge that he had insisted she have.

Had he been right? She still was not sure. Was the chance that Kate would find out by herself and confront him with the knowledge really preferable to the calm statement that her parents were not her parents, not really, but they loved her all the same? It had been absurd to tell her, stupid. Nancy brought the heel of her hand down on the cushion of her chair. Dear God, what she would not give to undo her father's decision to tell Kate that she had been adopted.

The memorial service at St. Peter's was scheduled after Kate went back to school, and they decided not to ask her to make another trip. That is how they put it when they discussed it, in terms of convenience, and expense too, for that matter, but Nancy found herself unwilling to give Kate another opportunity to express her sense of estrangement from the only family she had ever known.

Nancy had understood her father's attachment to St. Peter's, although her own attitude toward the school was, of course, more complicated. Father Gorman had been an old friend of her father's, a man whose learning he had admired, and partly envied. His pride in what he had done for the school financially was, by all accounts, more than justified. Nancy understood nothing about money. It was her father's area, and she was happy to be guided by him in that as in so many other things. Her friends might think of her as independent, but Nancy knew that she had been her father's daughter all her life. How hard it was to think of a future without his presence, his experience, his love. They had been bound together by the past and its secrets; he had been her confidant when she needed one. But he had been the best kind of confidant, one with whom words are unnecessary. They knew what they both knew and had made a common truce with it.

Jason had said that they could sit down and go over her father's will whenever they liked. There were legal steps he had to take, but in the meantime he could spell out the provisions of Mitchell Striker's will.

"I think he showed us that, Jason," Jim said.

The lawyer shook his head. "Not this one. This is more recent."

It provided distraction at least, and she and Jim met at Jason's office, which was located in a beautiful house that he had rescued from imminent destruction, restored to its original magnificence, and in which he both lived and worked. The house should have been dwarfed and rendered insignificant by the glass giants surrounding it, but it was they that had become functions of it, their glittering sides playing back to the eye reflection upon reflection of a structure that had been there since before the turn of the century. Jason's office suggested a grace of living and slower pace than the view from its window conveyed.

"Your father came to think that you have done very well and that consequently he would leave to you some real property and Nancy's trust."

"Do I have a trust?"

"Nancy," Jim scolded. Obviously she was supposed to know this.

"Trusts have also been established for your sons; they will derive income from them personally beginning at age eighteen and come into complete control at the age of thirty."

Nancy was paying attention now. What was her father's will with regard to Kate, his beloved daughter? It turned out to be phenomenal. The remainder of his wealth went to her.

"What does that amount to, Jason?"

He looked at them, one after another. "At current market value, six million dollars."

"My God."

"Jason, you shouldn't have let him do that."

"Let him, Jim? I think you knew Mitchell Striker at least as well as I did. He had made up his mind and that was it."

Nancy asked softly, "Did he give you any reason?"

"No."

She had always wondered if her father had confided in any of his friends. The discussion of the will went on, and Nancy was filled with foreboding. How would Kate react to her father's generosity? The news would have to be given to her carefully. For a moment Nan felt a surge of anger at the thought of her sister's possible ingratitude, but then the worry that this would precipitate something awful returned.

18

"I'm back."

Clara knew without turning who it was, but she could not stop herself from wheeling around, eagerly, to face Jerry Winegar. Nor could she stop the welcoming smile from forming on her face. In his absence, she had banished him from her life, easily resolved never to see him again. But the sound of his voice swept all that away, and she was startled at her feelings for this man who was still a stranger to her.

"Where have you been?"

"I've been to London to visit the queen."

"Oh."

She took it to mean that he had been to see another woman, but then he began to sing the nursery rhyme, "Pussycat, pussycat, where have you beeeen?" and she could believe that it was just a silly answer, an answer that wasn't an answer.

"Have you missed me?"

She was reduced to girlish reactions, and the worst of it was that not only was she engaging in giggling coquetry but she was a witness of the scene, a slightly overweight widow with a reputation for levelheadedness responding to this Lothario as if her life had been impossibly lonesome without him.

"You might have told me you were going."

"I'll remember that if I go away again."

"You should have been here for the great event."

And she told him about the evening at St. Hilary's Parish Center, Striker's not showing up, and then all the excitement when Father Dowling, coming over from the rectory, found the body in a car, parked, locked, and with its motor running.

"He gave Mitch absolution, but of course it was conditional, assuming he was still alive."

"Good for Father Dowling."

A feature of her marriage to Don had been his indifference to religion. He had treated it as an indulgence of hers, one he humored at best; she had never been absolutely sure that he believed any of it. Perhaps because of that, she enrolled his name in half a dozen societies that offered perpetual masses for the deceased, adding the name to those commemorated daily by the fathers of an order, a community, a house. She imagined Don in the next world, astounded at the spiritual capital that was being amassed for the benefit of his soul. Winegar, by contrast, was unequivocally Catholic—not pious or showy but matter-of-fact. Once settled in town, he had registered at St. Hilary's. And worked in the Ponader used car lot. This was something Clara had meant to confront him with, but confronted by his disarming smile, she couldn't. After all, he had quit.

They went off for lunch, in her car; he was without one at the moment.

"It was a rental."

"I see."

"From Ponader's Motors."

"Jason Broderick told me the oddest thing about you."

"That I had been in your employ?" He laughed and just like that all her doubts about him, which had been encouraged by Jason, were gone.

"Blake—he's your manager—told me that your lawyer had been asking about me. You realize I didn't know you from Eve when I took that job. It was just something to do when I first got back to Fox River, a way of orienting myself. It's the kind of job you get and hold because you can do it and there isn't the usual folderol."

"But you just quit."

"Just quit." Again he laughed and began to sing "King of the Road"—but then he grew serious. "I haven't been out of town, Clara."

"No?"

Talking with him was such a roller coaster, as if he were determined to keep her off balance.

"Do you know what Jude Thaddeus House is?"

"You were there!"

"A little volunteer work. For my sins."

"Your sins!"

He pinched her arm. "Those I hope to commit."

"Oh, you."

But she actually flushed, and the remote memories of that side of life flickered through her blood. Honestly. As if he understood her discomfort, he got them back onto the events of the past weeks. He had heard of Mitch's death, and he had tried to call her, but really he was so caught up in the demanding routine of Jude Thaddeus that he had decided to let the dead bury their dead. Never had the phrase struck her as it did then, but it served to characterize his motives for volunteering at a place that, however much she theoretically approved of it, she had never been able to spend more than a few minutes in. The derelicts seemed like escapees from hell. Watery-eyed wino women and slump-shouldered men, the two sexes almost indistinguishable in dress and manner. Clara found such weakness unintelligible. How joyless a life it was, and yet it had probably begun in a totally different setting, wines served in crystal glasses at tables covered with snowy linen. Who had not enjoyed the headiness of it in such a setting? The glimpse she had of those poor men and women burned itself into her memory.

"I don't know how anyone can stand to work there."

"Well, first of all, you don't think of it as work."

"I mean just being there. Those poor people. . . ."

"It helps to pick out one and tell yourself, that's me. I could be him. And of course that's true. They didn't start there. You would be surprised at the backgrounds of some of them. Maud had a story . . ."

"Maud."

"She started the place."

"But isn't she dead?"

"This story is part of the tradition of the house. It isn't so much a story as a quotation from the autobiography of Saint Teresa."

Apparently the saint had been given a vision of the spot in hell reserved for her if she lost her soul. Jerry Winegar spoke with great vividness and Clara almost shivered.

"Maud said that Thaddeus House was her way of avoiding her assigned seat in hell."

Again he seemed to sense her feelings and shifted away from the topic. They were in Evanston, in the hotel dining room, his suggestion. Afterward they would visit the bookstores that had proliferated there because of the university. This was yet another side of him. When Jason had told her the results of his inquiry, she had been able to remember Jerry Winegar as a shiftless charmer, almost a vagrant, but he had so many sides to him of which she had no inkling that she was constantly revising her estimate of who and what he was.

"Where did you come to Fox River from?"

"First tell me more about Striker's family."

"He lived with his daughter, in an apartment over the garage specially built for him."

Well, it was delightful to talk about Nancy and her family, the wonderful children and the way in which her father had been an integral part of the family yet still independent, in his own apartment, so much better than the prospect of a nursing home.

There were thoughts about the future that Clara did not want to have. That she had been provided for had been made abundantly clear by Jason; she would never face the prospect of destitution as the result of extended medical care. Perhaps worry about the economics of old age is a convenient buffer to the real worry—age, debility, death. Death would come. And she would be all alone when it did. Mitch's situation had been so different, and now he had his children and grandchildren to mourn him. Who would have masses said for her after she was gone?

"How many Walsh children are there?"

"Two boys. Nancy's sister lives with them too."

"Sister."

"Oh, she's considerably younger." Clara sat forward. "It's one of the things that made it easy to overlook Mitch's foibles, wanting to lecture about money and all that. Kate is adopted."

"That's the sister."

"Adopted sister."

"How old is she?"

"Twenty, twenty-one. She's in college." Clara paused, remembering. "She volunteered at Jude Thaddeus House too. Last summer."

"Is that right?"

"Mitch was so proud of her."

"I'll bet he was."

It was not fair to say, as Father Dowling did, that Marie kept a roll of those who attended the daily noon mass at St. Hilary's, but she would have had to be a mystic not to notice. Regulars of course she noticed, in the sense that their absence would have struck her, and newcomers were bound to catch her eye. The second time Winegar came, she wondered if he would become a regular. She remembered when he first came to the door and they had been chatting in the front parlor until Father Dowling came along and almost scolded her as if she were taking over his job. Did Winegar remember?

He had come in by the side door, the one near the sacristy that gave onto the sidewalk leading to the rectory. Marie was puttering with a birdbath when he came out.

"Well, haven't you become a stranger."

"No. That's how I began."

"It's Mr. Winegar, isn't it?"

"Jerry. And you are Marie Murkin."

She was absurdly glad that he remembered. She looked toward the door. Father Dowling stayed a few minutes after mass, making his thanksgiving, and then came to lunch. Marie had the thought that if she kept Winegar here until Father Dowling came out, the pastor would invite him to lunch. Captain Keegan had not been at the mass, she had noticed, and, of course, if he were there, it was almost certain that he would have joined Father Dowling for lunch.

"Have you found a place in the parish yet?" When he registered, Winegar had given the address of a hotel. Marie was forbidden to touch anything on the pastor's desk, but she had noticed the registration card Jerome Winegar had filled out.

"Not yet. Any suggestions?"

"Would you like me to ask around?"

"No, no." He looked at the house and then turned toward the school. "I met the fellow who looks after the school."

"Willie!"

"Is that his name? Clara Ponader introduced him."

"The Ponaders were once members of the parish."

"She said he lives in the school."

And then she got it. Was he actually inquiring about living in the parish plant? This disappointed Marie insofar as it suggested that Winegar was on a level with Willie, the little ex-convict Father Dowling had hired as maintenance man although he didn't do a lick of work, and if you didn't believe her, you could ask Edna. (This was something she often rehearsed and intended to say aloud to the pastor some day.) On the other hand, wouldn't it be something to have a man like this living on the premises?

"What do you do?"

"I've been doing volunteer work. At Jude Thaddeus House."

"You have!"

"A week or two." He waved it away as insignificant. Marie wholeheartedly approved of such places but had no desire to go near them. As far as she was concerned, Father Dowling had a bad habit of accommodating some people who might better be at Jude Thaddeus. But Marie's mind was racing ahead. Clara Ponader was a volunteer, helping Edna Hospers with the old folks. If Winegar had volunteered at Jude Thaddeus, if Edna had need of help, if there was the apartment on the third floor of the school, where the nurse's office had been, well . . .

This line of thought was interrupted by the appearance of Father Dowling, who came out of the church and started toward the house and then drew to a stop at the sight of Marie and Mr. Winegar.

"You remember Jerome Winegar, Father."

"Of course." He shifted his breviary and extended his hand. Cordial enough, but Marie wished it were a warmer welcome.

"He has been helping out at Jude Thaddeus House."

"Well, well."

Marie started babbling then—she couldn't help it—telling Father Dowling that their new parishioner was still looking for lodging in the parish, and wasn't it nice, doing volunteer work like that, the way Clara Ponader helped out at the school, on and on, and the two men grew uneasy under the onslaught of words until Father Dowling interrupted.

"Is lunch ready or are we on a black fast?"

"It will just take a jiffy."

"Want to take a chance on Marie's gruel? I'm living proof that it isn't fatal."

Winegar accepted with a laugh, and Marie skipped along the walk to the house. By the time the men passed through the kitchen, she had the meal well under way.

"Just be seated. I'm ready."

Well, the soup had been simmering all morning, so that was no problem. She got them started on that and then went back to her salmon salad. She felt an urge to sing, but what she did was frown. What on earth was wrong with her? The young man was a young man, years younger than she, and she must not misinterpret his courtly manner. Of course it is flattering to be treated like a woman by so good-looking a man, but it was just that. Still, she hoped that he and Father Dowling would get along, that one thing might lead to another.

After she had brought in the rest of the lunch, she sat in her kitchen and opened a book, listening to the low murmur of male voices in the dining room. It was the music of the voices rather than what they said that she heeded, since the words themselves were not always distinct, but the rhythm and pitch suggested harmony.

They sat on after she cleared the table. Then, as she was doing the dishes, she heard them go down the hallway and assumed they were going to his study. But a moment later came the sound of the front door closing. She dashed through the dining room and into the hallway where Father Dowling stopped at the door of his study to look quizzically at her.

"He left?"

"Yes."

Had she expected him to come say good-bye? "How did it go?"

"The soup was delicious. And the salad. He ate my piece of pie as well as his own."

She nodded, taking all this as a compliment, waiting. When he said nothing, she could not hold her tongue.

"I wonder if there is anything for him to do around here?"

"Do? What do you mean?"

"Well, he did volunteer work. You heard him."

"You mean at the school?"

"It's just a thought."

"Why, Marie, you old matchmaker."

"Matchmaker!"

"Marie, Edna may be alone but she isn't eligible. I hope you're not suggesting that we throw those two young people together."

Marie did not trust herself to answer. She made a face, as if to dissociate herself from any such suggestion, and went back to her kitchen. Edna! Of all the nonsense. And calling her a matchmaker. Oh, it would be just like him to kid about it with Edna. Marie picked up her book, feeling furious.

There are some men who fascinate women but not men, Father Dowling reflected when he had settled behind his desk in the study. Jerry Winegar was clearly one of those. His effect on Marie verged on the comic, though of course his deference and courtesy to her were to be emulated not mocked. It was her response that was so out of character. Now, Phil Keegan was a man's man, and many women clearly found that attractive, but it was impossible to imagine him fawning over them the way Winegar had over Marie. The priest sensed that this was Winegar's way with all women. It was a manner he dropped entirely when there was no woman present, but what replaced the gallant courtier was a personality Roger Dowling could not decipher.

Why Jude Thaddeus Home?

"I have a lot to make up for, Father Dowling."

"We all do."

But he did not want to talk about his volunteer work, which should have commended him but somehow did not. Perhaps what annoyed Father Dowling—the word did not seem too strong—about Winegar was the way the man managed to get him talking about himself. How did he like being pastor of St. Hilary's? How many parishioners were there? How long had the parish center been in operation? Finally, in desperation, Father Dowling asked Winegar to tell him more about himself.

"We met before, Father."

"You mean a few weeks ago?"

"No. Years ago. I was in a class you taught."

Father Dowling sat back and stared at his guest. Winegar's smile encouraged him to try to remember, but it could only have been when he taught Virgil at St. Peter's.

"A Latin class?"

"Arma virumque cano," Winegar began, then stopped with a laugh. "I'd better not try to go on."

"So you were at St. Peter's?"

"Yes."

This should have removed any barrier to liking the man. How could he not respond to someone who had spent his boyhood in an orphanage, even in so unique a one as St. Peter's?

"I suppose I have the grade book stored away somewhere."

"You gave me a B."

Should he remember the name Winegar out of a list of perhaps thirty students? In any case, he didn't.

"I'm going to be saying mass there on Monday. A memorial for Mitchell Striker, the man who was found dead in our parking lot a few weeks ago."

"Yes, I heard about that."

"He was a great benefactor of the school."

"On the board, wasn't he?"

"Was he when you were there?"

"Students don't know things like that—who the members of the school board are."

"I don't suppose they do."

Winegar got to his feet, and Father Dowling walked him to the front door. When he came back he confronted Marie. What he said sent her scooting back to her kitchen. Of course, he had gotten her drift from the moment she began to talk outside the church. She apparently did not see that offering such a man employment of the kind available at St. Hilary's would be a species of insult. What did Winegar do, he wondered? For so affable and talkative a fellow, he certainly revealed little about himself. But imagine! He had been in that Virgil class all those years ago.

The chapel at St. Peter's was a marvel, with mullioned windows, painted beams, a reredo in the Spanish style, and the stations set into the walls. Once the student body attended daily mass, but this had become optional. Perhaps the chapel could not accommodate all of them as it once had. Whatever the current parlous condition of the school's endowment, most of the scholarships that had been given over the years, many by alumni of the school, were independently managed. These would suffice to keep the school population near its original number at least.

Father Dowling was greeted by Bob Frankman just inside the front entrance.

"Roger, I recognized you at once."

At first glance Frankman seemed not to have changed at all. He was, of course, heavier, even paunchy. The old classmates shook hands firmly, seeking in the other's face the boy of long ago.

"I met a fan of yours the other day."

"Who would that be?"

"Keegan?"

"Phil. Did you recognize him? He was several years behind us."

"He didn't mention that."

"I've come to know him very well in recent years, but I have no memories of him at Quigley either."

"I have plenty memories of you."

"Please. I will retaliate if you start."

"Come on. You were the class star. I'm told you're at St. Hilary's?"

The tone said it all, but Roger Dowling had become used to it. There was no point in saying that he found his assignment perfect, that he regarded it as providential and an unequivocal blessing. That would sound like a man trying to make the best of a bad situation, and he knew it. So he smiled and bore the unspoken commiseration of his old classmate.

"Where did you meet Phil Keegan?"

"He came to see me. They're looking into Mitchell Striker's death. I think I was being regarded as a possible suspect."

"No."

"It's a long story. Of course, I never even knew the man."

"A fitting remark in St. Peter's."

Frankman thought about that before he got it. "I don't mean to repudiate Striker. I just never knew him. I came onto the board after he left. He was, of course, publicly critical of me because of some reversals in the school's investment."

"That was his obsessive interest. The night he died he was scheduled to give a lecture on investments."

Father Gorman arrived then, driven by the chaplain of Guardian Angels. He got out of the car and stood for a moment looking at his old domain, a radiant smile on his face. When he had come inside, he said, "I had thought I had seen this place for the last time."

"Don't say that!" cried Cottage, who had joined them.

"Let me say right now that I shall want my own funeral to be from this chapel."

Cottage reacted again as if allusions to mortality were inapplicable to the aged priest. Gorman was saying that he would have insisted on being carried to any memorial for Mitchell Striker, if that had been necessary, a remark that Frankman received with a frozen smile. Roger Dowling excused himself and went on to the sacristy to vest for mass.

The congregation consisted of benefactors, alumni, and well-wishers as well as Striker's daughter and her husband, who were seated in a front pew. Gorman was installed like a bishop at a prie-dieu in the sanctuary. The altar facing the people was a late addition, of course, a concession to postconciliar liturgical changes, but Roger Dowling was oblivious of them as he went through the rite, completely absorbed in his function. And this was his chief function as a priest, to respond to Christ's admonition at the Last Supper: Do this in commemoration of me. All over the world, at every hour of the day and night, somewhere the mass was being said, a memory of Christ's redemptive act and the salvation of mankind. Roger Dowling was a foot soldier in that great sacerdotal army, in the far-flung people of God. But on this occasion there was a special commemoration of Mitchell Striker. That became a source of discussion at the meal afterward.

"Once you would have had to translate his name into Latin," Gorman said.

"What would it be, Father?"

"I had hoped that you, as a Latinist, could tell me."

"Latinist. The headmaster is the Latinist."

But Cottage had no idea either of how "Mitchell" might be rendered in Latin. Father Dowling assured him that even in the old days it could have been left unchanged. "Or assumed to be a variation on Michael."

"It was a family name," Nancy Walsh said. "His maternal grandmother's."

"Aha," Father Gorman said, all his skills at small talk once more at his command.

"And I bear my maternal grandfather's Christian name. Isn't it marvelous how some names are passed down in a family, recurring generation after generation?"

"What are your children's names?" Father Dowling asked Nancy Walsh.

"Joseph and Nathaniel. Biblical names. Jim chose them."

They were not traditional Walsh names, it turned out; he had indeed simply drawn them from the Bible, which seemed a common source, when one thought of it.

"And Nancy?"

"My mother's name."

"And Kate?" asked Father Dowling.

"I think my father took it from Shakespeare."

"Kiss Me Kate?"

"Is that Shakespeare?"

"An adaptation."

"I don't think my father had a musical in mind."

This was protested by several. It was an excellent show.

"Father Gorman," Roger Dowling said during a lull in the conversation, "do you remember an old boy named Winegar?"

The old man became agitated, shifting silverware around, his eyes darting about the table. Aware that he had said something disturbing, Father Dowling hurriedly said, "Or rather, let me ask you this. Do you remember the term when I taught Virgil here?"

"My dear boy, I am eternally grateful to you for your willingness to pitch in." He turned to Cottage, "I hope you never have the experience of finding you are short a teacher at the beginning of a term. It was an experience I always dreaded, perhaps because it was something that happened only twice. Father Dowling alludes to one of those times."

The old man, an accomplished raconteur who had performed at some of the best tables in Chicago, was off and running. Roger Dowling settled back to enjoy the performance, as did others. Gorman had the knack of turning the most banal situation into high drama. When his narrative reached the point at which Roger Dowling had ridden to the rescue, it was difficult not to believe, at least for the moment, that this had been a turning point in the intellectual history of the Midwest, if not beyond.

Later, before leaving, the old man beckoned Roger Dowling to him. "Father, thank you for changing the subject as you did. You must have seen that I could not answer you under the circumstances."

"Is it something you can tell me?"

The old priest touched his arm. "Come see me."

Jim Walsh stopped to say good-bye, but Nancy just waggled her fingers from the doorway and then disappeared outside.

The press room in the courthouse was a favorite stop for Tuttle, chiefly because of the free coffee but also because from time to time he actually picked up a worthwhile tip from the indolent journalists who whiled away their day there, turning out stories on the legislative and judicial and administrative activities of Fox River. Neither singly nor in the aggregate did these represent a taxing load, so the courthouse print journalists were of the philosophical type that knows how to enjoy inactivity.

Entering from the courthouse rotunda, Tuttle called a universal greeting and headed for the coffeepot. He poured a styrofoam cup half full of the syrupy fluid that seemed on the verge of congealing as it ran thickly from the spout.

"Ho," Craven said when Tuttle took a chair across the table from him. A perky young woman turned from her computer and squinted at Tuttle.

"I'm Tuttle," he said.

She got up and came over to him and shook hands. "Sommers. I'm a stringer for the *Trib*."

"Welcome to the club."

"Tuttle's a lawyer," Craven said.

"A lawyer."

She was impressed. Obviously this was a young lady of some intelligence. Tuttle pulled out a chair for her.

"Of Tuttle and Tuttle." He tipped forward until his hat fell into his waiting hand, than flashed his plastic-coated business card at her. "Never hesitate to call on me. For ladies and gentlemen of the press, I normally work pro bono."

"Why would I need a lawyer?"

"You see. You already have a legal question. From whence do you come?"

"Whither goest thou?" Craven grumbled. Sommers ignored him.

"Spokane."

"Spokane!" She might have said Sri Lanka and not gotten a bigger reaction from Tuttle, who had once been to Iowa but hurried home before the flatness got to him.

"Did you see my story on the Striker murder?"

"Was that yours?"

Craven made a noise suggestive of incredulity. Sommers ignored him and so did Tuttle. He asked the young reporter if she was up on the latest developments. Her thick blond hair was worn short and sat like an inverted tulip on her round head, swirling whenever she moved, then falling precisely into place. Dark eyebrows accentuated blue eyes that seemed to open on a world that amazed and fascinated her. She wore an ankle-length shapeless dress of an off shade of blue, and her toes showed through her sandals.

"What latest developments?"

Tuttle hunched a shoulder and moved in the direction it indicated, toward the door, away from the skeptical Craven. "Will you keep a lid on this until I give you the go-ahead?"

She thought about it. Her lower lip was drawn between straight white teeth while her eyes searched Tuttle's face.

"I can't see your eyes because of your hat."

Tuttle tipped back the tweed hat. Her eyes narrowed as she continued to look at him. "What's your sign?"

At first he didn't understand. "My birthday's in September. You tell me."

"September what?"

"Twenty-fifth."

"Libra!" she cried. "I should have known. Yes. Okay. It's a deal."

Tuttle was unused to such deference from an attractive young woman. He found it exhilarating. He found himself less willing to lie to her than he had been when he spoke of the latest events in the Striker case.

"I'm on my way to police headquarters to speak to my contact there. You can come along as my cousin. Wait."

There was a phone on the table next to the door. Tuttle picked it up and punched out Peanuts's number. After a dozen rings, during which Tuttle tried out various pensive expressions, a woman answered impatiently.

"Give me Peanuts."

"How about Cracker Jacks?"

"Pianone. This is Tuttle."

"Oh, hey, whyn't you say so in the first place." Her voice was heavy with irony. Tuttle was about to ask for her badge number when she told him to hold it. Half a minute later Peanuts came on.

"Yeah?"

"Tuttle."

"Yeah."

"I'm on my way to the Great Wall and wondered if you want to come along."

"Sure."

"I will meet you in the courthouse rotunda in exactly three minutes. I will be with a young blond woman in a long dress. Don't speak to me. Follow me to my car, and we'll go to the Great Wall."

"Okay." There were few people other than Peanuts Pianone who would have reacted so blandly to such unusual instructions. But then his mind was presently filled with visions of Chinese food.

"And Peanuts? Bring everything you can on the Striker case."

"What is there?"

"Find out."

"In three minutes?"

"I'll wait. Don't come without it or the Great Wall is out."

He put down the phone, took Sommers's arm, and led her into the rotunda.

"Sommers what?"

"Lucy."

"That's nice."

"Tuttle what?"

"Just Tuttle. That's what everyone calls me."

"That's not fair."

"I'll tell you later."

People moved across the intricately patterned marble floor of the rotunda like pieces in a game understood only by God. It felt good standing there with Lucy Sommers at his side. Over her shoulder she wore a denim purse that bulged with contents, making that shoulder lower than the other. She shifted her feet to compensate.

"I love Chicago," she breathed.

"This is Fox River."

"I mean the greater metropolitan area."

"Right."

"I chose here because there aren't as many people as downtown. I never saw so many people in my life."

"How many in Spokane?"

"One less."

He looked at her. She smiled, nice little dimples, and her eyes widened. "Sorry. Bad joke. Since I left. One left. Forget it."

"That's funny."

"Is that why you're laughing?"

"Why did you leave Spokane?"

"I got this internship? Paid? It's the opportunity of a lifetime."

Tuttle looked around the rotunda and tried to remember a time when the world had looked that promising to him. This kid was a shot in arm, no doubt about it.

Fifteen minutes later Peanuts shuffled toward them.

"You got it?"

"You said not to talk to you."

"Just say yes or no."

"I got it."

"Let's go."

The girl swung in beside him as he headed for the door. He remembered in time to let her go through the revolving door first. A meter maid had a foot on his bumper and was writing out a ticket. Tuttle took it from her.

"Thanks, I'll take that. Take her badge number Detective Pianone. And write a commendation."

He was behind the wheel before she knew what had happened. Lucy scrambled into the passenger seat.

"He's the chief," Peanuts said as he lowered himself into the backseat. The meter maid stooped to get a glimpse, and Tuttle waved at her and pulled into traffic, nearly sideswiping a taxi that was a little late changing lanes.

"I hope you're hungry," Tuttle said to Lucy.

"It's two in the afternoon."

"Think of it as a late lunch. You have lunch, Peanuts?"

"Is it okay to talk now?"

Tuttle glanced at Lucy. Peanuts's oddity had either not dawned on her or she didn't mind. He liked that. Peanuts was the best friend he had and probably vice versa. It made you think.

At the Great Wall they ordered three dishes and a very large pot of tea. That took care of Peanuts. Tuttle opened the folder Peanuts had brought. It was empty. He reached across the table and took away Peanuts's plate.

"There's nothing in here."

"That's what we know about the Striker murder."

"Not good enough, Peanuts. You come across or starve." He passed the plate under Peanuts's nose so that the aroma could work its magic. Peanuts tapped his head.

"It's all here."

Tuttle groaned. To Lucy he said, "We might just as well eat first."

"I'm really not hungry."

"Neither am I. Consider it a professional duty. Peanuts will tell us everything."

Everything wasn't nothing, but it wasn't a great deal more. The lab had identified the brand of shoes that had made footprints in the backseat of Striker's car. The top of the front seat had yielded fibers, thought to be from a sweater the assassin was wearing. A small piece of plastic was part of the wrapper of a hypodermic needle. The day after the body was found, Dr. Pippen had returned to the scene and found a footprint matching those in the car in the mud next to the sidewalk leading toward the church. That was all, or at least all Peanuts had in his head.

"Good work," Tuttle said.

"What does it mean?"

Tuttle looked at Lucy. "That, my dear, is what separates us from the collectors of evidence. We must interpret it."

"So interpret it."

"After I eat."

On their way out of the restaurant they ran into Winegar. Tuttle had not seen him since the bar, when Winegar had gone off with a middle-aged woman he'd had a couple of drinks with. That left Tuttle with the bartender and his third diet Coke. Winegar was all smiles now, but they were directed at Lucy Sommers.

"This is Detective Pianone," Tuttle said to distract the good-looking bum.

"Private?" Winegar asked, his smile fading.

"Corporal," Peanuts said.

They left a mystified Winegar and continued out to Tuttle's car.

"Who was that?" Lucy asked.

"Just a guy."

"He's so good-looking."

"Plastic surgery. They can do wonders."

She didn't have a number where she could call Winegar, so Clara Ponader had to sit by her telephone like a teenager, wondering if the boy would call. Twice she had declined invitations from Marjorie to take in an afternoon movie at the mall, pleading an upset stomach.

"You ought to have that looked at."

"Oh, it's not serious."

"That's what my husband said and it was cancer."

"Marjorie!"

"I wish I had nagged him more at the time. He might still be alive today."

She made an appointment with her doctor just to stop this morbid speculation. Her stomach really had begun to feel upset when she was talking with Marjorie, and Clara didn't want to give her imagination free rein.

"Whatever happened to that good-looking man you brought to St. Hilary's?"

"Good-looking man?"

"Oh, come on. Silvery hair, suntan, slim."

"I don't know what happened to him. He was from out of town."

"I thought he had moved back."

"You know as much about it as I do." But her tone was peevish rather than indifferent. Anyway, Marjorie stopped talking about it, thank God.

Even Jason Broderick asked about Winegar, and Clara had the feeling that he was checking up on her. But he asked her out to dinner and that was a first, a date like that, but she found herself comparing the predictable Jason with the unpredictable Winegar. Jason's gallantry had a to-whom-it-may-concern aspect to it, like a generic drug: He could turn it on anyone and it would be the same. Winegar, on the other hand, had seemed to speak directly to her and to her alone.

Oh, such nonsense. Jason was an expert dancer, and it was pleasant to be moved so deftly about by him, though of course all eyes were on him. It might have been a better evening if she had not felt that she was the object of Jason's professional therapy.

"Has that Winegar fellow been back?"

"Back where?"

He dipped his head and looked at her over his glasses. "Has he called you?"

"No. You sound like Marjorie."

"Do I? Well, listen to your friends."

She called on Nancy Walsh, to get her mind on something else, and asked about the memorial service at St. Peter's, but Nancy didn't want to go on about it. Jason, on the other hand, had given her more detail about it than she had wanted. Clara wondered if Nancy thought she should have gone, but that worry evaporated while she talked to her.

"I'm going to leave Dad's apartment just the way it was, at least for now."

"Of course." Clara had followed Marjorie's advice and cleaned out Don's closets the week after the funeral, and she was never quite sure whether it had been the right thing to do.

"Every time I go in there I half expect to find him." Nancy went to the desk and moved a ring of keys lying there. "Those are the keys of St. Peter's School. I suppose I should turn them in, but I just can't."

"Have they found out yet who did it?"

"No."

"Haven't they any ideas at all?"

"That's what they ask us! Who would have wanted to kill Dad? The answer is nobody."

"Of course not."

Except that someone had. From what Jason had told her, information he had gotten from Chief Robertson, it was not just a random act of violence. It had the look of a planned killing, an assassination. It was difficult to imagine Mitchell Striker having that kind of importance for anyone.

"It can't be his heirs, not in this case."

Like most lawyers, Jason loved to divulge professional secrets, and he had given Clara a full account of Mitch's will. Giving that much money to an adopted daughter was surprising, until you saw how well provided for everyone was. God knows Nancy and Jim didn't need the money. Quite apart from Jim's practice, Mitch had handled his investments, and though Jason had no precise figures, he was certain the Walshes were very well fixed indeed. Their money would go to the Walsh boys eventually, so giving all that money to Kate made sense, when you thought about it. And besides, Nancy and Jim thought it was just fine.

"Wasn't your dad generous to Kate?" Clara said to Nancy now.

"How'd you know about that?"

Whoops. "Didn't you tell me?"

"I don't remember telling anyone."

"Then it must have been Marjorie."

"But how would Marjorie know a thing like that?"

"Would your father have told her?"

Thank God Nancy found that plausible. Jason would never forgive her if she let it be known that he told his clients' secrets to other clients.

"It is true, isn't it?"

"Not even Kate knows about it, Clara."

"I won't breathe a word."

"I'll have to talk with Marjorie."

"No. No, I'll do that."

"That ought to keep the wolf from her door," Winegar said when Clara mentioned Kate Striker's good fortune to him.

"More likely it will bring him there. Them. Wolves."

He smiled as if he regarded such comic scrambling after money from a lofty perch above the fray. What were his circumstances? She knew no more now than she had when they first met. The first meeting was one that in retrospect had been considerably edited. The literal version, which presented her as a bored and lonely widow lunching alone in a department store tearoom and susceptible to the advances of a good-looking stranger, was obviously not one she cared to cherish. In the amended version she entered regally, a piano played discreetly in the background, there was a general stir at her entrance, but slowly this handsome man rose to his feet and said in a vibrant voice, low but audible, "Clara?" From that beginning the scenario advanced to her great advantage, and to his; it was not that she felt the need for her own role to be upgraded; his had to be reimagined also so that it would be appropriate to him.

Except that she had no idea what was appropriate to him. She seemed to talk to him endlessly in the hope that something she said would trigger off a great confidence, give at least some hint of who and what he was. Who would have thought it would be the mention of the memorial service for Mitchell Striker at St. Peter's?

"I went there."

"To the memorial service?"

He looked at her. "To the school."

"You did!"

His eyes remained on hers. "I never graduated. I left during my senior year. I couldn't wait to go into the army." He smiled indulgently at this memory of his earlier self.

"But isn't the school for . . ."

"Orphans? Yes. My parents died in an accident, the kind you don't want to think about. The car trying to get across the tracks before the train arrives. They were dragged a mile before the train was able to stop."

"Dear God."

"I never really knew them."

Was she glad now to have at least this much information about his past? Of course she was, and her appetite for more had been whetted.

"How long were you there?"

"It's a prep school. There are four years."

And he had left at the beginning of his fourth. "Tell me about it."

"Is there anything more boring than someone else's story of their callow youth."

"It wouldn't be boring at all."

"Here is one tidbit anyway. The other day I told Father Dowling that I had met him before. He didn't remember—why should he? He knew me as a raw youth. One term he taught Latin at St. Peter's, and I was in the class."

This was precious information, especially because it linked him with others she knew. She made much of the fact that Father Dowling had not recognized him.

"It would have been amazing if he had remembered me."

"How long ago was it?"

He pinched her arm, not quite painfully. "I wondered when you would ask that."

"You don't have to answer."

"Then I won't."

She could find out for herself now, knowing what she did—ask Father Dowling when he had taught the class, check at the school, or have Jason do it, unless she didn't want him to know. If he knew, everyone would know. It turned out that Marie Murkin didn't know.

"Teach school? I have no idea."

The housekeeper did not like the implication that Clara knew more about the pastor than she did. Of course, this would have been before he came to St. Hilary's.

"Where was he stationed before coming here?"

"He was on the archdiocesan marriage tribunal."

"What on earth is that?"

"One of the most important posts in the archdiocese. At least it used to be. They hear requests for annulment."

"Ah."

Later that week she was at the country club for bridge, and after that broke up, she was going by the bar when she ran into Bob Frankman. He suggested a drink, and she let him order a glass of white wine for her. The bar at that hour was crowded, smoke filled, noisy with many voices. They ended up in the lobby in two chairs that were seldom used, there for decoration rather than practicality.

"Didn't I hear that you're on the board at St. Peter's School?"

He looked at her for a moment. "I am."

She leaned toward him, legs crossed, holding her wine in both hands. "Could you do a small favor for me?"

"Name it."

"It's just a whim and if you think you shouldn't, just say so."

"Go on."

"There was a boy at St. Peter's some years ago who left at the beginning of his fourth year. I don't know what year that was, and I would like to know. The only clue I have is that while he was there Father Dowling taught a Latin course and the boy was in the class."

"That was mentioned the other day at our memorial for Mitchell Striker."

"Was it?"

"What's the boy's name?"

"He isn't a boy now, of course. Winegar. Jerome Winegar."

"Winegar."

"Do you know him?"

"I've heard the name."

"Anything you can find out, Bob, I'd appreciate."

"Consider it done."

How easy that had been. She could hardly refuse to have dinner with Bob after that. She had another glass of wine at the table before they ordered because he asked for another scotch. The memorial at St. Peter's seemed to be the favorite topic of late. That and references to Father Dowling.

"He said the mass. It would have been impossible for old Gorman to do it, although he was there for the occasion. Roger Dowling and I were classmates in the seminary."

"You were in the seminary?"

He smiled. "I wish that didn't surprise you quite so much."

"I've always thought of you as, well, uxorious."

"I wish my wives had thought so."

A somber note. Bob's first marriage had been annulled, and his second ended in divorce. Nor did his interests in that line seem to be over, considering the fact that he was almost as constant an escort of different women as Jason.

"It's a long sad story," he sighed over the entree. "My only consolation is that I am right with the church."

Over brandy he asked how she was adjusting to being alone. Under the circumstances, that seemed a dangerous line of conversation. It had been an enjoyable evening, and she was grateful in advance for what he could find out for her about Winegar, but the thought of romantic entanglement with Bob Frankman did not appeal. He might be all right with the church, but his reputation around the club was something else. Even so, she looked forward to mentioning offhandedly to Marjorie that she'd had a date with Bob Frankman.

23

"You never told me you taught school," Marie said to Father Dowling in mock scolding tones. She had waited until serving lunch to him and Phil Keegan to ask the question.

"Did you?" Phil asked.

"Well, as a seminarian I taught catechism once in a while."

"In Latin?"

"Don't mention Latin," Phil groaned. Latin had been the shoal on which the ship of his presumed priestly vocation had foundered.

"What prompts the question?"

"Something Clara Ponader said."

"Clara Ponader!"

It was possible that Winegar had mentioned it to Clara. That he knew her was one of those items of intelligence he owed to Marie Murkin's sleepless vigilance. The way she put it, Clara was setting her cap for Winegar.

"Setting her cap?"

"You know what I mean."

"Does anyone use that phrase anymore?"

"I just did."

"That's true."

By such questionable means he diverted her from prying into the lives of parishioners or, in Clara's case, of someone who had been kind enough to volunteer to help Edna Hospers in the parish center.

He felt as concerned as Marie when he noticed Clara and Winegar in a car that she was driving. He supposed that it was possible that he had mentioned the class that had been all but forgotten before Winegar brought it up. What Father Dowling remembered was Gorman's reaction to the mention of Winegar at St. Peter's. "Come see me," he had said.

* * *

The old priest was in pajamas and robe and sitting in a chair at the foot of his bed and seemed to have aged a decade in the week that had passed since the service at St. Peter's. He brightened at the sight of the younger priest.

"Did I ever express my admiration for the way you conducted the service for Mitchell Striker, Roger? It was *absolument comme il faut.*"

"It must be pleasant for you to get back to St. Peter's."

"Oddly it isn't. It brings home to me that the school I love is here." He tapped his head and then his heart. "It goes on, I know, but it is Cottage's school now. I prefer my memories to being kept informed on current events."

"You reacted dramatically to my mention of Winegar."

The old priest's hands lifted in an *orate fratres* gesture. "I couldn't speak of all that, not with Mitchell's daughter right there at table."

"Nancy Walsh."

He nodded.

"What has she to do with Winegar?"

The old priest urged Roger Dowling to pull his chair closer. "Everything I tell you I tell you in utter confidence. With the proviso, however, that it is not my secret. I am not sure just how much of a secret it is. If it isn't one, this isn't because of any lack of effort on Mitchell Striker's part."

In the ensuing half hour, Roger Dowling came to understand why Father Gorman had waved him off the subject when it came up at table at St. Peter's. Nancy, because of her father's connection with the school, had accompanied him there from time to time. And that is when she caught the eye of young Winegar, as he then was. The rest took place outside the father's knowledge, but the two young people had grown close to one another. Too close. One day Nancy's condition became inescapable. She was pregnant. The only possible father was Jerome Winegar.

"Nancy came to me," Gorman said, and this was clearly not one of the memories he cherished. "I had faced many crises as headmaster of St. Peter's, but never anything like this. Boys do not become pregnant. She wanted me to marry them."

"How old were they at the time?"

"Arguably of legal age. But that was not the problem."

"What was?"

"In such a situation, Father Dowling, Barkis must be willin'."

88

"Winegar is Barkis?"

"He panicked at the thought of marriage. I should add that he was the most promising boy in his class. His academic performance was stellar. His admission to a first-rate university was assured. He was a very ambitious boy. Whatever infatuation he had felt for Nancy was chilled by the prospect of a wife and child before he had even finished prep school."

This was unacceptable to Mitchell Striker. He insisted that the young man marry his daughter.

"Imagine my predicament, Father Dowling. Who would not have sympathized with the young woman, and with her father? But a shotgun marriage? The boy could not be forced, and the fact that he would have to be made him a singularly unattractive son-in-law, or so I would have thought. Mitchell would not listen. There was only one acceptable solution and that was marriage."

"And he failed to get that solution."

"Father, I began by suggesting it was Nancy Walsh's embarrassment that explained my reluctance to speak of this at St. Peter's. That is only part of it. I am ashamed to remember what I did."

"What was that?"

"When it became clear that Winegar was not to be persuaded, or threatened, into marriage, Mitchell insisted that he be expelled from the school. There was a patina of legality in this; boys were held to a high code of conduct. There was no specific mention of impregnating the daughters of members of the board, but given the other things explicitly mentioned, this seemed a fortiori cause for expulsion."

"His academic hopes were the major reason for his refusal to marry the girl?"

"Yes."

"And he was expelled."

"I expelled him, God forgive me. He dropped off the face of the earth. Apparently he immediately entered the army and went off to equivocal battle."

"So he had courage in the usual sense."

"And a kind of principle. I was never sure whether I should admire him or, like Mitchell Striker, despise him. By acting as Mitchell's instrument, I conveyed to him that it was the last that I felt. The life he might have had was closed to him."

"I wonder what he has been doing all these years?"

"He has returned, Father Dowling. He has been here to see me."

"When?"

"The day before yesterday."

Father Dowling waited. The old priest's face was a kaleidoscope of expressions, as if his face could not keep up with his flickering thoughts.

"How was it?"

"Awful." He breathed the word as bishops used to breathe on those receiving confirmation. "Awful."

"He blamed you?"

"Worse. Far worse." The watery old eyes bore into Father Dowling's. "He forgave me."

The two priests sat in silence. It was their function to pass on God's forgiveness to repentant persons, and of course they themselves regularly confessed their sins. But the forgiveness that sent a shudder through the frail body of Father Gorman had been a weapon of revenge.

"What happened to the child?"

"It was not a subject Mitchell Striker and I ever discussed again."

"Surely it was born?"

The old priest looked sharply at him. "Yes, yes, no doubt of that. Any other course would have been unthinkable for Mitchell and I am sure for his daughter. During the dreadful negotiations, she said several times that she would have her baby in any case."

"I'm sorry to have been the occasion of bringing all this up again, Father."

"Oh, this has been easy. It was Winegar's visit that was difficult."

It is a bane of a priest's life that he becomes privy to the secrets of others, aware of troubles he can do little to alleviate, so that the mere knowledge of them becomes a burden of his own. From the time of that visit to Guardian Angels he could no longer view Nancy Walsh, or Jerome Winegar, as he had before, but equally he could do nothing to indicate what he knew. Perhaps it was not a secret, it certainly did not come under the seal of the confessional, but over and beyond his assurance to Father Gorman, the knowledge he now had involved the most intimate lives of two people, of at least two people. It would be unconscionable to be the instrument of further pain for either of them. Particularly for Nancy Walsh. Who was to say which of the two had suffered more? The fact that Winegar had sought out his old headmaster and made him suffer by a pose of magnanimity suggested that he still burned with resentment at the injustice done him long ago. A retaliatory injustice, no doubt; he had acquired obligations to Nancy and her child he was unwilling to shoulder. Father

Dowling could not help wondering how she had borne this burden over the years. Almost against his will, he found himself seeking the answer to that question.

When she read of Thomas More conversing with his daughters in the garden in Greek, Kate would think of those wonderful years during which her father had taught her Latin. Her foster father, she reminded herself, and tears welled in her eyes. Of course, Nancy thought she was cold and cruel, but no one else could understand what she felt, knowing that she was not a real member of the family.

Really adopted, really raised, really loved, yes, oh yes, all those things, but the one thing missing was their blood in her veins. And if not theirs, whose? Her roommates wouldn't have guessed how much she envied them—not their actual families but just the fact that there were families to which they unquestionably belonged. In every other way she preferred her own upbringing and the parents she had. Not that she had told her friends at college that she was adopted. She had insisted on that with Nancy, but with others she still regarded it with shame.

She sat at her desk in the room she shared with Barbara and Jane, Catullus open before her, dictionary, grammar, several recent translations of the poet on her desk, and all she could think about was the funeral. That her father had died, at his age, was not the shock, but the way it had happened.

A roommate she'd had in freshman year was raped that spring and had gone into an absolute tailspin. It had just happened, no warning, out of the blue, and afterward, when her world had been completely destroyed and she became fearful of everyone and everything, there was no one to punish. The man, boy, whoever he had been, had struck and gone and disappeared, leaving Joanne with the consequences. They had been only psychological, thank God, but that turned out to be bad enough. She dropped out of school and was now as vanished as her assailant. And now it looked as if Mitchell Striker's murderer would escape in the same way.

Kate could not bear to hear it described, but she had read the newspaper accounts. His death was written of as quick and painless. But microseconds could grow to hours in such a situation. No one could ever know the agony he had suffered.

Kate's love was classics, and that was a tribute to the time he had spent with her when it was clear that she had talents. Now, as she prepared for class, it was as if they were communing through the Latin poetry—communing with the dead by means of a dead language. Of course, Latin had never been dead except to those who failed to come alive to it. She had never read Catullus with her father, of course, nor Ovid. But the language was the same, and she had the sense that he was at her shoulder as she worked.

Dad had never worked with Nancy as he had with her, and Nancy was as bright as anyone Kate knew. Not that Nancy resented it, far from it. She seemed to take as much pride in her little sister's accomplishments as their father. Remembering the insistent way she had said to Nancy that Dad was not her real father, Kate wanted to take it back, to explain what she had meant, if she could. She would like to just be with Nancy now; they wouldn't have to talk a lot to enable her to make up for it. That was when she resolved that she would hop into her car immediately after class and drive home to Fox River. She packed a few things, considered calling to give Nancy warning, then decided that surprising her would fit in better with her reason for going.

Miss Griswold preferred Greek to Latin but she taught both. A week into the semester it was obvious that she regretted offering a course in Catullus. There were only three of them in it: Kate, a tall thin girl with thick glasses named Imogene, and an auditor from the men's college across the road. Catullus's shameless pagan eroticism tightened the lines around Miss Griswold's mouth and made Imogene clear her throat a lot. Today, fortunately, they had been assigned Catullus's tribute to his brother. Kate had breathed the poem's final words over her father's grave. *Ave atque vale.*

When she returned from class, there was a man waiting to see her. From behind his back, her roommates rolled their eyes and made swooning gestures. He *was* good-looking.

"I knew your father," he said when she acknowledged that she was Kate Striker.

She looked at him. "I don't recall ever meeting you."

"I knew him a long time ago." He looked at her appraisingly. "Maybe before you were born."

She waited. She wasn't going to tell him how old she was, if that's what he was waiting for.

"Did you come here just to see me?"

He shook his head. "No. I was passing through and remembered having heard you attended school here and took the opportunity to stop and mention your father."

"You haven't given me your name."

"Winegar. Jerome Winegar."

"Where did you know him?"

"I was a student at a school whose board of directors he served on."

"St. Peter's!"

"You know it?"

"Of course. It was one of his great enthusiasms."

"I'm sure it was."

"It was very kind of you to stop by."

"I never forgot your father."

She felt an absurd impulse to tell this stranger she was adopted, that Mitchell Striker was not her father and that she was not his daughter.

"Have you said these things to my sister?"

"Mrs. Walsh?"

"Nancy."

"Do you think I should?"

"She would be at least as glad as I am to hear that someone who knew Dad all those years ago still remembers him. I gather you hadn't seen him in the meantime?"

"I have been living in the West."

They stood looking at one another, not saying anything further. There didn't seem to be anything more to say.

"What's your favorite subject?"

"We don't major. If we did, it would be classics."

"Greek and Latin?"

"Mainly Latin."

"I studied Latin at St. Peter's. It's what I would have gone on to study in college."

"Why didn't you?"

"It's a long story."

"Well. Actually I'm about to head for Fox River, to be with my sister. I'll tell her of our talk. What was your name again?"

"Winegar. Jerome Winegar."

When Maud Weaver started Jude Thaddeus House, homelessness was not a favorite cause, and compared to some of the recent establishments, hers looked as if it shared the economic status of the men and women who wandered out its doors every morning and with twilight began to shuffle back again. Keegan had seen pictures of Asian dope addicts, emaciated men lying in tiered bunks, puffing on an opium pipe and looking with large dead eyes at the camera. The winos Maud set out to help weren't much better off.

"Do you hope to cure them?" Maud had been asked.

"No."

"So what's the point if they just keep coming back?"

"What's the point of washing your face if it keeps getting dirty again?"

"That's not much of an answer."

"Well it wasn't much of a question."

Finally everyone knew what motivated her, not because she said it but because eventually it dawned on those whose interest continued that she wouldn't go on doing what she did for any lesser motive. Christians are a mixed bunch, but Maud looked a lot more like the earliest ones than she did any of her contemporary fellow believers. She seemed to have no doubt about the truths of the faith; she accepted them as true because God said so. That, she seemed to say, was the easier part anyway. Essential, but easier. The hard part was to live it, and living it meant loving your fellow man, and winos were a typical sample of mankind.

"Typical?"

She would look at the questioner. "There are winos and winos."

She wasn't accusing anyone, just providing an opportunity to think. People who came to help her brought with them the unstated assumption that they were better than the ones they came to help. That easy conviction did not long survive being in Maud's company. Phil Keegan doubted that he could have put in a full day there.

"Winegar? What about him?"

Phil Keegan put the question to Haley, the egg-bald cadaverous man with the walrus mustache who had taken over after Maud died.

"What about him?"

"He been helping you out?"

"Has he done something?"

"Nothing I know about."

"He's been staying here."

It turned out that Haley meant Winegar had been sleeping at Jude Thaddeus as one of the clients.

"From what I've heard, he doesn't seem the type."

"What's the type?"

Well, that was the answer to Roger's question apparently, and Keegan wondered why he had raised it. So he asked the pastor of St. Hilary's.

"I think Marie's got a crush on him."

"But she likes all the boys."

Marie stood beside the table, undecided which of them to glare at. "Father Dowling is still annoyed because Mr. Winegar chose to ask me a few questions before I brought him to the study."

"I have to protect Phil's interests."

"Oh, for heaven's sake."

The more Phil looked into Winegar, the more fascinating the picture became. Blake at Ponader's Motors spoke of his former employee as if he were a legendary character.

"He could sell cars, don't get me wrong. A natural salesman. But from the first I thought he was wasted here. He was obviously an educated man. My suspicion was that he was on the sauce. You know, a professional man, successful at something, and he starts to drink and the next thing you know he's waking up in strange towns without any money. So he takes temporary jobs like this. Not that he told me it was temporary. I don't hire people by the month."

"Have you seen him since he left?"

Blake smiled. "A guy like that's a rolling stone. God knows where he is now."

"Did he drink?"

"Not while he was here. But he was a drinker."

"So that's your theory?"

"It's got to be something like that." Blake hitched up his trousers and looked out over the lot. "He wasn't meant to be a used car salesman, Captain, I can tell you that."

What had he been? What was he? More important, why was the Fox River captain of detectives going around asking questions about the man? Because there wasn't enough to keep him busy on the outstanding case facing the department, the murder of Mitchell Striker. Roger Dowling had gotten him interested in a man who, as a kid, was a student at St. Peter's and had been in a Latin class Roger had taught years ago. Hearing that someone had put in time in an orphanage engaged sympathy, no doubt about it, even when the orphanage was the unusual institution St. Peter's was.

In his office Keegan lit a cigar, ignoring the groans of protest of Lois, his secretary. The mayor kept threatening to make every public building smoke-free, but he hadn't acted yet, probably because he was a three-pack-a-day man, and until he did, Phil Keegan intended to enjoy his constitutional right to foul the air in which he worked. There was a message to call Cy Horvath, so he did.

"Remember Gerry?"

"No."

"The gruff old guy at St. Hilary's who had the crush on Barbara Rooney?"

"Oh yes. What about him?"

"He says he knows who killed Striker."

"Where is he?"

"In the building. I've got Agnes keeping him entertained. I wanted you to decide on this."

"Decide what?"

"Whether we take him seriously."

"Who does he say did it?"

"Father Dowling."

"Has he talked with anyone?"

"Someone named Sommers, a reporter for the *Trib*, thought we ought to know she's going to run a story on it."

"Geez."

Keegan pushed back from his desk, reluctantly stubbed out his cigar, and rose to his feet.

"You want to finish that cigar, it's on my desk," he said as he went past Lois.

Gerry was telling Agnes about the First Amendment when Phil and Cy joined them.

"Go ahead," Keegan said. "I've always wanted to learn about the Constitution."

"Why was I brought down here?"

"You want to leave?"

"Can I?"

"Sure."

He looked at the three expressionless cops as the silence grew. He fidgeted in his chair. "It's the only possible explanation." Nobody said anything. "You got a better one, I'm willing to listen."

"You have the floor, Gerry. Tell us what happened."

"I don't claim I saw it. I never said that."

"To the reporter?"

"I thought she was from here at first, but it doesn't matter. I have my rights."

"How did Father Dowling kill Mitchell Striker?"

"You know how he did it. The thing is, he's the only one who had the opportunity. We're all waiting in the school, Mitch comes and parks and sits there, probably thinking about his speech. Father Dowling comes along the walk from the rectory, Mitch can't hear much in the best of circumstances, but in the rain, well, the door is open and he gets in the backseat and bam, bam, it's over."

Suppressing a smile, Keegan nodded. "Fine. Any idea why he does it?"

"He tried to talk Mitch out of that lecture. Originally he wanted to do four and Father Dowling got him down to one. My idea is he kept telling himself he should have prevented it altogether. And that is what he did."

"Well that takes care of opportunity and motive."

"There's more," Gerry said.

"What's that?"

"It's out in my car. In the trunk."

"What is it?"

"The overshoes he was wearing, the ones that made the footprints."

This time it was Gerry who let the silence develop. Finally Keegan nodded to Cy. "Take Gerry out to his car."

Agnes sat looking at Phil Keegan. "Is it possible?"

"Let's check it out before that story appears."

26

When Nancy Walsh read the story accusing Father Dowling of killing her father, she felt a murderous impulse of her own. Who on earth was Gerry Major?

"He's a grouchy little man who is always following Barbara Rooney around," Clara said. "At St. Hilary's Parish Center."

The fact that he was a regular at the parish center gave his accusation a specious credibility. It was worse than treason for him to accuse the pastor of the parish that provided him with a place to while away his days.

"He claims that it was one of Father Dowling's shoes that made the footprints in and around Mitch Striker's car." Clara said. "He actually got hold of the shoes."

"How did he do that?"

"Just don't ask Marie Murkin."

Poor Father Dowling was besieged by reporters and television cameras and managed to remain serene as he denied having killed his old friend Mitchell Striker. It emerged that Captain Philip Keegan was also an old friend of the pastor of St. Hilary's. The media then turned their attention to the police department's alleged delinquency in pursuing the lead opened up for them by Gerry Major and the *Tribune.*

"Does the shoe match the prints?" Keegan was asked.

"Yes."

Pandemonium among the reporters. If the police had matched the priest's shoe to the prints found on the murder scene, why hadn't they made an arrest? Why hadn't Father Dowling been brought in for questioning?

"It wasn't his shoe."

"But it was the shoe that made the prints?"

"It looks like it."

"Then whose shoe is it?"

There were those who felt that the police should engage in a Cinderella-style search and try the shoe on every foot they could until they found the owner. Captain Keegan pointed out that, like most shoes, it was of a size that fit more than one foot.

Where had the shoe been found?

Clara Ponader was a good source of information, but Nancy hesitated to put all these questions to her. Anything she said might add to the circus atmosphere that was growing up around her father's tragic death. She didn't like that. She didn't like it at all. Captain Keegan should stop encouraging the press in thinking that the shoe that Gerry Major had found represented some great mystery. Finally she asked Clara where on earth the shoe had been found.

"In the school," Clara said in a confiding whisper. "In the basement apartment where Willie the maintenance man lives."

Willie, it seemed had been arrested on this basis and taken downtown for questioning. Clara did not know what was happening to Willie, but there were some who considered Willie, not Gerry Major, to be the traitor. Willie was an ex-convict hired by Father Dowling, and the shoe had been found in his room.

"What was it doing there?"

"Maybe he did it," Clara said.

The maintenance man at St. Hilary's? Willie turned out to be an insignificant little man, a history of losing etched in his pinched face. It was an unwelcome thought, that her father should have been killed for no apparent reason by someone there at the parish.

When she answered the phone and the caller identified himself as Father Dowling, her first reaction was that it was someone playing a grisly joke. Fortunately she said nothing before it became clear that the voice was unmistakably that of the pastor of St. Hilary's.

"Could I come see you, Mrs. Walsh?"

"Well, of course. Or I could come to the rectory, if that's more convenient."

"I'll come there."

After she hung up and began fussing about the house in preparation for his visit, it occurred to her that he must want to assure her that all these newspaper and television stories were complete nonsense. He needn't say that to her. She could have told him that on the phone. Still, she was glad he was coming. She put on coffee, and the house was filled with its aroma when he arrived.

He did talk about Gerry and the young reporter Lucy Sommers, whose gullibility had started it all.

"The real victim is Willie, of course. With his record, even an arrest is a permanent threat to his freedom."

"Was your shoe really found in his apartment?"

"It wasn't my shoe. But it was the shoe that made the prints in the backseat of your father's car and in the ground around it."

"Then it must be the killer's shoe."

He nodded.

"Was it his shoe? Willie's?"

"It was several sizes too large for him."

"But how did it get into his room?"

"That's the question the police have been putting to poor Willie for days."

"What's the answer."

"There is another question."

"What's that?"

"Who called Gerry and told him where to find the shoe—and that it belonged to me?"

"Oh, Father, all this is so demeaning to my father. I would far rather have it end as an unsolved murder than have this going on."

Father Dowling fell silent. She had refilled his cup twice since he had come. So it was true that he drank coffee like water.

"Nancy, the answer to all those questions could be found if we could come up with someone who had an opportunity to put that shoe in Willie's apartment."

"Yes."

Again he fell silent.

"You've thought of someone?" she asked.

"Do you know a man named Winegar?"

"Winegar!"

He put down his cup and clamped his knees with his hands. "Nancy, the other day Father Gorman told me a long and very sad story about a young woman and man, a girl and a boy, really. Your story. And Jerome Winegar's."

She stared at him and suddenly was conscious of every surface of her body, where she left off and everything else began. It was as if a bomb had been set many years ago and the clock had finally ticked to the moment when it must go off.

"My father managed things very well. After it was clear that I was just another wronged woman."

"You had the baby?"

"Yes."

"And?"

"It was adopted."

"Have you heard from Winegar during all these years?"

"No. He had decided that what had happened had not happened. I guess that meant that I ceased to exist, or never had existed."

"He has come back to Fox River."

"Yes."

"Has he tried to see you?"

"No."

"Why do you suppose he came back?"

"I don't know."

"If not to see you, who else would have drawn him back? You said your father managed everything."

Her mouth opened and remained open. Dear God. He did not need to say anything more. Suddenly she understood it all. And it made sense of what had been only an enigma. Revenge, after all these years, for having ruined his life.

"I haven't said anything of this to the police."

"The police."

"They are desperate for a lead. That's why they are wasting so much time quizzing Willie. Of course, they don't think he did it, but they can't ignore the shoe. Winegar had a motive. . . ."

"No! You mustn't tell them, Father. I can't have all that made public now."

"Not even if it might solve your father's murder?"

"It would be worse than murdering him. It would be the whole awful thing all over again."

The more she thought of exposure, and of what its ramifications would be, the more frantic she got. Father Dowling calmed her.

"I have said nothing because I do not feel I have a right to. Without your permission . . ."

She shook her head and her hair seemed to fly about. "I won't give it."

"Then that's the end of it."

She sank back in her chair.

"The end of it so far as you and I are concerned. Nancy, there is no guarantee that someone else won't independently see the significance of Winegar's return."

"Do you really think that he killed my father?"

"I think that he could have been motivated by your father's role in his leaving St. Peter's."

"He had him expelled." She said the words slowly, one at a time, as if their cumulative impact could only be felt in that way.

"I don't *know* he did it. Perhaps even after the most thorough police investigation, an arrest, a conviction, we could still wonder if he had. What do you think?"

"He could have done it." She looked at him. "What difference does it make now who did it? It is all over at last."

She spoke the words in order to try the feel of them on her lips, not because she thought they expressed the truth. She did not know anymore what she thought or what she felt about those events of so long ago. Except for one thing—she was certain of how she felt about that.

"Father, that must not be brought up now, after all these years. Jerome and me."

"I understand."

She trusted that he would not, by word, deed, thought, or omission, in the phrase he would probably use, tell anyone else about what he had learned of the baby she had borne to Jerome Winegar. Father Dowling's "I understand" encompassed her whole family, her husband and children. And Kate too, of course.

"I ask only one thing in return, Nancy. If Winegar gets in touch with you, if it is he who tries to resurrect the past, let me know."

She nodded. "Yes."

Half an hour after he left, Kate unexpectedly drove in.

"Is anything the matter?"

For answer Kate enveloped her in her arms and held her tightly. When she stepped back, there were tears in her eyes.

"That's what I came home to do."

"For heaven's sake."

"What I said about Dad? I'm sorry."

With a sob, Nancy gathered her into her arms, and the two women clung to one another for several minutes. Then, over cups of the coffee she had prepared for Father Dowling's visit but which the priest had not finished, despite his best efforts, they talked.

"The funniest thing, Nancy. Just as I was getting ready to leave, a man who used to know Dad stopped by."

Nancy looked at Kate, and it was as if she had known all along that this would happen. She knew instinctively who the man was. For the first time she began to fear.

"His name is Winegar, something like that, and he said he was a student at St. Peter's when he was a kid. He knew Dad then and . . ." She stopped. "At the time it sounded plausible, but that's pretty incredible, isn't it? Him visiting me." Then she looked at Nancy. "Did he speak to you?"

"No."

"Did you ever hear of him?"

"A boy who went to St. Peter's while Dad was connected with it?"

Kate smiled. "Okay. Dumb question. Anyway, he was very nice, and it didn't seem awkward then."

Kate intended to go back to campus the following morning, early, so it really was a flying visit. It did not seem to be the right time to tell Kate that she was now an independently wealthy young woman, thanks to Mitchell Striker.

The combination of Father Dowling's visit and Kate telling her that Jerome Winegar had visited her on campus filled Nancy with foreboding. Whatever Jerome's reason for returning to Fox River after all these years, she was certain that it concerned her and was not benevolent. His rejection of their child years ago had been devastating for Nancy. Later she would shrivel with embarrassment when she recalled the excited whisper with which she had confided to him their great news. A child had been the last thing from their minds, and yet now that it was clear she was to have one, it seemed an altogether fitting fulfillment of their love. It was as if having a child *had* been the point of everything, because this would be a flesh-and-blood expression of their love.

"You sure?" Jerome had said.

"Yes."

"What are you going to do?"

She had looked at him. "What am I going to do? Jerome, this is our baby; this is us." She took his hand to press it to her womb, but he tore it from her grasp.

"Nancy, we're kids. We're not married."

There had never been a moment when he had remotely hinted that he found the news happy. She, on the other hand, thinking that their sin might become known, but only as an understandable anticipation of their decision to be with one another forever, had been filled with wondrous joy. He had rejected that, and in doing so filled her with shame. By refusing to accept the child as theirs, by making her condition her private problem, he had altered everything. She had never felt more alone in her life, even with the child within her, because they had both been repudiated. She knew that her father's determination to rectify matters with marriage would fail. Jerome was determined to succeed. That lay at the bottom of his rejection of the news that he was going to be a father, and it made him vulnerable when he refused to bend to her father's demand. He who had swept away her hope and joy in turn had his own hope destroyed. When it happened, Nancy was beyond deriving any satisfaction from his fall. It was enough that for her father Jerome's expulsion from St. Peter's was a kind of redressing of the balance.

That night, after the kids were in bed, Jim left them to themselves and they went out to her father's apartment to talk. It was then that Nancy gave Kate some sense of what Mitchell Striker's will was like.

"He left us all a good deal, Kate. He left you a good deal."

"I wish he hadn't done that."

"That's like wishing he wasn't happy. He wanted to do this. It meant a great deal to him."

Nancy was certain that Kate would be no less indifferent when she learned the actual sum.

"I understand your attitude, Kate. But you will have to remember its effect on others. Something Father Dowling said suggested that people are already aware that you have become an heiress."

"If people treat me differently because of money, well, I can easily fix that."

"How?"

Kate's smile was radiant. "Give it away. I'll give it all to Jude Thaddeus House."

What had occurred to Nancy was that it was a rumor of the inheritance that explained Jerome Winegar's visit to her campus.

27

Phil Keegan's request for anything and everything on Winegar made sense to Cy Horvath, particularly because of what Keegan had already come up with.

"Put Agnes on it. Keep it discreet, but I want to know everything we can about that guy."

It was what they might have done earlier if Winegar had seemed in any way connected with the murder of Mitchell Striker. They would have done this to Willie even without the need to do so because of the story Gerry had given the young reporter from the *Tribune*. But the shoes that Gerry had come upon in Willie's apartment had solidified the assumption that it was not merely an accident that Striker had been killed in the parking lot of St. Hilary's Parish Center. Of course, they weren't Willie's shoes. Gerry's imagination caused him to leap to the conclusion that Father Dowling was the owner of the shoes and thus the killer of Striker.

"They were planted in my closet," Willie whined.

"Like a shoe tree?"

"Funny."

Agnes's remark was pretty funny, although Cy never laughed at jokes, not wanting to set a precedent. There were too many jokes he didn't see the point of, and more whose point he didn't think was funny.

"Who would do such a thing to you, Willie?"

"I don't know."

"What reason would anyone have to put those shoes in your closet?"

"This." He swept the room with a wide gesture. "To get me down here, to have you work me over, to try to send me back for good."

"Who hates you that much?"

"I don't know! Maybe you guys put them there so you wouldn't look so bad in the papers."

"Yeah. We've really gotten a good press with this. Getting Gerry to make asses out of us was difficult, but we managed to persuade him. He didn't care about us, but he didn't like getting you into trouble."

"So we're agreed they were a plant?"

"Shoes a vegetable? I'd say animal. Skin, leather, you know."

Willie had hired Tuttle to represent him. Well, why not? Tuttle clung to the courthouse like the smell of the disinfectant the cleaning crew used.

"Bring a charge or let my client go!" Tuttle cried.

"Yes, Moses."

Tuttle looked at Agnes, genuinely puzzled. She explained. He confided in her that he meant to start at the beginning and go right through the Bible, right to the end, the apostrophes and everything.

"Apostrophes?"

"The ones they're not sure of. Like the creed."

"The creed!"

"Catholics say it every Sunday." Tuttle closed his eyes and recited, "I believe in God, the father almighty . . ."

Agnes interrupted him. "Every church says that every Sunday."

"I envy you your biblical knowledge."

"I envy guys whose lawyer isn't so tight with the cops," Willie grumbled.

The implied doubt spurred Tuttle into activity. He was wasting his time gathering evidence to prevent Willie's indictment. He was wasting his time because they weren't going to seek an indictment, and they were wasting their time because nothing Willie knew shed any light on the murder of Mitchell Striker. In these circumstances, it was a relief to undertake a thorough investigation of the background of Jerome Winegar.

"You might check with Bob Frankman," Father Dowling suggested. "About the St. Peter's matter."

It would have been too much to say that the financier's cooperativeness increased when he saw that the supposed enmity between himself and his highly successful predecessor was no longer being seen as relevant to recent tragic events. But he was cautious.

"What did the headmaster say?" he asked Horvath.

"If he knows of what happened back then, he acquired the knowledge independently of the police."

Frankman took the point. How many people need know, or need be involved in the inquiry, before curiosity was directed at the records of the events leading up to the expulsion of Jerome Winegar?

Frankman promised a swift and prudent survey. His position gave him easy access to the archived materials of St. Peter's, and his study of them would not arouse curiosity.

"You and the headmaster get along?"

"Still?" Frankman asked edgily, then obviously wished he hadn't. His eyes lifted from Horvath to a window from which he had a glimpse of a marina north of his office. Before seating his caller he had pointed out his own craft, one of a blur of indistinguishable masts that moved like corked matchsticks in the incessant breathing of the lake. Like many deskbound men, Frankman found it necessary to see himself in temporary bondage, an outdoorsman at heart, the wind in his face, gnarled hand on the tiller, braving the elements.

"If I tell you I have turned the corner with the finances of the school and the crisis is over, I might sound like a Latin American government. But recovery has begun and Cottage knows it. Do you know much about investment, Lieutenant?"

"No." Just no. As he knew it would, not out of intention, but rather of experience with the effect his taciturn manner had on others, this rid Frankman of any inclination he might have had to explain his arcane skills. In that tendency, at least, he was like his predecessor.

"Okay. I'll get at it and tell you what's there by . . ." He looked at his watch. "Thursday."

"Mine tells hours."

Frankman grinned and turned his wrist so that Cy could get a better glimpse of his elaborate chronometer. A sailor's timepiece. His secretary, when told it recorded revolutions of the earth on its axis as well as its circuits of the sun, had thought it a completely new concept. "Of course, it's a toy."

"Like a boat?"

Frankman's continued smile was a matter of discipline rather than humor. "Till Thursday."

"What kind of help will you employ?"

"I'll do everything myself."

That freed Cy to concentrate on Winegar's contemporary movements. He found a voluble muscatel drinker with a thin sharp face from which stubble sprouted as if each whisker were individually willed, not only by God but by its bearer, whose curiosity had been aroused by Winegar.

"There are kibitzers on our fallen condition, Horowitz."

"Horvath."

"Kovacs. People who want to be among us, in the rabble but not of it, just looking."

"Social scientists?"

The toothless mouth formed itself into a cavity rimmed by quill-like whiskers. "Ha." The redolence of yesterday's fruit of the grape wafted across the table. The table was covered with white oilcloth and stood with dozens of others under the unforgiving neon lights in the dining area of Jude Thaddeus Center.

"Winegar was a watcher?"

Kovacs nodded. "But a watched watcher. I kept an eye on him."

That so obviously dry a man as Winegar would seek to share their lot might have been resented by others but not by Kovacs, an accountant in his previous life "before the fall." Sharp eyes narrowing, the cavity formed again.

"How long have you been here?"

"What is time?"

"You're a CPA."

"Was. Once I used to rearrange such acronyms to see how many combinations they yield. CAP, PAC, ACP . . . There is only a finite number with three. But with four letters, and five . . ."

Kovacs had been angered by Winegar's persistent prowling from table to table, seeking to pry into the memories of those he talked to.

"Like me?" Cy asked.

"Your interest is professional. You are well paid for what you do. Incidentally, I will be hitting you up for ten dollars when we are through."

Cy gave it to him then and there. "Earnest money."

"But money is never earnest, Howser."

"What kind of questions did he ask?"

"All kinds, but there was really only one."

"What was it?"

" 'Tell me about the volunteers.' Not the permanent staff. The volunteers."

"What did he want to know?"

"Anything we remembered. Why? I sympathized when I thought it was a relative, a child, he was asking about."

"Wasn't it?"

"The suggestion angered him. He got me drunk after I made it, but it was the last time he talked to me."

Kovacs's hand began to make regular trips to the pocket where he had put the ten. Soon the stores would open, and he would buy the only thing that now pulled him forward into the future. As Maud had seen, he had lost the will to be dry ever again.

"My dependency," he said in the jargon of the day.

"What do you think explained his curiosity?"

"All questions stop somewhere."

It sounded like one of the arguments for the existence of God that Phil Keegan claimed he and Father Dowling discussed when they got together nights in the rectory study.

And where had Winegar taken up residence since leaving Jude Thaddeus House? Agnes Lamb had reported back from an interview with Lucy Sommers that the young reporter had a new housemate. The description intrigued Cy Horvath, and he checked it out, and sure enough it was Winegar. Cy was not yet ready to interview the man himself. Everything he learned about Winegar came as a surprise, perhaps because the pieces of information failed to cohere into a single picture. From used car salesman to recipient of welfare to a kind of gigolo living off the modest earnings of a journalist intern. Unless he was independently wealthy, of course, and nothing suggested that. The young woman was clearly in awe of her lover, but he treated her with affectionate condescension, thereby increasing her willing subservience to him. It was her car he borrowed when he drove to Milwaukee. Following him, Cy was prepared to break off the pursuit when Winegar arrived at what turned out to be his destination. The campus of Manresa—a girls' college? Another surprise.

Keeping an eye on another man in that sea of femininity was no small task since any male stood out like an evolutionary freak. The questions Winegar had asked students revealed the purpose of his visit. Kate Striker. Their talk, given the long drive and the waiting about, was relatively brief. And Cy had no way of finding out what the topic of their exchange had been. The only way he could have found out would have been to ask one or the other.

Frankman's report was a disappointment: If there had even been a record of Winegar's stay at St. Peter's, it no longer existed.

"Maybe he didn't attend the school."

Frankman had no answer to that. Cy checked back with Keegan, who called Father Dowling. He suggested that Cy come see him and, in the rectory study, expressed surprise at the result of Frankman's search into Winegar's past at the school.

"He remembered that I had taught Latin for a term and told me he was in the class. I have no memory of him, Cy."

"Could he be making this up?"

"I must have the grade book I kept for that term. If he was in the class, he would be on the list."

"That would only prove that someone named Winegar took the class."

"Ah."

"Is there anyone still alive who would remember whether or not he actually was a student there?"

Cy had the impression that he had asked precisely the right question. "Father Gorman is still alive."

"Who is he?"

"He was the first headmaster and held the post until only a few years ago."

"Where is he now?"

Father Dowling offered to call the old priest. In doing so, the pastor of St. Hilary's learned that Father Gorman had suffered a stroke. The two men set off immediately for Guardian Angels. The old priest was being attended to there, sufficient medical personnel and equipment being on the premises. But the stroke had been severe and he was in a coma. Father Dowling said he wanted to stay with the old man, so Cy left him there.

On the way back to Fox River, he stopped in a bar and had a beer and sandwich and tried to construct a picture of Jerome Winegar. Cy was again struck by the way in which the pieces of information failed to form a picture. He finished his sandwich, put the plate out of his way, and began to list what he knew, or thought he knew, of Jerome Winegar.

1. He returned to Fox River and took a job at Ponader's Motors, where he exhibited a knack for selling used cars, but left after a month.
2. At that point he registered for unemployment compensation.
3. He also registered as a parishioner with Father Dowling at St. Hilary's.
4. He began to pay attention to Clara Ponader, the widow whose employee he had been, although it was doubtful that she had known it.
5. He was aware that Father Dowling had once taught Latin at St. Peter's and claimed to have been a member of the class.
6. He took up residence at Jude Thaddeus, where he irked Kovacs by his prying and by his inquiries about volunteers.
7. He took a long drive to the Manresa campus where Kate Striker, the daughter of the murdered man, went to school.
8. Earlier, he had been seen about St. Hilary's Parish Center in the company of Clara Ponader.

110

9. Frankman reported that there was no record of a Winegar having attended St. Peter's.

10. He is now living with Lucy Sommers, a reporter investigating the Striker murder.

Was there more? That was what he had at the moment, the points not quite in chronological order, but he had the sense that he could shuffle them and deal them out in any order and they would tell him as much or as little as they did now.

Father Gorman died that night while Father Dowling was still with him. It was two days later that the pastor of St. Hilary's called Cy.

"I found my grade book, Cy. He *is* on the list."

"Winegar?"

"Jerome Winegar."

"Do you remember him at all yet?"

"I'm afraid that any effort to recall him would be influenced by the image of the mature man."

If they were the same person, but that class list removed at least one possibility. However it might be with the official archives of the school, Father Dowling's class list made it clear that Jerome Winegar had attended St. Peter's School.

Was the man identical to that boy of long ago?

The question that interested Cy even more was why the records of the school did not record the presence of any Winegar at all.

When Tuttle learned that young Ms. Sommers had a live-in boyfriend, he was crestfallen in a way that was unprecedented in his celibate life. The long march through law school and the extended effort to pass the bar exam had left him little time for a social life even if he'd had the wherewithal and charm to undertake one. There had been moments since when his pulse had been stirred and, more marvelous still, when there seemed to be a reciprocal response on the part of the lady in question. But if there had been overtures, the hint of a beginning, Tuttle had been unable to carry them beyond that point. Hope of a far different sort had been stirred by Lucy Sommers's reliance on him.

"I curse the day I introduced her to him," he said aloud. He was in his office, alone, the walls his only confidants, and they did not respond. Solitude was his companion now. Even the inarticulate company of Peanuts Pianone would have been unwelcome in this mood.

It seemed to him now, against all the facts, that he had come to an understanding with young Sommers. The way she had riveted her attention on everything he said had encouraged him. Had he responded to what was not there? It pained him to think so. But her manner with Winegar, when he introduced them in the rotunda of the courthouse, had been equally deferential. A few days later her story appeared, and she became a celebrity in the press room.

And allowed the odious Winegar to move in with her. What a deadbeat. He was old enough to be her father. Tuttle was shocked and disgusted. And he felt betrayed.

But hunger of the ordinary sort put in an appearance, and the thought of food drove off the pain of being rejected. The pull of Chinese or Italian food was insufficient to drive off his need for solitary suffering, and he went off alone to Luigi's. Parked half a block from the restaurant entrance was Lieutenant Cyril Horvath, Fox River detective.

"Horvath," Tuttle said, stopping by the driver's door.

"What you doing here, Tuttle?"

It occurred to Tuttle to wonder why Horvath was parked outside Luigi's, clearly doing nothing but sitting behind the wheel of his car.

"Want to split a pizza?"

"I've already had lunch."

This was an odd suggestion as an impediment to having half a pizza, one that would never have occurred to either Tuttle or Peanuts Pianone.

"Later," Tuttle said, and went inside.

Too late, he saw that Lucy Sommers and the odious Winegar were seated at a table, a bottle of Chianti in front of them, the remains of a meal apparent on their plates. Winegar was looking directly at Tuttle when he came in, as if he had been keeping an eye on the door. His hand lifted in a salute, and Tuttle returned it but kept on moving to a far-off table. The appetite he had brought with him was gone.

He sat and stared unseeing at the menu while the sound of Lucy's laughter drifted to him, each peal transfixing him with sorrow. The waiter put a glass before him.

"Compliments of the gentleman." The waiter pointed at Winegar. Another salute. Tuttle returned it by lifting the glass. He tasted it. Ye gods. Chianti and ginger ale, a vile concoction. But he drank it to the dregs, in penance, in masochism, to punish Lucy, who was unaware of anything he did.

The waiter recommended the gnocchi, so he ordered it. An *insalata mista* too and bread, lots of bread.

"Want another of those?" The waiter referred to the awful drink he had just downed.

"Bring me some water."

His meal had just arrived when Winegar and young Sommers rose to go. The girl waved good-bye, her first real notice of him, and he smiled and waved as if his heart were not breaking within him. Before they were completely out the door, he scrambled to his feet and told the waiter he would take the meal with him.

"You wanted it to go?"

"I do now."

"Okay." Ah well, Tuttle's purpose in life was not to make waiters happy. At the front window, he watched Winegar hand the girl into her car and get behind the wheel. The car Horvath had been seated in looked empty now. But as Winegar pulled away, Horvath came into view. The waiter handed him a sack full of his lunch just as Horvath pulled away from the curb.

Luckily, Tuttle caught up with them, following the follower. Confirmation that Horvath was tailing Winegar raised his spirits. He realized that he wished his rival harm. Perhaps not a capital offense, but enough to put him away for twenty to thirty years.

The pursued car went at an unhurried pace toward downtown and pulled into an area in front of the courthouse set aside for picking up and dropping off passengers. Time ticked glacially by as Tuttle watched Horvath watch the couple. The girl leaned toward Winegar, who accepted a kiss on the cheek. Then the door opened and the girl ran up the steps of the courthouse and disappeared inside. A lesser man would have abandoned his own car and gone after her, determined to talk sense into her pretty little head with its inverted tulip of blond hair. Tuttle stayed with the pursuer and the pursued. Winegar's next destination was not at the end of a straight line. There was indetermination or whimsicality in the serpentine route he took to the parking lot at St. Hilary's, coming to a stop

113

almost in the very place where the yellow car of Mitchell Striker had been pelted with rain while inside its owner lay dead.

Horvath continued on past the entrance to the parking lot, but Tuttle parked on the street. While Tuttle watched, Winegar slipped out of the reporter's car and into another apparently waiting for him. Tuttle lay flat on the front seat of his car when the sleek town car emerged from the lot and after he heard it go past put his own car in gear and followed. There was no sign of Horvath behind him.

He got close enough to see that the driver of the car was a woman. Already he had traced in the dust of his dashboard the number of the license tag. What a perfidious knave, Tuttle thought, dredging the phrase up from the treasure trove of his boyhood reading. Yet how could he not admire even as he despised the brazenness with which Winegar used one woman's car to keep a rendezvous with another. His manner, to the degree that Tuttle could discern it, was as aloof and disengaged with this woman as it had been with poor little Sommers.

"Ah, frailty, thy name is woman!" he cried aloud, and was surprised to hear a sound in the seat behind him. He nearly drove into a parked car as he wheeled around and looked into the confused just-awakened expression on the face of Peanuts Pianone.

"Peanuts! What are you doing back there?"

"I went to sleep."

While he kept his eye on the town car, he gathered that Peanuts, unable to get an answer on Tuttle's office phone had walked over from the courthouse, seen the lawyer's car, and decided to wait for him inside it. Time passed and he transferred to the backseat for a nap.

"Where we going?"

"I'm on a job."

He drew Peanuts's attention to the town car ahead of them and to the man in its passenger seat.

"Does the name Winegar mean anything to you?"

"No."

"It will."

"Why?"

"Horvath has been following him."

"He's behind us."

And indeed he was, until he went past, paying them no attention, and got behind the town car. Tuttle had been sure Winegar had unwittingly given Horvath the slip. Now he was once more in Horvath's sights and Tuttle relaxed.

114

"What's the charge?"

"I'll leave that to Horvath."

"I dreamt about Italian."

Tuttle hoisted the sack from Luigi's over the backseat to a little cry of pleasure from Peanuts, who soon set to work on its contents.

Horvath made no arrest but took up his station outside the house to which the woman drove Winegar. After he had finished eating his Italian snack, Peanuts grew impatient and Tuttle, thinking of Lucy Sommers skipping up the steps of the courthouse, took his friend downtown.

"I want you to check out a license tag for me."

If God had not wanted Marie Murkin to look out and see Winegar get into Clara Ponader's car and be driven away, he certainly could have prevented it. Such a sight was worth a thousand words, but Marie was unlikely to get to speak any of them because there seemed to be no one with whom she could discuss the matter as thoroughly as it required. Certainly not Father Dowling, who would greet with skepticism the simple truth that she had glanced out the window and watched the man get out of one car and into another.

"Just about where you found the body of Mitchell Striker." She tried that sentence out in her mind, wondering whether it, added to a mention of what she had seen, might not disarm the pastor and persuade him that he had a professional obligation to discuss the matter. But she knew it wouldn't work, and she did not want to give him any more occasions to accuse her of being nosy.

Edna Hospers? Marie drifted over to the church for a visit and afterward started down the walk toward the school. She had prayed for guidance in the matter. Should she attempt to draw Edna into a conversation about the woman who sometimes helped her out in the parish center? For some reason Edna was unappreciative of the role Marie had played in

Clara's decision to volunteer. Marie would have liked to take credit for Dr. Walsh's visits to the center, for several hours each week, giving free dental checkups to those who wanted them. Dr. Walsh suggested this was a little memorial for Mitchell Striker.

She arrived at the parking lot and stopped, looking about the area where Mitchell Striker's car had been parked on that rainy night when he met his death right here. Marie sought to fix with her eyes the exact longitude and latitude of the place where Mitchell Striker had said good-bye to Earth and been hurtled before the judgment seat of God. The thought sent a delicious chill through her. Had Mr. Striker ever crossed that exact spot before, had he been given a premonition of what a special spot it was to be for him? To Marie that seemed the sort of thing a person would recognize, somehow or other. Had she herself ever occupied the place that would be the last on Earth she would every occupy? She thought of her daily rounds, her room, the kitchen, her favorite pew at mass. Would one of those be the place where she would breathe her last?

The trouble with thoughts of death was their peacefulness. When she thought of it, Marie imagined herself slipping painlessly from one world to the next, but just think of the way Mr. Striker had met his. Surprise, horror, violence. The most that could be said of it was that it was swift.

"Visiting the scene of the crime?"

Marie jumped at the sound of the voice. To her astonishment it was Edna Hospers.

"I didn't mean to startle you, Marie. You going to see Dr. Walsh?"

"No!" Marie, her wits about her again, said. "This is where it happened."

Edna nodded. "I know."

"Something else just happened here." The moment seemed propitious. "I frightened you?"

Marie shook her head, her eyes wide with significance.

"Clara Ponader just picked up Jerome Winegar and drove away with him. He drove in and parked that car and then she came for him."

Edna looked at Marie as if waiting for her to say more.

"Whose car is that?" she asked finally, pointing at the parked car. "His?"

Edna shook her head. "He doesn't own one. I guess he was renting one for a while, but that isn't a rental."

Marie was miffed at Edna's nonresponse to what she had told her. What difference did it make whether or not Winegar was driving a rented car?

116

"Is Father Dowling in?"

"Yes."

Edna went on past her to the rectory, leaving Marie two choices. The first was to dash back and in effect answer the door. The second was to continue on toward the school. But then a thought struck her and she went around behind the car Winegar had left and jotted down its license number. Father Dowling had come to the door and admitted Edna. Marie returned to the rectory, went around to the back, and entered her kitchen. She could hear Edna and Father Dowling talking, but she had no time to spare for that. She picked up the phone and called headquarters and asked for Captain Keegan.

"Who should I say's calling?"

"Marie Murkin."

"Purpose of call?"

"Personal."

"O-kay," the operator answered in a tone Marie might have found insinuating in a less distracted moment. Her mind was turning over rapidly what she was engaged in doing.

"Marie?"

"Captain Keegan, I know it's foolish to call you about a thing like this, but I didn't know who else to talk to."

"Has something happened to Father Dowling?"

"Good heavens, no."

"All right. So what is it."

She told him of the car parked in the parish lot, just about where Mitchell Striker's car had been parked, and that she was worried about it. She had been told that a man had driven it into the lot and immediately been driven away in another car.

"Just left the car there?"

"It's still out there."

"How long ago was this?"

"Within the hour. Maybe twenty minutes ago."

"Marie, listen. Don't go near that car. I'm going to send someone out to look it over. Where's Father Dowling?"

"In his study."

"Tell him to stay in the house."

"Edna Hospers is with him."

"Don't let her leave, understand?"

"How long will it be?"

But he had hung up. Marie sat on the edge of a chair and prayed that

117

the people Captain Keegan sent would come before Edna wanted to return to the school. If she had to stop her, she would have to say why, and Marie did not want to imagine what Father Dowling might say.

The study door opened and the voices became louder. Marie went through the dining room and into the hallway, where Edna and Father Dowling were chatting.

"What's this about a car?" he asked.

Marie looked at Edna. Traitor. "Oh, did you notice it?"

"I've given up looking out the window at parked cars. It's bad for my blood pressure."

Marie was saved by the scream of an approaching siren. Father Dowling fell silent, listening too. Marie willed the sirens toward the parish, bringing them in on the projected thought waves of her mind. When the two squad cars and the truck they had convoyed roared into the parking lot, the sound of their sirens was earsplitting. As they died down, men poured from the truck, wearing what looked like space suits, and began to surround the parked car. The three onlookers were drawn out the rectory door but were immediately directed back inside.

"There are many old people in the school," Father Dowling called. A wave of comprehension answered him and they went inside.

"Who called the bomb squad?"

Marie said, "I told Captain Keegan about the car."

"You telephoned to tell him there's a car parked in the parking lot?"

"It seemed the right thing to do." She looked right at Father Dowling, ignoring the presence of Edna, willing him not to say more. She was saved by a pounding on the kitchen door and then the sound of Phil Keegan bursting in from the dining room. He stopped at the sight of them, and a look of relief came over his face.

"Thank God, you're all right."

He thumped the pastor on the shoulder, shook hands with Edna, and actually swept Marie into his arms. Then he went past them to the door.

"How they doing out there?"

Marie, vindicated, as she thought, turned and proceeded into the kitchen as if in a vast liturgical procession, head high, arms folded, a beatific smile on her face.

The bomb squad found no bomb. The car was identified as belonging to a young woman who did not answer her phone. But the car was all but forgotten when, cleared to do so, Edna returned to the school and to her excited wards. This haven of peace had been a nest of excitement several times during recent weeks. And there was more to come.

Marie was at work in the kitchen, humming "Pomp and Circumstance," when the phone rang. She waited for a generous three rings, giving the pastor first shot at it, then picked up the phone.

"St. Hilary's Rectory." Each syllable distinctly pronounced and given appropriate pitch.

"Marie!"

"Is that you Edna?"

"Are they still there?"

"Who?"

"Father. Keegan. The police." Her voice slid up the scale into strangled excitement.

"Edna, what is it?"

"Marie, for God's sake, tell them to come over here. There is a body in my office."

In Father Dowling's pastoral experience, the obsequies of a person are seldom commensurate with the worldly estimate of the life that preceded them. And so it was with Gerald Major.

The body of the lugubrious little man with the big if aching heart was found in Edna Hospers's office on the first floor of the parish senior citizens center. Once her offices had been inhabited by the nun who was principal of the parish school, and something of the spit and polish and piety of that nunnish regime still showed in the waxed floor, glowing metalwork, and unclouded windows. The outer office, where students whose offenses exceeded the absolving power of the classroom teacher were sent to await the pleasure of the principal, and their own pain, had two hard benches under the frosted glass that formed the upper half of the wall dividing the outer from the inner office: mourner's benches, so to speak. A more yielding upholstered chair stood in a corner under a lamp whose shade looked capable of doing the shimmy or the Charleston, with its fringes and overlaps and period air. The couch—four cushions, plush, florid, and comfortably out of place, a yard-sale acquisition—had been added by Edna. The body of Gerald Major was laid out on the couch for all the world as if it had already received the professional attention of McDivitt the undertaker.

Edna's first reaction, as she told Father Dowling, was that the old fellow had crept in here for whatever reason and, finding her out, had seized the occasion for a nap on the sofa. She was wrong. He was dead. What explained her excitement when she called Marie was the fact that when she attempted to shake Gerry awake, his lifeless body rolled off the couch and dropped to the floor. The term deadweight assumed new meaning for her, as it would always afterward be associated with the sound of the body hitting the polished wooden floor.

No relay from Tinker to Evers to Chance had gone more smoothly than the passage of the grim news from Murkin to Dowling to Pippen. The assistant medical examiner, dressed in civilian clothes, off duty, had been listening to the police radio as she drove from a exercise session in the police gym to her apartment and had immediately set out for St. Hilary's. She was talking with the pastor and Phil Keegan about the apparent false bomb alarm when Marie came legging it along the sidewalk from the rectory. Pippen, galvanized by Marie's message, was already on the way toward the school when Edna appeared in the doorway.

Unlike her boss, Pippen was willing, perhaps too willing, to offer swift intuitive opinions on the matter at hand. Someone less skilled might have concluded as quickly that the rope knotted about the old man's neck, which had discolored the face and caused the tongue to loll out, was the cause of death. But soon Pippen had added that the death had not occurred where the body was found but that the body had been placed on the sofa sometime after the event.

The rope around his neck had a red wooden handle at one end and came to an elaborate knot at the other. Father Dowling thought it looked familiar. Phil said it looked like the pull rope used to start an outboard motor.

"Or a lawn mower?" the pastor asked.

Phil looked at him. "What lawn mower?"

In a shed that stood across the parking lot, once the playground, of the school, was housed the equipment used to keep the grounds in trim. There was a rider mower that Willie had steadfastly refused to ride and a small power mower used to trim and mow areas inaccessible to the larger machine. It was a vintage machine, whose barrel-like little gas tank had a cap on top, the parts of its single cycle motor exposed for the admiring eye, and a circular starting wheel around which a rope was wound before being pulled to start the engine, the operation usually requiring several tries as one adjusted the intake of air with the choke. The lab would later establish that the rope wound around Gerry's neck had been tied to a crossbar of the mower's handle.

"Don't walk there," Pippin had said, not in charge but saving the scene for the team from the lab. There were footprints on the oily cement floor of the shed.

Father Dowling crouched to look at them, and a frown came over his face.

"What were you looking at, Roger?" Phil said when they were outside again.

"I'll tell you later."

Agnes Lamb had arrived, and then Cy and the whole sequence of events was sketched for them by Phil, beginning with Marie's looking out the kitchen window.

"Winegar?" Cy said.

"You got something?"

"The owner of the car isn't home?"

"No."

Arrangements were made for Agnes to pick up a search warrant and to meet Cy at the address of the car owner. Phil's initial resistance to this suggestion was removed when Cy told them that Winegar had recently moved in with the owner.

"Why are you interested in him?" Father Dowling asked, uneasy.

"Later," Phil said. His presence was needed once more in the school, where Lubins, Pippen's superior, was introducing a characteristically glacial pace into the proceedings over which he had assumed charge. Pippen, however, remained on the scene, her kibitzing status doing little to speed up Lubins.

Meanwhile Father Dowling took the sad news to Gerry's daughter-in-law, whose name he had entered in the space on Edna's card reserved for the name of someone to be notified in case of an emergency. The old man had first written Father Dowling, then scratched it out and wrote Ursula Major.

"I told him you were always called first anyway," Edna said.

"This name cannot be right."

"Why not? He wrote it."

And what Gerry had written was, of course, right. Had his daughter-in-law been destined to fall in love with a man whose name, when combined with her baptismal name, produced such an astronomical result? Gerry, of course, had made much of the fact that he had been the only Major in the army who was a sergeant.

"Sergeant-major," Dowling had said.

"The war ended too soon, Father. I nearly stayed in just to reach that rank."

Mrs. Major received the news with an expressionless doughlike face. She had stood to hear it and now sat. "Cholesterol," she said in sepulchral tones.

"This wasn't diet, Mrs. Major." He longed to call her Ursula and rebuked himself for the impulse to levity at such a moment. But the daughter-in-law was treating the death as the QED of a patiently developed theory.

"I'm a nurse, Father."

"Ah."

"No one could tell him anything. He ate whatever he liked."

"He was killed, Mrs. Major."

"Killed?"

"Strangled."

"No!" Her shoulders slumped but her eyes lifted as she released a great sigh of air. "Dear God. I always feared he meant it."

"What is that?"

"He said he would destroy himself. The Koreans should have done it long ago, he said. What's an Edsel, Father?"

"Why do you ask?" Further information had simply invoked another theory from Ursula Major.

"He called himself that. An Edsel on the road of life."

"That was his phrase?"

She nodded with a jowly smile. The smell of baking came from the back of the house. It was a cozy place, brightly furnished and cheerful, but the daughter-in-law, like Gerry, was a devotee of the dour side of things.

"It was a kind of automobile," he said.

"A lemon?"

"Some people said so." But she was handing him a bowl filled with yellow candy done up in bows of cellophane.

He gathered that Gerry had brought his troubles home. Ursula knew of her father-in-law's unhappy passion for Barbara Rooney.

"Was it wrong of me to make a novena that he would marry her and move out, Father? He's no trouble in one sense, and just a gloomy Gus on the other."

"Gloomy Gus. Where did that phrase come from?"

"Old Maid." She offered to get the deck and show him. Gerry had bought the cards as a possible gift for Barbara, the name of the game an oblique warning if she should let this chance go by.

"Have you told Augie?"

"Augie."

"My husband."

"I came directly here."

"I better call him at work."

"Yes."

She waited, as if hopeful of being relieved of the responsibility. He asked her if anyone had threatened her father-in-law.

"Besides Augie?"

"Did your husband threaten him?"

"He threatens everyone. He threatens me." Her smile revealed a glistening gold filling. "Ever since the accident."

"He had an accident?"

"That's his story. He lost two fingers at work and the company is fighting his claim, saying he was careless."

There seemed little in this household that might have cheered up Gloomy Gus, although the smell of food rivaled the olfactory delights of Marie Murkin's kitchen.

"What was it that caught your attention on the floor of the mower shed?" Phil asked later when they were in the study.

"The footprints."

"The crew got good shots of those."

Father Dowling stood, turned away, and lifted his foot. Phil rose and studied the sole of the shoe like a blacksmith.

"It's not the same print."

"I know. Wait." He went down the hall and came back with a pair of rubbers.

Phil turned them over and began to nod. "Yeah."

"This time the match will be perfect."

"But what does a set of your footprints around your own parish prove?"

"Maybe they're not meant to prove anything."

31

The search warrant authorized Cy and Agnes Lamb to enter the apartment of Lucy Sommers to seek any indications of a link between the owner of the abandoned automobile and events at St. Hilary's. The wording was deliberately vague, so that both of the murders committed on parish property could be looked into.

"What's she got to do with those?" Agnes asked.

"It's her boyfriend we're interested in."

"He lives with her?"

"That's what we're told."

"What's his name?"

"Winegar."

"Never heard of him."

Neither had Hilda Lilienthal, the building manager, when they showed her the warrant and asked to be admitted to the apartment. The woman was in a motorized wheelchair in which she whisked about her basement apartment. There was the mandatory ramp enabling her to get to the street floor, but she almost never went higher in the building.

"Did you ring her bell?"

"She's not in."

Hilda frowned at the warrant, but Cy had a feeling her displeasure was directed at Agnes. Hilda reluctantly came with them up the ramp to the first floor and into the elevator. When its doors closed on them, Cy thought of how vulnerable the chair-ridden woman must feel whenever she left her familiar habitat.

The apartment was on the third floor. Hilda opened the door and then wheeled back from it.

"You won't need me anymore. It will lock itself when you leave."

"Would you like me to take you back down?" Agnes asked.

"I can make it." She was half peeved, half touched by the offer.

Inside, they went methodically to work. There was a living room, a kitchen, a bedroom, a bath. Cy took the bedroom and gave Agnes the bath.

"What are we looking for?"

"I don't know."

"That helps."

"You'll know if you find it."

The bedroom would have seemed that of a college coed but for the things that must be Winegar's hanging in the closet. Cy checked the brands of the clothes for signs of origin, he checked shoes and shirts. There were some items in one drawer of the dresser: underwear, socks, some change too small to bother with. On the basis of what he found, Cy would not have been able to say where Winegar was from for sure, although the indications were the West Coast.

"He uses an electric razor," Agnes said.

"That helps."

"If you have a beard."

The briefcase was in the front hallway. It had the initials JAW embossed on it. Inside were maps with a route traced from Portland across the west to Fox River. Someone had come quite purposely from Oregon to Fox River. The papers told little of the owner of the briefcase, except that it did indeed belong to one Jerome Winegar. The records were in an inside zippered pocket.

"This looks like a transcript," Agnes said. "St. Peter's School."

There were letters too, from Father Gorman, from Mitchell Striker, one of fairly recent vintage. These were the papers Bob Frankman had sought in vain in the school archives.

"Bingo," Cy said.

"Meaning?"

"He got kicked out of the school and the kicker was Mitchell Striker more than the headmaster. Three months ago Striker was asked by Cottage to respond to a request for a recommendation for an old boy. Winegar. Striker torpedoed his chances for the job."

Agnes got the picture. Cy had picked up the phone to call Captain Keegan to ask for an arrest warrant on Winegar when the man himself unlocked the apartment door and came in before he realized they were there.

"What the hell are you doing here?"

Agnes closed the door and got between it and Winegar. Cy had risen to his feet. He looked over the dapper Winegar. There was a tap on the door behind Agnes. She looked at Cy. He nodded. She opened the door.

"Hilda says that . . ." And then the girl saw Agnes, who took her arm and brought her in, again closing the door.

"You want to see the search warrant?" Cy asked her.

"Search warrant for what?" And then she remembered. "Look, I am a newspaper reporter."

Cy was about to put away the search warrant when Winegar asked to see it. Cy had laid the papers from the briefcase out on the coffee table, but Winegar showed no interest in them. Having glanced at the warrant, he asked Cy what they wanted of Lucy.

"Her car was found abandoned at St. Hilary's."

"You found it!" The girl was delighted.

"It's been taken downtown."

"Why?"

"There's been another murder at St. Hilary's." Cy kept his eye on Winegar as he said this.

"A man named Gerald Major," he said when neither of them asked.

Winegar shrugged. "Don't know him."

"He was strangled with a lawn mower starting rope taken from a shed on the premises."

It dawned on Winegar that they were here for him rather than the girl.

"Two weeks ago another old man, Mitchell Striker, was killed in his car in the parking lot of the school. You knew him, didn't you?"

"I read about it in the paper."

"I knew Gerry Major," the girl said. "I did a story about him."

"A story about Striker's murder," Agnes said.

"Claiming that Father Dowling had murdered Winegar's friend."

"Friend!"

"You knew him, didn't you?"

"No."

"Winegar, you're under arrest on suspicion of the murder of Mitchell Striker."

"Oh, come on. What reason would I have?"

Cy began to pick up the papers. "In your briefcase were the records of your departure from St. Peter's School. I had asked for them from the school, and they reported that they were missing from the archives. They were in your possession."

"Then you planted them here."

"Don't. Get a lawyer."

If Winegar had been tense when he first came in, he was relaxed now. He apologized to the girl for the nuisance, and she went to him and pressed

126

her forehead against his chest and began to cry. He put one arm around her, some comfort, but not much. He had too many troubles of his own.

"I've got a lawyer," he said to Cy. "Shall I call him?"

Cy pushed the phone toward him. When he picked it up, Agnes was on the alert, but phones nowadays are too light to make much of a weapon. In any case, Winegar dialed a number and waited in vain for it to be answered.

"Who's your lawyer?" Cy asked, taking the phone.

"A man named Tuttle."

"He's probably already in the courthouse."

On the way downtown with their prisoner, Cy called in to let them know they were coming.

"Make sure Captain Keegan knows."

Philip Cottage, headmaster of St. Peter's, the student body's affectionately named Big Cheese, tried to follow Frankman's argument that this sensational news was good for the school.

"A former member of the board killed by an expelled student nearly twenty years after the fact?"

"One, it shows the good sense of the school in getting rid of the kid. Two, our devotion to Mitchell Striker is clear, not least because of the special memorial service."

"Bob, it's bad publicity. You can see what it might suggest about the character of our students."

"One bad apple, and he was thrown out."

Cottage could not ignore the fact that this news drove out any lingering effect of the memory of Frankman's unhappy investment results and the public chiding he had received from the late Mitchell Striker.

Frankman was reacting as a member of the board no longer under a personal cloud. Cottage reacted as an old boy of the school himself. What he had known of the Winegar case had made him for the first time feel critical of Father Gorman. The priest should have supported the boy and defended him against Striker's vendetta.

"What exactly had he done?" he had asked the old priest when he went to visit him shortly after Striker's murder. Reminiscing about the former board member and financial genius, the old priest had sorrowfully brought up that old case.

"I did not act nobly or well."

"But what had the boy done?"

"It doesn't matter now. The charge was immoral conduct."

Gorman was right. It didn't matter now—or so Cottage had thought then. Had the old priest some premonition that there was a connection between Striker's death and his demand that a boy be expelled from the school years ago? Cottage had promised himself that one day he would acquaint himself with the details of the story. Now the whole community was being told of it via newspaper and television.

Cottage had left a tenured position in a Jesuit university for the post of headmaster, requested by Father Gorman to submit his name for the appointment. What an odd thing the human imagination is, likewise the private hierarchy of values it supports. On any objective view of the academic pecking order, there was no comparison between the position he had left and his appointment as headmaster of St. Peter's. His professorship had been tenured, his teaching load was light, he had ample opportunity to pursue his scholarly work and to communicate with colleagues around the world via the internet and World Wide Web. As headmaster, on the other hand, he served at the pleasure of the board of trustees, and once his five-year appointment was up, they need not renew it. Moreover, his duties left him little time for reading, let alone study. But he had never regretted his decision to become headmaster.

True, his office at the university was a featureless box, which when emptied of his books retained not an iota of sentimental pull for him. The office of the headmaster, on the other hand, was what one would expect from the building that housed it. His windows cranked open onto a quad, the bookshelves were integral to the room, the carpet was red, with the seal of the school woven into it. His desk was such that important treaties might fittingly have been signed on it. Above all, it was a room that had enjoyed continued existence over the years in his memory.

Here as a boy he had spoken with his already venerable predecessor. Here the first dreams of an academic life had come to him, dreams that perforce took their cue from Gorman's function and the office within which he performed it. When Cottage came back to St. Peter's as headmaster, he was not in his own mind taking a step down but the final step up to the pinnacle of his dream.

Frankman's unsteady stewardship of the school's endowment had been a shock, but they seemed to be recovering from it. Cottage had taken it as a personal rebuke when Mitchell Striker commented adversely on it in *Crain's,* the Chicago business magazine. The Winegar matter was infinitely worse. When he was called by reporters just before the first story on Winegar's arrest came out, he had refused comment, invoking confidentiality between school and boy. Now, as story after story washed over the jaded sensibilities of sensation-seekers, he felt that he had failed miserably in the one job he had really wanted after untrammeled success in every previous effort.

Frankman had examined the papers the police had found in Winegar's possession.

"They are authentic, no doubt about it."

Winegar claimed that these documents had been planted on him by the police, a story that required them first to remove them from the school archives and then stage the discovery in the apartment of the girl off whom Winegar was sponging. That was the clear implication of his relationship with the girl. The term "gigolo" was favored in accounts of it.

"It had to be an inside job," Frankman said.

And Winegar, even after all these years, qualified as an insider. Had he too carried memories of the school about with him all these years? They would have been tainted by the way he left, but he would have been the rare student if he had not found St. Peter's a true home, a place where he could acquire an identity, a sense of self and worth and the possibilities in life. If the charge against him was true, he had expunged all records of his stay there from the archives. That almost seemed more heinous than the killings of which he was accused.

Cottage had studied the photographs of Winegar and satisfied himself that he had no memory of the man, or of a boyish version of the man. If the recovered records were correct, Winegar's departure would have taken place during Cottage's first year in the school. It had not been a scandal at the time, certainly not one that reached down to the freshmen. Cottage found himself feeling more and more sympathy for the accused man. But he did not tell anyone, not members of the staff or of the board, not Frankman, when he decided to visit Winegar in jail.

If he expected a defeated man with the burden of a public charge of two murders on his shoulders, he would have been surprised by the swift, confident entry of Winegar. He headed for the table that divided the room and indicated a seat across from him.

"You're the new headmaster."

"That's right."

"Congratulations. It must give you a profound sense of achievement to sit in Father Gorman's chair."

It was the kind of remark he had become used to from alumni when he met them.

"I am sorry to meet you in such circumstances."

"I have done nothing, headmaster. Please be assured of that. I have killed no one. And I certainly did not break into the school and remove those records."

"They seem to have made a heavy case against you."

"It is still difficult to convict an innocent man."

How easy it was, talking with this good-looking, self-possessed man, to forget the charges against him, charges that did not look implausible in the light of the record turned up since his arrest. Winegar's had been a career of humdrum jobs, well below his capacities and talents, punctuated by sudden rises in fortune that regularly ended with him under a cloud of suspicion and forced to move on. He seemed to specialize in susceptible women. There was about him the look of a man who had lived on the surface, capitalizing on his charm and physical attractiveness. But Cottage could not help wondering what Winegar might have become if he had not been expelled from the school and seen the dashing of all his hopes.

"What was that all about anyway?"

Winegar smiled and shook his head. "A gentleman never tells."

"That suggests there was a woman involved."

Winegar grew serious. "I wouldn't want you to think it was anything else."

"Of course not."

Winegar was relieved. Cottage liked that. Despite himself, he liked this man. If he was a rogue and there had been a woman involved, wouldn't he just spill it all? For no purpose, just to spill it. If he was a rogue. But he drew the veil of secrecy over the woman in the case, the sort of action— granting the premise—that one would expect of a St. Peter's boy.

"You have a lawyer?"

"Of sorts. A man named Tuttle."

"You're not satisfied with him?"

"I am lucky to have him."

Cottage resolved to talk to Tuttle and see what might be done about strengthening Winegar's defense. Cottage had no experience with murderers, but he did not think this man had killed two other human beings. That conviction wobbled when he considered that he had not always proved himself a good judge of people. He had thought Frankman would continue the heady record with the school endowment that Mitchell Striker had set. But the man had employed an investment device that, when it led to huge losses around the world, was described as little better than a confidence game.

Her adviser, Jason, booked a flight for Clara Ponader to St. Petersburg, where she rented a car and drove to Sarasota and settled into a resort on Longboat Key. For two days she haunted the shops in St. Armand Circle until they no longer held any secrets for her. Twice a day she talked with Jason.

"He seems to be keeping you out of it."

"I'd die if he mentioned my name."

It was the recurrence of the term "gigolo" in the newspaper reports Jason faxed to her that made Clara shiver with shame. To be linked with such a man in the present circumstances would be a posthumous betrayal of all Don had been to her. Walking along the beach under the complaint of the gulls, watching pelicans crash dive into the waters of the gulf, with the sun hot upon her and the rhythmic sound of the surf in her ears, she felt purged of the infatuation she had felt for Jerome Winegar.

Her memories had altered under the pressure of his arrest and indictment. Quite apart from her own humiliation, if her name was now linked with Winegar's, what would the Walshes think of her for gadding about with the man who had killed dear old Mitch Striker? Winegar now seemed to her to have been a slick trickster who had used on her the wiles

131

he was said to have used on any number of other vulnerable women over the years. It had been his occupation, really, preying on widows like herself.

The age given for him in the newspapers meant he was young enough to be her son, another potential source of embarrassment. The gray hair had made him seem older, and of course his flattering attention had reduced her to a giggling schoolgirl. Her cheeks burned at the memory.

Seated by the pool, surrounded by the stories sent her from Fox River, she tried to piece together what the man had done.

The fact that he had gotten employment at the used car lot suggested that from the outset she had been his target. Jason had spoken with the manager and came away with the clear impression that Winegar had gotten information about her from Blake. It was, of course, possible that what he learned had turned his attention to her for the first time.

In any case, he quit the job after a month, applied for unemployment compensation, and lived in a shabby hotel until he actually took refuge at Jude Thaddeus House. She found this inexplicable, given his fastidiousness and vanity. The money he was receiving from the government would have allowed him to stay on in his hotel. Throughout this time, he had been seeing her. There had to be occasions in which he had come from Jude Thaddeus to go to dinner with her.

And then he moved in with the girl. If he was decades younger than Clara, the girl was more than twenty years his junior. Clara's shame did not lessen with the realization that even after he had moved in with the girl he had continued to come to her. Her one boast was that she had not slept with him as the girl clearly had. This was not a boast she could publicly make nor expect to be believed if she did. But she took consolation from it, there by the gulf, safely distant from the events unfolding in Fox River.

It was hard enough on Clara to interweave his dealing with the girl into their meetings, but to think that while she knew him Winegar had killed two men, brutally, and broken into the archive of the orphanage to destroy the record of his connection with his first victim was devastating. Clara could have wept at her stupidity and blindness.

At the time of Mitch's death it had been easy to say, because it was true, that Winegar had decided not to come with her to the lecture, but that did not mean he wasn't at St. Hilary's that night, lying in wait for his ancient enemy.

Planting the shoes, prompting Gerry to find them and identify them as Father Dowling's, seemed to present no insuperable difficulties for a man who had been leading so duplicitous a life.

Killing Gerry too seemed easily within the range of dreadful things Winegar might do. Lure the man to the mower shed and strangle him there, move the body to Edna's office in the school when that was appropriate.

Sorting through these awful events, Clara found it easy to put Winegar in the chief role in each episode. No wonder Bob Frankman had been unable to find Winegar's St. Peter's record. Thank God he had been arrested at last. And thank God too that she had escaped into the anonymity of a Florida beach.

"Everyone else seems to have gone down there," Marjorie White said when Clara, desperate for the sound of a familiar voice, telephoned her friend.

"Have they?"

"The Walshes are spending a week on Siesta Key. How I pity those of you who can afford to escape this awful weather."

Marjorie was not exaggerating. Like others from the north, Clara took daily satisfaction from the Weather Channel, which graphically proved the wisdom of being here rather than there. She was on the verge of inviting Marjorie down, but she bit her tongue. Perhaps she would have done so if her potential guest had not mentioned that the Walshes were in the area.

"What else is new besides the weather?"

"Nothing. I suppose that's why they won't leave off going on and on about the Winegar case."

The Winegar case. That impersonal designation made it seem more than a thousand miles away. Clara did not press Marjorie for information. There was no need to.

"Jason says he has never seen anything like it."

Jason had told her of his recommendation that Father Dowling sue the *Tribune* for libel. Lucy Sommers had been let go as a stringer for the Chicago paper.

"Did she go home?"

"No. To Jude Thaddeus House."

"Ye gods."

"As a volunteer, I hasten to add. She moved out of her apartment and is living there. The current Mary Magdalene, I guess." Was that a subtle reference to Clara's liaison with Winegar? Was she doing penance on the burning sands as Lucy Sommers was doing it in the soup kitchen?

"Jason and I ran into Bob Frankman the other night." Jason and I?

133

That was the second mention of the lawyer. Had Marjorie landed the fish at last? It would have been too dangerous a subject to pursue. Clara felt safe, but on the shelf. That night she phoned the Walshes.

"You're here?" Nancy said in tones of unfeigned delight. "What are you doing tomorrow?"

"I thought I'd run down to Naples."

"Take me along. Jim wants to do nothing but talk to the world via his fax/modem."

The following day, Clara was delayed by a bridge raised to let a small sailboat inch through. Traffic had grown to epic lengths in both directions before the bridge went down. There was a bottleneck at the junction with the Tamiami Trail that delayed her further. If she had not been on her way to pick up Nancy, Clara would not have noticed.

Midnight Pass was not what it had been, but the Walsh place was. As if to illustrate Nancy's complaint, Jim was set up in the front room, computer plugged in, sending and receiving messages. Is a doctor ever free from his patients?

"Don't get him started," Nancy said affectionately, rumpling his hair. "His patients and his broker."

"Thank God Jason does all that for me."

Jim seized on the remark, and Clara realized that she had never told the Walshes of Jason's role in her financial affairs. Jim blew through his fluttering lips. "Daddy used to take care of everything," Nancy said.

"Do you buy and sell yourself?" Clara asked Jim.

"Does Jason have you in the Tokyo exchange?"

"I never ask."

Jim was shocked. In the car Clara said to Nancy that Jim might want to talk to Jason about investments.

"Oh, he likes to complain about it. He won't admit how dependent we were on Daddy in such matters. And his faith in Bob is more or less restored."

"Bob Frankman?"

"Dad didn't know, but Jim wanted to put some money with a more daring broker." Nancy waved it away. "Tell me about the mall in Naples."

34

His client was a goner, Tuttle had little doubt of that, but then most of his clients were. Minimize the damage, take what you're given, plea bargain—these were precepts of the Tuttle code, and he was only too happy to be in a position to apply them. The question was, how could he get something more than a public defender's compensation for representing Winegar? The accused, sticking to his predestined role, insisted that he was innocent.

"All they've got is circumstantial evidence," Tuttle assured him.

Circumstantial evidence, in this case, had the look of a noose. Could Winegar establish his whereabouts on the night Striker was killed? He had a problem even locating the night in his memory.

"It was raining," Tuttle said helpfully.

"I never go out in the rain."

"Didn't you live in Portland?"

"That's why I left. My feet were becoming webbed."

There were obvious gaps where the missing papers once had been. Tuttle had picked up the rumor that the prosecution was consulting an expert who claimed he could tell how long the papers had been out of the temperature-controlled environment of the archives. Even without that, Tuttle thought a jury would easily accept the suggestion that Winegar had removed them. After all, they had been found in his possession.

"I figure I surprised them in the act of planting them in my briefcase."

Winegar described the expressions on Horvath's and Lamb's faces when he let himself into the apartment, making them sound like inept and corrupt policemen. Tuttle imagined the jury thinking that Winegar was letting himself into the apartment of an almost underage girl he had been sponging off and whose car had just been impounded because Winegar had left it in the parking lot at St. Hilary's when he was driven off by another woman.

"Leave her out of it," Winegar said when Tuttle suggested that Clara

Ponader could establish his alibi at the time Gerry Major was murdered. Winegar had an annoying habit of acting as if he were innocent until proven guilty.

Meanwhile the prosecution was interpreting the rules of discovery as narrowly as possible. Thank God for Peanuts. With his friend as conduit into the police files, Tuttle felt he knew more than Pep Ardmore, the assistant prosecutor assigned to the case, a rangy redhead in a pinstriped suit whose hair fell over her face unless she threw back her head and looked straight up. Tuttle had the sense of talking to the back of her head whenever they met.

"Have you deposed Father Dowling yet?"

"Of course."

"About the shoes?"

The footwear the pastor of St. Hilary's had given the police from the front hall of the rectory, identical to those that had made the prints on the floor of the mower shed, showed no traces of having been worn in the maintenance shed.

"That's in our favor," Tuttle told Winegar, and he was serious. "Once they get the jury thinking of things being planted, we have a chance with the St. Peter's documents."

"They really were planted."

A jury would shrug off such an assurance from Winegar and accept it as gospel from Father Dowling.

Tuttle asked Pep to come have coffee with him across the street.

"Coffee! I never drink coffee."

"Okay. Have a beer."

Alcohol was out too. They split a bottle of mineral water that tasted like an emetic to Tuttle. He ordered coffee.

"That'll kill you."

"That's okay. I left a note in my office."

"You'll see," she warned. There wasn't much meat on her bones. Her favorite topic was the way Tuttle's client, the accused, had manipulated and abused the women in his life. Clichés rolled off her tongue like newly minted coin.

"The girl asked him to move in."

"Do you believe that?"

Unfortunately, Tuttle did, and against the grain of his desire. His attraction for Lucy had only increased with knowledge of her disinterest in him and her doormat behavior toward Winegar. Pep seemed not to know that she had sought refuge in Jude Thaddeus House. Until he interviewed her, Tuttle didn't owe the prosecution that information. On two occasions he had sat at a table there, with his tweed hat pulled over his eyes, watching her wait on the derelicts who moved disinterestedly along the chow line. What a waste. Not just here but because the worst still lay ahead for her. The prosecution would put her on the stand, and Pep would pull out the stops to establish that Winegar had exploited her. She would deny this, and that would prolong her time as a witness and feed the public details of her sharing her bed with a man old enough to be her father.

Tuttle took consolation from the fact that the discrepancy between his age and Lucy's was not as great as that separating her from Winegar.

Agnes Lamb turned up a clerk at Target who thought she remembered selling the rubbers to Winegar, but it turned out she thought she was being asked about condoms. None were found in Lucy's apartment. Tuttle felt sick when Peanuts passed this information on.

"This will never go to a jury," he assured Pep.

"I won't plea bargain."

"Plea bargain. Are you kidding? This case will be thrown out."

It didn't matter what Pep would do, the prosecutor's office wasn't going to waste money if Winegar would plead guilty to a lesser charge. But what if they saw publicity value in taking it through the courts? Tuttle himself found the prospect of exposure to publicity pleasant, but it would be a public loss too.

"Talk to Edna Hospers," Winegar urged.

"Did you have something going with her too?"

"Hey," Winegar said.

"She'll vouch for you?"

"She'll tell the truth. You know about her husband."

"I'll talk to her."

"Talk to Willie too."

Sure. He could put Willie on as a character witness. Ex-con swears accused is a nice guy? And Edna on the stand would be certain to be asked about her husband, who was doing time. Pep the feminist would give no quarter.

"Let's work out your alibi," Tuttle suggested one day, if only to show Winegar the kind of trouble he was in. He had a large sheet of paper in front of him. He drew a line from top to bottom a quarter of the width from the left side. "This column is the day Striker was killed in his car."

"Are they sure about that?"

Tuttle was not given to outbursts, least of all directed at someone who represented income, however modest, but he nearly lost his temper then.

"Do you doubt he was killed?"

"You said in his car."

Tuttle looked at him. "Good point. I'll check and see if they can rule out that it happened somewhere else."

"They seem so sure Gerry Major wasn't killed where they found him."

"Right. So why not say Striker was killed who-knows-where and driven in his own car to the parking lot of St. Hilary's? Is that your suggestion?"

"I just asked a question."

A wise lawyer does not want to know whether his client is innocent or guilty; he definitely does not want to be told if the client is guilty. One little question that no one else had asked, and Tuttle had the feeling he was seated across the table from a man who had committed two murders. Winegar didn't look any different than before. Why should murderers look any different? Tuttle had no idea why Winegar had waited this long before giving him a little help. But it was dangerous to introduce this suggestion until Winegar's alibi had been established.

"What were you doing that day?"

"I was with Mrs. Ponader."

"She was at the school when the body was found."

"I meant earlier."

"Let's establish times. Exactly how long were you with her, from when to when?"

Winegar shrugged. "I won't be able to remember details like that."

"Let's find out. Was it morning or afternoon?"

"Afternoon. We met for lunch."

"Where?"

"Dayton's."

"At lunchtime?"

"Twelve-thirty."

"Okay, at seven-thirty she'd been at St. Hilary's school for maybe fifteen minutes. When did you leave her?"

He wasn't sure. Nor was he sure where he was afterward. The time during which the murder took place was a vast vagueness to Winegar. Tuttle did not believe a word his client said. In desperation, he stopped by St. Hilary's Parish Center to talk with Willie the maintenance man.

Willie would never see fifty again, but he dressed and acted exactly as he must have as a teenager: longish hair swept back and glistening with pomade, a T-shirt under a blue denim shirt left unbuttoned to his belly button, Levi's worn short, exposing his white socks, and loafers equipped with large cleats on the heels. His shirt pocket bulged with a package of cigarettes from behind which a comb was visible.

"You're Winegar's lawyer? I hope they put him away for life."

"What did he ever do to you?"

"Nearly had me put away for life."

"He didn't arrest you; the police did."

"Because he set me up, putting those overshoes in my apartment and telling Gerry about them."

"Do you believe everything the police say?"

"What do you mean?"

"You're just repeating their accusations against Winegar. Look, you say someone planted those overshoes in your apartment."

"They did."

"Okay. But why Winegar? He's got nothing against you, does he?"

"What are you getting at?"

"Do members of the police force ever show up around here?"

Willie let the thought sink in. Captain Keegan and Cy Horvath were frequently seen on the parish premises. Tuttle observed that they knew where Willie's apartment was. Winegar did not.

"Think about it."

"Somebody planted those overshoes."

Tuttle tipped back his hat and put his hands in his back pockets. "Nice place you got here."

"It's all right." But there was pride in Willie's voice.

"I suppose they keep you pretty busy."

"The job has responsibilities."

Tuttle let the little man go on about the duties of a maintenance man. He did not quite say that his tasks were more important than those of the pastor, but he came close.

"When they were questioning me, this place was a mess. That's the only good thing came out of that. They saw the difference I make around here."

"Did you know Gerry?"

"Like I know the other old people who come here. Very little."

"The body was found right here in the school?"

"I haven't slept well since it happened."

"You haven't?"

"Would you? Knowing a man had been strangled and left here so the police would take me in again and put me through their whole routine."

"That your bedroom?"

Willie clammed up. The little guy was scared. Did he think Tuttle would go downtown and tell Winegar, who would . . .

"I'd like to report to my client that you've been helpful."

"I don't know anything that would help him."

"You all alone in this building at night?"

Willie liked that topic no better than he had a simple question about his bedroom. Fear is a fearsome thing.

"If you were asked if you had seen Winegar on the parish property, what would you answer?"

"You mean seen him ever?"

Tuttle nodded. "He was here a couple of times, you know."

"Yes, I do."

"Do you remember when Striker was killed?"

"I'm not likely to forget that. Or Gerry."

"Of course not. I will now ask you a question, and I want you to think before you answer it."

"I always think before I answer a question."

"That's a good policy."

"You bet it is."

"Did you see Winegar here on either of those days—the day Striker was killed or the day Gerry was killed?"

"No."

"I didn't think so."

"That doesn't mean he wasn't here."

"Do you have reason to think he was?"

"Who else killed those guys?"

"You think Winegar can just make a call and someone will show up here and kill someone?"

Willie's thought processes kept pace with Tuttle's words, and he got the implied point.

"What good would it do him if I said he wasn't here?"

"You said you always thought before answering."

"I didn't see him here."

"That's right." Tuttle rose. "Thank you for your cooperation."

Willie came with him to the door, where Tuttle inspected the lock, humming, then slapped Willie on the back and sauntered out to his car.

At the Great Wall he bought the Szechuan special for Peanuts and another for himself. Peanuts picked up an egg roll and ate it like a candy bar.

"You know where you've gone wrong, Peanuts?"

Peanuts just looked at him while continuing to consume the egg roll.

"You don't see the significant similarity between Striker's and Gerry Major's deaths."

The wariness left Peanuts's eyes. He did not take responsibility for the department.

"Gerry was killed outside somewhere and his body brought inside and put in Edna Hospers's office. You know what that did to Willie's nerves?"

"Who's Willie?"

"You know Willie. The maintenance man who lives in St. Hilary's school."

"He lives there?"

"He's sort of a custodian."

Peanuts snorted. "That's funny. Living in a school."

"Gerry was killed first and then brought inside the school." Repetition is the mother of learning. This was a maxim he had learned from his father and had proved by taking each year of law school at least twice.

"You said that."

"The same thing happened with Striker."

"He was found in his car."

"His dead body was put in his car."

Peanuts shook his head. "I never heard that."

"Who you been listening to, Agnes Lamb?"

Fire glowed in Peanuts's eyes.

"Do yourself a favor, Peanuts. Find out if anyone down there has ever thought of the similarity between those two murders. And let me know."

The report was negative when Peanuts called back. It wasn't much, but it might suffice to confuse a jury.

The only problem with the suggestion was that it did not solve the problem of Winegar's whereabouts when Striker was killed.

It was Jim Walsh who told Kate of the provisions for her in Mitchell Striker's will. Six million dollars? She hadn't realized her father had been so wealthy.

"Did you and Nancy get the same amount?"

Jim tucked in his chin and looked at her.

"Didn't you?"

"His rule was to give to those who haven't, not to those who have."

"But that isn't fair."

"Of course it's fair. It was his money."

"Jim, I don't want millions of dollars."

"You've had it ever since he died. Has it changed anything?"

"But I didn't know about it."

"You don't have to think about it."

Then Kate had a great idea. "I'll give it to Jude Thaddeus House."

"That's a worthy cause," he said carefully. "You'll be able to help a lot of people."

"I mean just get rid of it. Give it all to them."

"They would have no use for that much money."

"Well, neither do I."

"I'm beginning to be sorry I told you. Look, let me suggest something."

Jim offered to act as her trustee so she could quite literally forget she now had such a fortune. Properly invested, the money would be as good as forgotten; she wouldn't have to give it another thought.

"I would still own it."

If she could have, she would have signed it all over to the Jude Thaddeus House then and there. Not only did she not want that amount of money, she did not want to be the chief beneficiary of her foster father's will, as she obviously was. Jim had not uttered a word of complaint, but Kate thought he wasn't a fan of the view that he and Nancy should have been left out.

"I'll give it to you and Nancy."

He became flustered and embarrassed. She couldn't do that. People wouldn't understand; she should see that. She took it to mean that it would call attention to the fact that she was an adopted daughter who had been passed over in favor of the true daughter, when exactly the opposite was true. The more she thought about that, the more puzzling she found it. She and Dad had been close, very close, until she learned that she had been adopted. All this money was meant to make her forget that! She was sure that was the idea behind it. Jim again offered to look after the money for her, see that the investments were sound and productive.

"Who's been doing that?"

"Jason Broderick."

"Isn't he any good?"

"He's very good." Jim let that sink in. "Do you want to just leave everything in his hands?"

It made more sense to let Jim and Nancy control the money, however they wanted to do it. And then she had her second big idea.

"I do want some of it."

"I'll arrange for an increase in your monthly allowance."

He seemed relieved when she did not object. What had occurred to her was that she now had the means to find out who she was. The money would pay for the search into her past, into her origins. Knowing that Dad was providing the means for that, Kate felt a tenderness for him she had not known since learning she was an adopted child.

She also felt an odd kinship with Winegar, the man who was accused of killing her stepfather as well as another man. Winegar had been an orphan at St. Peter's.

The Walshes had asked Father Dowling to stop by. When Kate came back into the main house from the apartment where she and Jim had been talking, the priest was there. Later she found herself alone with him, and the subject had turned to the case against the man accused of killing her stepfather. Apparently Winegar had been forced to leave St. Peter's because of Mitchell Striker's objections.

"Objections?"

"The breach of some school rule," he said, seeming to speak cautiously. "A serious one, obviously."

"Did you ever meet him?"

"Yes, I have."

"He came to see me. He drove all the way to campus to say he was sorry about Dad."

"That is unusually thoughtful."

"He was very nice. I didn't have time to talk for very long, not that there was anything more to say, but now I wish I hadn't rushed away from him." She looked at the priest. He was easy to talk to. She could imagine confiding in him—oh, not going to confession; she didn't mean that, though he seemed the priest for that too—but just to talk. Kate felt a tremendous pressure to make the secret of her life public, at least to say it out loud to someone. I am an orphan; I am not really a member of this family; my father is not my father; my sister is not my sister; my nephews are not my nephews. . . . And like a sob from deep within, the question arose: Who am I? Dear God in heaven, who am I?

"It's all so awful," she managed to say.

"Come talk about it. At St. Hilary's."

"When?"

"Whenever you like."

"I will."

"Good."

This gave her far more of a sense of having accomplished something than had her talk with Jim. Yet she had given Jim control over that unimaginable amount of money, and all she had done with the priest was to make a vague promise to go see him. Only it was not at all vague in her mind.

Her friend Judy came by to take her to the club for tennis, and Kate was glad to get away from the house. Jim had said nothing more, but she had the sense that he was treating her as if she were an heiress. That is what she was, at least for the moment.

"We won't even mention it to Nancy, if you don't want me to."

She had agreed with that by not disagreeing. She just wanted to stop talking about the money. He was right, she supposed, about Jude Thaddeus House. What would they do with millions of dollars? The great attraction of the house was its poverty, matching that of those who went there for shelter, food, warmth, one another. Those zombielike people did cluster together, sitting as often as not in silence. Kate's heart had gone out to them, but it had always taken an effort to deal directly with them. They seemed another species.

The people at the country club seemed another species too. All the others belonged, fit in, but Kate felt she was there under false pretenses.

"I think I'm engaged," Judy said after they had played a halfhearted set and collapsed with Cokes.

"You *think* you're engaged."

Judy's thick ponytail bounced as she nodded. Her lips opened gradually like a flower in a film until her smile glistened briefly. She looked at Kate, then looked away.

"It's special."

"Who?"

"You don't know him."

"School?"

"Uh-huh."

"How long?"

"Most of this semester."

"Wow."

The smile had folded itself back into a plush pout of her lips, and her eyes, with the sunglasses off, seemed tired. She turned to Kate and looked at her for a long time without speaking. And then, "Can we really talk, Kate?"

Kate took her friend's hand. The conversation had moved improbably to the precipice of a revelation. The mention of an engagement had only been a preliminary.

"After what you've been through, with your dad and all, I think you . . . you seem older, all of a sudden."

Kate said nothing. It was not a moment for flip remarks. She already sensed what the confidence would be. And she was right. Judy was two months gone. Was that the basis of the sort-of engagement?

Judy nodded. "If I don't have it."

That too seemed something Kate had already known. Her grip on Judy's hand tightened, and she leaned forward to bump heads in solidarity.

"Are you going to?"

"Have it?"

"What are you going to do?"

"Why should there be any problem, Kate? If it were someone else, I know what I would tell her." Again her eyes found Kate's, and if the smile tried to come back, there was an almost wild look in her eyes. "What would you tell me?"

Kate's first impulse had been to tell Judy to solve her problem. Everyone knew what that meant. Wasn't this what all the marches and speeches and blather had been about? Judy had gotten in trouble, and it shouldn't be allowed to ruin her life. Kate found that she could not say this.

Luckily Judy had not really expected the big answer then and there. What she needed was the chance to talk it out.

"He's the only one who knows. I haven't told anyone. Oh, thank God for you, Kate."

Kate agreed to stay with Judy, and she called home to say she would be spending the night there. Mr. Foster cooked hamburgers on the grill, and they ate on the patio: Judy, her parents, and her little sister, who had so much metal in her mouth she wouldn't smile. She kept ducking her head and, whenever she just had to, spoke from behind her hand. Nobody mentioned Mitchell Striker, but Kate had the sense that his ghost haunted them, and even little Louise looked at her as someone singled out for such an awful fate. What would her parents make of their daughter's dilemma?

"Oh my God, Kate, I can't tell them. Could you?"

"I don't have a mother."

The remark transformed the conversation. Of course, Judy would think she was referring to the death of her stepmother two years ago, but Kate began to have the eerie irrational feeling that Judy was the unknown woman who had given birth to her twenty years ago. Was this how it had been? She had never imagined her mother was a girl before, a student, someone confused and fearful as Judy was. She had no clear image of her at all, and that permitted Judy to fill the void. We're talking about me, Kate thought. I am someone else and Judy is my mother and they are talking about me. It put a very different stamp on the conversation.

"Either way, I'm scared to death."

"Either way?"

"I wonder what it's really like. Some people make it sound like a visit to the dentist, others give you all sorts of gory details." Judy's hand rested on her stomach as she talked, but she couldn't possibly feel anything yet, could she? All the lore about babies was a confused jumble in Kate's mind.

"It's been two months?"

"Meaning I am probably in my third month."

"The first trimester."

"It sounds like a course. Only I don't get credit."

"You could just have the baby, Judy."

"What do you mean?"

"You don't have to get rid of it."

"Kate, I told you. He isn't threatening but . . ."

"Forget about him for a minute. Let's just talk about it, look at every side of it. You've got time." She laughed. "We've got all night."

They talked about everything, about how wonderful the boy was—Kate had no difficulty imagining him as a boy; she could supply a face from guys she herself had gone out with—how sweet and tender. He had spent nights with her, and Judy just glowed with the memory. But now she was pregnant and had to figure out what to do, and she seemed on her own. He didn't want a baby. Sure, they would get married, but not under that kind of pressure. Afterward, they could finish school as they had meant to, and then, later on . . . No date had been set for the wedding. More and more, that distant wedding sounded like a way to persuade Judy to get rid of the baby and ease his burden as much as, maybe more than, her own. Resenting the guy was like resenting her own father.

About midnight they began mixing white wine and ginger ale and sipping that. Judy cried and then laughed and then cried again. Kate felt that they were reenacting an ancient female ritual: the pregnant woman seeking the company of other women whose sense of their own fertility was

146

made acute by the ripening body among them. The abstract notion that she too could have babies became concrete in Judy. Despite all the flippant remarks about being safe and watching out and all the rest, as if they were all doing it like crazy and had to dodge the consequences, Kate had never slept with a boy, not in that full sense. There had been near times, once when she would have, she was sure she would have, but he couldn't wait and his interest drained away, and she found herself consoling him like a mother. Poor baby couldn't make a baby.

When Judy finally fell asleep, snuggled up beside her, Kate lay awake, watched light and shadow form and reform on the ceiling above, glad that Judy had trusted her and confided in her, unable not to see her friend's plight as the one her mother must once have faced. The thought that had come when she talked to Jim became a resolve as she lay there. She could now afford to spend whatever it took to discover who her parents were, who her mother was, at least, and how she had come into this world. Beside her, Judy whimpered and Kate took her in her arms and rocked her back to peaceful slumber. Who was the mother and who was the child? Every woman was both, she supposed, every parent. She slipped into sleep as if into the vast labyrinthine mystery of the race.

"A night watchman, Willie?"

"It makes sense, Father Dowling, the things that have been happening around here."

"You think a night watchman in the school would have prevented them?"

"It would establish an atmosphere."

"I must say that this comes strangely from you, Willie."

The little man moved backward as if from a blow. He took the cigarettes from his shirt pocket, then put them back. He was nervous and fidgety and had been ever since Marie had ushered him into the study with all the pomp a devil in Dante accords a damned soul.

"I know, I know. I'm finding it hard to sleep nights."

Marie Murkin would have asked him if he slept better during the day, but Willie was clearly distraught. The school was a large, lonely, and echoing place at night, but Willie's apartment was snug. Father Dowling pointed this out.

"Your door locks, doesn't it?"

"I'm not sleeping down there."

"You're not!"

There was a nurse's office located on the third floor of the school with a cot on which ailing children had lain, and it was to it that Willie crept of an evening.

"You feel safer upstairs?"

"I do."

"Have you brought your television up there?" Marie claimed that he watched television day and night, though how she could possibly know this was unclear. Willie shook his head.

"What would be the point of moving if I had that thing going?"

"You mean it would be heard."

"Exactly. I take along my radio that has an earplug."

"Ah."

"It's not the same thing. Play-by-play isn't what it used to be. Except for Harry Caray."

Father Dowling could understand how anyone, Willie included, would be affected by the deaths of Mitchell Striker and Gerry Major on the premises, and Willie had a special reason to feel edgy about Gerry, since the body had been discovered in Edna's office. Was he superstitious or afraid?

"Afraid?" Willie laughed, but he did not smile.

"If you'd like, I'll come over and bless the school."

"There's no way we can add a security man?"

"Why don't I talk to Captain Keegan about it?"

"Keegan! No, Father, no." Whatever else Willie was afraid of, he was more fearful of being thought friendly with the police, his years at Joliet having permanently located him on the other side of the line from police, guards, detectives, and the like. The suggestion of a night watchman was as far as Willie could go in the direction of fraternizing with the enemy.

"Why are you so worried, Willie?"

The janitor shifted his loafered feet. "Do you know a man named Tut-tle, Father?"

"The lawyer?"

"Winegar's lawyer. He came to test my memory about his client. He threatened me."

"Are you sure?"

"You learn to hear things that aren't said, Father. The hint was that unless I provided Winegar with an alibi, well, bad things would happen."

"How can you give him an alibi?"

"By swearing he wasn't here the night Striker was killed."

"Was he here?"

"I didn't see him."

"Well, then swear to that."

"It won't be enough, Father."

Willie was worse than a scrupulous penitent. He was frightened, and nothing would allay his fears.

"Would anything else enable you to sleep?"

"You don't have a place for a man here in the house do you, Father Dowling?"

A crashing sound came from the kitchen and Willie jumped. But only silence ensued. "I'm afraid not, Willie."

"Oh, I mean in the basement, something like that."

"I can't have you sleeping in the basement, Willie. Not when you have a nice apartment of your own."

He assured Willie that everything was going to be peaceful in the parish from now on and brought the visit to a close. He closed the front door after the maintenance man and went back to the kitchen. Marie was sweeping shards of glass into a dustpan. She looked up at Father Dowling, every bit as panicky as Willie.

"Is that man moving into the rectory?"

"Marie! Is this an announcement?"

She rose, eyes closed, arms at her side, her mouth a basted line as she bit her closed lips lest she say something profane. He assured Marie that Willie would remain in the school. She tried not to look overly relieved.

"It's just that you're such a pushover, Father."

"I know, I know. But you've held the job for so long."

But she would not be teased, now that her mind was at rest.

"The night watchman is not a bad idea, though. That's what he's supposed to be. Caretaker, living there and all. Of course, he's worthless. He's not even a good janitor."

"Are you suggesting I replace Willie?"

"You might have asked him to do what he's being paid for."

He did mention it to Phil Keegan later.

"Any further trouble here would be more unlikely than what has already happened. And we've got the man in jail who did that. Does Willie think someone else might be killed?"

"Tuttle came to see him."

"If Tuttle scares him, he needs more than a watchman."

"He claims Tuttle threatened him."

Keegan listened to the account, then shook his head. "It's all bluff even if it is true. Another complaint to the local bar wouldn't help Willie or hurt Tuttle. It just shows how desperate Winegar is."

"Wouldn't you be desperate if you had Tuttle for a lawyer?"

"Tuttle's not as bad as you think."

"Now, there's a ringing endorsement."

Later, while he and Phil were playing pinochle, the phone rang, and Kate Striker asked if she could stop by the parish house the next day.

"Is morning or afternoon best for you?"

"Morning."

"Is nine okay?"

"Nine," she repeated dubiously.

"Let's say ten."

The next morning Marie was on the alert for the young woman from nine-thirty on.

"It's such a wonderful family, Father, and to think of Mitchell Striker coming to such an end. And right here. We're lucky the family didn't decide to sue us."

That was something that had never occurred to Father Dowling, but given the litigious mood of the moment, Marie might have a point. One of Edna's concerns was that the program at the parish center might open them to such suits. There was a somewhat fustian phrase in the registration form that absolved the parish from responsibility for the natural or accidental demise of the senior citizens who spent their days under Edna's tutelage. It was unclear whether it gave them any semblance of a defense against one being murdered there.

"They say she's rich as Croesus because of his will."

"They?"

"I hear things."

"Sometimes I think you hear things that haven't been said."

"Milll-ions," Marie whispered, and went off to answer the front door.

Kate Striker was at that most attractive age, when the future with all its possibilities looms ahead and idealism comes easily. Soon she would embark on the great adventure of life like others her age, marrying, entering the priesthood or religious life, beginning a professional career. From that point on, deeds would fall within awaiting categories, however flexible. Before that point, one has yet to choose the categories. Father Dowling had always enjoyed talking with people of that age, but the enjoyment became keener as he grew older and realized more keenly what a crossroads the young are approaching. Soon they will make decisions that necessarily involve trust and confidence in others. Life was largely a matter of how well or badly one kept the pact made with oneself then.

But Kate had not come to talk about her future. The future was a postponable interest until she understood her past.

"I was adopted."

"I learned that only after your father's death."

She made a little face. "I didn't know it myself until a few years ago."

"I regret that I didn't know your parents better. Or your sister, for that matter. Your father had been making use of our parish center. He would have known many of the people who go there from the time he himself lived in the parish."

"I don't remember that."

"Oh, neither do I. That was before my time."

"Now both my adoptive parents are dead. That makes me an orphan, in a way, even at my age, but, of course, it doesn't. Father, I intend to find out who my real parents are."

"I see."

She waited and so did he. "Don't you approve?"

"I'm not sure what I would be approving, if you needed my approval, which of course you don't. What is it you wish to know?"

"Who my mother is! Or was."

"And your father?"

"Yes."

"And what then?"

She looked at him for a moment. "I don't know."

"Let me play devil's advocate. There are two unwelcome results of such an inquiry. You could find out who your real mother is and not like what you find at all. Or you could be jeopardizing a whole lifetime she has built up since giving birth to you and which does not include you."

Kate nodded. "The second can only happen if I act on the knowledge. First, I have to know."

"This kind of inquiry seldom leaves things as they were before."

"What do you mean?"

"Do you plan to hire a professional investigator?"

"Is there such a thing?"

"You mean one specializing in tracing adopted children back to their real parents? I don't know. There are investigators. I am told that not all of them deserve the trust a client puts in them."

"I don't understand."

"You know what Francis Bacon said: Knowledge is power. This kind of information can be used for good or ill."

"Don't you think I have a right to know?"

"I understand your wanting to know. There seem to be too many rights nowadays."

"Father, I've got to know."

He could imagine to some degree how this would grip her once she gave it a chance. What he could not really imagine was the sense of isolation she must have. Existing in a family, but not one in flesh and blood with it. The mother who had borne her might have died in childbirth so far as Kate was concerned, but she would know the identity. Father Dowling doubted that she would rest until she had discovered her origins.

Kate began to tell him of a friend who had gotten pregnant and was being asked by the boy to get an abortion as a condition of marrying her later. That she should see her own situation replicated there was understandable. When Kate was conceived, there would have been far less likelihood that her mother would have even considered abortion.

"You don't like talk of rights, but I don't like the suggestion that my mother had a right to kill me."

"Giving you up for adoption might have been a great sacrifice for her."

"What if she should want to see the child she had to give up then?"

"Before you hire anyone, let me make some inquiries."

"Where?"

"Catholic Social Services. What is the date of your birth?"

She gave it to him and then sat back. "Can you just call them up and find out?"

"Good Lord, no. I doubt that anything like this can be a simple matter. What I want to find out is the best way for you to proceed. If your adoption went through CSS, they will of course have a record of who the mother is. That does not mean that they can or will give out that information."

"Not even to me?"

"Let's proceed a step at a time."

"I thought when I called you that you would be able to think of something."

"Thinking is easy. Let's see if I can be of help."

"Obviously you agree that I ought to find out."

"Kate, at this point I am not sure that option is open to you. I will help find out if it is. You yourself may change your mind about the wisdom of this."

"I don't think so."

"I didn't think you'd think so now."

"This is just between us, isn't it?"

"Have you told anyone else?"

"I think I should tell Nancy."

Barbara Rooney had been a pain in the you-know-what since Mitch Striker's death—in fact she had been a pain before, but after the object of her infatuation was found dead in his car, she insisted on casting herself in a tragic role.

"I wish now we had made it public, Edna."

"Made what public, Barbara?"

"Mitch and I." A significant look at Edna, then she allowed her lids to close.

"Oh, I think everyone knew."

"What do you mean?"

Careful, careful. "It is difficult to hide such things."

"Did Mitch say something to you?"

"Why would he do that?"

At the wake she had to be ushered away from the casket several times.

But she would get into the line again and inch toward the bier and the prie-dieu placed in such a way that mourners could at once pray for the repose of Mitch Striker's soul and get a good look at McDivitt's handiwork. Many of these mourners could be said to be shopping around, and McDivitt had put his best foot forward. After praying half aloud, punctuating her orisons with theatrical sighs, Barbara would rise and position herself at the head of the casket, as if she were the principal mourner.

"What's wrong with that woman?" Marie Murkin had asked Edna.

"She had a crush on Mitch."

"That's ridiculous."

Other people's crushes always are. But Marie had a way of making a bit of a fool of herself over Captain Keegan. And, like several other women, over Jerome Winegar.

"Is he a nephew?" Barbara asked Edna the first time Clara Ponader brought Winegar with her to the senior center.

"Whose?"

"Clara's."

That day at mass Father Dowling had read the gospel story of the servant who, forgiven all his debts, proceeded to throw his debtors into prison. Edna had overlooked, and still overlooked, much folly from Barbara's fixation on Mitchell Striker. She was not inclined to encourage Barbara's criticism of Clara's susceptibility to Winegar.

Edna had noticed when Jerome looked her over, but it never went beyond that. One reason could have been his discovery of her marriage, but most likely it was the extent of her responsibilities. A man like that would not think a spouse in prison represented any impediment. She was glad she had not been put to the test. Was she herself susceptible to Jerome Winegar's charms? She certainly understood those who were, even though she instinctively distrusted the man. He was so smooth, it seemed natural, doubtless because he had been at it all his life. Edna had pretty well immunized herself against him when she learned that he had been at St. Peter's as a boy. An orphan. Add the tug of sympathy to his other attractions and it might prove too much.

"I dread the reading of the will," Barbara said. Her significant look had become practiced.

"Whose?"

Barbara forgave her with a smile. "Mitchell's, of course."

"Tell me why."

"The family seems not to have known how close Mitchell and I had become. That proved very difficult for me at the wake and funeral."

154

At the church Barbara, all in black with a lovely mantilla over her head, had been seated with the family by an usher whose misinformation must have come from Barbara herself. This got her a ride to the cemetery, where she nearly fell into the open grave when she pushed through the family to get a ringside seat. Afterward she lingered by the grave, stirring the autumn leaves with her restless feet, and managed to be abandoned there when the vehicle she had come in left.

"It is difficult to get a cab from the cemetery," she said with all seriousness.

"Think of the precedent."

Barbara was still pondering the remark when Edna, on that occasion, escaped.

"I don't think I could enter into another relationship, Edna," she said the next time she saw her.

"Oh, come on."

"Something in me has died too."

Yes, Edna thought, and you dye what grows on top of it. Parish center romances refused to stay put. Clara Ponader was in Florida but she called from time to time to apologize for not being there to help.

"You just have a good time, Clara."

"A good time," Clara repeated, as if unsure of the meaning of the words.

"Not that we don't miss you."

Clara asked about the others. It was strange to think of her in the Florida sunshine missing the drab doings in Fox River.

"Has Marjorie been coming regularly?"

"Not lately."

"I'm not surprised."

"What's going on?"

"Do you know Jason Broderick, the lawyer? No? No reason why you should. He takes care of things for me; he always took care of things for Don. My late husband. Jason and I are old and dear friends, so I can tell you this without in any way being critical. He has a childish habit of flirting with every woman possible. Old friends excepted, by and large. What I mean is, he is indiscriminate."

"What is he after?"

"Oh, nothing really. Dinner, dancing, being seen with someone new. That's it. He has broken more hearts of women who assume there is something in the offing. But there are only more dates—dinner, dancing, being seen."

"Sounds pretty nice to me."

"I would put in a word for you, Edna, but you're much too young for him."

Edna felt no need to remind Clara that she also had a husband and three kids to look out for on her own.

"I put in a word for Marjorie, and it seems to be working out."

"Dinner and dancing and being seen."

"Edna, it will never be anything more."

When Nancy Walsh came by to tell Edna how much she and her family appreciated the way her father had been made to feel at home in St. Hilary's Parish Center, Edna replied that he had been a much appreciated figure.

"He had been looking forward to explaining investments to the others," she added.

"It was a kind of obsession with him."

"He certainly was enthusiastic."

"He would have been willing to give four lectures, not just one."

Edna did not like to encourage in Nancy Walsh a misconception of her father's involvement with the parish center. But she could hardly say that, apart from Barbara Rooney, most people began to edge away from Mitch when he got going on his favorite subject. His only subject, for that matter. Laying up treasure in this world when the next world loomed seemed an odd preoccupation, but people do not set aside the habits of a lifetime just because they are old.

"He managed our investments," Nancy said, speaking as if the whole world had investments to make and advisors to guide them in the doing of it.

"He offered to look after the center's holdings. Of course, there aren't any."

"Was my sister ever there?" Nancy asked abruptly.

"Your sister?"

"Kate. Kate Striker. She's much younger than I am."

"Here at the center?"

"I guess that means no. She's still in school and is a great idealist. Last summer she helped out at Jude Thaddeus House."

"I couldn't do that."

"Neither could I! Oh, I give them money, but that's easy."

"You think she might have wanted to volunteer here?"

"I think she wouldn't find it demanding enough."

"Oh."

156

"I don't mean it isn't work. Particularly for you. But she would be afraid of enjoying it, and that takes away from the reason for doing it."

"Well, she sounds different anyway."

"I wish she would volunteer there. It would be a nice way to remember Dad."

"I always need volunteers."

If Nancy saw what this meant, she sidestepped it deftly.

"I suppose she could have gone there to see Father Dowling," Nancy said.

Nancy went on from the school to the parish house and asked to see Father Dowling.

"Nancy Striker," the housekeeper said, looking up at her as if she might deny it.

"How did you know?"

"Because your family once lived in the parish, and I was working here then as now."

"What's your name?"

The housekeeper's brows converged, as if she thought Nancy should know. "Marie Murkin."

Eventually Nancy was put in a parlor, and Marie went off down the hall. A moment later the tall figure of Father Dowling stood in the door. He was so warmly welcoming, she wished she had come to him far sooner, and she followed him down the hall to his study.

"Was Dad ever here?"

"Yes. Why?"

"It smells like his apartment. You realize that almost no one smokes anymore."

"I won't, if you'd prefer."

"Oh, go ahead. Just breathing in here is addictive. When I quit I had to resort to patches and acupuncture and all the rest. I was considering hypnotism when I realized it had been a week since I'd smoked and that was that."

"Good for you."

"I'm not so sure. So many nice people still smoke, and so many of us who quit are, well, forget it."

Talk about smoking made for a prologue into the purpose of her visit. She had no doubt now that she should spell it all out for him.

"Father, one of the really sad effects of my father's death has been my sister's reaction to it. My sister Kate. My parents adopted her, but she was unaware of this most of her life. She was told less than two years ago. Her first reaction was, I think, gratitude, and for a time she was even closer to my parents. My mother died and she grieved as deeply as I did. How could she not? She was the only mother either of us had ever known. My father's death has had a far different effect. Now she insists on saying that she is not his real daughter."

He lit his pipe and the aroma was glorious. She might have been talking to her father, and the words just tumbled from her. How long she had needed to say these things, to confront the situation rather than just ignore it and expect Kate to do the same.

"This all sounds quite normal to me."

"That's what bothers me."

"How so?"

"It seems to be a national trend now, adopted children demanding to know their real parents, effectively ignoring what those who adopted them have done for them."

Who would not have read the stories of children insisting that they be told who their real parents were, and birth mothers, as they were now called, wanting back the child they had given up for adoption. Often a terrible tug-of-war ensued in which everyone involved was a loser.

"Your sister can't be expecting to go back to her parents, not at her age. Even if they could be found."

"It is a rejection of the love my parents gave her."

"Not all such searches are successful, Nancy."

"Just to start one would be bad enough."

"For you?"

She sat back. The question was a reminder of how momentous a conversation this was. To have started it was already to have done something extremely serious. "Of course."

"Have you ever imagined yourself in her place?"

"That's difficult to do," she said carefully.

"Is it? I wonder. I ask myself what my own inclination would be in that situation. I'm afraid the answer is that I would want to know. It wouldn't be a rejection of anything. Perhaps once I knew, I would be satisfied, and my previous affection and gratitude for those who had adopted me would return, perhaps greater than before."

"Things are more complicated in her case."

"How so?"

"I think she would discover something that would devastate her."

"Who her mother is?"

"Who her father is."

"You know?"

"Yes."

The silence was an easy one, somehow neutral, as if he were leaving it entirely up to her whether she should tell him. Had she meant to go this far? To stop now would negate the whole purpose of having come.

"The reason my father forced Father Gorman to expel Jerome Winegar from St. Peter's was that he had fallen in love with a girl and she had become pregnant. This became known. My father wanted Jerome to marry the girl so that the child would be theirs, but he refused. His refusal meant he would be expelled. He knew that, but still he refused. My father never forgave him. But he had the girl looked after. Her baby came and my parents adopted her."

"Kate."

"Yes."

"Does Winegar know this?"

"No."

"You mean your father never told him?"

"My father would never have willingly spoken to him. There were some sins he felt only God could forgive. And this was one of them."

"Abandoning one's own child?"

"And its mother."

"Could he have found out himself?"

"I don't think so. Given the circumstances, my father went to special pains to make sure that the facts were concealed."

"So information about the baby would not have been included in Winegar's records at St. Peter's?"

She smiled a small smile. "No."

"The case against Winegar is strong enough as it is, but the police have no inkling of this, I'm sure. The expulsion and your father's role in it are sufficient. In any case, whatever the precise reason for the expulsion, the recovery of the papers seems to make the underlying reason irrelevant."

"Even if I thought this information were necessary to have him convicted of killing my father, I would not want it known."

"This has aspects of a Greek tragedy, Nancy. A man repudiated in his youth returns to a city and kills the man responsible for his exile, not realizing that that same man has raised his child."

"Do you think the newspapers and television would view it so philosophically?"

"There is another possibility."

"What?"

"After all, he would know who the mother was. Maybe after all these years he had contacted her and returned to Fox River. Would the mother know the story of their child?"

She sat for a moment, considering the question. "My father took such pains to conceal what he was doing that I doubt the mother could discover what had happened to her child. He did not use half measures."

"No. I should say not."

"Which takes me back to Kate. You can see now why her curiosity strikes me as far more than just another adopted child's wanting to know who her parents are."

"Oh yes."

"Imagine if she should learn that her father is a murderer and that his victim was Dad."

"If your father was as careful as you say, it sounds unlikely that her quest will be successful."

"Do you think she's already decided?"

"I couldn't say."

"Would you talk to her?"

"Nancy, if I did, the conversation would be as confidential as this one."

"I don't ask that you tell me what is said."

"Of course I'll talk to her."

"And advise her not to undertake a search?"

"Let me talk to her. For all we know, your fears stem more from what you know than from what Kate actually intends."

He offered her coffee then, but she refused, not because she didn't want a cup but because the purpose of her visit had been reached and she did not want to prolong it. From the house she walked to the church; she went past the Blessed Virgin's altar, genuflected to the tabernacle, and

160

went on to kneel before the image of St. Joseph, foster father of the Lord. She asked him to dissuade Kate from her intent to find her real parents. After that she knelt before Mary and thanked her for having been able to say only enough to make Father Dowling understand the situation. And she asked Mary's intercession for all her children.

Plover, the prosecutor, had picked up rumors that the defense was investigating the possibility that the dead body of Mitchell Striker had been driven to the parking lot of St. Hilary's, so Captain Keegan called Dr. Pippen to ask whether the lab evidence admitted that possibility.

"That's an interesting suggestion, Captain." She spoke as if to congratulate him on his ingenuity.

"Thank you. It did not originate with me. The defense lawyer is said to be toying with it. The defense lawyer is a guy named Tuttle, so my impulse is to laugh."

"Bad science, Captain. Bad science."

"I'm not a scientist."

"Let me get back to you."

That phrase was on a list of fatuous phrases he and Roger Dowling had drawn up, but he forgave her. The lovely Dr. Pippen conferred new life even on clichés. Her already overheated imagination needed little prompting. Bad science! Her idea of good science was an endless exploration of any and everything that might conceivably have happened. He half regretted passing the rumor on to her. Within days, this had turned into deep remorse. Lubins called in a rage.

"What the hell assignment did you give Pippen?"

"Assignment?"

"She's put all available resources on the task of coming up with ways Striker's body might have been brought to where it was found."

"I asked her a question."

"Phil, you ought to know better."

"Can I put the question to you? Could anything be made of the claim that he was killed somewhere else and brought to where he was found?"

"In a lab or in a courtroom?"

"A courtroom."

"Hell, anything goes in a courtroom. You know that."

"But nothing doing in a lab?"

An angry silence. "If there's anything to it, Pippen will find out. She'll make a lovely defense witness, helping them suggest that little men from Mars did it all."

"I'll buy you lunch."

"Please," the pathologist said. "Not while I'm working."

The thought of Tuttle attempting to persuade a jury cheered Keegan, but not for long. Chief Robertson asked him to come in.

Robertson was not a cop's cop. He was a politician's cop, the mayor's man on the force, whose antennae twanged to PR ramifications and little else.

"What's this new evidence in the Striker case?" The desk before Robertson was devoid of paper, so they were starting from scratch.

"You mean the caliber of bullet?"

"Has that come into question too? No, I mean where the crime took place."

"We are working closely with Plover of the prosecutor's office to prevent any courtroom surprises."

"I thought this was open-and-shut."

"Have you been to court lately?"

Robertson took this as an allusion to the shady dealings of his political friends. "What kind of question is that?"

"A dumb one. There is no new evidence in the case."

Robertson sat back and his belly expanded. Had he been holding it in? "That's a relief. The mayor needs this one."

What the mayor needed was a thirty-day retreat in a Trappist monastery, but then so did Robertson. So do I, Keegan added to himself, not seeking immunity.

"The prosecutor going to pin both of these murders on him?"

"Maybe he'll confess to the second after Pep Ardmore gets a conviction on the first."

"Pep Ardmore?"

"An assistant prosecutor. It's her case."

"She any good?"

"Yes."

"I never did like Mitchell Striker."

"How so?"

"A sanctimonious pain in the ass. Of course, he belonged to the other party. Fed them all kinds of lines about financial shenanigans in the administration. The people of this town are lucky the mayor is always reelected."

Well, there were two schools of thought about that, and they didn't come down to the two parties. Mayor Grimes had inherited the job from his father, whose father had been an alderman. The ballot box was supposed to be an alternative to hereditary monarchy, but in Fox River they came to the same thing. Voter turnout was about 20 percent because there was never serious opposition. It was interesting to learn that the mayor was at least bothered by accusations. The newspapers and television had decided there was something cute about the way he manipulated the city, since they generally approved of his policy of transforming citizens into recipients of political patronage.

Keegan assured the chief that the department would do everything possible to keep the prosecutor informed.

"If the defense has anything, they have to divulge it."

"That's the rule," Robertson said with the tone of a man who knew all about rules.

Cy Horvath said that Peanuts would know even if he didn't know he knew.

"Yeah?"

"He hangs out with Tuttle. I'm sure that Tuttle finds out everything Peanuts knows. Of course, Peanuts doesn't realize he's giving out secrets. That can be a two-way street."

"Put Agnes Lamb onto him."

But Cy shook his head. "He wouldn't give her his badge number."

"Why?"

"Because she's smart and he's dumb."

"As long as he's got a reason. So what do you suggest?"

He was volunteering. Keegan accepted. Then he sat down and wondered if Plover and Ardmore really could lose this case. It sure as hell looked open-and-shut to Phil Keegan.

Item. Jerome Winegar returns to Fox River after years of absence. Why? He takes a nothing job, quits, goes on welfare, even sacks out at a home for derelicts, meanwhile jollying the widow who owned the car lot where he was temporarily employed. If he has come back to town for a purpose, it is none of these.

Item. The body of Mitchell Striker is found in his car, which is parked in the lot at St. Hilary's in a pouring rain. Striker is bone dry, there is little evidence of the rain inside the car except for a muddy footprint in the backseat. The assumption is that the assailant hid back there, surprised and killed Striker, and ran off through the rain. A footprint similar to that inside the car was found outside.

Item. The connection between Striker and Winegar slowly became clear. Striker the investment wizard was the financial adviser for St. Peter's School and worked miracles with its endowment. Winegar makes the mistake of telling Father Dowling he had taken the Latin class Dowling once taught at St. Peter's.

Item. The former headmaster is the source of the information that Winegar had misbehaved seriously as a student but that it was the vendetta of Striker that explained his expulsion. A bright future is thereby extinguished, and Winegar's life has been a hand-to-mouth affair ever since. A strong motive.

Item. Gerry Major, who had received anonymous information, calls a reporter, and a story appears telling of the discovery of the boot that made the prints at the Striker murder scene and pointing the finger at Father Dowling, a clearly idle threat since the boot is not the priest's.

Item. Gerry Major is strangled with a starter rope from one of the St. Hilary lawn mowers, and his body is put into the office of Edna Hospers, thereby scaring the hell out of an ex-con named Willie, who is one of Father Dowling's private charities. The only connection with the Striker murder seems to be that Gerry was the chosen conduit of misinformation. Most likely he was killed because he could identify the killer.

Item. All data relating to Winegar have been removed from the St. Peter's archive but are recovered among Winegar's things in the apartment of the young journalist mentioned above with whom he has been living.

Item. Winegar has provided no alibi for the time of the murders, and his defense against theft of the records is that they were planted on him.

Phil Keegan glowered at his list. He seemed to have left nothing out. In the aggregate the items provided motive, opportunity, and sufficient circumstantial evidence to enable a prosecutor to get a conviction of Jerome Winegar. But Robertson's reminder of the goings-on in court and the whimsies of juries filled Phil Keegan with foreboding. Despite his assurance to Robertson, Pep Ardmore seemed a slender reed on which to lean.

This was the sort of case she was capable of losing. This was a case that could be lost by anyone in the prosecutor's office.

"What's wrong with Ardmore?" Plover asked, his manner suddenly defensive. "She's a good egg."

"Of course she is."

"She wouldn't be working for me if she weren't."

"I don't doubt it."

"So what are you saying?"

"Do we want a promising young prosecutor like Ardmore being beaten by a lawyer like Tuttle?"

"Beaten? How could she be beaten?"

"Fairly? Not in a millennium. Have you heard the judge to which the case has been assigned?"

"When did that happen?"

"It will be announced tomorrow."

"Who?"

"Lipsky."

"My God."

"I came as soon as I heard. You and I have our own stakes in this."

Plover gestured to a graph pinned to a corkboard on his wall. All the cases his office was engaged in. There was a star next to Winegar. A star indicated a case had already been won, a graphic indication of what Plover thought of Pep Ardmore's chances.

Phil wished he hadn't agreed that Cy should debrief Peanuts of his unconsciously acquired knowledge of what Tuttle was up to. No one had checked out Lucy Sommers since the publicity about Winegar living with a woman half his age had died down. Was she even in town? He decided to find out.

"Police," Phil told the woman in the wheelchair who came to the door.

"You're not the one who was here before."

"No."

"He had a black gal with him."

"I emancipated all mine."

She decided that was funny. Phil was glad Agnes wasn't there, but she must have picked up vibes from Hilda when she was here before.

"Miss Sommers in?"

"This isn't a sorority house, Captain. They don't check in or out."

"I understand you didn't know Winegar had moved in with her."

165

"I don't know any Winegar."

"Do you read the papers?"

"What for? I've enough bad news of my own."

"He will be going on trial for murder. He was living here, with Miss Sommers. Why don't we just give her a ring?"

"I don't want to see anyone," came a thin voice over the communications system.

"This is Captain Keegan," he said, leaning toward the device. "I'll be up in a minute."

"I won't let you in."

"I won't go away."

"I haven't seen her in days," Hilda said before he stepped into the elevator.

"Well, this isn't a sorority house."

He knocked regularly for ten minutes before Lucy finally opened the door. She wore a baggy sweatshirt and jeans and was barefoot. Her hair was mussed up enough to look in style.

"I'm very sorry to bother you, Miss Sommers."

"Then why are you?"

"This isn't a personal call. As a policeman, I often have to do things that I would not do if acting in my own name. I respect your privacy. I know you've gone through a bad time."

"They fired me. I lost my internship."

"And someone took advantage of you."

"I won't talk about that."

"I mean the story you wrote. That was a setup, obviously. First Gerry Major, then you. If we hadn't made an arrest, you might have been the third murder victim."

Her eyes widened, making her look even more waiflike than before. Keegan was reminded of his own daughters at this vulnerable age. Some people do dumb things and others don't, and who's to say why? A lot of it seems to be whether or not they have a chance to do it. Little Miss Sommers won an internship and went off to Chicago to become a journalist and ended up the object of a sensational story, discredited in her profession, alone.

"Why don't you go back to Washington?"

"I was advised to stay here."

"We can bring you back at our expense if we need you."

"I don't want to go back."

"They may not even have heard of what went on here."

"Oh yes they have. The first thing I did was get my folks a subscription so they could read my paper every day, even if it was a day or two late. They know about it, all right."

"Have you talked to them?"

"Well, I listened." She glanced toward the phone.

"When this is all over, come see me."

She looked at him suspiciously. "What do you mean?"

"At my office. I might be able to find something for you if you're still looking."

"I'm a good girl, Captain. I won't have you thinking I'm not."

Dear God. What did she think he meant?

"I know you're a good girl. I was just thinking how easily one of my daughters could have gotten into such a mess."

She started to cry. Jeepers Christmas. A more obvious parallel was Winegar himself. He too had been cut off from a promising future by what the records called "immoral behavior." Poor little Lucy probably thought she was just acting like a city girl when she let Winegar move in. And now her career was blighted, perhaps beyond repair. No newspaper would easily forgive a reporter for involving it in such a mistake while being personally involved with a principal of the story.

"I suppose you have been asked to refresh your memory about the important dates in the case."

"It's silly to think people remember things that weren't important at the time."

"What about the night Mitchell Striker's body was found?"

"What was I doing?"

"That involved Winegar."

"I didn't know him then."

"Ah. Where did you meet?"

"At the courthouse."

"The courthouse!"

"I was in the press room and met this lawyer and we left and ran into Winegar and he introduced me. Jerome looked at me and . . ." She shrugged.

"Did he ever talk about himself?"

"How can you expect me to tell you things about him? You know what we were to each other."

"He killed two innocent people."

"I don't believe that."

"Murderers aren't all that different from you and me."

"Captain, he told me he didn't do those things. He told me not to worry. He is sure everything will come out all right."

If trust was only invested in the trustworthy, it wouldn't be the risky thing it is. Keegan had no desire to convince her that her boyfriend was a killer. The trial would establish that.

"Just repaying your visit," Kate said when Winegar came into the room and looked quizzically at her before taking a chair on the opposite side of the table.

"I'm surprised they let you in. Usually it's only relatives. Or lawyers."

"Your lawyer gave me a pass."

"Ah, Tuttle. A monument to the triumph of persistence over talent."

"Well, you seem cheerful."

"Why not. I am in terrific physical shape, I get lots of sleep, eat wholesome food, read elevating books."

"When is the trial?"

He folded his arms and leaned toward her. "Let me say this as simply as I can. I did not kill your father."

Kate looked into his eyes and found it impossible not to believe him. All his lawyer had to do was put him on the stand and have him speak directly to the jury and he would be free.

"He wasn't really my father."

"What do you mean?"

"That's one of the reasons I wanted to see you. Reading about your background, at St. Peter's . . ." She leaned toward him. "Were you an orphan?"

"I still am. We think it only applies to kids. Eventually, everybody is an orphan, if he lives long enough."

"The Strikers adopted me."

"Lucky you."

"Did you feel lucky when they picked you for St. Peter's?"

"Lucky? I felt that I had died and gone to heaven. The place I was in before? Well, I try never to think about it. They didn't encourage me to apply for admission to St. Peter's. They operated on the charming principle that orphans are predestined to the lower rungs of life and thought I was just being pushy. Well, I pushed and applied and was admitted."

Something of the glow of that old triumph illumined his face. The first time she had seen him she had been struck by how handsome he was, but that was no longer a factor. He was just himself. It was a funny thought, that good looks play a passing function before you really know a person, and then everybody just looks like himself.

"I'm an orphan too."

"Because Striker's wife is dead?"

"In that way too, I guess. But if they weren't my real parents, I'm not a real orphan. But I suppose I may be with respect to my real parents too."

"So you think we have something in common?"

"Yes."

"And that's why you came here." He looked around the visiting room with distaste.

"Do you know who your real parents are?"

"No."

"Did you ever try to find out?"

"I was afraid to find out, once I got into St. Peter's. You have to know what that meant. I had been rescued from a hellhole where my most likely future was auto mechanics or one of the building trades. The first time I sat down in Father Gorman's office, I resolved never to look back. My life was just beginning, and I meant to make the most of it. That was the point of the school, of course. I even imagined I would become a priest and come back to St. Peter's, maybe as headmaster."

"Why didn't you become a priest? You could have gone into a seminary and continued your education. . . ."

"You sound like Father Gorman. He looked into it, but the reason for my expulsion stood in the way."

"What did you do?"

He shook his head. "Let's talk about you for a while."

"Oh, there's nothing interesting about me."

"Dull people don't say such things. When I saw you on campus, I had a sense of how you fit in there, how well you're doing."

"It's just school."

"And your great love is classics."

"You remember. Yes, classics. I was drawn to something absolutely useless. The only thing you can do with Latin and Greek is teach them to other people. And enjoy them for themselves. Do you remember your Latin?"

"*Et sic sic sine fine feriati.* Sextus Propertius. 'And so it is that we make endless holiday.' I'm afraid I remembered it because it's useful with a certain kind of girl."

"You never married?"

"Married. No, neither a priest nor a husband be. When I was given the boot, I couldn't escape the thought that those who said I was reaching beyond my grasp were right. None of the good things of ordinary life seemed meant for me."

"But you had girls?"

"That's a very different thing. One of the things I feel liberated from in here. I have become a celibate."

"I went to see Father Dowling."

"My old Latin teacher—at least for a term."

"About my background, who I am, all that. I wondered what he would say about my finding out, if I can, who my parents are."

"They could be dead, you know."

"Knowing that would make them more real for me than they are now."

"I suppose that's true."

"I can afford it, so I think I'll hire someone to investigate it."

"Be careful."

"That's what Father Dowling said."

"Most investigators are former cops."

"That's not a recommendation?"

"I said former."

"Father Dowling is going to make some preliminary inquiries for me."

"Well, I wish you luck."

"Are you worried about the trial?"

"I'd be willing to forgo the honor, as the man said who was tarred and feathered."

"Is there anything I can do?"

He thought about it for quite a while, watching her as he did.

"Someone I hoped would come see me is the girl who was with me when I was arrested. We were living together. Not a very honorable thing to do on my part, but I was desperate. But it wasn't just that. I don't want her to think I just used her."

"Would you like me to talk to her?"

"I don't know what I would expect you to say."

"I'll tell her you're still the man she was attracted to."

"Why would you do that?"

"We orphans have to stick together."

"For all I know, she's left town."

Kate took down the address and name, glad to have something she could do for him. When he told her he would never be convicted, he was as convincing as he had been when he told her he had not killed her stepfather.

41

His sessions with the two sisters, Nancy Striker Walsh and Kate Striker, had left Father Dowling with a renewed sense of the mystery of human existence. There were those who accused religion of introducing myths and stories and superstitions that must be done away with if human beings were to gain a clear understanding of themselves and the world. Even if God did not exist—an impossible supposition—there were ineradicable mysteries sufficient to stir our awe and wonder, not least those that arise from the free decisions of human beings.

Freedom and choosing are glorious things, but they can be abused or engaged in thoughtlessly. Even when we do the right deed for the wrong reason, we are always bringing about far more than we ever intended. Much of the joy and sorrow of life arise from this fact. But not all critics are rationalists. Others dream of the programmed human being, one whose choices can be reduced back into factors over which he has no control—genetics, environment, upbringing. But then, identical circumstances should produce identical personalities. A nonsensical theory at best. There were so many boys in the Victorian age whose parents fell afoul of the law and landed in debtors' prison, but only one Dickens.

Freedom, the bane or glory of human life, will never be explained. The only law that guides it is Providence, a law that is hidden from us. Such long thoughts were induced by the tale of the two sisters. There is an Ambrose Bierce story in which two people communicate only by tapping on a common wall in a boarding house; they never meet. Nancy and Kate, living side by side all the latter's life at least, were in many ways unknown to each other.

Kate said that what she wanted was to know who her parents were. That's all. But of course she assumed that the discovery would be happy, or at least satisfying, and would enable her to go on with a sense of her own identity. How much of a human being is tied up in the blood? The genetic code of each is at once unique and the product of mother and father. It was those shared characteristics that Kate longed to understand.

"Tell her to forget it," Monsignor Barth said, interrupting Father Dowling.

"Can't it be done?"

"All too easily." Barth reached back and eased his window up a few inches, looking furtive. "What are your views on smoking?"

"Asleep or waking?"

"You still smoke?"

"It is one of my few virtues."

"You don't mind if I have a cigarette?"

"Only if you smoke alone."

Barth skipped around his desk and locked the door to the outer office. "Laura is a fanatic. Douses herself in perfume and then complains about tobacco." He shook cigarettes from a package with a nervous hand and leaned across the desk to light Father Dowling's. Having lit his own, he sank back into his chair and inhaled beautifully.

"Remember the seminary, Roger?"

"Of course."

"I mean the way we smoked. Students, faculty, everyone smoked. The faculty corridor was sweet with the smell of it. Who was it who told me that when he got a glimpse of an opium den in Saigon it reminded him of the faculty corridor at Mundelein? It was the accepted clerical vice."

"Chesterton said that only Americans call wine and tobacco vices."

"I'm down to seven of these a day."

"I'd rather not smoke at all. I normally smoke a pipe."

"A pipe! They'd all go on strike here if I lit a pipe. A cigar, they'd bring charges."

The way Barth smoked was all too reminiscent of the seminary: the cupped cigarette, the frigid air from the open window meant to cleanse

172

the room, the frequency with which he dragged on it. Had they all taken their cue from the movies of the thirties? Eventually they finished their cigarettes; Barth got rid of the evidence and left the window open. Father Dowling was glad he had retained his scarf, wearing it stolelike over his shoulders.

"She won't forget about it, Emil."

"Then she will regret it. The vast majority of such inquiries lead to heartache or worse. Does she understand the kind of tragedy that usually lies behind a woman's giving up her child to adoption? Ninety-nine percent of the time she is unmarried. She may or may not know who the father is. Chances are that after all this time she has lived it down and gone on with her life. I have known cases where, despite the documentation, the birth mother, as we now call her, flatly denies having borne a baby at the time in question. How would your parishioner like to go from not knowing her mother to being denied by her?"

"You're preaching to the choir, Emil. Of course, I don't have your experience, but common sense suggests that such a past could be a minefield of unpleasant surprises."

"Did the adoption go through here?"

"I don't know."

"Who were the adopting parents?"

"Striker. Mr. and Mrs. Mitchell Striker. I don't know Mrs. Striker's name."

"Fox River?"

"Yes. In St. Hilary's Parish at the time."

"At the time?"

"Affluence bore them onward."

Emil Barth wrote down the name, then looked at Father Dowling.

"Is this the Striker whose body was found a few weeks ago?"

"Fifty yards from my parish house, in the parking lot of the school."

"Just a minute. We've got all this stuff computerized now."

Emil's fat little fingers flew over the keyboard of his computer, following some system of striking keys he must have devised himself. He frowned at the screen, hit some more keys, frowned some more.

"No record here, Roger."

"I wonder how he arranged it?"

"There are lots of ways. We've complicated it beyond belief now, putting people through the damnedest anguish and delay. Roger, if we could just put together the kids and the parents who want them it would be almost a perfect match. More black kids than black parents, but white parents want a baby, period. I've always thought that intermarriage would take care of racial prejudice. Now I think adoption may run interference for it. At least, it would if we let it."

Emil gave him the names of other local agencies, then put through some calls to colleagues, and within half an hour the results were in.

"Nobody's got a record of it, Roger."

"Isn't that strange?"

"Not really. It's basically a legal not a social thing. A good lawyer can find ways to do things that are perfectly legit and yet bypass us. He may have to go out of the state, even out of the country, but he can find a way."

After he left Emil's office, Roger Dowling stopped at a cigar store, where he picked out a good serviceable pipe. He added a pound of mildly aromatic tobacco, slightly laced with latakia.

"They're a gift," he explained. "Could you wrap them."

"Wonderful choice, Father. Would you like it sent?"

"Can you do that?"

"Cheaper than the post office."

So he wrote out Emil's name and address, not his office address, and included a card.

> Dear Emil,
> *Fumare humanum est, miserere divinum.*
>
>   Roger

The following day he put through a call to Kate and got her roommate. He left the message that she should call him. Within an hour she called back.

"Did you find something?"

"Something negative."

"What do you mean?"

"There is no record of it in any of the Chicago social agencies, Catholic, public, any."

There was a long silence on the other end of the line.

"I'm sorry, Kate. I should tell you that before a friend of mine tracked this down, he urged me to dissuade you from pursuing it."

"Did he say how it might have been done?"

"He said a good lawyer can do anything."

"Thank you, Father."

"When will I see you again?"

"I feel guilty taking up so much of your time."

"Good. Haven't you heard that priests thrive on the guilt of others?"

174

42

Jason called Clara from St. Petersburg and asked for directions to the sybaritic spa at which she was easing her arthritic limbs.

"St. Petersburg! What are you doing there?"

"I meant Russia, but the travel agent made a mistake and here I am. I have a car."

She gave him directions and while she waited went to have her hair done and fought the impulse to call Marjorie and mention just en passant that Jason was visiting her. And then she had a horrible thought. Marjorie had succeeded where platoons of other women had failed, she and Jason were on their honeymoon, and it was Marjorie who had arranged a triumphal descent upon Longboat Key. Clara was in a very mixed mood when she strolled out to the guard gate to be there when Jason arrived. She did not want him treated with the usual disdain the guards reserved for nonresidents.

He was alone, dressed for the North, all smiles, and he gave her a kiss on the cheek when she got into the passenger seat to direct him through the maze of the club's private roads.

"This is no Jaguar," he lamented. Was he already missing his own car?

"With a twenty-mile-per-hour speed limit, does it matter?"

"Where do I register?"

"Jason, you can stay in my apartment. I have three bedrooms; I don't know why. It's as big as a house."

"My dear girl, your reputation."

"Jason, I have known you long enough to know that you are all thunder and no rain."

"Well, as long as that's understood, and there's a lock on my bedroom door."

"There is. On the outside."

Oh, what fun it was to have him here. It came home to Clara how bored she had been, and Jason's jolly insouciant air made her panic when the news of Winegar's cavorting with some Lolita of a journalist seemed unseemly. Why did she think the whole world had an eye on what she was up to? The sad, and liberating, fact was that nobody cared. Except, of course, Marjorie and a few others.

"How is Marjorie?"

"It's funny you should ask."

"Is it?"

"She's why I'm here."

Clara felt her heart sink. Her old friend was going to best her after all.

"She's a lovely person, Jason."

"I couldn't agree more. And a good one. But, oh, Clara, there can be too much of a good thing. Why must a woman always be uxorious? A simple friendship, a companion, someone with whom to revel away the evening, why is that not enough?"

"Marjorie wants more?"

"God forbid that I should say an ungallant thing about a lady."

He had unpacked, he was more appropriately clad, and they were on the balcony having drinks of Jason's concoction. Below them, residents disported themselves in the pool. Beyond was the beach, where bright blue shelters stood in rows, and then the gulf, blue, blue-gray, white caps rolling ceaselessly toward the shore. "This is why we fought the war," Jason sighed when they first sat and sipped their drinks. Clara could not help getting the conversation back to Marjorie. Relief that Marjorie had not snared the career bachelor was being augmented by the joy of hearing that Jason found Marjorie a bit too eager.

"Some women cannot dance without leading. Even when they are not dancing, if you take my meaning."

Of course she came to Marjorie's defense sufficiently to keep Jason going on the need he had felt to fly off without warning so that Marjorie would be able to understand the place she had in his life.

Later they had dinner in one of the restaurants downstairs. Then there was dancing to a Caribbean group, and Jason was in his element. He moved Clara gracefully across the patio, around the pool, and back to the improvised dance floor. Others took admiring notice; the musicians seemed to play for them alone; for the first time in her life Clara felt like the belle of the ball. During a break, when they were sharing a piña colada, a woman Clara had not spoken two sentences to stopped at their table.

"Is this Mr. Ponader?"

176

"Good heavens, no!" Clara cried. "This is my lawyer, Jason Broderick."

Jason rose and kissed her hand, and she floated away with the news. Clara and Jason had created a sensation, but a safe one, not like her imprudence with Jerome Winegar. They didn't get around to that topic until morning, over the eggs Benedict that Jason had prepared.

"The media are entering stage three," he said authoritatively.

"What are the first two?"

"Stage one, in such a case as this, is to sensationalize, to express horror, to suggest that the streets are unsafe and the police are delinquent. You were there for that, so I needn't go on."

"And then?"

"Then some journalist begins to take an interest in the monster they have created. It turns out that the killer is a man of flesh and blood, he has friends, he has faults and foibles but virtues too. In Winegar's case, it was the girl that provided an avenue into stage two."

"There you're wrong, Jason. She was part of the first stage."

"True, but in another role. Then she was the exploited child being ravished by the homicidal maniac. Now she is seen as his effort to join the human family, to form a relationship, to get in touch with himself by reaching out to another. But you know all that crap. Pardon my French."

"So what is stage three?"

"Underdoggedness. Now the media take the side of the accused against the combined forces of official and, of course, corrupt society. Any suggestion, however wild, that evidence has been manufactured, that perhaps the bodies themselves were borrowed from the morgue in order to incriminate poor Winegar, is given credence. It has already begun."

"How?"

" 'My Brief Life,' a series of interviews with Lucy Sommers, girl reporter, by a former colleague, Brad Nailles. Cloyingly sentimental. We learn of her collection of stuffed animals brought with her from Spokane, of the original Apple computer on which she works, a gift of an aunt who died of cancer before her dream of becoming a writer was realized."

"You didn't send me those."

"My sadism has limits, my dear. Would you, out of the abundant goodness of your heart, get us another cup of coffee?"

"I was such a coward, running off like this."

"Nonsense. I would have had you drugged and carried off against your will if you had refused. A reputation is a delicate thing, and one must not expose it to dangers."

"The Walshes and Kate Striker have had to tough it out."

"Ah, but they are the victims. Mitch, too, is undergoing a metamorphosis according to the demands of stage three. He has become the prime mover of all these events, the man who heartlessly turned on an erring orphan and drove him into the cold, thwarting his life all the more cruelly because of the hope the years at St. Peter's had instilled in him."

"And he will no longer be given credit as benefactor of the school?"

"Credit! His generosity is now recognized as sinister, a symptom of some aberration. All those boys. No good deed shall go unpunished."

"What about others? How will they be twisted to fit this third stage?"

Jason, whose mouth had been running like the well-tuned motor of his Jaguar, paused. A gear shifted silently, and he went on.

"Kate Striker is suddenly transfixed by the idea that she is an adopted child."

"That's right. She is adopted. How easily one forgets such things."

"Apparently not."

"I don't mean Kate."

"She has told more than one person that she will spend what it takes to find out who her true parents are."

"Good Lord."

"Yes. In ordinary circumstances one might wait for the mood to pass, sympathize, empathize, above all not criticize, and she might have second thoughts. It could remain as the sort of impossible thing anyone might do one day, such as undertake a search for one's flesh-and-blood relatives, construct a genealogical tree, you know the sort of thing."

"But that's different."

"Have you done it?"

"We talked about it."

"As I have thought about it. And not done it. There are those who offer to do the task for you, prove that you are descended from royalty, the Puritans, Adam and Eve, whatever you like. Some of these offers are shady. Others perhaps not. The Mormons have a vast archive, and the Irish government will help you trace your way back to the hovel in which your ancestors lived like animals during the Great Famine."

"Why does it have to be awful?"

"How many of the relatives you know are you delighted to be related to?"

Clara laughed. "Have you ever lost an argument?"

"In or out of court?"

"We're playing tennis at ten."

"I insist on it. Tennis at ten, in heaven at eleven, on the shelf at twelve, and in the sun by one. . . ."

"Do you think Kate Striker could find her ancestors?"

"Striker ancestors? Mitch had it done. He has a bound book, certificates, everything but a dueling scar."

"I meant her own. Her parents."

"No."

"Just like that? No."

"Do you think Mitchell Striker would have left a trail that might draw his adopted child off into the darkness from which he had taken her?"

"I think you're in stage three."

"That is the simple truth, not a stage."

She paused in the act of wiping fingers sticky with jam on her napkin. "You were his lawyer then, weren't you? You know all about it."

"Yes and no."

"Yes, you were his lawyer?"

He nodded. "What could you possibly not know?"

"Oh, I could hug you. And I would, but we mustn't be late for tennis at ten."

If it had been anyone other than Father Dowling who had told her that there were no records anywhere in Chicago of her adoption by the Strikers, Kate would have suspected it was less than the truth. But if she doubted him, she did not know whom she could trust.

"I'm almost relieved," Nancy said. "I said almost."

"Are you surprised?"

"Oh yes."

And Nancy wept when she took her in her arms as if she were as disappointed as Kate. It was the sort of thing that called for conflicting reactions. How could she not see that Nancy would interpret her curiosity as ungrateful, as a wish to repudiate the wonderful people who were Nancy's real parents even if they weren't hers. Kate knew by now that there was no point in explaining to others her longing to know her true origins.

So she got them away from the subject with something she thought would prove her continuing closeness to them all.

"Jim has offered to worry about the money for me."

"He has?"

"I thought he might have told you."

"Not yet. When did you talk about it?"

Kate smiled. "When I made a grand gesture and told him I would just give all the money away. To Jude Thaddeus House. Or spend it on detectives to find out who I am."

"I wish you'd left it with Jason."

"Maybe that's what Jim will decide. I think he mentioned that."

"Well, you are indifferent to it, aren't you?"

"My allowance is to be increased."

"I should think so."

The legal chatter she had sat through with Jason and then with Jim anticipated Father Dowling's report that there was no record in any of the local adoption agencies of her entry into the Striker family. But surely there had to be. Unless her adoption had been some unregistered deal with the mother. Could that have been?

"Jason has been the family lawyer for a long time, hasn't he?"

"Lawyer and friend."

Kate called his office and was told he was out of town and would she like to make an appointment when he returned.

"Could I call him where he is?"

"Is it an emergency?"

She could not call it that. "I'll call him when he gets back."

"Would you like me to leave a message to that effect?"

"Thank you."

After she put down the phone, she felt drawn from her room and through the house to the apartment where her adoptive father had lived. Nancy had vowed to leave it just as it was, at least for now, and Kate had the eerie feeling as she closed the door behind her that her father would say hello and then look around one of the winged-back chairs that angled toward the fireplace. She actually checked them to make sure he was not there.

Along one side of the room beneath shelving that rose to the ceiling was a long table on which stood his computer and printer and scanner and fax and all the other electronic apparatus that had enabled him to carry on the diminished financial adviser career that included only his family and one or two close friends. An oversize monitor was placed on a shelf above the computer, and the wheeled upholstered chair, with a special back that afforded extra support for her father, was one in which he could move swiftly along the table to get at the various machines. The filing cabinets were set under the table, one at either end, the kind with two horizontal rather than three vertical shelves.

Kate sat in the wheeled chair and pushed away from the table so she had a perspective on the whole. Untouched as everything looked, it had been thoroughly examined by the police. Had they gone through the file cabinets? Had some indifferent eye seen the document she sought?

She spun in the chair and then pushed herself toward the file cabinet she was then facing. The top drawer rolled outward effortlessly, revealing a parade of carefully kept files, tabbed, color coded, perfectly in order. Correspondence. It was filed by year rather than subject or addressee, and a glance told her that what she sought was not in this drawer. Nor would it be in the bottom drawer. She was scooting down the length of the table when the door opened and Nancy slipped in. She gave a little start when she saw Kate.

"You can't keep away from here either, can you, Nancy?" Kate rounded her eyes and smiled.

"I like to just come here and sit. He's here, I think. I can feel his presence. Don't tell Father Dowling. He'll think I'm getting superstitious."

"Why would I tell Father Dowling?"

"Any priest. But particularly not him."

"During one of my regular visits to the rectory?"

"Kate, it was just a manner of speaking."

She let it go. The reaction was partly explained by her feeling that Nancy had caught her at something. After all, she had not suggested that they go back to the apartment and see if there was any record of her adoption there.

Nancy sat in one of the winged-back chairs and became invisible. Kate envied her the ease with which she could fill her mind with images and memories of her parents. She could do the same so far as the Strikers went; they had been Mom and Dad to her most of her life, but they could never again mean to her what they meant to Nancy. She got out of the chair and walked to her sister and sat on the arm of the winged-back chair.

"Want a fire?"

"Oh, let's. That would make it perfect."

"I'll do it."

It was a gas log, simple, clean, turned on and off at will. It was not the sort of innovation of which Mitch Striker approved. As a boy he had chopped wood for a wood-burning stove.

"I mean a cooking stove," he had once explained.

The stove was still in the summer place in Wisconsin, a summer place that he coveted as a boy when he had been hired by the then owners to chop wood and perform other tasks. Eventually, it had indeed become his.

"That's America," he would say fervently. "All around us are paper-boys, shoe-shine boys, girls behind the counter at a fast-food place, forming the ambition to own it all when they grow up. And any of them could. It's possible." And he would look them each in the eye. "I did it."

Had he spoken that way to Winegar and the other boys at St. Peter's? Of course Father Gorman was pointing them in the direction of academic success, but Mitch Striker would have seen that as a field of competition too, one where hard work is rewarded with excellence, preeminence, success.

With the fire dancing on the log it could not burn, Kate took the companion to Nancy's chair.

"I wish now we had talked of this while Dad was still alive."

"Of me?"

How tender Nancy's eyes were when they turned to her and nodded.

"Do you think he would have told you?"

"I would have begged him to."

She so obviously meant it that Kate's heart turned over. How could any real sister love and understand her better than Nancy did?

"I've been wondering if he kept any records of it here."

Nancy pushed herself forward, hands on the arms of the chair, then levered herself to her feet.

"Let's find out."

Kate followed her to the first cabinet, the one she had already looked at, and let her discover for herself that it was not the right one. Nancy became distracted by various items, and Kate was afraid she would become absorbed in them. But soon they had gone to the other cabinet.

Nancy slipped her fingers under the recessed handle and pulled. It did not roll open. She tugged.

"This one's locked."

"Where's the key, I wonder?"

"I have to think."

Despite herself, hating herself for doing it, Kate wondered if Nancy had done all this knowing the important cabinet was locked and the search would have to be given up.

But they spent an hour looking for the key, stopping with Nancy's promise that she would find it or they would open it by force.

"I almost feel I could open it with my bare hands."

"We don't know it contains anything, Kate. Let's not get our hopes too high."

And in the dark side of her soul Kate interpreted that to mean that Nancy already knew the cabinet would not yield the information she sought.

As Father Dowling had thought she might, Nancy Walsh came by to ask what he had told Kate.

"How is she taking it?" asked Father Dowling.

"Of course she's disappointed."

"Will she accept it or want to go on?"

"I doubt that she herself knows just now. There is no record of the adoption at all?"

"It didn't go through any of the usual agencies. Of course, there must be a court record."

"Then she can find out?"

"I am not the one to answer that question, Nancy. We live in an age of information. Anything and everything that has been recorded has been made easily accessible. It is the very glut of such information that poses the problem."

"Dad actually had a CD with every phone number in the country on it."

"Did he find it useful?"

"He may have used it once or twice, seriously. But for several hours it was a new toy. Do you use a computer, Father?"

"I admire from afar."

It became clear to Father Dowling that Nancy Walsh did not think this setback would change Kate's mind.

"She had a brainstorm that there might be something in my father's files, and I helped her look. I could hardly stop her, and if she found out the truth, I wanted to be with her at the time. But all the way I was praying that there would be nothing."

"And there was nothing?"

"We found nothing, thank God."

"Who did his legal work?"

"Jason Broderick."

Father Dowling consulted his old friend Amos Cadbury on the matter, and the distinguished lawyer listened with all the judiciousness of a lifetime of jurisprudence.

"Delicate matters, Father Dowling. Delicate matters. The firm is currently involved in two cases I would never have dreamt possible. One involves what we are pleased to call surrogate motherhood. Once poor women hired themselves out as wet nurses; now they rent their wombs. But nature will have a say. The girl who was impregnated with the seed of another's husband in order that the barren couple might have a child, now is reluctant to give up the child."

"Whom do you represent?"

"The barren couple! Not even Solomon with all his wisdom could find a way to please them both. Legally, our clients are in the right; they have a prenatal agreement, valid as can be. The poor girl is being pilloried for greed; I suppose she can be said to have committed technological adultery."

"What is the other case?"

"We are, as you know, reluctant to take divorce cases. To principle has now been added the threat of sheer volume as reason for our reluctance. The case is peripheral to the divorce. A couple—driven, ambitious, even avaricious—decided not to have children until they had achieved their financial goals. At the same time they wanted the children of their youthful vigor. They availed themselves of the services of a laboratory specializing in reproductive matters and contributed sperm and ova. Several embryos were produced and then frozen. These arrested children are a bone of contention in the divorce."

"Who is your client?"

The old eyes rolled upward. "The laboratory. When they became our client, they were involved in less ambiguous projects. Father, there are days when I am certain I have lived too long. Human beings do badly enough with limited control, but such technology reveals that folly can go hand in hand with undreamt of scientific achievements."

"The church disapproves of both of the procedures you mentioned."

"As well she should. A child as an artifact!"

"Can an adoption take place without a legal transaction, Amos?"

"Nowadays? No. Not a formal adoption. In the past people took in orphaned children—relatives, sometimes not—and raised them, and the child took the name of those who raised it, and that was that. Who is likely to ask a person who has always or even for a long time used a given name if that is their name? Of course, there are possible moments of embarrassment."

"The birth certificate?"

"Precisely."

"I suppose there is some computerized way one could discover if there was a legal adoption made in the greater Chicago area twenty years ago."

"There is. Give me the name and I will have one of our paralegals . . ." He stopped. "One of a pair." The noise he made seemed to be laughter. "She will look it up in a quince. What is the name."

"Katherine Striker."

Amos laid his hands on his desk and looked solemnly at Father Dowling. The silence grew.

"Father," he said finally. "I deeply regret it, but I cannot continue this conversation. Please do not ask me why. I assure you that my reasons are compelling."

"Say no more." Father Dowling rose. "We must have dinner together soon."

"I hope you mean at the rectory."

"If you'd like."

"Why would you ever dine elsewhere with a cook like Marie Murkin?"

"I will tell her you said that."

"Do. Do."

Amos came with him through the maze of offices and waited with him until the elevator came. Not another word was said about the question Father Dowling had asked. The very refusal to go on was eloquent, and as he dropped soundlessly to the street in an elevator with music played almost subliminally, he drew the obvious inference. Mitchell Striker had consulted Amos about the adoption.

Professional confidentiality can be as exacting as the seal of the confessional, at least with one as conscientious as Amos Cadbury. But there were situations, like the one he had just left, in which something of the confidence is betrayed no matter what one does. Amos had acted impeccably, whatever had called into play his sense that he could say no more, but in saying no more he had said much. But what, exactly? It was only an inference that it meant that Mitchell Striker had employed Amos Cadbury in the adoption process. But Amos had indicated that there was a database in which the information might be lodged.

Jason Broderick, he learned when he tried to reach him, was out of town and would return Father Dowling's call upon his return. "A return call in every sense."

"Yes."

Bad jokes are best perpetrated face-to-face.

There were many lawyers in the parish, but he hesitated to approach them for fear of starting just the sort of rumor that Nancy was so intent on quashing. Finally he walked over to the school and tapped on Edna's door.

"Just a minute," she called, as the principal might once have called out to a student come for punishment. And then she looked up. "Father, come in."

She leaped to her feet and came across the room to him.

"You're busy."

"Not too busy to see my boss."

He had closed the door after coming in and now took the chair she indicated.

"The family all right?"

"Yes." Wariness crept into her eyes. She was one to whom tragedy had come once and left her suspicious of normalcy.

"Carl?"

"They're all just fine."

"Carl is the computer genius, right?"

"He better be, the time he puts in on that thing."

"I wonder if he could do a little job for me."

"Involving the computer?"

"Yes."

It doubtless did the soul of a man his age good to sit at the feet of a child for instruction, but when Father Dowling got together with Carl Hospers some hours later and marveled at the equipment the boy had put together with a minimum of expense, Carl began to speak in strange tongues. Father Dowling held up his hand.

"Carl, not only am I computer illiterate, I am complacent with my illiteracy. I want to use your knowledge, not acquire it."

Carl looked at him as if English gave him something of the same trouble computerese gave the priest.

"There are, I am told, legal databases."

"Sure."

"Can you get into them?"

"Legally?"

"I wish you hadn't asked me that. I want to make a confidential inquiry about something highly confidential. Before I give you any information, I will have to swear you to utter silence on the matter. If you can get into . . ."

"Access."

"Used as a verb?"

"I guess."

There were purists who objected to "input" and "output," but Father Dowling felt these had a solid Germanic ring to them. It was the nominalization of verbs and the turning of nouns into verbs that grated on his ear. But thus it is that language has ever grown. One can live at the point where solecisms are becoming grammatical and suffer the pain of novelty. Hopefully.

As it turned out, the database that seemed most promising was not restricted to subscribers, as a few preliminary inquiries by Carl made clear. Father Dowling then gave him the name Striker, reminding him that this was a solemn secret between them.

The little fingers moved over the keys as he frowned at the monitor and followed the instructions that began to appear there. But then came a request for the name of the attorney making the inquiry.

"Amos Cadbury," Father Dowling said, groaning silently with guilt.

Several more taps of the keys and there it was. Father Dowling leaned forward to peer at the screen.

"Should I print it out?"

"Can you do that?"

For answer, Carl hit more keys and the printer began to hum with life. When the printout was ready, Carl asked if he needed anything else from the database.

"Oh, this is what I wanted."

And in a trice it was all removed from the screen and sent back into whatever distant star is the habitat of databases. He handed Carl a ten-dollar bill.

"What's that for?"

"Not much I suppose, given the cost of all these gadgets."

"Most of this is secondhand. Have you ever seen *Computer Shopper*?"

He came forth with a huge catalog of a magazine that, alarmingly, seemed to appear monthly. It seemed that everything from the newest equipment to parts for the most ancient of computers could be found advertised in the magazine. A card fell from it indicating the cost of a subscription, and Father Dowling added the requisite amount to the ten-dollar bill so that Carl could go on paging blissfully through this electronic treasure trove for another year. Meanwhile he had folded the printout carefully and put it in the inside pocket of his suit jacket. He did not take it out until he was at his desk in his study in St. Hilary's Rectory.

What he read was a revelation. Mitchell and Martha Striker had adopted a child on 4/10/77 in the courtroom of Judge Seneca with Amos Cadbury as legal counsel. Sex of child, female. Father: unknown. Mother: Nancy Striker.

He filled his pipe slowly, struck a match, and held it until it nearly scorched his fingers. He struck another match and brought it to the bowl of his pipe, and soon he was enveloped in clouds of delicious smoke. The tears of things, in Virgil's phrase, had never been more present to him. It was too late to wish that he had not discovered this. Yet as he sat there, puffing meditatively, it seemed to him that he had somehow already known it, that Nancy had unwittingly conveyed this to him during their conversations.

Kate felt that Jason Broderick was avoiding her, which was silly, because he was on vacation and probably thinking of anything in the world but calls that came into his office in his absence. She had been unable to find out when he would return. His office seemed genuinely not to know. So Kate needed an alternative.

She had to do something, that was clear. She would not go on wondering whether Nancy was really on her side in this, doubting what she said, if only momentarily. Such temptations to mistrust Nancy could only multiply unless she independently discovered the truth. She imagined herself discovering her true origins and then remaining silent, no longer bothering Nancy with the matter. She herself would know, and that was enough.

It was because Winegar's lawyer was Tuttle that she went to him. Remarks about the little man in the tweed hat had suggested that he was not the jewel of the local bar, but Kate was not prepared for the modesty of the setting in which she found him.

The building in which he had his offices was mainly empty, apparently because the owner had staved off the destruction ball of urban renewal with a last-ditch suit that no one expected him to win. Consequently his renters had fled to safer quarters. Tuttle, however, remained.

Among the casualties of the interregnum was building maintenance; there was dust everywhere, scraps of paper, a general air of having been. It was something like a campus building during the long summer vacation.

The rippling glass in the outer door read TUTTLE & TUTTLE ATTORNEYS AT LAW, and she knocked on the frame, turned the knob, and looked in. What was designed as a secretary's office had become a sort of storeroom. In one corner a stack of newspapers rose toward the ceiling like the Tower of Babel; a typewriter stood dustily on a stand beside a desk on which boxes, papers, junk mail, and what looked like pizza containers were piled.

"Peanuts?" cried a voice from the inner office.

Kate picked her way through the debris and looked around the half-opened door. The first thing she saw were the soles of very large, very wide shoes, one crossed over the other. These were attached to baggy trousers that led toward a pudgy body sitting at so acute an angle that the chair touched the wall. The top of a tweed hat was where a face ought to be.

"Mr. Tuttle?"

A great scrambling ensued as he righted the chair, tipped back his hat, rolled up to the desk, and slapped his hands upon it in a businesslike manner.

"At your service."

There had been moments in her life when she knew she had made a mistake but felt obliged to go on nonetheless. There had been dates of that kind, courses signed up for, an agreement to try out for a play. Kate's impulse now was to frame some merciful lie and leave. But there was something so hopeful and expectant in the little lawyer's eyes that she removed some journals and a paper from the chair he indicated and sat.

"Is that today's *Trib*?"

She looked at it. It was three days old.

"I've been looking for that."

It had been sitting in plain view, but perhaps that is how things became invisible in this office.

"I hardly know where to begin."

"Then begin at the beginning, go through to the middle and on to the end."

"*Alice in Wonderland.*"

"My dear father's favorite. I read it to him once more on his deathbed."

"Was he your partner?"

"The senior partner of Tuttle & Tuttle, now arguing for my soul before the heavenly court."

She liked him. He was absurd and a mess, and this office would bring out the housekeeper in anyone, but she liked him. Besides, he was Winegar's lawyer, and if a man accused of murder entrusted himself to Tuttle, there must be more to him than met the eye. There had to be.

"I want advice on how to proceed." She squared her shoulders and looked him in the eye.

"You haven't told me your name."

"I'm sorry. I visited your client in jail. Winegar."

"You did?"

"I felt sorry for him, and I felt sort of in the same boat with him."

Tuttle frowned into his hat, then replaced it. "I have to tell you that other young ladies have felt his charms, to their sorrow."

"Oh, it's nothing like that."

He peered at her and seemed satisfied. "Good. He is, of course, innocent as charged, whatever other peccadilloes must be charged to his account."

"He seems so sure he'll be proven innocent."

He wagged a finger. "No lawyer would put it that way. The burden of proof is on the prosecutor. My client is, as of this moment, as innocent as you or I before the law."

Was that what he meant when he said his client was innocent?

"Not that you and I are in the same spot, young lady. He is in prison and charged and must stand trial. But he has Tuttle to defend him."

It was a dramatic sentence which, however, lost its power when she heard him say it and realized he referred to himself.

"But you have not come here to speak of my other client. Can I presume that you wish to be my client?"

"I want your advice."

"A token sum, then, if you please. Shall we say twenty dollars? This simply seals the bargain, gives you a claim on my time and services, and can be considered as a payment against your account." She gave him twenty dollars.

"I am an adopted child."

The money having disappeared into an inside pocket, he leaned toward her. He was waiting. It occurred to her that what was so singular a truth for her was not so for Tuttle, perhaps for no one else. Did she expect the world to break into tears at the news that she had been adopted?

"My adoptive parents were Mr. and Mrs. Mitchell Striker."

She had his full attention now. "You are the daughter of the late Mitchell Striker?"

"The adopted daughter."

"And you have paid a visit to Jerome Winegar in his cell."

"I used your name when they asked for identification."

"You identified yourself as Tuttle!"

"No. As your employee."

He seemed unsure whether to approve or disapprove. "You will have noticed that the outer office is empty."

"I thought it looked pretty full."

"Touché. I meant empty of personnel. I am temporarily without secretarial and paralegal help."

"Doesn't that make preparing your case difficult?"

"Difficult to the point of impossibility for anyone other than Tuttle."

"Is Winegar paying you?"

"He has given me a written promise of fifty percent of the royalties of an eventual book detailing the injustices to which he has been subject."

"But nothing now?"

"He has nothing now."

Kate took a checkbook from her purse and opened it on the desk. The lawyer pushed back his hat as if to get a better look. She held a pen poised over the check.

"Eleven, six, ninety-five," he said almost in a whisper.

She entered these and then Tuttle & Tuttle. "How much is customary in such a case?"

"You refer to Winegar's defense?"

"Yes."

"I can hardly say offhand. If you like, I will prepare a statement for you to study. . . ."

"I'm making this out for ten thousand dollars." She did this and tore the check free and handed it to him. But he sat back and folded his arms and smiled sadly at her.

"Why not for half a million, or a million." The smile disappeared. "Did you come here to mock Tuttle, to make lofty comments on my outer office?"

"Don't you think this check is good?"

"A college girl comes in here and dashes off a check for ten thousand dollars. . . ." His voice slowed as he spoke. He unfolded his arms and took the check, holding it far out in front of his face so he could look at her and it at the same time.

"It looks genuine."

"It is.

"And you are giving me this as a contribution to the defense fund of Jerome Winegar?"

"Exactly. Let me write that on the check."

He gave it back and she wrote the legend on it and returned it. This time it went where the twenty-dollar bill had gone.

"Then you have accomplished your purpose."

"Oh, that isn't why I came. I want to hire you for another matter."

"Go on."

"I told you I was adopted. I do not know who my real parents were. I want you to find that out for me. Don't do anything but find out. Will you do that?"

"Have you thought this through?"

Would she have to go through all the pitfalls and dangers with Tuttle as well? But his homily had a somewhat different spin.

"Chances are those that were yours, so to say, have lost track of you as well. Who knows what evil times they might have fallen into. So comes now you, looking like Marie, the queen of Romania, and they are going to be all over you like bears over honey."

"Step one is to find out who my parents are. And what real relatives I might have. If you are right, I shall have to be careful. My primary wish is to find out."

"Well, if you've made up your mind."

"Can you find them?"

"Only a fool boasts before success. But I will take the assignment, and that should answer your question sufficiently."

"I want this to be utterly confidential."

Tuttle brought a hand to his lips, made a twisting motion, and then threw away the imaginary key.

"I haven't seen that since grade school."

"Another memento of my dear departed male parent."

This devotion to his father was clearly genuine, and Kate found it moving. Her own gratitude and affection for Mitchell Striker could never approach this link of flesh and blood that could not really be severed, even by death.

"I wonder what my father is like."

"My father was, among other things, a student of Aristotle. The great sage—I refer to Aristotle—once said that anyone who asks if he should honor his father needs punishment, not instruction."

Kate found herself wanting to take notes of this extraordinary creature's sayings.

"Whoever he is, he'll be your dad and that's enough."

Tuttle might be a comic figure and the least distinguished member of the local bar, but Kate felt drawn to him in somewhat the same way she had been drawn to Winegar. She had no illusions about either man, but she had no delusions either. They were what they were.

"Who would your father's attorney have been, I wonder."

"Adoptive father."

"Adoptive father, of course. Mitchell Striker."

"Jason Broderick."

"A good man, a good man."

"I have been told that none of the Chicago adoption agencies was involved."

"Who could tell you such a thing?"

"Do you know Father Dowling?"

"Know him! I pride myself that I have been able to do him a service from time to time." Tuttle's brow proved to be clouded when he removed the tweed hat. "You have spoken to him of this?"

"Yes."

"A priest, of course, knows how to keep a secret."

"Oh, I trust him completely."

"As well you should. Your priest and your attorney, bound by similar sacred oaths of confidentiality. How did he learn that there were no records?"

"He didn't say."

"It is convenient to have had that avenue explored." He hunted in his desk and finally brought out a piece of paper with only a few lines typed on it. He turned it over.

"Do you have a pen?"

She gave him a pen.

"Now I want you to supply me with as many of the particulars as have come to your knowledge. I want you to relax and remember anything you may have been told over the years as to your origins."

"But I only learned I had been adopted two years ago."

He wrote vigorously, apparently finding that significant.

"Did you ever ask your adoptive father about your parents?"

"No. I don't think it would have done any good. I sensed that he would never enter into that topic with me."

"It had to be kept a secret from you."

"Yes."

Tuttle's cheeks inflated as if he were about to play the trumpet. "That suggests that the truth may be less desirable than you think."

"Anything is better than not knowing."

He looked at her with narrowed eyes. Then he nodded. "I believe you. Miss Striker, I will do my best."

There is a tide in the affairs of men that taken at its full leads on to new business cards, a secretary from Manpower, and a supply of white shirts from Target to replace the plaids and off-color linen Tuttle had favored to make frequent laundering unnecessary or at least the need for it invisible. The girl from Manpower was named Irene and seemed to have been born with the disapproving look with which she swept the outer office. She immediately picked up the phone and called a cleaning service. Tuttle let it go. He had always ended up being bossed by his employees.

"What do you want me to do?"

"Just put some order into things for now."

"Where is the computer?"

"There is a typewriter."

"The typewriter is obsolete."

"Do you know what I paid for that typewriter?"

"I am more interested in what you are willing to pay for a computer. They can be rented, you know."

He told her to rent one and got out of there. This woman was a one-woman spending machine. He walked over to Jason Broderick's office and dropped one of his newly printed cards on the receptionist's desk.

"I'm returning his call."

"Mr. Broderick is out of town."

"He already left?"

"He has been gone a week."

"Business that bad, huh? Tell him the committee cleared his name completely and threw out the charges."

"Charges? What committee?"

"I'm not surprised he didn't tell you. I suppose he gave you no indication when he might ever be back?"

The woman was in a panic now. Tuttle out of habit picked up his card and sailed out of the office. It was amazing what a little money in the bank and a couple of paying clients—well, two clients and one payer—can do for one's spirits. He had half a mind to stop by Amos Cadbury's office and twit that patrician receptionist of his.

"Do you subscribe to WESTLAW?" Irene asked when he got back.

"I prefer boxing."

That got him past her and into his office. He closed the door. He opened it again.

"If you had to check out an adoption that took place twenty years ago, how would you go about it?"

"Give me the names and dates."

Tuttle printed them out carefully and retreated to his office, leaving the door ajar. He listened to Irene on the phone, brisk, efficient, announcing that she was calling from Tuttle & Tuttle. He had half a mind to have her put through a call to Amos Cadbury. She pushed his door open.

"Amos Cadbury."

Tuttle just stared at her. Had he hired a clairvoyant? This woman was beginning to frighten him.

"Amos Cadbury handled the adoption for the Strikers."

"Good work."

Her heels seemed an inch higher than necessary, and she gave the impression of balancing on them as she stood there. Her frown was being turned on his office.

"What a sty. Should I have them clean up this office too?"

"Them" was a trio of suburbanite women who hired themselves out for special cleaning jobs under the title of Lady Macbeths and the motto of Out Out Damned Spot.

"Not this time."

"They may turn down the job when they see my office anyway."

"Who were the parents of the adopted child?"

"That's not in the database."

"Should it be?"

"I'm surprised it isn't."

"Faulty records."

"Incomplete."

"Put through a call to Cadbury's office, would you?"

He tried to relax when she went back to her desk and phone and got through to Cadbury's office. The side of the exchange he could hear suggested that she was having a battle of wits with the battle-ax in Cadbury's office who had been Tuttle's nemesis since the first time he met her. On the few occasions he had been in Cadbury's office, he half expected the crone to ask if he had come for the trash.

"You seem to be persona non grata over there," she said when the battle was over.

"No luck?"

"Weren't you listening?"

"Well, keep at it. I'm going to the courthouse to visit my client."

"If you had WESTLAW, I could compile some precedents that could be useful in the trial."

"I must have let my subscription lapse."

"You need a computer."

"When will it be here?"

At that precise moment, as it happened. Boxes were added to the boxes already in the room, but Irene seemed unperturbed by the new additions. Quite the contrary. She fell to with great enthusiasm and in half an hour had the system up and going and had opened an account with WESTLAW.

Tuttle took the stairway to the street floor and went up an alley behind Kane's Bar and emerged across the street from the courthouse. In the rotunda he stood and felt caught up once more in the majesty of his profession. Here he had stood with his father after his second failure to pass the bar exam. Tuttle senior had put his arm around Tuttle junior's shoulder and reminded him that this was the arena in which he was destined to go *mano a mano* with his peers. Tuttle's shoulders had firmed under his fa-

196

ther's arm; he had looked up with cleared eyes at the mythic figure of justice looking down from the dome above. All his doubts fled. On his fourth try he passed the exam but, alas, by then his father had drifted up there with justice and the rest of them.

He looked in the press room when he passed it and was surprised to see Lucy Sommers plinking away at a computer keyboard. He went in and pulled up a chair.

"It's good to see you back."

Her smile unfolded when she turned and recognized him. "I am the Chicago correspondent of the *Northwest Precipitation.*"

"Good for you."

"I am working on a series on the Winegar trial."

"Lucky you, my dropping by like this."

"Can I ask you a few questions?"

He looked at his watch. "It would have to be at lunch."

"Where?"

"I'll come back for you."

"Great."

He left her there, once more the bright young thing she had been when he first met her. Perhaps her dalliance with Winegar had not left a lasting mark.

She brought it up over the egg rolls, as if it were important that he understand how it had been.

"I am not a promiscuous woman. In fact, I had never been sexually active before."

Tuttle found such conversations embarrassing, turning the intimate into the public matter of fact.

"I had decided I wanted to be a single mother."

"One at a time?"

"Unmarried. Just me and my baby. I needed a man and I chose Winegar. He is smart and handsome and seemed genetically desirable."

"Did it work?"

"No."

"Good. That takes care of that."

"I was lucky. I have now decided I do not want to be a single mother. Even the president's against it."

"So am I."

"Oh, I knew that. I did think of you, though."

Tuttle blushed fiercely; his ears felt hot enough to drop into the sweet-and-sour soup that had just arrived.

"Thank you."

"Now we can eat."

And eat they did. Tuttle mentioned his secretary offhandedly, and Lucy showed no surprise. He grumbled at the cost of computerizing one's office, and she said it had to be done. She asked when the trial would begin.

"Jury selection is scheduled for two weeks from now."

"Will it last long?"

"Not if my motion to dismiss is given the reception it deserves."

"I'm interviewing you."

"Go ahead."

After a lifetime of bad luck, Tuttle was made humble by the string of good fortune that had come his way in recent days. Somehow it was his father's work; he was sure of it. Thus he was not prepared to be snubbed by Peanuts Pianone.

He turned and stared at the shuffling figure of the police officer who had just passed him with his nose in the air. He ran after him and grabbed his arm.

"Peanuts, if this gets around, you're off the force."

"What?"

"Your eyesight. You just walked by me without even seeing me."

"I saw you."

"What's wrong?"

"You wanna be a big shot and take people out for lunch, that's okay with me. You wanna put the dragon lady in your office so's your old friends gets the hustle when they stop by, okay. But don't be surprised if people start walking by you without seeing you, know what I mean?"

"What are you doing tonight?"

"It's Monday night."

Monday Night Football. The only way Tuttle could stand it was to have the picture on TV and Hank Stram and Frank Buck on the radio. In a sports bar that was hard to do. But friendship is more important than the aggravation of listening to three motormouths at once.

"What got into your client?"

"What do you mean?"

"Trying to escape."

Tuttle looked into the have-a-nice-day face of his old friend and then took off, sprinting toward the jail.

Marie Murkin, on tiptoe at the kitchen sink, looked out the window at Willie, who was once more coming toward the house from the school, moving fast. But even as she looked, he slowed down and, sure enough, when he came to the statue of St. Francis there on the lawn, wheeled around and headed back toward the school. Honestly. That was at least the fourth time he had done that.

Marie faced a dilemma. Should she or should she not go in and tell Father Dowling that the alleged maintenance man of the school had finally lost what little mind he had? If she didn't, she had two other choices. Either just ignore Willie—there was a good chance that he was doing what he was doing just to annoy her—or go out there and make him snap out of it.

Laying out the possibilities cleared her mind, and Marie pushed through the back door and waited on the porch. When Willie, head down, came hurrying toward the house, she moved swiftly down the porch steps and up the walk to confront him.

"Willie!"

He just kept coming, his chin on his chest, hands clasped behind his back, getting closer and closer to St. Francis. By now it was clear that he was doing this to annoy her.

"Willie!"

He stopped and raised his head and went through various theatrical stages of recognition.

"Mrs. Murkin! A lovely day for a walk, ain't it?"

"What are you doing?" she demanded.

Theatrical surprise. Oh, he was a rascal. "Just a walk, Mrs. Murkin, as God is my judge."

"Willie! Now, you've been coming up to this spot and going back again and again, and I want to know why."

Defeat, capitulation. He threw out his hands. One of them stayed out. A finger pointed. At St. Francis.

"What about that statue?"

"I am making a novena, Mrs. Murkin. This is five and I have four to go."

"What kind of novena is that?"

"Why, walking from the school to the statue and back and saying as many Our Fathers as I can as I go."

"You call that a novena?"

"It always works, Mrs. Murkin. I recommend it to you. St. Francis never fails."

"It's St. Jude who never fails."

"I don't have a shred of prejudice left. I thought he was an Italian. I better get back to it." But he remained where he was.

"What are you asking for?"

He looked furtively about. "Can you keep a secret?"

As if anyone other than a silly woman like herself would give a hoot what he was up to. "Yes."

"I'm praying that you'll come with me to the center dance on Saturday."

Marie Murkin was filled with confusion. There was indignation, of course, then anger at his lack of class consciousness; she was, after all, more or less in charge of the parish house, easing life for the pastor, looking after all manner of things, and he was a janitor, forget the fancy title, who spent most of the time he was supposed to be working in his apartment in the basement of the school watching games on television. But there was flattery too. That he should aspire to enter the former auditorium with her on his arm and then waltz gracefully around the floor with her was a recommendation.

"Dance," she said with unsuccessful disdain.

"A stroke of genius on Edna's part. Everyone is quite excited."

Although she was the age of some of those who came to the parish center that had been established for senior citizens, Marie looked with lofty benevolence on the activities Edna organized. Several times she had sought to establish her rule there and been rebuffed by Edna. When she did go over there it was with something of the air of the grande dame. Waltzing around the floor to the amazement of the arthritic oldsters had its appeal.

"I'll not come with you, Willie, We're both already here. But I will give you a dance, yes."

The man actually fell on his knees in the direction of St. Francis. "See?" he cried. "See? He never fails."

Awed by her own power as much as by the saint's, Marie went back to the house. No sooner was she back in her kitchen than she saw that she had made a great mistake. Her presence at the dance could easily be misinterpreted as a statement as to her age. Dancing with Willie, on reflection, was difficult to see on a par with Jeanette MacDonald and Nelson Eddy. She'd been taken by surprise; that was the only explanation.

As luck would have it, the dance was a major topic of conversation in subsequent days. Edna came to consult with Father Dowling about it. It was decided that Jaime Badajoz and a group he was putting together would provide the music, with records being used to give them a break. Barbara Rooney tried out as a vocalist, producing a crisis.

"They don't want to tell her, Father, and hope that you will."

"Tell her what?"

Edna whispered, "She can't sing."

"I am not going to tell Barbara that she can't sing. What judge am I of that?"

"You would be conveying their opinion."

"They are going to have to convey it themselves. Or let her sing."

"I told them you'd say that."

"Didn't they ask you to tell her?"

Edna smiled. "And you have no one to pass it on to."

"I certainly do. Marie, are you in the dining room?"

Marie had half a mind to steal back to the kitchen and ignore him. But she had an idea, and she marched into the study with it.

"The solution is simple."

"What is it?"

"Have her form a trio. Like the Andrews Sisters."

Edna just stared at her, but Father Dowling was delighted. It was the perfect solution. He explained to Edna that the Andrews Sisters had been very popular shortly after the glacier passed through. He was quite taken up with the idea.

"But who will be the third, Marie?"

"The third?"

"Barbara and you, but you'll need someone else for a trio."

"Does canon law allow it, Father?"

"A trio?"

"The pastor to sing at parish dances. You could keep us on pitch."

Ah, how sweet is victory. The pastor was rendered speechless by her deft countermove. Marie fairly floated back to the kitchen, and later, when Phil Keegan stopped by, she kept a keen ear out to see if Father Dowling would mention the singing trio. He did insist that Phil come to the dance. To her surprise Phil agreed.

"Will they polka?" he asked Marie.

"We'll have to wait and see."

At table Captain Keegan grumbled about the rehabilitation of Lucy Sommers, whose series done for a paper in the Northwest had been picked up by the *Fox River Herald.*

"Tuttle has given away the whole defense before the trial begins. The title of that installment was 'Body Chess.' The moving about of bodies. Without any proof, his claim is that Striker was brought dead to the parking lot just as Gerry was brought dead from the mowing shed to Edna's office in the school. Find your body mover and you have the one who committed the crimes Winegar is unjustly accused of."

"That's it?"

"That's the big one. All Tuttle needs is one juror dumb enough to accept it and hang tight and the trial is over."

"And Winegar is free?"

"They could try him again."

Captain Keegan did not sound confident of that. Marie broke in to say that she didn't know what was happening in this country, the way obviously guilty people were getting off because of the incredible things that juries could be made to believe. The pastor, predictably, had reservations.

"If I were on a jury, I would want to know more about the theory."

"There's nothing more to know."

"Can the prosecutor show that it makes no sense?"

"Roger," Phil said, appropriating Marie's point, "what bothers me is that a theory can make no sense and still influence the jury."

"Tuttle's theory would explain how little evidence of the rain there was inside the car."

"There was a muddy footprint in back."

"Just the one."

"Yes."

"There are ways to explain that. The killer deliberately makes it to encourage the view that the killing occurred there."

"You sound like Dr. Pippen."

"I do? Maybe I will fit into your trio, Marie."

48

Cy Horvath listened to Dr. Pippen's review of the pathological evidence in the death of Mitchell Striker. Death had been due to the effects of the amount of Demerol that had been injected into him.

"It would have been a pleasant death," she said dreamily. "Did you ever have a total anesthetic?"

"I had a root canal."

"That wouldn't have been total."

"Have you?"

"For an appendectomy. Hours afterward you come to, certain that it is all still to happen. It has to be carefully monitored. That's why the anestheticist has to be there, and you get to pay a special bill."

"Where would Winegar have gotten access to Demerol?"

"Dr. Walsh reported a theft from his clinic. Needles, drugs. What we found in the apartment matches what he's missing."

Among the things found in Lucy Sommers's apartment was a lethal supply of the anesthetic that had killed Striker. The amount of medicine found there had led to the assumption that Winegar was a hypochondriac. Only a few days before, an intern in the medical examiner's office had pointed out the presence of the anesthetic among the items taken from the apartment. Pippen brought out a shy young man with Bugs Bunny teeth and a shock of yellow hair that all but concealed his eyes. Cy felt a twinge of jealousy at Pippen's show of big-sisterly affection for the boy, whom she treated as if he had discovered penicillin. But Winegar had not used so sophisticated a method on Gerry. In Winegar's background was a stint as medic in Vietnam, which perhaps answered the question as to his knowledge of the effects of the substance.

"How could he have injected this with no sign of a struggle?"

"He must be very good at it."

"It's been years since he did it."

Pippen had no answer to that. She tossed her thick honey-colored hair in a way he wished she wouldn't. She was a large woman, perfectly proportioned, beautiful, and it was a major trial of Cy Horvath's professional life that he was fascinated by her. Keegan and Lubins made fun of her, but they were chauvinists who really did not believe that a woman could be a good pathologist. It was her tendency to imagine unlikely scenarios to explain how murders might have happened that was their principal target of criticism. Cy had come to take her for coffee in the police commissary, wanting to review the pathological evidence but also hoping that she would suggest some wild scenario to account for what they knew. Finally, over coffee, he had to prompt her to do this.

"Father Dowling said he found the body toppled onto the passenger seat. Why toppled? Maybe that's the way he put him there. He kills the old man, gets him into the car. No, wait." She was warming to it now. "He is hiding in the backseat of the car."

"That's what we're supposing."

"But at the parking lot. Say it was somewhere else, earlier. In the garage, when the victim got into the car. The killer is in back; he quickly gets the needle into him; the victim goes all blubbery right away. Then he topples over. The killer gets in front, drives him to St. Hilary's. Meanwhile, rain has begun to fall. He gets out of the car and then, for whatever reason, opens the back door, makes a muddy footprint, and goes cackling into the night."

"And plants the boot in Willie's apartment," Cy said.

"And calls Lucy Sommers."

"The plant lady."

"What?"

"Have you been reading her series?"

"No."

"She accepts a theory like the one you just came up with. Adding that Gerry Major's body was also put somewhere other than where he was killed. Then we have a planted overshoe, planted documents, and, of course, planted anesthetic."

"And the accusation of Father Dowling," Pippen said.

"Yeah."

"Whose overshoe was it?"

"Retailers have stopped keeping records of purchasers of overshoes. It was manufactured in Hong Kong and is carried by four discount chains locally," Cy said.

"Well, that pins that down."

"Inside was found grit matching that found on Winegar's shoe. It came from Ponader's Motors' used car lot, where he briefly worked."

"A plant within a plant, no doubt. It sounds like a solid case."

Then why were they all worried? They had drawn Pep Ardmore, but she was up against Tuttle, for crying out loud. Cy knew that a part of the official unease stemmed from the confidence of the accused that he was both innocent and would be exonerated. Sticking with Tuttle was either madness or a manifestation of confidence, as if nobody could lose this case.

"What happened at the jail?"

"Trying to escape."

"Did he?"

"He thought the guard was behind him when he wasn't, and took a couple of turns that would have had him on the street if he continued. But he came back."

"Did he realize what he had done?"

"Nearly walked off? Yes. The guard went crazy, trying to cover up his own mistake by accusing Winegar. If he'd have shut up, he'd still have a job. He and Winegar were the only ones who knew."

"Mr. Cool."

Cy got away from Pippen so he could think. It wasn't that he didn't think when he was with her, but his thoughts were not the kind a happily married man was supposed to have. Peanuts was in the squad room, and Cy waved to him to come along. This slowed his pace, since Peanuts was carrying about 150 pounds too many, but he felt they ought to get some work out of the guy. God knows they had gotten no information about Tuttle. Cy had talked to Pianone for an hour, using every tactic, but it would have been difficult to prove from what Peanuts said that he even knew Tuttle or was sure who Horvath was. But today he was, for him, voluble.

"Tuttle's got a girl."

"It's a free country."

"Winegar's girl."

"What?"

"The killer. They lived together."

"Oh, that girl."

"Yeah."

That was about it, but for Peanuts this was Fidel Castro–length garrulity. He fell silent, giving himself a rest.

Having reviewed them verbally with Pippen, Cy wanted to go through the sequence of events again by way of the actual physical sites. Ten minutes later they pulled into Ponader's Motors. A bright-eyed salesman came wading toward them through the parked cars, hugging a clipboard, the sunlight gleaming off his bared dentures.

"See what you can get as a trade-in," Cy told Peanuts, and went into the office to talk to Blake.

"The guy works here what, a month, and you'd think that's all that ever happened around here. I'm thinking of putting it in the ads. Get a killer deal from the killer lot."

"It might work."

"To put me on unemployment too. You realize he left here, went downtown, filled out a card, and he's on unemployment."

Cy looked at him.

"Thanks, Blake," he said, and turned to leave.

"Was it something I said?"

"Maybe. I'll tell you later."

Outside, a bewildered salesman was circling the car and glancing at Peanuts from time to time.

"He says he don't want a police car."

"Get in."

Peanuts got in and rolled down the window. "You take used taxis," he said accusingly.

Miguel Esteban, the head honcho at the unemployment office, was not sure that Cy had the right to see or that he had the authority to show him the record of Jerome Winegar's application for unemployment compensation. Cy turned to Peanuts and said with one closed eye, "Go down to Judge Fink and get back here with a court order as soon as you can." He turned to Esteban. "You may have read that Winegar goes on trial for double homicide next week."

"Jeez, why didn't you say so?"

"Who's Judge Fink?" Peanuts asked.

The world is a database, Cy decided, when Esteban took him back to records and a sleek female with frosted hair and a glad eye called up the record for him.

"Just sit down and take your time, Lieutenant." She was turning her charms on Peanuts, who was immune. Cy sat before the monitor and read.

Winegar, Jerome. Born February 24, 1956, Fox River, Ill. Parents: mother, Elena Winegar. Last place of employment, Ponader's Motors.

That was the essential piece of information so far as unemployment was concerned.

"Get everything you need?" the woman with frost on her roof asked suggestively.

"More."

What a disappointment. He had come here with the conviction that some element of Winegar's past would come to the fore and provide some basis for his eerie confidence in his own chances.

"Hurry back," she was saying to Peanuts.

"Why?"

She gave up. Cy dropped Peanuts at Tuttle's and returned the car to the garage. Going up on the elevator he had a thought that seemed the continuation of the one he'd had talking with Blake at Ponader's Motors. He hit another button and continued on up to records.

His helper here was male and seemed to regret it. He hovered but was helpful. A marriage record for Elena Winegar? Tippety-tap on the keyboard, a kaleidoscope of images on the screen, and then it stopped.

"There she is."

"Thanks."

Seventeen years before, Elena Winegar had married Robert Frankman.

Chips Pommfrits had a way of chuckling when he talked that must have made the performance of certain sacerdotal acts difficult. Hearing confessions, for instance, or preaching a serious homily. The words and music would be at odds with one another. But it was a perfect voice with which to tell Father Dowling that Chips was class secretary and was aiming at 100 percent attendance at this year's reunion.

"You mean the retreat?"

"Bolingbroke, who spent five years in Guatemala, is giving it."

"What was he doing in Guatemala?"

"It was his sister parish, and he went down on a visit and got permission to spend some time there, and it stretched into five years because of the unrest. He has some hair-raising anecdotes."

"Ah." With this information Father Dowling was certain to make his retreat elsewhere, perhaps with the Trappists in New Mount Mellary in Iowa.

"When I say one hundred percent, I mean it, Roger. Not just those who were ordained. I am casting a wide net, asking those who left and those who have been laicized. We're all one class, sharing the same memories."

"That is an innovation."

"Know who just agreed to come?"

"Who?" he asked when it was clear Pommfrits's question was not rhetorical.

"Frankman, as in Robert, as in millions. You've heard that he's become a wizard of the stock market."

"He and Bolingbroke should have a lot to talk about."

"We all will. Can I put you down?"

"In what sense?"

"Ho-ho. Is that a yes?"

"Let me check and call you back, Chips. I wouldn't want to be put down and then find I'm unable to come."

"I'll give you my number."

"Aren't you in the book?"

"Just the parish secretary. My personal phone is unlisted."

While not all clerical get-togethers were his cup of tea, Roger Dowling was all for priests seeing one another frequently. He sometimes thought that those who became disenchanted and left the priesthood had permitted themselves to become too isolated from their fellow priests. Of course, one has lay friends too, but the shared experiences and memories, to say nothing of holy orders, makes for a special affinity among the clergy. And those who had been in the seminary but failed to go on shared at least in the past and often had fonder memories of the seminary than those who had gone on to ordination. As witness Phil Keegan's roseate recollections of Quigley. And Bob Frankman's legendary nostalgia for his days in the priesthood.

"It's a ploy," his classmate Noonan had once grumbled. "You expect that from people selling insurance and brokers."

"It seems an odd sales pitch."

"It works."

"But surely priests don't represent a fertile field for an investment counselor."

"You'd be surprised."

There was the distant sound of singing coming from the kitchen, unusual for Marie Murkin, but then Father Dowling remembered. Tonight was the dance at the parish center.

Originally intended for only the regulars at the parish center, the dance had been opened to all interested parishioners and their friends. In effect, to anyone. The presale of tickets guaranteed that it would break even, and the prospect of a profit was in the offing.

"It will all go to the center," he told Edna.

"Thank you, Father." Something in her tone told him she had already assumed this.

He tiptoed through the dining room and looked into the kitchen. Marie sat at the table, a songbook before her, piecing out the melody of a tune unfamiliar to Father Dowling. He tiptoed away again. He wondered if they had found a third for the trio, someone who knew how to sing and who could carry Barbara and Marie.

As it happened, recorded music made up the vast bulk of the dance music. Jaime and his group were reduced to intermezzo status, but then no one could dance to their hot Latin rhythms anyway. While Barbara and Marie sang, there was an unfortunate glitch in the public address system, and only those in the immediate vicinity could bear witness against the songbirds. Feeling uneasily like a squire, Father Dowling made the rounds, saying hello and deflecting congratulations to Edna. Cy and his wife were there, two large people with surprising agility and grace when they stepped onto the dance floor. Cy performed intricate pirouettes and nimble-footed routines without a change of countenance, his impassive expression somehow emphasizing the quality of their achievement. Mrs. Horvath made up in liveliness of expression for her husband's lack of it. All in all, a well-matched complementary couple.

The Dailey twins, to everyone's amazement, executed rumbas and sambas with expertness despite their defective hearing, their smiling partners responding to the directive hand laid on their hips and the authoritative pressure of the hand that held theirs, moving them through movements they had never made before, certainly not as successfully as this.

"Arthur Murray," one twin explained.

"Dance Studios," the other added.

Only in this gathering would that allusion have rung a bell. Barbara Rooney, her eyes widened to receive praise for her singing, moved about the auditorium unnoticed. Father Dowling sought not to encounter her, lest he be tempted to lie about her talent. But she outmaneuvered him.

"I can't help but think of Mitchell," she said with moist eyes.

"Ah."

"I suggested that the dance be called the Mitchell Striker Memorial Dance, but Edna thought that might be off-putting."

"I think the dance is meant to get our minds off recent sad events."

"I shall never forget him," Barbara said fervently.

"Gerry Major?"

She stepped back, her mouth falling open. Words failed her.

"Did his son and daughter-in-law come?"

Barbara did not know. She moved away from him, her mouth unprettily open. Phil Keegan was in the bar, at which Willie presided.

"Willie tells me these are going to be monthly events."

"Just passing on a rumor, Father."

"Don't."

"Aren't you enjoying yourself, Father?"

"I've said hello to most people here, and I've been thinking how comparatively peaceful my study is."

"Why don't we go over there?" Phil said.

"What a splendid suggestion."

When they were settled in, fending for themselves since Marie was at the dance, Phil lit a cigar and the pastor touched a match to his pipe.

"Cy came up with an odd bit of information yesterday."

"In what connection?"

"The Winegar case. Do you know who married his mother? Robert Frankman."

This was news indeed. Father Dowling jotted down the dates. There were years between the birth and the marriage.

"So Frankman wasn't the father."

"I don't suppose it means anything, Roger. But it gives us a fuller picture of the accused."

"You already knew that he was an orphan."

Perhaps Phil meant that to know more about Winegar was to find it more difficult to think of him simply as the man who had killed other men. It may not be that to understand all is to forgive all, but it makes condemning more difficult. The more we know of the criminal the less different from ourselves does he seem.

Father Dowling had taxed his memory, trying to come up with images of that Latin class he had taught so many years ago, but to no avail. He had found the grade book he had kept, and it was strange to find at the end of the list Winegar, Jerome. You would think that the final name on a list would have some claim on memory. The grade was B, he had given only one A, a further claim on memory, but no image, no event, came. He did not even remember the room in which he had taught. He had been busy then, too busy, and had wedged the class into an already crowded day. He could not believe that he had taught much of a class, but at that time he had been much closer to his own first reading of Virgil and it would have been less of a task. What he did remember was the ease and insouciance with which he had taken on assignments, answered requests, counted on his energy to keep a packed schedule. Ah, youth, as Virgil did not say.

Not to remember Winegar made him feel guilty, and it did not help that on the two occasions he had gone to visit the man in prison he had managed to see him only once.

"I am not a credit to the parish, Father Dowling."

"You're innocent until proved guilty."

"Do you operate with a legal sense of innocence and guilt?"

"The other is between you and God."

"And my confessor?"

"Is that a request?"

"Not this time, Father."

It is what brought him back again, a few days later, but Winegar was with Tuttle, and the priest had not seen Winegar. Despite the reminder of teaching him Virgil and despite the proof of the grade book, Father Dowling's dominant memory of the man was the visit he had paid to the rectory on the day he registered as a parishioner. None of the envelopes he had been given that day ever showed up in the collection basket.

Now what Cy Horvath had discovered connected Winegar in an accidental way to Father Dowling's past. Bob Frankman, his classmate, had applied for and been granted laicization and had married twice since. The first wife, Elena Winegar, incredibly, was the mother of the man accused of killing Mitchell Striker and Gerry Major. Had the son ever known her? Father Dowling sought to find out.

"My whole life was lived in institutions, Father. I am a beneficiary of a very efficient and generous system."

"You were never adopted?"

"My mother apparently kept me for a while before placing me in the orphanage. One's eligibility declines rapidly with the years."

"You never saw her again?"

He shook his head. "What could she be for me but a face in the crowd?"

And vice versa too, the priest supposed. Still, it was tempting to think that she might have known of her child's rescue from oblivion and selection for St. Peter's, might have followed his brilliant years there, only to see them blighted by the vindictiveness of Mitchell Striker. She had almost as much motive to murder Striker as her son. But would she have waited all those years to act if she could be imagined to know? Who other than the victim of Mitchell Striker's vengeance could carry the hurt with him all those years, letting it fester and become malevolent, a motive for murder?

He wondered too if Bob Frankman knew of the connection. It almost seemed a motive to attend his class reunion. Almost.

As a boy, Bob Frankman had an altar in his room at which he would pretend to say mass. His mother made vestments for him, an alb from a sheet, the chasuble from a white bedspread that had the thickness of the real vestment, stole, maniple, cincture, the complete outfit. For a chalice he had a silver sherbet dish. His mother made unleavened bread and cut disks of it for altar bread, and he used Welch's grape juice for wine. Sometimes his parents would come and watch him go through the whole mass, for all the world as if he were already ordained.

That he would be ordained seem foreordained. There was no other future he even contemplated as a kid. He went first to Quigley, the day seminary, and then on to St. Mary's at Mundelein. He never had a date; he looked at girls as decorative, but, of course, they were all informed of his vocation. Everyone knew that Bob Frankman was going to be a priest. His years in the seminary were untroubled and pleasant, simply the time that must be put in before that great day when he lay facedown in the sanctuary with his classmates and listened to the cardinal praying over them. He had the sense of already having done this.

When other newly ordained priests were enjoying a heightened sense of zeal as they performed for the first time the tasks of an assistant pastor, Bob Frankman was seized with a sense of boredom. Nothing seemed new to him, everything was something he had done a hundred times before. Mass? He had said mass in his room since he was a kid. He had played at all the tasks of a priest for so long that the real article left him deflated.

His confessor told him he was suffering from spiritual dryness. It was an answer he might have given himself; indeed he had over the years whispered such wisdom to imaginary penitents. The lives of others, laypeople, suddenly took on for him the look of something utterly strange and unknown. He sensed as he never had before the attraction of females: their mannerisms, their voices, their eyes, the soft plush turn of their lips.

His confessor told him that sin requires assent, and apparently he had not been guilty of lust, but he must take these disturbances as a warning. Celibacy is difficult; it requires vigilance. Increase your devotion to our Blessed Mother.

His own lips moved with the words spoken to him. Of course, of course. But the rote answers now collided with a stirring in his blood he had never really felt before. It certainly had not seemed to him to promise anything remotely competitive with the priesthood.

His few years of active priesthood seemed in retrospect to have been an incessant flow of temptation and turmoil. But victorious. He had not succumbed. Oh, he had lived dangerously, allowing himself to prolong sessions with groups of girls just to hear their chatter and laughter and see the flash of their eyes. Their lithe bodies moved in ways that seemed to comprise the secret of the universe from which he had turned away forever. But he did not fall. Nothing went beyond a velleity. He became an expert in the calibrations of the human act, all the variations from a first awareness of attraction through the scale to the deed openly done. His imaginative involvement was restricted to the initial innocent aspects of action.

Elena Moore was hired by the pastor out of the goodness of his heart as much as because he expected to get much work out of her. "A troubled woman, Father Frankman, but a good one. Oh, the vicissitudes of life. We will be patient with her."

She was hired as assistant to the housekeeper and was given cleaning jobs about the house and did the laundry as well. There was a wild beauty about her reminiscent of faces in the crowd in a Renaissance painting: Her large eyes rivaled those of Rembrandt's girl in a turban, and no shapeless dress could conceal the richness of the body beneath it. From the first time he saw her, Bob Frankman was infatuated with her. He avoided her; he scarcely spoke to her; he just nodded abstractedly when the pastor mentioned how well she was working out after all.

He noticed that she noticed him. It was the custom in the house to wear a cassock when one received visitors but not at other times. Bob bought some nonclerical shirts and a pullover sweater. He began to jog, and this provided an opportunity to wear a jogging suit about the house. He realized that he was preening before the girl. And that she noticed.

"You never talk to me," she said one day, lifting her eyes to his.

But he had. He had told her all about himself; they had discussed a dozen topics not remotely related to the parish house or his priesthood; he had asked her about herself and she had answered, expanding on the fragments he had heard from the pastor. All this in his mind, of course. As a boy he had lived the priesthood in imagination; as a young man he established a whole friendship in his imagination. When she spoke to him, it began to come forth into the real world.

"I've been married," she told him.

"I didn't know that."

"How could you? It didn't last."

He became angry as he listened. Who was this Moore who had treated her so badly? A seaman from Great Lakes who had been transferred to a ship and sailed out of her life. Their marriage had been a thing of six months.

"By a priest?"

She nodded. The naval chaplain.

"If you should ever want to marry again . . ."

Her smile dissolved him. She shook her head and turned away. That was the moment during which his life made a decisive turn. There are things that cannot happen, that we are unable to do, that nonetheless happen and are done. Words are lacking, but this is deeper than speech. Free acts are predestined too. He put his hand on her arm, her head turned, doelike eyes looked into his, more pressure on her arm and she was close against him and nothing would ever be the same again. That night, without any verbal agreement, she came to him.

She was frightened, shocked, when he told her he would leave the priesthood. He had to grip her wrist tightly to prevent her running away. He explained that it was possible. He would submit a request.

"You will always blame me."

She spoke as one for whom love did not last. As a token of his earnestness, he vowed not to touch her again until he had been freed. His pastor was astounded when he told him he had applied for laicization. His confessor told him repentance was enough; he need not leave the priesthood. He listened patiently. They did not understand that in his heart he had already left.

He was laicized and married Elena before a justice of the peace because her previous marriage prevented her from marrying in the church. Within a month he knew it had been a great mistake. Not to leave the priesthood, but to marry Elena. So long as he could imagine the details about her and control her as he daydreamed their life together, everything had been fine, but the flesh-and-blood Elena was emphatically there. More beautiful than before, with a perfection of feature and, as he now knew, of body that was breathtaking but mindless. She might have been a body without a soul. It was a requirement of his existence that reality be convertible to imagination, that things have significance as well as existence. Elena lived in the isolated moment.

When he presented her to his parents, he might as well have driven a sword through them. For the first time he became aware of Elena's commonness, her vulgarity. She was inescapably the cleaning lady from his rectory. His parents would have liked to think that she had seduced him, that he was temporarily mad, but if she had seduced him, it was as he had imagined her.

He fought the realization that he had made a mistake. For some years he was able to sublimate their life together and pretend that it was as he imagined it. In compensation for this effort, he became a hardheaded man of business. A manipulator of money. A broker. The entry-level job provided a way to learn the market. Within a year he was the peer of his boss and was rewarded. Rewards came regularly, and in the world of money the reward was money. Two years after returning to the lay estate he was a rich man.

Wealth did not improve Elena. She became more ostentatiously vulgar. The favor of a prince was the ruination of Cinderella. She began to drink. Later, looking back, he could acknowledge that he welcomed her weakness, even subtly encouraged her decline. He discerned in it the possibility of escape. The money he gave her before arranging the Mexican divorce should have meant independence, properly managed, but she scorned the thought that he might act for her.

What would he have done without Colleen's understanding during that period? She marveled at his patience and generosity with Elena. With her he could discuss the fact that of course his marriage was not really a marriage, only a civil affair, and when it was civilly dissolved it was gone indeed. He was free by civil law and free by canon law. He made his peace with the church, making a good confession. Colleen wore white. They were married from her parish, Wilson who had been in the seminary with him, though not a classmate, presiding. But invitations went out to every member of his class.

The real priesthood failed to meet the demands of his imagination, and so it had been with his marriage to Elena. Colleen bore him two sons, they lived a parody of suburban life, his wealth pullulated, he became a pillar of his parish and reestablished many of his clerical friendships. He refused to take a fee for any help he could be to the parish of a friend, or to the friend himself. There were any number of priests with condos in Málaga and property in Phoenix because he had nursed their meager savings into affluence. He had learned by having it that money is not the answer to life.

Some premonition led him to open accounts elsewhere in the world that did not come under the surveillance of the IRS. This was a knack he had learned from others, merely a device to make money grow. The tax man could be a grim reaper, and a moral theologian worked out for Bob a convincing argument that the income tax was contrary to natural law. And of course no man-made law in conflict with natural law can bind.

Colleen had an affair with Earl, a man at the club, a swarthy little fellow whose domed bald head was tanned from his daily round of golf. They became partners on the course, and one thing led to another. Frankman was very calm while she explained to him what had happened. He went to the man and shook his hand and wished him and Colleen every happiness after the divorce.

"What divorce?"

"Surely you mean to make an honest woman of her."

"I've got a wife."

"You should have thought of that before."

Earl's portfolio was with Frankman and Associates. He was not a stupid man. He agreed.

Colleen came to him with what she thought was the news. They agreed that since she had broken up two families the only thing to do was to form a new one.

"You must apply for an annulment."

"On what grounds?"

Many men and women, like himself, were left psychologically incapable of contracting a valid marriage. There were many cases. Tribunals had become very sympathetic.

"You're taking the blame?"

He closed his eyes and patted her hand. Blame seemed a small price

216

to pay for his freedom. He had not reckoned on the psychological effect of nullifying the marriage.

One morning in Lisbon he got out of the shower in the luxury hotel where he was staying and caught a glimpse of himself in a full-length mirror. He was overweight, there was a great deal of sag in the stomach, but that wasn't it. Naked, defenseless, he saw himself as what he had become, not physically, but spiritually, morally, as a human being. He was terrified. An image of the bather at Pompeii caught in the flow of lava and preserved for all to see centuries later. In that baked carcass a soul had once dwelt for a few years and then been called before the throne of God. Never before had the stakes of life seemed clearer.

He had become a priest and been laicized. He had entered into a civil marriage and divorced the woman. He had married in the church, had two children, then had that marriage annulled. There was a woman in Chicago with whom he enjoyed vacations. She was to join him in Lisbon in two days. Once he had had a soul, an imagination. Now he was only the sum of fleeting deeds that did not add up to a meaningful life. He leaned toward his image in the mirror and whispered, "You are damned."

But the words clouded the mirror as he spoke them, and no one alive is damned. He still had a chance. He wired the woman that his plans had changed. He rented a car and drove to Fátima and advanced across the great patio on his knees. He was certain that his life would change, that everything up until now had been merely a prelude to the real life of Robert Frankman.

When he heard that Mitchell Striker was retiring and that this included his position on the board of St. Peter's School, he enlisted his colleague's support and was elected to succeed him. It was understood that like Mitchell he would husband the school's financial resources. In fact, with the new financial opportunities that had opened up and a device he would normally have used only when his own money was at stake, he had in effect bet on advances that yielded enormous benefits—if they worked. The alternative was best not thought of.

"Try it," Jim Walsh had said when he explained it to him.

"This is not just risky."

But Walsh was game and it worked and he realized a profit that made him gasp. It was doubly sweet turning such a profit for the son-in-law of Mitchell Striker. Walsh swore him to silence, which seemed unfair; Frankman would have liked Striker to know of the coup, but the customer was always right.

That success for Walsh and another for himself emboldened him, and he took the gamble on behalf of St. Peter's as well as another on behalf of Walsh. He lost more in one day than he had earned for clients during his first five years as a financial manager. Stories of brokers hurling themselves from Wall Street windows in lesser situations came to him. He went immediately to Cottage.

The headmaster was a typical academic for whom money is more mysterious than the law of special relativity. Frankman emphasized the positive.

"It may be months before we're back to where we were."

"Oh," Cottage said.

"I pledge a significant profit for the year as a whole."

"That would be nice."

Frankman had the sense that he could have absconded with the whole endowment and Cottage would have been able to absorb the news. But there were those who understood what he had done. Frankman tasted the full wrath of Mitchell Striker.

"You owe it to the school to resign at once."

"I intend to earn it back."

"Your methods make that unlikely."

"My methods have enriched a wide clientele, Mitchell, and you know it. That is why you promoted me for this seat on the board. It is your own reputation, not mine, that concerns you. I shall restore what has been lost and show a profit before the end of the fiscal year."

"Have you reported to the board?"

"I went to Cottage immediately."

"Cottage."

It had been one of the most painful experiences of Frankman's professional life. There was a moment of self-doubt. Had he lost the Midas touch? He had not. Already the endowment was beginning to grow again. Frankman had worked out an intricate but supersafe plan, and it was proceeding like clockwork.

In Zurich he met an expatriate American at a conference, and over dinner it emerged that the man, J. J. Laville, was a product of St. Peter's School. Laville extolled the training he had received there. He had gone on to Fordham, then the Wharton School, accepted an overseas assignment, and found it just to his taste to be an American abroad.

"Father Gorman was like a, well, father to me."

"His death came as a great shock to the school. While he lived, it was not yet understood that the school has entered into its second act."

"Cottage is a good man." Laville said.

"Ah, you know him."

"I helped him with his Latin."

This seemed to be true. "The death of my own predecessor was considerably more tragic, and mysterious," Frankman said.

Laville had not known of this and was avid for details. It was certainly no surprise that the news of Fox River did not get to Zurich. Cottage had sent a special letter to all alumni informing them of the death of Father Gorman.

"Striker was actually murdered?"

"That is the charge."

"Who did it?"

"Did you know a man named Winegar?"

Laville, already interested, nearly came across the table at the mention of the accused's name. "Of course I knew Winegar. I thought of him as soon as you mentioned Striker. Striker hounded him from the school. Ruined his life, quite literally."

"You have just stated the motive for the murder."

Laville scarcely ate, he was so excited by this news from his old school. Over brandy he began to wax philosophical, and Frankman was beginning to regret having brought the matter up.

"What exactly did Winegar do? What did immoral conduct mean in those days?" Frankman asked.

"He got a girl pregnant."

"Why did Striker get so militant about it?"

"Oh, that's the key to the whole thing. Winegar was dating Striker's daughter."

"Better not. Think of what people will say," Jason said when Clara suggested that she return to Fox River with him.

"Over a week in the same apartment and you're worried about returning on the same plane?"

"I won't tell if you don't."

"I can hardly wait."

She did drive with him to St. Petersburg in his rented car, planning to spend a few days with friends there. When she got back to the condo, she gloried in having the whole place to herself. Having Jason around had been fun, but she came to realize that she had invested everything she had in life with Don and simply could not summon what it takes to make her life conform with another's.

And all the frantic phone calls from Jason's office stopped. Marjorie had called while Jason was here, and with gestures and mouthing, Clara had threatened to tell her who was with her, but she was glad she hadn't when Marjorie began to talk of the dance at St. Hilary's.

"A sort of benefit for the old people."

"It sounds dreadful."

"*Au contraire.* We had a lovely time. Barbara sang."

"You went with her."

"Don't be silly. Barbara and the housekeeper sang, but someone turned off the speakers and we got through it all right."

"What kind of music was it?"

"The kind Jason loves, a mixture of the old and the new, well, the relatively new. Nothing spastic."

Clearly Marjorie was trying to convey the thought that she and Jason had attended the dance together, and Clara could not resist prompting more lies out of her, but finally she let it go. You just couldn't do that to anyone you hoped to see again.

Besides, the whole hennish pursuit of Jason appeared to her in a new perspective now. He was a brilliant man, a conversationalist and raconteur without equal, but a bore to be with day after day. Jason was made for dances, for dates, for special occasions. For the long haul you needed someone with ordinary virtues too.

Still she was lonely after a day or so, missing all her friends, and Fox River. Jason's advice was to stay out of town until the trial was over, but that would have been cruel and unusual punishment. Besides, if there was any talk going around, Marjorie would have brought it up. The truth seemed to be that her folly with Winegar loomed larger in her own mind than it did in anyone else's. Jason had actually thought she might be called as a witness for the defense, and if there was any danger of that, she would certainly stay put in the Florida sunshine.

"How long are you going to be away?" Nan Walsh asked when Clara called her. "We've missed you."

"What's the weather like?"

She listened through the gloomy report. Of course, she had already checked the Weather Channel. It was abundantly clear that going back had its punitive aspects too.

"Has the trial begun yet?"

"Not till next week."

Nan answered all her questions, but she did not go on about the trial, understandable when you remembered it was her father's murder you were talking about. Or was it Nan's realization that Clara had been escorted here and there by Winegar? Clara was beginning to think this call was a mistake when Nan mentioned the series on the trial being written by Lucy Sommers.

"The girl he was living with when he was arrested?"

"Apparently she is completely rehabilitated after her silly story accusing Father Dowling."

The way Nan said it made it clear to Clara that she was not classifying Clara among the girlfriends of Winegar. That was when she became convinced that Jason's concern for her reputation was exaggerated. She made arrangements to return the following day.

And when she stood waiting for a cab outside O'Hare in a gray cold day with what snow was visible all dirty and pocked and the people around her looking pinch-faced with cold, Clara asked herself why she had been in such a hurry to return. But once home with coffee on and listening to the ancient phone messages, she began to be glad. After erasing all the messages, she called Marjorie.

"Oh, you wouldn't want to be here today," Marjorie began.

"But I am. I just got in."

"So did Jason!"

"Where was he?"

"Oh, he's being mysterious about it. Why don't the three of us do something tonight?"

"Marjorie, I was hoping that just the two of us could catch up."

"Did I tell you Barbara's wearing black?"

"Oh, save everything until we get together. Name a place."

"Dayton's Tearoom?"

Shades of Winegar. No thanks. "How about the Crillon Grill?"

"Who's paying?"

"This is on me." And to take the sting out of Marjorie's relative poverty, she added, "But you better have lots of gossip."

She was disappointed in what Marjorie had to offer. Absence from home seldom produces an exciting list of what one has missed, either because it does not seem exciting to the stay-at-home or because nothing much has happened. But Marjorie got good mileage out of Barbara's going into high mourning for a man who probably had not noticed the way her tongue hung out every time she looked at him.

"Are you still going to St. Hilary's?"

"The thing about volunteer work is, once you start, it seems that you're letting down the side if you stop."

Was this a criticism of Clara's fleeing south? Clara did not feel the least bit guilty. She had given some good days to the effort, and that was it. No matter how long she helped, some day would be the last day. Marjorie saved Willie for the last.

"You remember Willie, the superintendent of parish buildings?"

"I thought he was the janitor."

Marjorie made a face. "I don't think I ever really spoke to him before the dance."

"He was there?"

"Clara, he lives there. He has a lovely apartment right there in the school."

"Lovely?"

"I peeked in one day. Of course, it's a man's place."

"What does that mean?"

"A mess. I asked him if anyone else had ever cleaned up the place."

Marjorie was moving circumspectly toward her point, and Clara realized that the wrong remark on her part would stop the narrative.

"He dances?"

"Do you remember the lindy? I don't recall ever doing it particularly well when I was young, but with Willie I feel like Ginger Rogers."

So much for the idea that Marjorie, on the phone, had been trying to pretend that she and Jason had attended the dance together. What would she have learned if she had picked up on Marjorie's enigmatic phrases then? It was far more fun to hear her on this subject in person.

"Has he ever figured out why he was the target of the murderer's shoe and the body of poor Gerry Major?"

"He spent time in prison."

"He did!"

"As the eyes and ears of the state's attorney. They invented a criminal record for him, to make it plausible. He was responsible for gathering information that was decisive in any number of highly publicized cases. He lives in fear that his double life has been discovered."

222

"But why take a job as janitor?"

"Buildings superintendent," Marjorie insisted. She paused, ran her tongue behind her upper lip, cocked her head, and looked at Clara. "What I tell you now is confidential. Very confidential. I feel I owe you this as an old friend—you have the right to be curious about my associations; I think we have each given that right to the other—and I trust you as I could only trust an old friend."

Despite herself, Clara hunched forward, as if sparing Marjorie the need to do more than whisper.

"It is another assignment."

"Ah."

"Does that shoe, does poor Gerry's body, mean his mission is known? Father Dowling has urged him to take extra precautions. There was talk of a security guard."

"Well, I should think so."

"Willie says no. One, if he has not been found out, that would give him away. Two, if he has been found out, a mere security guard cannot afford him adequate protection."

"Marjorie, how exciting."

Marjorie sighed. "And all I wanted was a dancing partner."

Amos Cadbury was only somewhat older than her father had been, but to Nancy Walsh he seemed an old man, whereas her father had never seemed that. Amos wore nothing but black suits—very expensive, well-tailored black suits—a snowy white shirt, and then a necktie with just a soupçon of color. The studied understatement of his dress lent to that little bit of color the chromatic power of a bright light. Thin wrists emerged from stiff French cuffs, the tapered fingers touched at their tips, and the tips of his index fingers pressed against the thin line of his lips. He was studying Nancy with half-closed eyes. Finally he removed the fingers from his lips and spoke.

"I have been trying to decide whether the confidentiality I owe your late father can be transferred to you. My decision is clear from what I have already said."

Kate had passed on to her Father Dowling's discovery that none of the Chicago social services had handled her adoption, but that raised the question of the judicial record. Jason had finally returned from wherever and simply shook his head when she asked if he had done the legal work for her father in the adoption of Kate.

"You represented my father in the adoption," she said to Amos Cadbury.

"I did."

"Does that mean that someone could obtain that judicial record for Kate and she would learn everything?"

"No."

"It doesn't!"

"Let me approach the manner circuitously. There are certain things a lawyer may not do on pain of heavy penalty, perhaps disbarment, things which he nonetheless may feel very inclined to do and feel furthermore that his inclination is moral and even noble. For example. A parent begins to act out of character in his final days, gets angry with one of his sons, and in a rage scribbles a will disowning that son. A totally irrational thing from start to finish. The lawyer comes upon the last will. It is undoubtedly in the hand of the deceased. The lawyer destroys that will; both sons inherit; no one but the lawyer and the soul of his client know what he has done."

"If nobody knows, he cannot be punished."

"The lawyer knows. His deed is ambiguous in its moral aspects, however unambiguous legally. His conscience will always return to the sore tooth of that memory."

"How does this apply to Kate's adoption?"

"The judge to whom I took the matter was not a credit to the bench. That is why I went to him, as a penitent may seek out an easy confessor when he has too heavy a burden. I suggested to him that it would ease the mind of my client if certain names did not enter into the record. He obliged me. If someone should obtain that record for Kate, she would find that her mother was a young woman who died as a result of complications of childbirth a week after Kate was born."

"Who was she?"

"I have no idea. The judge happened to know of the death. It does not matter who she was."

"That seems cruel."

"I meant that it could be any false name."

"How much did my father tell you?"

"Everything."

"So you know who the mother of Kate is?"

"That was a principal consideration in my decision to transfer your father's confidentiality to you."

The office seemed quieter. Nancy was aware of sounds that had their origin in her head rather than the outside world, almost subliminal, what her father had called the Music of the Ears. With her father this point had been approached several times, but only approached.

"I always suspected that is how it was."

"Didn't you know?" The old lawyer was startled.

"Dad would never let me discuss the subject with him. We both knew what had happened to me, and he had taken care of that beautifully, and when I came back, they had another little daughter."

"Your daughter."

"Yes."

She had guessed, conjectured, hoped. But the ruse her father had insisted on made Kate a sister to her, so that it was difficult to imagine that this was the child she had been trained to think was gone from her forever, taken from her at birth lest any attachment be formed that would make giving her baby up more difficult. She had not even known the sex of her child. She had been pregnant; she had waited out the long months with other girls in a similar situation; she had gone into labor and returned to her room without the burden of her child but with no infant to hold. She sobbed now at the memory of it.

What she had never felt was guilt, at least guilt coming from her parents' attitude toward her. She could not have asked for more unwavering support than they gave her. Once her father accepted that the solution he considered honorable was not going to happen, all his efforts were spent in making this as easy an experience as possible. Every possibility of embarrassment was neutralized. The one thing that had never been considered was abortion.

"And now Kate wants to know the truth," Amos Cadbury said, having waited respectfully until she regained control of herself.

"Yes."

"The only way she can possibly learn it is from you."

Nancy knew that she herself might have been gripped with curiosity about where her child was and contemplated a professional search if she had not felt she already knew the solution her father had hit upon. His daughter would give birth to her child out of wedlock and he and his wife would adopt her, grandparents becoming foster parents. The precautions Amos Cadbury had been induced to take were not meant as precaution against the child's eventual desire to know her origins. Rather, her father wanted to make it impossible for Jerome Winegar ever to discover where the child he had repudiated was. The trail was to be nonexistent. Those same precautions now prevented the child from discovering who her father was.

"Will you tell her?"

"How could I then conceal from her who her father is?"

"Ah."

Her husband knew nothing of any of this. There was no reason that he should. The decision was her father's, and it had been conveyed to her with great circumlocution. He became adept at not talking about this one subject, yet they seemed to have communicated on it constantly over the years.

To tell Kate would be to tell Jim, that is how she had viewed the problem. That had been the source of her uneasiness when Kate began to insist that Mitchell Striker had not been her real father. Implicit in that was curiosity about her real parents, and the thought that Kate could somehow learn the truth and force her to speak to Jim of that long-ago event filled her with panic.

Far more undesirable would be Kate's discovery that Jerome Winegar was her father. Ironically, the money her father had left Kate now made it easily possible for her to acquire whatever help she wanted in order to discover the past.

"Six million dollars," Jim had said. He actually looked pale.

"It's only fair. Look what Dad's done for us."

"Nan, I've been dealing with another broker."

"But Dad takes care of our affairs."

"Do you know a man named Frankman?"

"He succeeded Dad on the board at St. Peter's."

"Right. He's more or less a protégé of your father's. He told me of a scheme that seemed too good to be true, so I let him put a token amount into it and earned profits of an unbelievable sort. I saw a chance for a single transaction that would put us forever beyond any possible worry about money."

"We needn't worry now."

"Imagine three times what we now have."

He had made a play to triple their money. The scheme failed. Meanwhile Frankman was embarked on a long-term plan to restore their worth. It was too late then to go back to her father.

"Frankman did the same thing with the St. Peter's endowment."

"We were in on the same scheme."

There is no set amount of money that permits one to bid good-bye to any further consideration of money. Some achieve this attitude while possessing nothing. Saint Francis and all kinds of just plain people have simply stopped worrying about money. The practical think them chuckleheaded or naive, but the truth was that someone who would worry about ten thousand a year will be able to worry about ten million a year just as easily. The billionaire is sleepless at the thought that he could be wiped out tomorrow.

Wealth was no longer chiefly possessions, unless money itself could be called a possession. It was numbers moving ethereally across a screen in her father's office, printouts with estimated sales value of the stocks one held—but stock prices varied daily, and one's wealth was a function of those variations.

She was not pleased, accordingly, when she learned that Jim had offered to take over the guidance of Kate's money. But she believed him when he said he would never again take part in the kind of scheme Frankman had proposed.

Gloria was a short disfigured woman whose body had been put together wrongly. Her shoulders rose permanently behind a head topped by an obvious wig; through heavily framed glasses, sharp eyes looked up at Frankman.

"The police have gone over it again and again," she said.

"That must have been a nuisance for you."

"It was." Around her neck was a heavy chain from which hung a large timepiece, her father's, who had been on the railroad. "Of course, records are here to be consulted."

Gloria's long involvement with St. Peter's encompassed the time when the data recorded in the earliest of these records was simply the present. She had followed him into this temperature-controlled haven as if she too were to be preserved as an essential feature of the school's history.

"This temperature is good for allergies."

Frankman found it cold.

"Father Gorman wanted to throw out things when they accumulated. I had to argue and argue, I can tell you. When he gave in he said, 'Okay, Gloria, and you can take care of them.' "

"You've done a good job."

Could she detect behind his patient interest in her life story an urge to pick her up and shake her? He wanted to see again the box from which the Winegar papers had been removed.

"You were the only member of the board to show any interest in them."

"The new boy's enthusiasm."

She grimaced. "Don't talk to me about new boys."

Boys are notoriously cruel, and Gloria's disability had not been spared. It became a school custom to touch her back for luck before an exam. Once she had been kidnapped for a lark and spirited off to a dormitory. Her cries of rape had mystified her captors. She was dedicated to the written record of the school, but she had entered into its oral tradition. Gloria Mundi, she had been called by the erudite, Midge by the insensitive. In the school she had acquired an importance that would have been denied her almost everywhere else, the world being a cruel place. Perhaps that is why she stayed on as keeper of the records.

"The lock has been repaired," she explained, running crooked fingers over the door. "They photographed it and dusted it and looked at it through strange contraptions. Do you realize that for years and years it was only the outer door that was locked?"

"Who would think of records as in danger?"

"Exactly. You're one of the few that has understood the matter."

"In my business, records are important." But how evanescent they were; their lifetime was the statute of limitations on income tax.

"They asked who consulted the records?"

"They did. Your tour wasn't a consultation, of course."

"You didn't mention that to them?"

"Certainly not."

That visit had begun as a simple getting-acquainted call, but Gloria had given him the full treatment.

"Mr. Striker was no more sympathetic to keeping these records than Father Gorman."

"Is that so?"

"He came in here and looked around and just shook his head. He considered it a waste of space. Put it all on film, he said. Put it on a computer. The amount it cost to keep the room cool, the acid-free boxes, and the sheets of paper that go between pages of records, it drove him crazy."

"The bottom line."

"Exactly. He never liked me."

"Why do you say that?"

She looked around, moving her head as a bird does. "I knew too much."

Gloria had been in Father Gorman's office not as secretary but as an assistant to the secretary during the Winegar events.

"Oh, he became an angel of vengeance, I can tell you. The conversations he had with Father Gorman, wearing him down, talking about the school, the good of the school, the example set for the other boys. He had his way in the end. Father Gorman was a saint, but he couldn't stand up to that. Not everyone knew why Mr. Striker was so determined."

Frankman waited with a receptive smile.

"His daughter was sweet on the boy," she whispered.

"Aha."

"They were very secretive. She would come in a car and he would go out and they would sit together, the way young people do."

"You saw them?"

"When you are little, people overlook you." Her lips were heavily rouged, and when she smiled, her face with its waxen skin became a mask of comedy. Frankman laughed appreciatively.

"And now all that is left is this."

She pulled out a box and opened its lid and showed him the tab with Winegar's name on it. She pulled out one of the folders to show him how papers were preserved. The name Elena lifted to his eyes. He said nothing.

Given the setback he had suffered with the school's endowment and the publicity swirling around Winegar, Frankman found that he could not forget the name on the form that Gloria had shown him. The name was unusual but not unique. He did not want to be pulled into the Winegar matter on top of the public criticism he had received from Striker, a criticism he knew must influence the other members of the board, no matter how otherworldly Cottage's reaction had been. He had to know.

He had actually called in young Komfort to give him the assignment when he had the wit to realize that was stupid. The last thing he wanted was anyone else to make a connection between himself and Winegar—if the Elena Winegar listed as his mother provided such a connection. He went over to city hall himself to see Chief Robertson, just a chat in the course of which he casually mentioned the wonderful way they kept the records of St. Peter's School. Robertson, of course, wanted to show him how the records were kept in city hall. Criminal records. How about marriage licenses?

"Come on."

Robertson had waddled down the corridor, carrying his belly like a bass drum, with Bob Frankman at his side. Records were kept here as Striker had wanted the school to keep its, computerized. It made sense to Frankman, if not to Gloria, who raised a metaphysical issue.

"Then you have records of records, copies, not the record itself."

"But the information . . ."

"I hate that word." Against her will, she had sat down with a computer person, but Father Gorman had intervened and saved her.

The girl at the computer in the courthouse was a technician who clearly had no interest in the data she called up, if she even noticed it. Frankman had often wondered if typists knew what they were typing. It seemed to go from the eyes to the fingers without passing through the mind.

"Try Frankman," he said, and there was the record of his parents' marriage. And when Robertson was distracted, Frankman said to the girl, "Try Winegar. Name of the bride."

And there it was. The marriage Elena had told him of. She had been Elena Winegar at the time, and it was her first marriage. He had the girl tap out Robertson, and when the chief returned, they had a good laugh over the girl checking up on the chief like that.

"Wondering if I'm eligible," Robertson said, and his large wet eyes rolled speculatively toward the girl.

Frankman returned to his office with the conviction that the papers filed under Winegar in the St. Peter's archive represented a ticking time bomb. He talked to Gloria later, after they had turned up in Winegar's possession.

"They won't give them back," she wailed. "Not till after the trial."

"What was the point in removing them?"

"I don't know! It wasn't that he was ashamed of having been here. Far from it. Did I tell you he came to see me?"

In Gloria's memory, Winegar was one of the few boys who hadn't teased her. "Oh, they thought it was fun, but he didn't make fun of me."

"You remember him?"

"I do. When he came and we talked, it was as if no time had passed. He was a sweet-talker as a boy too. He had a way."

"Do you suppose he was casing the place?"

"I find that hard to believe."

"What did the police think?"

"Oh, I didn't tell them. He has enough trouble. Besides, they found the records in his possession."

"Yes."

"Let's just get away for a few days, the two of us," Nan said. "I can get someone to look after the kids, Jim won't care, and we can just talk."

Kate supposed she meant talk about Mom and Dad. Nan was suffering a delayed reaction from the horror and probably felt a need to dredge up as many memories as she could, as complete in detail as her memory would provide. Kate could not rid herself of a sense of make-believe when she entered into such reminiscing with Nan, but the fact was she enjoyed it too.

"Okay."

"The trial starts next week." Nan said this as if it were another reason to spend a few days in the family cottage in Wisconsin.

Mitchell Striker had found the place years ago when he had taken a boat trip up the Fox River to its source in Wisconsin. He had asked for and got a summer job there. The original still stood, a rough cabin not twenty yards from the shore, but over the years the larger place had been built, rustic only in motif and architectural style but as convenient as anything in the city.

"I learned to swim in that lake," Kate said.

"So did I."

After they got settled in, they took out the small boat and let the wind carry them soundlessly down the length of the lake. Coming back was trickier, involving much zigzag tacking.

"That's my speciality," Kate said.

"I taught you how." But Nan gave up the helm and kept her head out of the way of the swinging boom.

It was good just to be together, doing things, not needing to talk. Despite herself, Kate had been making a psychological retreat from the past that she remembered in favor of a past she did not know.

Her efforts to rely on professional help had failed. Father Dowling had drawn a blank at the social services; Tuttle reported that the judicial record contained surprising information.

"Who was my mother?" she had asked him.

"I am positive the woman whose name is there is false. Judge Seneca handled it."

"But what is her name?"

"She's dead," Tuttle said. "And she couldn't be your mother."

"Dead."

"Of complications in giving birth to a boy who didn't make it either."

"But why?"

"Seneca should have ended up in jail himself, but he was a survivor. I argued my first case before him. Vagrancy."

Kate didn't care about the judge or Tuttle's first case or anything else. She still wanted the name.

"There's something else."

"What?"

"She was black."

It was cruel to come that close and find the door shut in her face. Her adoptive father had obviously taken every precaution to make finding out who she was impossible.

Tuttle said, "What surprises me is that Amos Cadbury was the attorney of record."

"Would he know who my mother really was?"

232

"I don't know. Ask him."

Kate felt that she was applying hot irons to Cadbury's bare flesh when she asked him questions.

"My dear child, I cannot help you. But pray consider this. If your father took such pains to keep the information from the judge in the case, do you think he would have told his lawyer?"

"Are you saying he didn't?"

"Imagine that he did. Imagine that he exacted the most solemn promise to keep that information forever secret. I am not saying he did this. But imagine that he did. And now imagine that you come and put questions to that lawyer. What is he to do?"

"Tell me."

"Break a most solemn promise?"

"But I have a right to that information."

"I think that is true."

"Well."

"But you do not have the right to demand that I break my word."

"My lawyer said the judge was a crook."

Amos Cadbury was silent for a moment. "That is a fair appraisal."

"He falsified the record."

"Then he must answer to God for it. In fact, he already has."

Was the information she craved locked away in the narrow patrician head of Amos Cadbury, sealed with his word of honor, inaccessible to her?

"Amos Cadbury knows who my mother was," she told Nan.

Nan looked alarmed and searched Kate's face, as if worried what she had learned and what it might have done to her.

"Oh, he wouldn't tell me."

"Oh, Kate." Nan hugged her almost painfully. "How cruel."

"I think if I had the power I would torture him until he told."

"He's only trying to do what he thinks is right."

"How can it be right to deprive me of the knowledge of who my mother was."

That was when Nan suggested they go off to the lake together.

When the sun went down, the temperature dropped, and they put on sweaters while they prepared dinner. Kate grilled hamburgers while Nan made a salad and heated up some frozen french fries. They decided to eat inside. Making a fire did not seem inappropriate, and soon it was crackling and there were leaping flames and they sat down to eat.

"Should I turn on the television?"

"Let's not."

It was just a suggestion; Kate had little interest in news of the present day.

"I wonder if there is anyone living besides Amos Cadbury who knows."

"Your mother?"

"Do you think she knows what happened to me?"

Kate pursued that possibility through dinner, but Nan said little. After the dishes, they set up a card table in front of the fireplace and got out Scrabble and began to play. But neither of them had their heart in it. Eventually they pushed the game away and sat staring into the fire. Outside a wind came in off the lake and rustled the pine needles in the trees surrounding the cottage. A log snapped and sent out a shower of sparks that died before they landed. The clock on the mantel became audible.

Nan said, "I had a reason for suggesting we come up here."

"To talk about me? We've been doing that."

"No. To talk about me."

"Oh, Nan, I'm sorry. I'm so obsessed with this that I've become a self-centered bore."

Nan squeezed her hand. "If you didn't talk about it, I would know you were holding back."

"That's true."

"I want to tell you something I've never told anyone. Not even Jim. Ever since you said you would do anything to find out who your parents were, I've wanted to tell you this. Let's sit on the couch."

Kate folded away the table. They angled the couch toward the fire and sat at either end of it, looking at the burning logs rather than each other so that Nan's story seemed addressed to them both.

"When I was just a girl I fell in love with a boy, and I had never felt that way and was certain that it was predestined. I didn't think I could ever feel so strongly about someone. We had a baby."

"A baby!"

"Well, I had the baby. His interest disappeared when I became pregnant. It was the most devastating rejection I have ever known. I had loved him; I was willing to do anything for him. I considered that we were already married and that he felt the same way. When I realized I was going to have a baby, I was so eager to tell him."

Nan's breath caught and she fell silent. Kate moved along the couch until her shoulder was pressed against Nan's. She might have been a confessor turned discreetly away from the penitent. Kate was overwhelmed by what Nan was telling her and rendered speechless by the thought that she had kept this secret all her life and now was telling her because this gave them something in common.

"He made it clear that the baby was my problem. Problem. My God, I felt holy with that new life inside me that was the two of us together. He was cold. He took no responsibility."

"Oh, Nan."

"I wanted to die. I thought of coming up here and going out in a boat and having an accident. My baby and I would drown together."

Kate's eyes swam with tears and her throat constricted at the thought of Nan in such a plight. Nan's hand went to the back of Kate's neck. Kate closed her eyes, and tears ran down her cheeks.

"What did you do?"

"I talked to Mom and we talked to Dad."

"What did he say?"

"He thought that everything could work out if, young as we were, we married. When I told him the boy's reaction, he became enraged. He had already asked who the boy was. He said he would talk to him."

"To no avail?"

"Kate, I no longer cared. I had felt the coldness of his rejection. I knew he wouldn't give in, and if he had, I didn't want him on such terms."

"So what happened?"

"Dad arranged things perfectly. I was said to be going abroad for the year. I spent months in a home with other girls in the same condition. I went into labor, and when I came out from under, my baby was gone."

"Oh, Nan."

The two of them sat there crying helplessly and hopelessly, and Kate marveled at Nan's ability to have held this back. How terrible it must have been to hear her vowing to find out who she was while all along Nan was nursing this heartbreaking secret.

"Did Dad tell you who adopted the baby?"

"No."

"And you never found out?"

"I think that if I tried I would run into the same kind of problem you have been having. Mitchell Striker never did things halfway."

Once the story was out, they went over it again and again. This was a vast unknown side of Nan, and Kate had an insatiable desire to know more about it. She had never loved Nan more than she did then. This revelation, after all these years, had been made for her sake, no matter the pain that would be involved in the telling.

All her life, Kate had gone to Nan as much as to her adoptive parents, they had shared so many confidences over the years, and all along there had been this great unspoken secret. A resolution was born in her. If Nan could bear her burden, then Kate intended to bear hers.

Later, using the twin beds in Nan's boys' room, they spoke on into the dark. Tiredness came, but before they fell asleep, Kate found what she had been looking for.

"There's only one solution, Nan."

"What?"

"I'll be your baby and you can be my mom."

Winegar was in a manic mood on the day of the trial, and Tuttle wished his client would realize the seriousness of his situation. He still did not seem to believe that, apart from a miracle, he was going to be found guilty.

"Baloney. Do you know how to remember the Spanish for judge? Gee whiz."

Tuttle waited but that seemed to be it. What a guy. The prosecutor, having decided that conviction was assured, took over the case from Pep Ardmore, relegating the birdlike redhead to second-in-command. Tuttle and Plover had a pretrial conference with Judge Lipsky, who said he wanted everything to go strictly by the rules: The accused was going to get as fair a trial as anyone ever had in this city. It was the sort of thing a judge said when he assumed that the result of a fair trial was not going to be favorable to the accused.

Now Plover and Ardmore and two lesser types from the prosecutor's office were at their table. Winegar had been brought in and looked brightly about the courtroom, for all the world like a host wondering if all his guests had arrived.

The judge entered with some pomp, the star of the show, trying to combine the dignity of office and the assurance that he was really just one of the boys. He was one of the first judges to allow television in his courtroom, but unfortunately none of the local stations considered the trial worth carrying. There had been some hope, voiced as a fear by Lipsky in the pretrial consultation, that the sensationalism of this case might bring in the media. A local gospel temple had sent a team consisting of a fellow in a blue suit with all three buttons of the jacket fastened and a handheld camera he seemed unsure how to use, and a tall woman with an overbite who had the look of someone who knew the day and the hour. Of course the print media were there, with Lucy Sommers prettily among them. A less professional lawyer might still resent the way his client had stolen away his girl. For weeks Tuttle had listened to Patti Page sing "The Tennessee Waltz" on his Walkman. Lucy waved at him now and Tuttle waved back, but once bitten twice shy.

The judge admonished the venire and jury selection began. Tuttle's main concern was to get as many women as he could on the jury; he was counting on Winegar's effect on women. Plover seemed equally concerned to keep women off. Obviously they could not both win their objectives. They ended up with seven women and five men. And then the serious business began.

Plover's first move was to establish that there had been a murder, and he concentrated on Mitchell Striker's death. Barbara Rooney, oddly dressed in black, was called to testify to the fact that Striker had been due to give a lecture on financial investment in the golden years at St. Hilary's Parish Center. Plover had chosen not to ask Father Dowling to testify. You never knew what the clergy might say under oath. Dr. Pippen settled into the witness chair as if she meant to be there for some time.

Her testimony was technical and boring, or it would have been if given by a less stunning young woman. She wore a plum-colored suit, her hair was pulled back and braided, giving her a faintly Viking air, and she spoke with easy intelligence.

"So it is your testimony that Mitchell Striker was killed in the way you mentioned while sitting in his car waiting for the rain to let up so he could go into the school and give his speech?"

"That's the most likely scenario, yes."

Plover glanced at Tuttle, indicating that he knew that the defense had just been given a gift by the assistant medical examiner. And on cross, Tuttle went for it.

"When you said that the prosecutor's story about what happened to Mitchell Striker was the most likely scenario, you were suggesting that there are other likely scenarios."

"There always are."

"Let's confine ourselves to this case. Take this scenario. Someone somewhere else does Mr. Striker in in the way you have so competently testified to. The body is then driven to the parking lot of St. Hilary's school and left there. Is that likely?"

"Up to a point."

"What's wrong with it?"

"Why take the body there? Why take the body anywhere?"

"Those are good questions."

"They certainly are."

"And remain so even if we do not know the answer to them."

Beside him, Winegar whispered a cheer. Indeed, Tuttle was impressed with himself. Pippen agreed that together they might think of any number of explanations of why the body had been left precisely at St. Hilary's.

"Do you intend to testify, Mr. Tuttle?"

"No, your honor."

"Then let us leave it to the witnesses to get the facts before the jury."

"Yes, your honor. Dr. Pippen, all the facts as you know them about the condition of the body could fit the supposition of someone bringing it there already dead."

"I can't rule it out."

On redirect, Plover said, "Even if one were to grant the wild hypothesis fabricated by the defense, what difference does it make where Mitchell Striker was killed?"

"You mean he'd be dead either way?"

Plover had a good point if trials were pure logic. But shaking the jury's confidence that the place of the murder was certain was useful to the defense.

The night of the first day of the trial Tuttle had dinner with Lucy Sommers, at a Chinese restaurant some distance from Fox River so Peanuts wouldn't walk in and pout because he hadn't been asked. She wore a sport jacket and olive green slacks and professed to be awestruck by Tuttle's performance. He took his tweed hat off and hung it up and left it off through the whole meal. Of course, he had not worn it in court either.

"You've got a natural curl," she said.

"I'm having fried rice with three delights."

"I don't know why you aren't mad at me."

"Why would I be mad at you?"

"Because you were nice to me and then I took up with Winegar. I'm sorry about that."

"He has that effect on women."

238

"That is why it is so demeaning. It's impersonal, it happens to every-body, nearly, so it doesn't mean anything."

"Have you been watching the jury?"

"You mean Miss Boobs."

"She's married."

"Well, she ought to cover up anyway. She spends half the time trying to catch Winegar's eye."

"You know the case that was found in your apartment, the needles and things?"

"What about them?"

"Did you ever see them in your apartment before the police impounded them?"

"No."

"Winegar claims that someone planted them on him. He said he hasn't given a shot since he was a corpsman in the army."

"It might have been the man who asked if he could look around my apartment, out of nostalgia. He used to live there."

"Who was he?"

She shrugged. "He gave some name. I didn't pay any attention. Of course I let him look around. It was after that that Jerome noticed that stuff. He felt we should get rid of it."

Tuttle was both angry and happy. Angry because he should have been told this long ago, happy because this was better than just establishing the possibility that somebody could have put those needles in the apart-ment. That nostalgic former tenant had to be found. He asked Lucy for as accurate a description as she could give of the man, but for a reporter she turned out to be pretty useless. Tall or short? Neither really. Old or young? Kind of middle-aged, you know. She was sure he had hair, but she wasn't sure what color it was.

"Would you recognize him if you saw him again?"

"I did see him again."

"Where?"

"Let me think." This was before Winegar had guessed that this alleged former renter of Lucy's place had left behind the incriminating evidence. After a while she smiled helplessly. "I don't remember."

He tried to explain to her the importance of what she had told him. The defense of Winegar depended on explaining away all the incriminat-ing and compromising evidence by saying that someone had deliberately diverted suspicion to Winegar. But Tuttle was working with a faceless un-known X, little more than something the jury could imagine and then take to be grounds for reasonable doubt. Only Lucy was in a position to put a face on that mysterious personage.

"You've seen him. You've got to remember what he looks like."

Her response was to write a special sidebar to her series in which she addressed the man who had claimed to be the previous renter of her apartment. The landlady, Mrs. Lavada, was quoted as saying that the previous renter had been a little old lady, and there was a scowling photograph of the keeper of the gate.

> You know who you are. Come forward now, when you can save the life of an innocent man. Today I shall be helping artists prepare a picture of you from my memory of our meeting, but I hope it will not be necessary to search you out as if you were fleeing the chance to help prove the innocence of Jerome Winegar.

"Brilliant," Tuttle said when she called to ask what he thought of it. He was wearing his tweed hat, pulled far over his eyes, wanting the mindless dark this afforded. Brilliant, indeed. Publicly ask the man who had planted evidence on Winegar to come forward and help exonerate the man he had meant to incriminate.

"Was that your idea?" Winegar asked.

"I'm a lawyer. I don't have ideas."

"Did you know she was going to do it?"

"I would have pulled the plug of her computer if I did."

"It sounds like she's making it up," Winegar said.

It became impossible for Father Dowling to avoid discussion of the Winegar trial. In the rectory, Marie Murkin was convinced of his innocence.

"I looked him in the eyes," she was saying over the phone. "I spoke with him. That man is no murderer."

Marie spoke as if out of a vast acquaintance with killers.

"It's a shame to waste money on trials when you could just look them in the eye and render a verdict."

"I am speaking of this man, Father Dowling, and you know it."

"Do you think he's guilty?"

"I think every man's guilty!" And her eyes sparked with defiant incoherence.

Over in the school, the debate raged. Edna kept out of it, the trial doubtless bringing back painful memories of her husband Earl, but Willie held forth with a claim to some authority on the matter. Like Marie, he was an intuitionist.

"You get a feel for these things," he said with narrowed eyes, looking around at an audience made up of men and women whose acquaintance with crime had been practically nil. "When you've been penned up with them, an undercover agent for the forces of justice . . ." He paused when he noticed Father Dowling had come in. "Let me tell you a story."

And he shifted into another gear, drawing on his inexhaustible fund of anecdotes about prison life. Edna drew the pastor aside.

"I wish they'd talk about something else."

"Well, it's almost a parish event."

Marjorie White turned, her finger lifted to her lips, and when she saw it was the pastor talking with Edna, flushed red with confusion.

"Let's go to your office, Edna."

"Marjorie hangs on his every word, Father."

"I long ago gave up trying to understand the attraction one man has for a given woman or vice versa."

"He has given her a real line about why he was in prison."

"Did he say undercover agent?"

"That must have been when he was in bed."

Phil Keegan groused about the way the first day of the trial had gone.

"Plover is no great shakes, but Tuttle is supposed to be a joke."

"Well, the burden of proof is on the prosecution."

"He did it, Roger. Don't you start thinking some poor innocent man is being railroaded."

Phil, like many policemen, lived in the conviction that the aim of the judicial system was to render careful investigative work irrelevant to the verdict of guilt or innocence. But there were mistakes in evidence as well as in the judgments of juries. Father Dowling considered himself blessed to be an operator in the realm of mercy rather than justice. Not his own mercy, of course, any more than justice belonged to Phil Keegan. But the two men had different perspectives on the same act. A legal judgment of guilt, or innocence, left the act morally untouched. The guilty are sometimes found innocent and sometimes, no doubt, the innocent are found guilty, but neither judgment affected the moral condition of the man involved. Mercy assumed the guilt of the one pardoned, and all men fall short of the ideal, are flawed and imperfect, yet all are in pell-mell pursuit of the good, the real good. But, oh, what sorry substitutes for that good we settle for. We distance ourselves from what we really want, and cannot ourselves repair the damage we cause. This was the arena in which the priest operates, as the agent of God. He himself, of course, has no more personal insight into the real condition of the human heart than anyone else. But he was there to make available to the penitent God's forgiveness.

Father Dowling had not seen Winegar lately, so he was unable to apply the Marie Murkin test and know if the man was guilty or innocent. A good part of his own uneasiness stemmed from that fact. Did Winegar see him as part of the enemy forces, the man who had discovered the body of Mitchell Striker? He did not want to force himself on the man, but Winegar's visit to the rectory, his reminder to Father Dowling of that Latin class at St. Peter's so long ago, seemed a basis on which they might at least talk. By all accounts, however, Winegar needed no boost to his spirits.

"If he wasn't smart, I'd say he was dumb," Phil said. "Apparently he is happy as a lark, all the guards love him, he speaks Spanish to the Spanish, a little Italian. They call him Professor Winegar."

"What did he do during all those years, Phil?"

The curriculum vitae of Jerome Winegar that had been put together might or might not provide the portrait of a man brooding over the event that had turned his life away from a university education and who knew what future beyond. Perhaps he might have become Professor Winegar after all. Instead, his life had been one of undemanding and temporary jobs—after his stint in the army. He had done two tours in Vietnam, the second completely voluntary, almost as if he didn't care whether he lived or died. He had distinguished himself as a medical corpsman, but there were no medals or any record of heroic deeds. Perhaps at a time and in a place where heroism of a dogged kind was routine, no such special citation was needed.

He was discharged in San Diego and stayed on there. He worked at a driving range, he managed a mall movie theater, he clerked in a used bookstore in Los Angeles, he did this and that, and the years just slipped away. How many lives would look like that if reduced to a record of what a person had done to earn enough on which to eat? He had never married, but he had left in his wake dozens of dazzled females. Eat, drink, and be merry? It was melancholy to think that rallying cry came down to something as humdrum as the life Jerome Winegar had lived.

And now this morning the paper had run an odd open letter to the unknown man who had come to the journalist's apartment pretending to be the previous tenant. The suggestion was that this person had left behind the needles and paraphernalia that formed the basis for the prosecution's contention that Winegar had both the skill and the means to murder Striker in the strange way this had been done, by injecting a massive dose of anesthetic into his neck.

Father Dowling read the story in disbelief. Was this supposed to bring the man forward? The story had the undeniable ring of the fabricated. If true, the woman had known it to be true since it happened, yet brought it up only after the trial began, and in this public way. It seemed part of the strategy to claim that Winegar had been the object of some great conspiracy to indict him for murders someone else had committed.

It was absurd to think that it was in the interests of the police to manufacture evidence against Winegar. All he would have had to do is offer plausible accounts of his whereabouts at the time of the two murders, and this he had not done. There had been sufficient prima facie reasons to suspect him, and then when his expulsion from St. Peter's came to the fore, a strong motive for the first murder was given. Poor Gerry Major posed a puzzle, no matter how one considered it. But the discovery of the St. Peter's records in Winegar's possession had been the coup de grâce.

"I do wish they would stop mentioning the school every other sentence," Cottage lamented over lunch at the Cliffdwellers, where they were the guests of Bob Frankman. Frankman agreed.

"It makes it sound as if St. Peter's is an ineffective Boys Town."

"This is the first time that any graduate of St. Peter's has ever been in trouble of this kind."

"Graduate?" Father Dowling asked.

"Well, he would have graduated. He was the most intelligent boy in the school at the time. I was his junior and can testify to the esteem in which he was held," Cottage said.

"Will you testify?"

"Do you know this man Tuttle?"

"He refused?"

"I think so. It was such an ambiguous reply, I wasn't sure. But I haven't heard from him since."

"Perhaps classmates of his should make some kind of statement."

"I advised against that," Bob Frankman said. "It would just increase the visibility of the school in the matter. Besides, those things always sound like special pleading. 'We don't know if he's guilty but when we knew him, etc., etc.' "

"The truth is, Father, he cut his lines with the school and everything connected with it when he left. Several of his classmates have called me, and that is the message I receive. Winegar for them is a mythic figure from the past who almost ceased to be when he left."

"Did they know why he left?"

"A serious breach of morals." Cottage shook his head. "It would have been better to say what it was. Such a phrase invites the most fanciful interpretations."

"Frankly, Striker comes through as an SOB in the whole matter," Frankman said.

"That's the prosecution's line."

The three men agreed that the story of a brilliant orphan driven from the school by the merciless wealthy member of the board could not hurt Winegar in one sense.

"But of course the thrust of it is to say that if anyone had a motive for murder, it was Winegar."

Cottage said, "I wonder if he had made any effort to find his mother during those years. Not right away—he could hardly want to go to her and tell her what a failure he had been—but eventually."

"Would he have known her?"

"Many boys have subsequently reunited with the parent or parents who gave them up for various reasons. I myself came to know my father well before he died. Many of the alumni have become quite distinguished and the source of great pride on the part of their parents. Their success justifies having put them in St. Peter's."

"If Winegar's mother is still alive and aware of what he is accused of, she won't be taking pride in it." Frankman's tone suggested that he thought this line of talk exaggerated. But then he was not an alumnus of St. Peter's as Cottage was.

"It might be a stronger bond," Father Dowling mused. "If she knew what he was going through, she might very well make herself known to him."

Frankman rather abruptly changed the topic to the finances of the school, on which he had happy news for Cottage. It was an odd way to make the report, with a third party sitting in, but he did not dwell on it. Later, when Cottage said he had to get back to his desk, Frankman asked Father Dowling to stay a minute, and they went into the library, where the furry face of Hamelin Garland, one of the founders of the Cliffdwellers looked down at them.

"Are you going to the reunion, Roger?"

"I was going to ask you the same thing."

"I believe I will. It's a wholesome idea, asking everybody back."

"I'm told that Chips is planning a picnic next summer, so that families can come as well."

"Is that so?"

Frankman had children, Father Dowling knew, but currently no wife. Noonan on the Archdiocesan marriage tribunal had rolled his eyes when he mentioned the annulment, and of course Father Dowling had not pressed his old colleague on details. The picnic did not strike Frankman as quite as inspired as the reunion.

"What did you think of Cottage's mention of Winegar's mother, Roger?"

"That you didn't think much of it."

"Was I that obvious?"

"It was a charmingly romantic idea, I think. St. Peter's produces unique alumni, in my experience. At the same time hardheaded and sentimental. But who knows what it is like to pass those years without parents?"

"Anyone who went to the seminary."

"Oh, we were grown men by that time. And Quigley was a day school."

While they sat there, the afternoon edition of the *Tribune* was brought in. On the front page was the computer-generated Identi-Kit portrait of the alleged previous tenant of Lucy Sommers's apartment. The two men looked at it.

"It could be anyone," Frankman humphed.

"He looks familiar."

"That's what I said."

"No, I mean it. Good Lord, Bob, it looks like you."

57

If Winegar's fate could be decided by a poll of newspaper readers and watchers of television news, he would be a free man. The sequestered jury was supposedly unaffected by the sudden shift in media attitude toward Winegar. The unspoken suggestion was that Winegar was a poor orphan boy who had fallen afoul of the powers that be and was being made to pay for it. Phil Keegan was damned mad.

"Plover is incompetent," he raged.

"Replacing him would be to throw in the towel," Cy said.

"If Winegar were black that trial wouldn't last two days."

This was an unusual remark for Agnes Lamb, who had discarded Victim status and made a career for herself as a police officer. Phil could see her running the whole department someday.

The three of them went over the case point by point, as if to prove to themselves that they had dealt the prosecutor a winning hand.

The murder site of Mitchell Striker had been cordoned off and the curious old people from the parish center kept at bay, so that when Pippen and her crew as well as the crime lab team arrived, the scene was exactly as it had been found.

Death had been caused by an injection of a massive amount of Demerol at the back of the neck, making it clear that this was murder and not suicide. The method of murder suggested an unusual expertise on the part of the killer.

"Any diabetic could have done it," Agnes said.

"How many diabetics are there?"

"You'd be surprised."

It didn't matter once they found the hypodermics in Lucy Sommers's apartment. They weren't hers; Winegar had been using her car and left it at St. Hilary's, which turned out to have been a rendezvous point with Clara Ponader.

"Is there any woman this guy doesn't turn on?" Cy wondered.

"He leaves me cold," Agnes said.

"But you're a racist."

"And don't forget it."

The car was impounded and the hypodermics found in the apartment and the needles were compatible with the one used to kill Striker. What was Winegar doing with them? Was he a diabetic?

"They're not mine," he had insisted during questioning.

"Are you saying they belong to the girl?"

"No."

Just no. Arrogant, carefree, not conceding any significance to what had been found. Phil had always considered those needles to be the item that took the case beyond the circumstantial. And now Lucy Sommers had published a cock-and-bull story claiming that some mysterious stranger had shown up at her apartment and she had let him look around unwatched and later they found the papers in Winegar's briefcase. The mysterious stranger must have planted the drugs and needles at the same time.

Cy had photocopied the computerized likeness of the alleged former tenant so they could all scowl at their own copies.

"The beard is a nice touch," Agnes said.

"It's like one of those trick pictures that gives you a face upside down as well."

Phil turned his. Sure it did, if you like a nose above the eyebrows. No, the mustache served as a single brow. Menacing. He turned it back.

"A picture of nobody."

"Or of anybody."

The man in the picture had been seen in at least a dozen places since the picture appeared, and the time of a lot of good officers was being wasted checking them out. One woman thought it was her husband. Before he shaved off his beard. He hadn't worn a beard for two years. And that had been a promising call.

They were still in conference, grousing, when Phil's secretary came in and put a message in front of him. He glanced at it and then looked at the secretary, his first thought being that this was some kind of sick joke.

"What is it?" Agnes asked.

He slid the message to her. He said to Cy, "The body of Lucy Sommers has just been found."

The three of them went together, driving in silence to the apartment building, where a hysterical Mrs. Lavada had found the body in the elevator. Pippen was there, inside the elevator car; the body had not yet been moved. Phil sent Cy up to the apartment, by way of the staircase, to check that out. The crime lab was waiting for Pippen to finish with the body.

"How about this weather, Captain?" a chinless technician with a ponytail said cheerily.

"Yeah."

How else are people whose daily work is the pursuit of clues to guilt or innocence supposed to pass their time if not in conversations about the weather? Findley the criminalist, as he now called himself, said the flowers in his yard were beginning to come out.

"What'll I get when spring really comes?"

"Good question."

Pippen finished and came out and Findley went in. Phil got her verdict as he stood in the doorway, looking over Findley's shoulder. The girl lay with her back against the far wall of the elevator car and her legs along the left wall, on her side, as if centrifugal force had slammed her into the position. The face was not pretty. She had been garroted.

"Like Gerry Major?" Phil asked.

"More or less," said Pippen.

She didn't say it. She didn't have to. Phil could sense the case against Winegar go up in smoke, and for the first time he doubted that the guy was a murderer. But it was Agnes who put it into perspective.

"He's on trial for killing Striker, not Major."

Her point was that the evidence linking Winegar to the slaying of Striker was as good as it had ever been. The assumption had always been that he had also killed Major, but that was not what he was on trial for. She was absolutely right, and it didn't mean a thing.

Tuttle moved for a mistrial the following day and the motion was denied. Before Lipsky made the ruling, Tuttle had a chance, with the jury absent but with a full complement of television cameras newly present, to draw the inference from the finding of the body of Lucy Sommers. The little lawyer actually broke down in court as he spoke of the reporter, and it seemed to be genuine grief. The judge gave him time to recover and then denied the motion, but Tuttle achieved a kind of immortality then and there. The jury was brought back, the prosecution completed its case, and Tuttle asked for a directed verdict of not guilty.

This was refused.

The defense decided to let its rebuttal of the prosecution suffice, and the case went to the jury. Tuttle's strategy became a major subject of discussion as the jury failed to reach a verdict and decided to call it a day, resuming their considerations the following morning. Phil called Roger Dowling and got an invitation to come to the rectory.

Phil entered the house to be met by the aroma of Marie's meat loaf. He had a beer in the study before dinner, avoiding the subject of the day. Marie had an annoying little smile and came and went humming.

"It had to be him," he said finally at table.

"It sure looked like it."

That said it all. Father Dowling, like Marie, was certain the verdict would be innocent.

"If it was that obvious, they wouldn't be taking so long."

Marie moved around the table, removing plates, bringing dessert, pouring coffee, humming.

"You and Barbara Rooney going on the road, Marie?" Phil asked.

"I don't understand."

"I thought you were rehearsing."

"Just happy."

Back in the study they got engrossed in cribbage. Marie interrupted before going up the back stairs to her apartment.

"Could I get you anything else?"

"Got any crow?" Phil asked.

"Is that a bourbon?"

And still humming, she went off to bed.

Marie had begun her novena to St. Anthony of Padua on the day the trial began, and it hadn't even taken nine days for the saint to do his stuff. It was mean to go around humming like that when she could see how mad Phil Keegan was at the turn of events. In her room it occurred to Marie that it was the death of that poor young girl that had turned the tide, and she thought St. Anthony could have found a less violent way to answer her prayers. She knelt by her bedside and said a rosary for the repose of the soul of Lucy Sommers.

Honestly, it was just more than Marie Murkin could understand, the conduct of young people nowadays. You always expected a boy to stray, not all of them, but many, maybe most. The thing is, they could sow their wild oats with no one the wiser, but a girl might fall just once and face permanent consequences of her act. At least that is the way it used to be.

It was contraceptives that had done it, and no one would ever convince Marie otherwise. Girls thought they could fool around the same as boys because of those things. They actually passed them out like mints in some schools, and what kind of message was that supposed to be? It was an illusion, as often as not. Why else were there so many abortions if contraceptives were so foolproof? Bring that up and you were told that young people needed more education. Imagine going to school to learn that!

Poor Lucy Sommers had come to the big city and let a man old enough to be her father move in with her, just like that. Marie shook her head and then realized she was saying the rosary. She couldn't remember whether she was saying the glorious mysteries or the sorrowful. She gathered up her rosary, got up, and sat in her chair. After she gave the girl a good think, she would pray for her.

Good-looking as he was, Marie would have taken a switch to Winegar for taking advantage of a young girl like that. By all rights, her reputation should have been ruined, and for a time it had been, but that was part of the current craziness. She had been turned into a kind of heroine, just as Winegar himself had been. It was all quite diabolical, turning everything on its head, good becoming evil, evil becoming good. Marie wondered what kind of a conscience the girl had had. Maybe she hadn't been guilty, subjectively.

She took that up with the pastor at breakfast.

"I hope you're not judging the state of her soul, Marie."

"Of course not."

"I plan to say mass for her today."

"I said a rosary for her last night."

"I'll say mass anyway."

She ignored that. With Father Dowling, you had to keep your eye on the main point or he would jolly you out of it every time.

"Young people nowadays are told such crazy things, it's hard to see that they know the difference between good and bad."

250

"Everybody does, Marie."

"I mean, get it right."

"Ah."

"The thing is, if she thought it was all right to let Winegar move in with her, and God knows there were people enough after the fact who acted as though it was all right, maybe she didn't do anything wrong."

"Invincible ignorance?"

"Whatever."

"Don't underestimate the persistence of the natural sense of good and evil. The cultural ambience is a great influence, but people regularly become critics of their own culture. What do they appeal to then?"

"I mean this specific thing."

"Premarital sex?"

"Yes."

"You think young people think it's all right?"

"I'm sure some of them do."

"Marie, I have met few people who did not develop an argument justifying what they are doing. Not many people can stand the thought that they are actually doing something wrong. So they think about it and begin to see that what they are doing is right."

"But they're just kidding themselves."

"Do you think they know it?"

"They should."

"I agree. But meanwhile they follow their conscience."

Marie was not sure where the conversation had taken them. And she said so.

"I'm just trying to keep up with your moral theology, Marie. You remember what St. Thomas said."

"As if it were yesterday."

He laughed. "You'll remember, then, that he said that while one must follow his conscience, it does not necessarily excuse what he then does."

"Does that make sense?"

"I'm afraid it does."

"Well, I'm still glad I said a rosary for her."

"Just so you don't judge the state of her soul."

As she did her housecleaning, it occurred to Marie that if Winegar was freed, he might soon be seen around the parish as before. She wasn't too sure what she thought of that. She had found it hard to believe that the man had actually killed anyone, but he sure had cut a swath since coming back to Fox River. Don't forget that when he left that girl's car here, he had gone off with Clara Ponader.

Marie was caught up with her housework by eleven, the hour at which she often turned on her television, but today she drifted over to the school, just to see what the old folks were saying about the new turn of events and, while she was there, to ask Edna if Clara Ponader was still helping out.

On the sidewalk she ran into Barbara Rooney, who came out the side door of the church wearing a black mantilla and a sorrowful expression.

"I have been praying that they do not let his killer go free."

Barbara's silly assumption of a widow's role after Mitchell Striker's death should have been nipped in the bud, so far as Marie was concerned. The woman had made an absolute fool of herself at the funeral.

"Do you know who did it?"

"Everyone knows who did it!"

"We'll see."

"I made a solemn promise that I would go on a hunger strike if they let him off."

"What good would that do?"

"I shall have the moral satisfaction."

Marie was glad when they got to the school and she could free herself of the bogus widow. What would Barbara's departed husband say about this display?

The news came over the television in the game room minutes after Marie had entered. A hung jury.

"Does that mean they'll hang him?"

"They ought to hang the jury."

"But he was innocent."

"Innocent!"

Marie turned from the babble of voices to face Edna Hospers. "Did you hear that, Edna?"

"Does that mean he's free?"

For some reason Marie got the impression that Edna resented this more because of her husband Earl than for any other reason. Twice Father Dowling had traveled to Joliet to speak before the parole board on Earl's behalf, to no avail. But you could only resent Winegar's good luck if you thought he was guilty after all. And Marie knew where she and St. Anthony stood on that.

"I suppose, but I don't know."

Barbara Rooney, in a rage, stood in front of the television, blocking it from view, delivering an impassioned speech. Marjorie White and Willie came into the room, drawn by the excitement, and Marie saw Marjorie take her hand from Willie's as they entered. Honestly. She went back to the rectory and marched to the study door.

"The verdict's in," she announced.

The pastor looked up through a cloud of pipe smoke from the book he was reading, waiting.

"A hung jury."

He absorbed that for a moment, then put his pipe in the ashtray beside him. "I wonder if they'll try him again?"

"Try him again!"

"I think that's the prosecutor's prerogative, Marie."

"What ever happened to double jeopardy?"

Kate's friend Judy didn't return her calls, and then one day they ran into each other in the Art Institute and Kate knew immediately why Judy had been avoiding her. They went to the restaurant and had coffee, and Judy talked about her plan to spend the following year in France.

"My college has a year abroad program in Nîmes."

"What part is that in?"

"Provence!"

"What a deal. I read that book."

"Kids love it there. It's not like another year of school at all. I mean, you travel, and you hang out in these great cafés under the plane trees, sipping wine." Judy closed her eyes and sighed.

Kate was dying to talk about the things in her own life but then decided that she didn't have to with Judy, so she ought to enjoy the recess from her troubles. Even her roommates had been keeping a close watch on the Winegar trial, and when Kate mentioned offhandedly that she had visited him in jail, there was an immediate division of opinion: either she had shown contempt for her father or she had been a model of Christian forgiveness.

"Neither. I was curious."

But if Judy knew of those events, she kept clear of them. The order of the day seemed to be chatter, talk that was at least a foot off the ground and finally didn't matter. All the enthusing about Provence was the expected outlook, but it was not yet based on anything in Judy's own experience. Would she see the real place if she went there with all these canned experiences already in her mind?

"Want a refill?" Judy asked.

"Sure."

"I'll get them."

The atmosphere had changed when Judy came back. "I'm not going with him anymore."

Just like that, as if no time at all had intervened since that day at the club and all the stuff about Provence hadn't been said. Kate didn't trust herself to say anything.

"What he wanted me to do? I did it." Judy stared at her and tears welled up in her eyes. Kate put her hand on Judy's. "My God, it was awful."

"Do you want to go outside?"

"I'll be all right."

But she didn't want Judy to be all right. By God, she had a right to cry about something like that. She had done it for that stupid boy and it hadn't mattered.

"Tell me about it."

"Are you sure?"

"Of course I'm sure."

She would have walked barefoot over ground glass not to hear it, but Judy had to talk, had to say it, had to tell about it, had to explain to her, because she had confided in her after tennis one day. It was so much as it had been with Nan at the lake, because that was what having her baby had been like for Nan, the emotional equivalent of an abortion: She had been pregnant, and then she wasn't, and there was no baby to show for it.

"He said he didn't want me to have his baby. But it was my baby, goddammit, not his."

They sat at their neat little table in the antiseptic room, the setting meant for talk about exhibits carried on in unnatural tones, yet they were discussing life and death. Kate thought of how men could just turn away from what they had done, as the boy Nan had fallen in love with did, leaving the girl with the problem. How infinitely better Nan's solution had been than Judy's. Somewhere Nan's child was alive, whereas Judy felt only violated and damaged and guilty. She didn't give a damn what all the marching, shouting, braless women said, it was the worst thing she had ever been through.

Neither of them had really wanted the second cup of coffee, but they sat on there through wave after wave of customers until Judy had gotten it all out of her system and they could leave.

"I'll bet you're sorry you ran into me."

"I've been calling you."

"I know."

"Let's get together next week."

"Where?"

"Here?"

"I can't stand museums."

"Marshall Field's?"

"Let me call you, Kate."

Maybe this was all Judy had really needed. There wasn't much more to say. Kate hoped that the sun and cafés and wine of Provence would heal the wound Judy bore. She herself was filled with an overwhelming gratitude to her unknown mother for having had the courage to bear her and give her up rather than go through the horrendous experience Judy had just described.

She heard the news on the radio driving back to campus and didn't know what she felt. A hung jury. That apparently meant that at least one of the jurors prevented a unanimous decision one way or the other. The commentator seemed sure that it was a single vote for conviction rather than acquittal that had ended the trial. He assured his listeners that the jurors would doubtless be telling all shortly.

Kate continued toward Wisconsin for several more miles and then decided to go home. Whatever else might be said, the man accused of killing her father had managed not to be convicted of it, even if he hadn't been exonerated either. What would Nan's reaction be?

"She took the boys to soccer," Jim said. He seemed surprised to see her.

"The jury reached a verdict."

"It's a scandal," he said.

"I heard on the radio that they can try him again."

"Don't count on it."

"You look different."

His mood changed and he grinned sheepishly. "Well, I kept the mustache anyway."

"That's what it is."

"Nan says now I won't be mistaken for the picture that appeared in the paper."

"I wonder how she's taking this verdict."

"I think she wants the whole thing to be over and done with. I don't blame her. After all, what's to be gained by locking up somebody? It can't bring Mitch back."

"How you doing with my money?"

"Okay, okay. Why do you ask?"

"Wouldn't you be surprised if I didn't ask?"

"You sounded before as if you never wanted to hear of it again."

"Nouveau riche." But he didn't get it. He looked kind of naked without his beard. She felt like telling him she liked him better with it, but that might sound as if the less she saw of his face, the better she liked it.

"I miss my beard, Kate," he said, as if conscious of her thoughts. "I think I'll let it grow out again."

"That might be a good idea."

"The boys hardly recognize me."

As if on cue, they thundered in the back door and Nan followed them. She kissed Jim's bare cheek then wrinkled her nose. "What do you think of paleface here?"

"I thought he was an intruder when I walked in."

"Have you heard?"

"Yes."

"I ran into Bob Frankman, and he is sure the prosecutor will simply drop the charges."

"What does Bob Frankman know?" Jim said angrily.

"Probably nothing. He's shaved off his beard too. Anyway he was just repeating Jason Broderick."

"The famous criminal lawyer."

"Had a bad day?"

Had his beard concealed his expressions? Jim seemed nervous and upset. "That verdict didn't help."

Nan seemed to take on Jim's mood, and Kate went off to where the boys were watching the television they had turned on as soon as they got home.

"Do you know Marjorie White?" Phil asked, and Father Dowling said of course he did.

"Why?"

"Edna sent her to me."

Father Dowling could feel Marie's presence near the kitchen door, betrayed by the eerie silence rather than anything else.

"I think I know why."

"Okay, tell me."

"She has been beating Marie's time with Willie."

The crash from the kitchen could have been an accident. Phil turned at the noise. "You all right, Marie?"

A further ten seconds of total silence and then Marie appeared, pushing regally through the intervening swinging door. "Did you want something, Captain Keegan?"

"I thought you fell."

Marie's wild expression indicated that she took this to be a continuation of the pastor's teasing. She stomped back to the kitchen, bewildering Phil.

"What's wrong with her?"

"Marjorie asked you about Willie, right?"

"Some cock-and-bull story about him having been an undercover man in prison, working for the police."

"Is that what you told her, that it was bull?"

"Of course."

"How did she take it?"

"How do you mean?"

"She and Willie have been seeing each other, in the phrase."

"No kidding." Phil thought about it. "Well, I didn't do him any good, did I?"

"That'll teach him to lie," Marie said, coming in as if nothing had happened. "I had half a mind to tell Marjorie myself."

"A housekeeper's work is never done," sighed Father Dowling.

But Marie was not to be baited. She wanted a more detailed account of Phil's talk with Marjorie.

"I just told her, that's all. I didn't know why she asked. I supposed she thought it was bunk and wanted to know for sure."

"But didn't she say anything?"

Father Dowling said the grace after meal and went on to the study, leaving Phil in the remorseless hands of Marie. From his window he looked out to where Mitchell Striker's car had been parked that rainy night; he thought of the body tipped sideways onto the passenger seat, the doors locked, the motor running. Someone had murdered the man, and if not Winegar, who?

He realized that he had been convinced that Winegar killed Striker. God knows he had a stronger motive than most killers. A vindictive act, years ago, that had shattered his life's dreams, a boy who apart from his selection for St. Peter's might not have had any such dreams at all. But he had been selected and he had excelled, the best boy in the school. All that had been taken away from him in punishment for having gotten Mitchell Striker's daughter in trouble. It was difficult to know if Father Gorman himself had known the name of the girl involved. It would have been like Striker, given his general handling of the matter, to have kept that information from Gorman. But he had convinced the headmaster that his best boy must be expelled, and expelled he had been. Thinking of Winegar's unimpressive, checkered career since leaving the school, of the drinking that had plagued him throughout the years, it was easy to imagine the resentment grow and a steady hatred take possession of him. When, fatefully, he returned to Fox River, the return seemed the culmination of a plan for revenge.

But a jury had been unable to reach a verdict.

Phil came into the study and said, "Plover is recommending a retrial, but then he thinks he did a good job."

"What do you think?"

"That he should save the city the money."

"I wonder if he did it?"

"Did Cain kill Abel?"

"You're that sure?"

258

"Roger, I'm as puzzled as anyone by what happened to that girl reporter. It doesn't make much sense unless you think we've got two killers, one for Striker and the other a strangler."

Lucy Sommers had been canonized by the press; she was one of their own who had given the last full measure of devotion, a martyr to the cause of a free press, a veritable Joan of Arc of the First Amendment. The poor girl herself disappeared behind all this inflated rhetoric. Her parents came from Spokane, and Phil asked Father Dowling to talk to them.

"They're Catholics."

Sommers was a plumbing and heating contractor in Spokane, and his wife was a nervous bony woman who kept looking around as if she was certain fingers were being pointed at them.

"Could she be buried here, Father?"

"If you wish, certainly."

"We don't want to bring her home. There's been talk." A dry sob, but that was all. No tears. Maybe she had cried herself dry already.

"We're not ashamed of her."

"Neither is God."

Sommers grabbed his hand and began to shake it vigorously, blinking his eyes rapidly. Plumbers don't cry. Father Dowling's heart went out to them. Their daughter had gone off to Chicago in triumph, had caused a scandal, then become a heroine for reasons they did not care for, and now she was cruelly dead. He suggested that they have a private ceremony.

"You won't want a big fuss made over her."

"No!"

McDivitt did things nicely, although there was no wake. Phil got the word out that her parents must have taken the body back to Spokane. At eight o'clock in the morning, Father Dowling said the funeral mass. The parents were in the front pew; there were a few regulars, and Edna. Marie Murkin, of course, ex officio as it were. And Tuttle, of all people. He rode to the cemetery with the Sommerses, and Father Dowling rode in the hearse with McDivitt.

"That was very nice, Father."

"I was going to say the same to you."

"They're all different, aren't they? Deaths."

"Like lives."

The little undertaker nodded, his cottony white hair thick over his ears, a pearl gray homburg on his head.

The coffin was placed on a device over the camouflaged newly dug grave, and Father Dowling read the prayers, invoking the great host of

259

the faithful, living and dead, and asking the Lord to receive his daughter Lucia into life eternal. Mrs. Sommers had saved tears for this, and her husband put his arm about her and tugged her to him. And then it was over.

He said good-bye to them there, dodging the money Sommers tried to give him.

"Give it to your favorite charity."

"I want masses said for her."

"I'll do that in any case."

When he got in beside McDivitt, Father Dowling heard Tuttle asking the Sommerses if they liked Chinese food. It seemed they did. McDivitt told his driver to take them wherever they wished.

"Do you suppose they know he represented the man she lived with, Father?"

"No."

Nor would Tuttle tell them. Father Dowling had never thought better of Tuttle than he did at that moment.

Jason was his usual charming self, gallant as the devil, ordering their meal, selecting the wines, sending a note to the orchestra to insure that "Sentimental Journey" in the Les Brown arrangement would be played. In each set there was a little gem of that sort—"Let It Snow," shades of Doris Day, "You Belong to Me," à la Margaret Whiting—he even crooned in her ear, until Clara could believe she was a teenager again attending a dance at the Catholic Youth Center. That was where she had met Don Ponader, only he didn't dance, so they had just sat through the music, but she hadn't really minded. But now, with Jason, it was as it should be. Except that he was a tad preoccupied.

"What's the matter?"

"Is anything the matter?"

"You look as if our Florida vacation had been discovered."

"If only it would be. I've dropped hints everywhere. My reputation needs a boost. Women are taking me for granted."

"Poor you."

"Not at all." And it turned out that this was what had been preoccupying him. "Nor are you. Are you happy with the way I'm handling your financial affairs?"

"As compared to what?"

He laughed. It was a variation on the silly joke he had told in Florida. A man is asked how his wife is. Compared to what?

"I'll ask you flat out. Has Robert Frankman ever suggested that he could work wonders for you?"

"You mean with my money?"

"Uh-huh."

"Jason, one of the last things Don said to me was that you would look out for things. I could trust you. I have. Do you think I would even listen if Bob Frankman said any such thing?"

"He is very good."

"I thought he made a big goof with the St. Peter's endowment."

"Even Homer nods. He is recovering the loss. He put money into something that is the financial equivalent of shooting craps. You win big or lose it all."

"Please don't explain it to me."

"I'm not sure I could, and I'm supposed to understand such things. I wonder if Bob Frankman could explain it."

"It sounds dumb to me."

"When you lose, yes. But he has won too. Jim Walsh put some money into it and trebled his investment."

"That's good, isn't it?"

"That's good."

"Don't let anything happen to you, Jason. I don't know what I'd do."

"How touching. Why the concern?"

"Did Jim Walsh turn to Frankman after Mitchell Striker's death? I understood that Mitchell looked after the family investments. Nancy told me so."

"Good question."

"Surely it wouldn't have been while Mitch was still alive. That would border on an insult."

"Not to mention ingratitude."

"It seems almost an insult that Jerome Winegar is going to get off scot-free."

"Not quite. They could try him again."

"I think he did it, don't you?"

"You know him better than I do."

Just a little edge to that remark, but Clara said nothing. She deserved to be rebuked for that foolishness. But then at the time Jason had paid no attention to her, she was bored to death and had to make do with afternoon teas with Marjorie White, for heaven's sake. Poor Marjorie. She had fallen for the St. Hilary's janitor.

"He's quite a dancer," Jason insisted.

"Marjorie won't talk about it."

Except in general terms. She had finally gone to Father Dowling and had found it a very reassuring meeting. The pastor had told her anecdote after anecdote of the mistakes people can make when they are cut loose from their moorings, losing a spouse, suddenly alone. He was so understanding, and Marjorie was able to see her feelings for Willie as an expression of her own loneliness rather than any response to the man himself.

"I am too trusting, Clara."

"There are worse faults."

"That's just what he said."

"Willie?"

"Clara! No, Father Dowling."

Admittedly she felt superior to Marjorie, now that Jason was being so attentive, but nobody had to tell her how lonely it was being alone after years with somebody. She even missed the things she hadn't liked about Don. So really she sympathized with Marjorie. Widows are all in the same boat. It's different with men.

"Can you find anyone for Marjorie, Jason?"

"I was thinking of asking her out myself."

"You do and I'll call Bob Frankman."

She wasn't suggesting anything beyond what they had, companionship, fun, the bittersweet nostalgia of dancing to tunes you had loved when you were in your teens.

"Don't answer the phone if he calls," Jason said the following day.

"Bob Frankman?"

"No, your other boyfriend. Winegar. They've decided not to retry him. Plover dropped the charges."

"He's free?"

"That's the idea."

Mad magazine had a section called "Good News You'd Rather Not Get" that Tuttle had tried unsuccessfully to explain to Peanuts. Congratulations, we found the guy who firebombed your house. Peanuts wanted to know what was wrong with that.

"Your house has to be firebombed first."

"That's dumb."

"That's the idea. This is *Mad.*"

Tuttle felt that way when Plover announced that he would not retry Winegar on the charges. Winegar was free. There was a photograph in the paper of Winegar shaking Tuttle's hand, beaming with pleasure. Right after that shot, he had swiped Tuttle's tweed hat and put it on.

"Hey, that's my lucky hat."

"You're telling me?"

There were analyses of the defense in the local papers. Tuttle was asked to speak to a class at the Loyola law school. Success seemed as much a matter of luck as failure. And Tuttle still thought Winegar had done it. Killed Striker anyway. Somehow he was responsible for Lucy Sommers's death too, even if he had been locked up at the time. Tuttle wouldn't even talk about her with Winegar.

"Too damned vulnerable," Winegar said.

But everyone was vulnerable with a guy like that running around loose.

"I owe you, Tuttle."

"Forget it."

"You trying to tell me you were working pro bono?"

"No, pro Cher." It was a joke he had heard in the courthouse. Winegar didn't think much of it.

Tuttle wasn't Catholic, but some of his best friends and all that, so at first he had found the funeral for Lucy Sommers a little strange, but he was glad he'd gone. Talking to her folks had been hard because the mother wasn't sure whether her daughter had died in disgrace or not. Getting killed is no disgrace, by and large, but what he liked was the conviction that, dead or not, she still existed. Like his own father. Phil Keegan had once accused him of ancestor worship because of the way he had his father's name in the firm, Tuttle & Tuttle. Maybe that's why he liked Chinese food.

Why was it people like Lucy paid and people like Winegar walked away from all the trouble they caused? Tuttle felt a bit responsible himself, having been the one who introduced Lucy to Winegar. He thought about that. How often was he likely to run into Winegar in the courthouse, back then, that is, and he just happened to ask Lucy to come along while he checked out the police investigation with Peanuts, so out of the press room they had come and run into Winegar. It might not have happened. Anyone who bet on it happening would be an idiot. But it had happened. Maybe it had been written into her life from the beginning and there was no way it could have been avoided. But think of all the things he had to do and she had to do and Winegar had to do, getting the timing just right, and all three of them free to do or not to do. It made your head swim. He tried to express that to Peanuts.

"You mean Providence," Peanuts said, chewing an egg roll.

"Fate."

Peanuts's frown pulled his forehead into a line with his nose. "Providence."

Peanuts was a Catholic, and dumb as he was, he could spiel off his catechism, all of it imprinted on a mind that was scarcely used, but he had that. So did the Sommerses. And Father Dowling, careful not to pretend that he had God's unlisted number, said the kind of things Tuttle would have liked to hear in similar circumstances. He had liked hearing them then.

Winegar seemed just to write off the girl. Once she had been alive, now she was dead. Period. That's why Tuttle could see him killing Striker, if not Major.

"I had reason to kill him, Tuttle; I kid you not."

"You mean from when you were a kid."

"Those are the best reasons."

"You carried a grudge all those years?"

"What if someone had tried to kick you out of law school, what would you think of them?"

Lots of people had; nearly every prof he had took him aside and told him maybe he should think of another way of earning a living. But his father hadn't lost faith in him and Tuttle stuck it out, taking the course over when he flunked it, amassing the credits. When the old man held that diploma declaring Tuttle Juris Doctor he looked so proud, Tuttle would have gone through the whole thing again just to give him that moment.

"Think we'll have to do it again, Tuttle?" Winegar asked.

"Let's wait."

And then the ruling came, and there was all the hoopla, and afterward Winegar said, "You like Chinese, don't you Tuttle?"

"Sure."

"I am going to treat you to the biggest Chinese dinner you ever had."

They went to the Nanking and had a great meal, only Tuttle wished it were Peanuts rather than Winegar sitting across the table from him.

"Why did you come up with the body being moved?" Tuttle asked when they were done. "Striker's."

"Because that's the way it happened."

Tuttle felt suddenly clammy all over. Was Winegar saying he had done it? He was grinning, watching Tuttle's reaction.

"Don't worry. I'm not confessing, Tuttle."

"Just guessing?"

He shook his head. "I saw it. I was there. I saw the car drive up and the guy get out. Leaving the motor running, the way people sometimes do at the ball park, but who would have been that anxious to hear Striker talk?"

"What were you doing there?"

"I wanted to hear him but not really be there. Willie had shown me around the place, and I was waiting in his apartment for the talk to begin when I figured I could kibitz from the hall. I just wanted to hear Striker's voice again."

"You saw the guy who did it?"

"I saw a guy get out of a car that turned out to have a dead body in it."

"You recognize him?"

The grin widened. "Maybe."

"You better tell Keegan."

Winegar's manner became icy. "This is a privileged communication, Tuttle. You mention this and I'll have your . . ." He paused, and the grin came back. "Tweed hat."

Confidentiality didn't cover information about a crime, not when it wasn't a crime of the client's, but what information had Winegar given him that he could pass on to anyone as an officer of the court? Basically what Tuttle wanted to do was put the whole thing behind him. His biggest triumph, and he would have been willing to pass on it, the way things had turned out.

"You want to let a killer walk around free."

"Up to a point, Tuttle. Up to a point."

Cy Horvath felt as bad as Keegan and Agnes Lamb when the prosecutor dropped the charges against Jerome Winegar and the judge let him go. But then he wondered if they hadn't been too easily satisfied. Complacent. The evidence had been there, no doubt of that, but it had been almost too easy. Dr. Pippen had come over to commiserate with the detectives, and Cy took her to the cafeteria for coffee.

"Whatever Winegar did or didn't do, there's somebody else."

"The one who killed Lucy Sommers."

"Try this. That it's the same person who put the St. Peter's records in the apartment."

"Wow."

"Just try it, I said. Of course, it doesn't make sense. Putting the records there to incriminate Winegar when killing the girl got him off the hook."

"Nice try."

"Maybe there's more than two."

That was the trouble with Pippen; she had too lively an imagination. Cy was sorry he had started on this line of thought with her, and he joshed her out of it, wanting to keep it to himself.

"How about four?" he said.

"Why four?"

"So they can play bridge between murders."

"Do you play bridge?"

"Honeymoon." He was about to add, with my wife, but he didn't, and that was always the problem talking with the beautiful assistant medical examiner. She was a lot of woman and pretty as a picture, and he ought to know better than to sit around having coffee with her, trying to impress her with his detective skills.

Some skills. Alone, he returned to the puzzle, taking a car and just driving. They could get in touch with him if they needed him. He went back to the thought of someone stashing those school records among Winegar's things. When they assumed Winegar had taken them, they figured he would know his way around his old school. If it hadn't been Winegar, if those records had been planted, the one who did it had to get hold of them first. And who could do that?

Old Miss Gloria was surprised to see him again and even more surprised that he wanted to talk about the missing records. When would they be returned to her archives? Cy assured her that the judge would release them and that he personally would bring them to St. Peter's so she could put them back where they belonged.

She got out the box, lifted its cover, separated the contents to show where the Winegar records belonged.

"Nothing else taken?"

She looked sharply at him. "What does it matter now that they've let him go?"

"I'm just reviewing the evidence. Was there any sign that other boxes had been opened, or had any boxes been moved around?" The gray acid-free boxes were placed neatly on shelves specially made for them. Gloria told him everything else was just the way it always was.

"Including this box. It was in its proper place. I'll admit this, Lieutenant Horvath. If you hadn't discovered those records, I don't know when I might have realized they were missing."

"How could anyone get into your domain?"

"That's what I would like to know."

"Weren't there signs the lock had been forced?"

"Yes. There were scratches on the door, as if it had been pried open."

"As if?"

She closed the door and showed him the marks, still there. "They make you think the door can be opened that way. Maybe it can. But I tried it and couldn't do it."

"You tried to force the door?"

"To force it open would require half destroying it. Even so, when I get this repaired, I want to make sure it's more secure."

He asked to see the key for the lock; it was a fairly standard one that would provide no great challenge to an experienced thief. Who else had a key to the archives?

"The headmaster."

"Just him?"

"The cleaning crew."

Cy had talked to them before; this whole conversation was redundant. Except that now what stuck out was that the one who had taken the records had come just for that, knew where to look, and removed them, and the theft might have gone undetected except for what might be an effort to make it look as if the door had been pried open.

"My first thought was the students," Gloria said. "God knows what they would want with these records, but boys are strange creatures. Anyway, I kept quiet about the door until the records were found on Mr. Winegar. I didn't want to get the boys in trouble."

Before, all this had been taken to point to Winegar, who would want to remove those records because they would provide the motive for his killing Striker. But if someone else had removed the records in order to incriminate Winegar . . .

Who would want to insure that the case against Winegar was tight and unmistakable, as the discovery of those records had seemed to make it? Winegar had come to know a few people since returning to Fox River—Blake at Ponader's Motors, those at Jude Thaddeus House, Clara Ponader, Lucy Sommers—but none of them would seem to have any reason to incriminate Winegar, even if they had known about the records.

That was the key. How many people knew of the old quarrel between Winegar and Mitchell Striker? By all accounts, knowledge of it had been kept to a very few. Old Father Gorman, the headmaster, and Striker himself. What had been meant by a serious breach of moral discipline? Given that St. Peter's was a boys' school, the phrase suggested something deviant, but then there would have been at least two candidates for expulsion. Father Gorman was dead, Striker was dead. Who among the living would know what had happened? Striker's family? It was a long shot, but why not? He called the Walsh house and got a recorded message, at the end of which the number of Walsh's dental office was given. So he called that.

"Sorry to bother you, Doctor, but there is something I would like to ask your wife."

"About what?"

"You heard that they let Winegar go?"

"We certainly did."

"Well, your father-in-law is still dead, and we intend to find the one who did it."

"You already did and they let him go."

"Maybe there is evidence we should have found and didn't."

"Can he be tried again?"

"A hung jury is not a verdict."

"I don't think Nancy could go through all this again. Why don't you just let it go."

"Let a murderer go?"

"The judge did."

"That's the way it looks, sure. But what if it is someone else?"

"Oh, for God's sake."

"I'd like to talk to your wife."

"She's out of town, Lieutenant. To get away from all this. I am not going to tell you where she is."

Cy had been hung up on before, but he had never learned to enjoy it. Well, he would talk to her when he talked to her. Chances are she wouldn't have the least idea anyway about an episode at a school where her father had happened to be a member of the board.

He began to imagine someone whose interest had been the school itself. If Winegar's motive was known to that person, getting the records known would have the effect of exonerating the school. Here was an atypical St. Peter's boy. Paint him black as tar so that he would be seen not to be a regular St. Peter's boy. And after all, he had been expelled.

Cy felt that he was going in circles. Back downtown, he put the car in the garage and went upstairs. Phil Keegan called to him when he went by his office, and Cy went in.

"Tuttle was in."

"Enjoying his triumph?"

"Not at all. He thinks Winegar killed Striker, but it isn't anything he really knows. Besides, it's all complicated by the fact that he was the lawyer in the case."

"Just a hunch?"

"Talk to him. He's down the hall with Peanuts."

Tuttle and Peanuts were spooning food from paper cartons and kept on doing it after Cy came in. Tuttle told Cy the same thing he had told Phil Keegan.

"Where is Winegar now?"

"He said he was going to look up an old flame."

64

He had acted as if their meeting was just an accident, but Marie Murkin was not deceived. Jerome Winegar did not just happen to be in the neighborhood of the church when she had gone over to make a little visit.

"As I live and breathe," he whispered, taking her hand. "It's Marie Murkin."

He said it as if they were old friends, and the way he smiled almost convinced her they were. They couldn't talk in church, not properly. Father Dowling had a little homily about those who have the great privilege to be around the sacred daily and sometimes become too familiar, too casual. "They talk in church, for example, as if they were in line at the supermarket." What did he know of the supermarket? And why did he always come along on the few occasions when she did talk aloud in church? In the line of duty, of course.

"No, this side," Winegar said to her.

Meaning he did not want them to go out the door that faced the rectory.

"Father Dowling wanted to come see me when I was on trial, and I deprived him of the chance to perform that corporal work of mercy."

"Whoever talks of the corporal works of mercy anymore? Well, you certainly look none the worse for wear."

"It is a spartan and healthy existence, being a guest of the state. No alcohol, no late hours. I was ashamed to be seen in that fallen condition."

"And now you're free."

"Free," he said. Had a monosyllable ever before conveyed such melancholy? "An accusation is as good as a conviction, Marie. I am sure that most people think I killed Mitchell Striker and that I have gotten off on a technicality."

"A man is innocent until proved guilty."

270

"Is that the gender-specific or inclusive use of the term?"

Marie knew when not to speak. She hadn't the least idea what he meant, but it sounded like teasing to her.

"There are those, though you are not among them, who would take my coming here to be an instance of a criminal returning to the scene of his crime."

Marie felt a little shiver. He took her arm and they began to walk.

"I have heard so much about it that I wanted to come have a look at it. Unobtrusively. And what better disguise than to be strolling in the parish precincts with the rectory housekeeper? Where was the car found?"

She took him to the very spot and then became caught up in the drama of the thing. "You have to remember it was raining cats and dogs and the car was parked right here and the rain was pelting off the roof. The motor was running, the lights were on, but the car seemed to be empty. Father Dowling could see it from his study."

"Then he might see us."

"If he were in his study."

"And he isn't?"

"He's gone off to his class reunion." Why did she feel he already knew that the pastor was not on the premises?

"Class reunion! I didn't think he was the type."

"Oh, he isn't, not really. He decided to go only at the last minute."

Winegar now stood, arms akimbo, looking about. "So this is where Mitchell Striker departed this vale of tears. One of the reasons I returned to Fox River was to speak to him, about old times. Alas, that was not to be. It is probably for the best."

"What will you do now?"

"Did you ever dream of living certain events over again, Miss Murkin?"

"Miss Murkin!"

"Ah, so it's the Widow Murkin."

"It is."

"Then you will understand me better. My life has reached a point where it is inescapable that I have made a hash of it. I knew that even before this terrible charge was made against me. For years I resisted, but finally I was drawn back as if by a magnet."

Did he think he could become a schoolboy again and this time avoid being expelled from St. Peter's?

"Being accused of murder clears the mind. I am guilty of so many things that the charge, while inaccurate, seemed almost deserved. There would have been a vast cosmic irony if I had been made to suffer innocently for the death of Mitchell Striker when so much of my life has been lived under his aegis."

They walked back and forth in the parking lot, and Marie imagined the old people looking out and seeing them and trying to guess what they were talking about. Or what he was talking about. It was the sort of thing he should have been saying to Father Dowling, almost a confession, and Marie became more confused as to why he was telling her these things.

"A woman understands," he said, as if reading her thoughts.

"Will you go away again?"

"Perhaps, perhaps."

"Where are you staying?"

"I am back at Jude Thaddeus House."

Marie was shocked. She believed in saving money and avoiding airs, but the idea of an able-bodied man like Jerome Winegar living down there with those derelicts was incomprehensible.

"How can you stand it?"

"The important thing is that I can afford it."

"Do you have to pay?"

"That is my point. No."

Marie's hip was bothering her now. She didn't mind a good walk from time to time, but this was becoming a marathon. She told him she must get back to the rectory. He walked along with her, he who had been avoiding the pastor; maybe he hadn't known the pastor had gone off for several days. He suggested they sit when they came to a bench flanked by two magnolia trees.

"You must be wondering why I am going on like this."

"It's very interesting."

"Do you know a young woman named Kate Striker?"

"I do."

"She came to see me while I was in jail. I found that remarkable. It turned out that she had been a volunteer at Jude Thaddeus House. Youthful idealism, perhaps mere enthusiasm, a romanticizing of the down and out, but I was impressed. You have been here longer than Father Dowling, I believe."

"Oh my, yes."

"Do you remember the Strikers adopting that girl?"

"I know that they did."

"Do you know anything of the circumstances?"

Marie searched her memory; she would have given anything to be able to go on about it. It seemed a negative judgment on her knowledge of the parish that she could provide no details at all.

"It was a lucky day for her, of that I'm certain. He left her wealthy, you know."

"I've heard rumors."

"That young girl is a millionaire."

"For heaven's sakes."

At the registration table, they were given toy birettas made of paper with a pom-pom that reminded Father Dowling of valentine cards. Pink and yellow birettas. This had been the standard headgear, in black, during their seminary days, but no one wore a biretta anymore except a few eccentrics—and, of course, bishops. So it was a nice touch, and Chips Pommefrits beamed at the praise.

"What a turnout!" he exulted.

The order of the day was casual dress, perhaps so the difference between priest and layman would not be emphasized, or between active and laicized priest, for that matter.

"Is Bob Frankman here, Chips?"

"He assured me he was coming."

"But you haven't seen him."

"He'll be here, Roger. He may be the only self-made multimillionaire in the class."

Grosslander had inherited wealth and had lived most of his life pretending to be poor, so he did not represent competition for Frankman. Clearly Chips regarded it as a coup to have the successful investment counselor accept his invitation to come and mix with his old classmates.

It was in the hope of seeing Frankman that Father Dowling had changed his mind and decided to come.

This first day was for festivity and reacquaintance, although perhaps three-quarters of the priests had been aware over the years of what the others were doing. Or thought they knew. Roger Dowling was again struck by how less than seismic for others are the events that are turning points in one's own life. His somewhat ignominious departure from the marriage court, his treatment in Wisconsin—drying out, in the expressive phrase—and, that completed, his assignment to Fox River as to the archdiocesan ultima Thule, had been a series of earthquakes in his personal life. As he went through them, he had assumed he was the cynosure of every eye, an object of comment, of pity, of contempt, perhaps even of *delectatio morosa* on the part of a few. These had been more or less public events, certainly not hidden from the clergy. Yet they had not loomed large for many others. His presumed upwardly mobile ecclesiastical career had suffered an irreparable blow, but from experience he had learned something of the vicissitudes and reversals of life. The greatest lesson of all was how little this had loomed in the lives of others. Yet it had been his salvation.

His presumed exile had been a coming home to the real purpose of his vocation. To be a pastor, to be the priest for the members of his own parish, to be in the arena where he would save or lose his own soul in administering to others, had brought a new clarity of mind and satisfaction of soul. One of the great truisms of spiritual conferences finally became a truth for him. It is in our failures that God can speak to us most directly.

How little he himself knew of the inner dramas of his classmates. In large part these were closed to him, by definition unknowable to another human being. What a marvelous and baffling mystery human lives are. He had learned to stand in awe of the persons with whom he came into contact as a pastor. The greatest danger was to think he already knew what was coming. It was the surprises that one looked for as signs that underneath the most humdrum externals the essential drama of life went on.

His love of Dante grew as he savored the way the poet worked variations on the one thing needful, salvation or damnation, the ultimate success or failure of a person's passage through time. So it was with his classmates. Perhaps many imagined that for a priest, given his function, given what occupied him day after day, that issue was not in doubt. Why else would the media seize upon real, and sometimes merely alleged, misbehavior by priests? This seemed to go beyond mere weakness, to be worse than hypocrisy. But it merely underscored the fundamental truth, immortally expressed by Yogi Berra, "It ain't over till it's over."

"Roger?"

It took a few seconds before Roger Dowling mentally restored the hair and removed about ninety pounds from the man who addressed him.

"Jimmy Marston."

"The same. Or rather not the same. You look cadaverously trim. What's your secret, yogurt?"

"No. The best cook in the western part of the archdiocese."

"Vegetarian?"

"More mineral, I think."

"Carbonated or plain?"

A poor joke gone wrong is a frightening thing. He assured Jimmy Marston that it was metabolism rather than diet or discipline that explained his lack of avoirdupois.

"*Avoirdupois!* Have some peas! Is Maurice here?"

Maurice had achieved immortality with this inaccurate translation of the phrase. Jimmy himself had known a brief fame for having pronounced "misled" as "mizzled" during a reading in the refectory. How incredibly innocent and distant those days now seemed.

A bar had been set up under a tent on the lawn. Inside it, men milled about a trestle table laden with various drinks. A keg had been tapped and some emerged from the tent with plastic cups filled with more foam than beer.

"I hope it's Lite," Jimmy said.

"I think I'll have a diet Coke."

"What a rebuker you are, Roger. Is that Polish sausage I smell?"

The afternoon air was beginning to fill with the aromas of the feast to come. Ed Morley at first gathered and then dispersed a small group with a disquisition on the games and banquets in the *Aeneid,* the sacrificed animals becoming the food of the contestants and observers.

"You've kept up with Virgil?"

"I have. Thirty lines a day, Roger, just as when we were boys. I know yards of it by heart. You will say I would have spent my time better with the Vulgate Bible or perhaps Augustine. But, as the twig is bent . . ." Morley wore rimless glasses that seemed to emphasize his lack of eyebrows. His hair was unnaturally dark. Did he or didn't he?

"Are you still at Visitation?"

"Good Lord, no. I have gone on to Nativity. Is Presentation next? Or Assumption?" He batted his eyes as he spoke; clearly he enjoyed himself. Perhaps his audiences at Nativity were more captive than here. "You're in Aurora, aren't you, Roger?"

"Close."

"I saw Borealis earlier."

This was the nickname of a classmate named Borland who had come from Aurora. But a crowd was gathering around McGrade, whose mimicry had been legendary and apparently had improved with time. He was doing impressions of their old professors and was urged on by delighted listeners. Do Fox. Do Moriarity. Kelly, please do Kelly.

"I'd swear Moriarity had returned from the grave if the words weren't coming from McGrade's mouth."

"Bob Frankman! I was just asking Chips about you."

"Oh?"

Bob held a cup of beer, which he drained while looking at Roger over its rim.

"Want another of those?"

"Not really. It's not cold enough for me."

"Care to walk?"

He did, and they strolled over the campus and into the building where classes had been held and came to a room where Bob stopped. "Now, if we could put McGrade in there and close the door, we would really be in a time warp. How it all comes back."

"Doesn't it?"

"Two men have spoken to me who are unaware that I've been laicized."

"You have children, don't you?"

A fleeting pained look. "I do."

They opened the classroom door and went inside and sat. Father Moriarity had taught Moral and was known as Trent's Last Casuist. The finest shades of difference among human acts had held no mystery for his Jesuit mind.

"How simple life seemed when we sat here."

"Mo always made at least some grudging reference to prudence."

"I don't mean that, or just that. Our own lives seemed simple then. So many years of this, ordination, one assignment after another, our own parish. It sort of drifted away into an indefinite future."

"Which held a few surprises."

"How much of my situation do you know, Roger?"

It was a prelude to an unexpected narrative. Roger Dowling had not realized how complicated Bob's life had been. The usual account of the man, the one Chips accepted, was that he had left the priesthood and made a bundle in the stock market and would help you do the same if you asked him. The story from Bob's viewpoint was rather one of failure. Two marriages, both dissolved, one civilly, the other ecclesiastically.

"Leaving me canonically as single as I've ever been."

It was the thought that these momentous decisions had somehow been annihilated that seemed to be the point of the narrative.

"Like forgiven sins."

"Or a hung jury." It was an awkward transition, but Roger Dowling wanted to change the topic to the one that had brought him here today in the hope of seeing Frankman. A casual, unplanned meeting would be the best way to discuss recent events involving St. Peter's School and St. Hilary's Parish.

"What a travesty, Roger. The people have a right to expect better than that of a prosecutor."

"The case was lost out of court, don't you think? When that girl was killed?"

"Why should that have affected the charge he was being tried on? How many other killings went on while court was in session? They don't make Winegar less of a murderer."

This was oddly irrational for a man who made his living by his wits.

"Well, he's free and we may have heard the end of it."

"Do you think so?" Bob was almost eager.

"They aren't going to try him again for Mitchell Striker's death, and they can hardly accuse him of the girl's death."

"But will he stay around?"

"I've no idea."

"Why did he come back, Roger?"

"If he didn't come back to kill Mitchell Striker? Who knows? Why did we come to this reunion?"

"What do you mean?"

"Nostalgia. The pull of the past. Memories."

"His memories of Fox River sound pretty awful, don't they?"

"If his life consisted of one thing. But he had years at St. Peter's, years of triumphs. He was the best student in the school during all his time there. He is obviously brilliant."

"That's hard to believe."

"Why?"

"Genetics has something to do with intelligence. Given his background . . ."

"Do we know what it was?"

Frankman made a dismissive gesture. His hand was fat, and he wore a ring on his little finger. "I'm generalizing. You're right. What do we know? But that's just it, an orphan, given up for adoption." He seemed to be searching for a point.

"Like all the other students at St. Peter's."

"Of course, of course."

"Speaking of adopted children, Bob. I've been asked to say something to you. Mitchell Striker has an adopted daughter named Kate. His daughter Nancy and her family were well taken care of by Mitch, while he was alive, and apparently he did wonders with their money."

"I'm sure he did." Frankman's manner had become more confident as they moved into the area of his professional accomplishments.

"He left the adopted daughter a very large amount of money. Nancy Walsh would like someone to look after it."

"I see. How much are we talking about?"

"I believe she said six million dollars."

Frankman's eyebrows raised in stages, and his ringed hand went to the cheek as if to stroke the beard that was no longer there. "That was very generous of him."

"Kate is indifferent to the whole thing. She even spoke of giving it all away."

Frankman laughed. "Giving away six million dollars is more complicated than she imagines." His brow clouded. "Losing it is somewhat easier." He seemed to wait for Roger Dowling to say something. "But go on."

"Nancy Walsh thinks that someone like you should handle the money now that her father is gone. But she doesn't want to be known as the one who suggests this. That is why I'm her intermediary. I wanted to meet you without making an appointment, which is why I'm here."

"Very hush-hush."

"It's a delicate matter. Kate only learned a few years ago that she was adopted. At first she seemed unaffected by it, but more recently she has become anxious to find out who she really is. Her efforts have not been successful and aren't likely to be. Mitchell Striker seems to have made very sure that her origins would remain unknown."

"It's odd that he would have thought of that."

"How well did you know him?"

"I take it back."

"I gather that when Kate was talking about throwing it all away, Jim Walsh advised Kate to let someone handle it. In the meantime, he is doing it."

"Jim!"

"Nancy says he doesn't have the time to do it, and he's a dentist, not a financial manager."

"He's got to be a better dentist."

"Oh?"

"I can't discuss it, Roger. Nancy Walsh would like me to manage her sister's money, is that it?"

"That's it. But she can't just ask you to do it. Actually, I am going to make the suggestion, but before I do that, Nancy agreed that your willingness had best be consulted."

"How do you plan to approach the girl?"

"I don't have a plan."

Three days had gone by and Kate had heard nothing. She stayed put in her campus room, because it was here that he had visited her, it was here that for the first time they had talked. There would be a kind of fittingness if he should seek her out there. Where else would he look? He could hardly come by the Walshes', the man whose trial for the murder of Mitchell Striker had ended in a hung jury. No, she decided, he would come here.

Only he didn't. In her head she worked out a scoreboard, his one visit against the times she had visited him in jail. Imogene had made a gargling sound and rolled her eyes when his picture appeared in the paper, and Kate realized that with her it wasn't anything like that at all. Once, for weeks, she had seriously thought that the life of a nun would not be so bad. Not a movie or television nun, more like Maud Weaver, only Maud hadn't been a nun. Kate could imagine herself never marrying.

What a gamble it was when a man and woman were attracted to each other. Nan's story brought tears to Kate's eyes whenever she remembered it, or remembered Nan telling it, and the closeness between them while she listened, was not typical. It was sick to think that all men were like that. Of course, you had to watch them, but that was different. Any boy was a bee taking nectar where he could get it. But the cold cruel repudiation Nan had gotten was rare. So what did looks get you? If Nan wasn't beautiful, Kate didn't know the meaning of the term. She had a serene Spanish beauty that was conscious of itself only in rejecting the notion that beauty matters. Yet that boy had seen a pregnant Nan only as an impediment to his life, to his future. Judy's experience was another instance of that, so it did happen; Nan's rejection had not been unique.

If only people wouldn't treat it as some sort of game or sport, talking of "having sex" as if it were a self-contained entertainment. Then, oh my, what a big surprise when the activity had the result it was biologically shaped to have. Maybe there was nothing new about wanting the fun and not the effect, but now it seemed that the effect wasn't taken into account at all. Except to say that if pregnancy occurred, the girl had the constitutional right to go through the hell Judy had gone through.

But it was the mysterious unknown out of which she herself had come that obsessed Kate. Whoever her mother and father were, they hadn't wanted her, or couldn't keep her, and the love she hoped had brought them together wasn't sufficient to welcome her. Not that she was complaining that they hadn't just gotten rid of her, her mother going the Judy route. However unwillingly, her mother had given her life. She would not exist at all if it hadn't been for her, and him—just pronouns, that's all she had— and it made her want to cry out in anger that she could never know who they had been.

Winegar was in the same spot. It was awful that he had been accused of killing the man to whom she owed so much, the adoptive father she loved and missed, not like Nan, but even so. Winegar said he hadn't done it, but isn't that what people accused of crimes always say? But the jury had not convicted him. Before the trial, talking with him, she had told him they were alike.

"Being orphans?"

"I think of orphans as poor and hungry."

"As in widows and orphans?"

"There are lots of rich widows."

He looked at her for a moment. "Well, I'm poor."

She said nothing. She could hardly say, "I'm not, I'm rich." But she was. At first she wanted to refuse the money. Then she thought it gave her the means to find out about herself.

Winegar had had a lifetime to think about being an orphan, and what he had to say on that occasion sounded almost cynical. He hadn't ever really tried to find out who his mother had been. Suddenly it seemed incredible that none of the investigative reporters had looked into that aspect of the mystery of Jerome Winegar. They had written about everything else, certainly, whether to blame or praise him. But as far as Kate knew, no one had checked the records to discover his origins. And that's when she had the great idea.

She could do for him what she couldn't do for herself. As she considered this, she was almost afraid he would show up on campus; now she didn't want to see him until she found out if the records showed who his parents were. Excitedly she picked up the phone and then paused. Her impulse had been to call Tuttle, but Tuttle was Winegar's lawyer and . . . She didn't know what followed, but maybe he wouldn't do it without telling his client. So she called Amos Cadbury.

She told the woman who answered who she was and that she wished to see Mr. Cadbury as soon as possible.

"Just a moment."

While she waited she did not have to listen to canned music or a local radio station or any of the other gimmicks employed lest people be left alone with their own thoughts for a few seconds. Jim had the worst kind of Muzak, the arrangements reduced to four notes; imagine listening to that with a toothache.

"Miss Striker?" The woman was back. "Did you have some time in mind?"

"I'm at school, in Milwaukee. I can drive down right now. It wouldn't take but two hours."

"Then it is urgent?"

Why not? "Yes."

"Very well. Come when you can and Mr. Cadbury will see you."

She was almost sorry she hadn't called Tuttle. At least she would have been able to talk with him. But then Tuttle had only one big win to his credit, while Amos Cadbury, she had been assured by her father, was the most successful lawyer in town, everything a lawyer should be.

Another difference was that if she had been going to see Tuttle, she would have gone just as she was, but with Amos Cadbury the question of what to wear arose. She realized that this was her upbringing showing; she would be going to his office as the daughter of Mitchell Striker, and the responsibilities that went along with that were many. Among them was that you did not show up in the office of Fox River's most successful lawyer, a man who was everything a lawyer should be, wearing jeans and a George-town sweatshirt.

"Is that an invitation?" Imogene her roommate asked when Kate told her she was going to go home but expected to be back tomorrow.

"Not this time." She made a face. "Family business."

"I'd go home myself, but nobody would notice."

Imogene was one of nine children, and her mother's parents lived with her folks. That was in Waukesha—hardly more than a waukesha from campus; it wasn't clear whether it was Imogene or her folks who most wanted her to live on campus.

When she drove through Waukegan she could hear her adoptive father mention that Jack Benny came from there. Orson Welles came from Waukegan too and maybe Spencer Tracy too, but it was always Jack Benny he remembered.

She was on I-294 when it occurred to her that Amos Cadbury might refuse her request. After all, what business was it of hers who Jerome Winegar's mother was? The idea that had seemed so simple in her dorm room became as snarled as the traffic in which she now found herself.

A recurring item in Amos Cadbury's monthly confession was the sin of pride. Ironically enough, one of the things in which he took pride was the faithful practice of his religion. He had lived into a time when few people availed themselves of the confessional—or reconciliation room, as it was now called, a phrase that made him wince—yet most received commu-nion. It was said that the sense of sin had become so attenuated as to be all but absent from the hearts of Catholics. Amos's pride was his thorn in the flesh and, paradoxical as it seemed, it kept him penitent.

There had been a time, when he was in midcareer, that there had been talk of his taking the bench. But he disdained the two ways of becoming a judge, either by political patronage or by the will of the voters, who were guided by the political parties, so perhaps in the end there was only one way. The most exalted title of the judge, justice, was one he aspired to deserve if not to wear. Fairness, equality before the law, to each his due— phrases that were cant for many were holy to Amos Cadbury. The few departures from the high ideals of his profession of which he had been guilty thus wounded him all the more. When Genevieve, his administrative assistant, came in to tell him of Kate Striker's phone call, Amos was filled with foreboding.

"I wonder what it's about?"

"Should I ask?"

"Oh no. I'll see her in any case."

"She wants to come immediately."

"Am I free?"

There were few clients who would not willingly wait to see Amos Cadbury, her manner seemed to say, and even as he acquiesced in the thought, he felt the squeeze of conscience. Genevieve reminded him of his scheduled appointments.

"And you are dining with Mr. Frankman at the Cliffdwellers."

"Ah yes."

"I keep wanting to call him Father."

"Better not."

"He was the assistant in my parish."

"He is in good standing with the church."

Genevieve cleared her throat, a sufficient comment on that. In his heart of hearts, Amos agreed: Laicizations, like annulments, were in the power of the church to give, in quite definite circumstances, but they were scarcely to be celebrated. As a student at Notre Dame, in a philosophy class, Amos had heard that not even God can undo what has been done. Forgive it, perhaps, but not make what has been not to have been.

"That would be a contradiction, gentlemen," old Father Brennan had said. He wore a biretta in class and carried a chalky eraser around in his pitching hand. He always hit the boy he aimed at. "A contradiction cannot exist. It is nothing. And nothing is impossible to God."

Zing went the eraser, and a second-string quarterback moved quickly enough to get hit on the back with it. That great white chalk mark, like Ash Wednesday ashes, could not be removed in class.

The point was that it is not a restriction of God's omnipotence that he cannot make the past not to have been, since to have been and not to have been is a contradiction, and a contradiction is nothing, so it is not *some-*

thing God cannot do. Amos had loved philosophy, which was touted as a good preparation for law. But canon law seemed able to do what God could not do. No, that wasn't fair. An annulment is the judgment that no marriage took place, not that it had taken place yet had not taken place.

These thoughts were prelude to his appointment with Mrs. Rondeau, who wanted to establish trust funds for her grandchildren. This was the express purpose of her appointment. Amos had not suggested trusts, and he spent half an hour explaining to Mrs. Rondeau that she could give ten thousand dollars to each of her grandchildren every year free of income or inheritance tax on their part. She could give an equal amount to each of her children. The whole discussion was academic, in any case. In disposable cash, Mrs. Rondeau had less than one hundred thousand dollars, and at last count she had twenty-three grandchildren.

"I've also thought of savings bonds."

"An excellent idea."

She was old, as old as he was. Her husband had been a swashbuckling man of business to whom banks lent money on the strength of his name. It was assumed all round that he was rich as a lord. This proved to be far from the case, but Mrs. Rondeau had never grasped the true nature of her circumstances.

Genevieve had rescheduled the rest of his appointments so that when Kate Striker came into the room, young, fresh, and beautiful, Amos rose stiffly and wondered why he had feared a visit from such a handsome young person.

"You're going to think I'm crazy."

"That I very much doubt."

But his foreboding returned. He remembered discussing this young lady with Father Dowling, a discussion that had brought back what he had come to think of as the nadir of his career. With Father Dowling he had been able to invoke professional confidentiality. He had waived that in the case of Nancy Walsh, though of course there were things he had not said. How he might handle questions from Kate Striker herself he did not know.

"There are judicial records of adoptions, are there not?"

"Of course."

"I've been told that they're no help in my case. But that has to be an exception."

"It is."

"Good. Well, I would like to have you find out who the mother of Jerome Winegar was."

"Jerome Winegar." No one hearing Amos repeat the name would have had any inkling that he was astounded beyond belief. At one and the same time, she had allayed his fear and surprised him in a totally unpredictable way.

"He is an orphan. That's why he was at St. Peter's. I talked to him about it."

"You talked with Jerome Winegar about this?"

"I visited him in jail."

He looked at her. *When I was in jail, you visited me.* How seldom he himself had had the opportunity to perform those deeds that are the condition of salvation. Some of them perhaps. Increasingly now he visited the sick and with almost equal frequency buried the dead.

"Tell me about it."

Always let the client talk. Be slow to give advice. Within reason, agree with what the client wishes to do in any case. Amos had learned that, by and large, the client wishes the lawyer to endorse what the client has already decided to do. As often as not, the decision is as good as anything the lawyer might suggest. He had lectured to law students on the matter. None of his hard-won lore was of any help in the present case.

"As I understand it," he said carefully, "he expressed no curiosity about his origins."

"That's what he said."

"You don't believe him?"

"He has to care."

"Maybe preferring ignorance is a way of caring."

"I want to find out for him."

"But if he doesn't wish to know . . ."

"I may not tell him. I will decide that later."

He sat in silence, whispering a little prayer to St. Thomas More, his professional colleague.

"I can afford it. I was left lots of money."

He smiled at this. He did not like to think how much of his practice had to do with quarrels over money, directly or indirectly. It may not be the root of all evil, but it was the source of most legal business.

"It is a relatively simple matter to discover."

"Will you do it?"

"Yes."

She sat back and sighed. "I'm so glad. Driving down here, I kept thinking that you wouldn't want to do it, that you would think it stupid."

"I haven't said that I think it wise."

68

Maybe his brains weren't in his feet, but his charm was, and Willie had known it since he was a kid. He could count on the toes of one foot the girls who had treated his attempt to get something going with anything but laughter. They couldn't believe he was serious. He accommodated his style to that, adopting a self-mockery that was a kind of preemptive strike. But just put him on a dance floor and he was the beau of the ball.

He had a friend named Lloyd who played the piano by ear. Nobody in his family played any musical instrument, but Lloyd sat down at a piano one day and began to fool around, and the next thing he knew he was playing boogie and jazz like he'd just come up the river from New Orleans. There were nights when they didn't pay for one drink because Lloyd could play any song you could hum and people loved it. Willie's dancing was something like that.

He just knew how to dance. Give him a little music, and he could do what Fred Astaire did in the movies, but it was the lindy that was his specialty. When he first heard the phrase Lucky Lindy, he thought it referred to the dance. Maybe it did. Using your feet for dancing is a self-contained thing. In the movies they dance down the street, but try that in Fox River and you'll be up on charges. Willie's fatal charm was confined to the dance floor.

A girl who had loved it when the other dancers stopped and formed a circle so everyone could see her and Willie do it the way it was supposed to be done, often had trouble remembering his name when the dancing was over. It was his fate to be excellent at an essentially trivial activity.

Marjorie White had seemed an exception. At her age, what was left but dancing? He took advantage of Dr. Walsh's visits and had his teeth cleaned and polished; he smiled a lot while he danced. Marjorie's old man had left her enough to get along, although she whined about how much other women had; women like Clara and Barbara.

"Barbara!" Willie shook his head. "What's wrong with her?"

"You mean wearing black?"

"That and moping around. How long's she been a widow?"

"It's not her husband she's wearing black for. It's Mitchell Striker."

"She is nuts."

"People say I'm nuts too."

"Yeah?"

"There are those who are skeptical about your stated reasons for spending several years in Joliet."

"That was the agreement. If it ever came out, they would deny it."

He had given her the story half as a joke, but she swallowed it, and then he was stuck with it. But it was the same old problem. On the dance floor she was a great partner, responding to every move, the slightest pressure, intuiting what he was going to do. They were great together, on the floor. But off, he had to tell her lies. And eventually she stopped believing him. The magic was gone and she saw him for what he was, an ex-con janitor in a parish school in Fox River, Illinois.

He wasn't complaining, don't get him wrong. He had had it worse, a lot worse. Marie Murkin was a pain and Edna Hospers was distant, but Father Dowling was a prince. Three squares, an apartment, the kind of work that people couldn't quite tell whether you had done or not. A corridor is a corridor, whether or not it's swept every day.

A couple days ago, Winegar stopped by and said he'd been over to the rectory to say hello to Marie Murkin.

"Sure you were."

Winegar laughed. "You're right. I really came to see you."

He was the kind of guy you wanted to believe even when he let you know he was lying.

"Come into my parlor," Willie said, opening the door of his apartment.

"I wondered where you took the ladies."

"Whoa. Never on church property. It's a rule of mine."

"How's Marjorie?"

"Marjorie who?"

"She caught on to you, huh?"

"Not everyone has your luck."

"Some luck. A girl has to be killed before they admit I'm innocent."

"Is that what they admitted?"

"You think they're going to try me again?"

"I hope not."

Willie meant it. He hated trials; he hated the way they usually ended; he hated parole boards and all the rest of it. For himself and for anyone else. Winegar leaned over and punched his arm. Willie offered him a beer, but Winegar had a Coke.

"On the wagon?"

"I think it's lost its charm for me, Willie. All my life, when things went bad, I could trace it to booze. That was a bit of a scare, being tried for murder. It clears the mind."

"You're right. I only drink beer myself now."

Winegar smiled, as if he knew what that was worth. "You know this parish pretty well, don't you?"

Willie shrugged. He could sense he was going to be asked a favor.

"You know a family named Walsh?"

"Striker's daughter?"

"That's the one. What do you know about her?"

"Nothing."

"What do you mean, nothing?"

"They don't live in the parish. I guess they used to, but that was back in the Ice Age, when Marie Murkin was young."

Winegar laughed. "I won't tell her you said that."

"Anything I know about the Walshes I read in the paper."

"Kate Striker came to see me in jail."

"Who's she?"

"Striker's adopted daughter."

"No kidding. So why you asking?"

"Asking what?"

"About the Walshes."

"Because you won't give me the lowdown on Marjorie."

"She's a great dancer."

"Dancing is the vertical expression of a horizontal desire. Or, as T. S. Eliot put it . . ."

"Those his real initials? T. S."

"They stand for Thomas Stearns."

"Not where I come from."

"Didn't you say that Nancy Walsh sometimes helped out here?"

"No."

"No, she doesn't?"

"No, I never said it. Maybe you mean Clara Ponader."

"She here now?"

"I haven't seen her for weeks. Maybe she's in mourning too."

"I don't get you."

He had thought Winegar might have noticed Barbara Rooney. "I meant during your trial."

"She never came to see me."

Was he serious? "Why you asking about the Walshes?"

Winegar looked as if he wished he hadn't asked. "You got another Coke?"

Father Dowling went into the front parlor, where Barbara Rooney, a portrait of dignified desolation, sat on the edge of a chair, hands in her lap. She looked up when he came in, her eyes wide with the wisdom of the tragic heroine. Marie had been putting off Barbara, suggesting that the pastor's schedule was more demanding that it was, and for once Father Dowling was glad for her tendency to interfere. But there are things that, though they may be postponed, cannot be avoided.

"Barbara, how good to see you." Moral theologians had a way of explaining that such remarks are not lies. As it happened, Barbara herself was in the grips of a problem in moral theology.

"I do not wish to go to confession, Father. First, I need some advice."

"Ah."

"I think you must have heard that before his tragic death, Mitchell Striker and I . . ."

He waited. What he had heard and what she thought he had heard were probably very different things. Her eyes became yet more expressive, changing as a landscape changes under low moving clouds, now bright, now dark, now bright again.

"Mitchell and I, well, even at our ages, the heart remains vulnerable. We had arrived at an understanding. One of souls. It had not yet reached expression."

"I see."

"What was Cardinal Newman's motto?"

Good Lord, this was worse than he feared. "Heart speaks to heart."

Her hands went up in a helpless gesture. "That's it. That's it exactly. He knew, Father. He *knew.*"

"Across a crowded room?" Ezio Pinza, wasn't it? ("Autumn Leaves"? "September Song"?)

"Yes!" She lifted her clasped hands and moved them rapidly. If she were holding them over her head, it would have been the gesture of the winner of a boxing match.

When calm returned, she told him that she felt closer to Mitchell now than she had while he was alive. She had enrolled him with several religious houses that said masses for the dead in perpetuity. She had also asked Father Dowling to commemorate Mitchell Striker in his mass, a little gesture at local business even while she went national. If Father Dowling had made a guess at this point as to Barbara's problem in moral theology, it would have been the propriety of this kind of concern for Striker's soul when her concern for Matt Rooney's had been more restrained. How wrong he would have been.

She shifted her weight and fixed her eyes on the floor.

"Father, is it possible to have impure thoughts of the dead?"

"I'm not sure I understand."

"When I said ours was an affair of the heart, I meant that."

"Of course."

"But the heart is bodily, Father Dowling. It is flesh if anything is."

"I think you're right."

"At first it was simply dreams. Very consoling dreams. Now it has become daydreams. In them, he has become increasingly ardent." Her eyes flashed at him, then returned to the floor.

Her question might be stated as, can one commit necrophilia in the heart? It was a delicate moment. What he, despite himself, saw as high comedy was anything but to her. So he said the things one says in such cases, to teenagers, but not only to teenagers. Barbara's conscience, despite the imaginary nature of Mitchell Striker's attitude toward her— Edna told him that no one had ever seen any indication whatsoever that the late investment adviser even knew who Barbara was—was a refined one. In an age when orgies are considered a discussable practice, it was good to hear someone speak of the subtler shades of desire. There was, of course, the danger of scrupulosity. No way occurred to Father Dowling to convey to her that, ardent as Mitchell Striker had posthumously become, he had been unaware of her in life.

He took Barbara to the front door and watched her walk off toward the school, drifting wraithlike through her inner world. O the mind, the mind has mountains, frightful, sheer . . .

As he stood there, Amos Cadbury arrived. The contrast between the arriving lawyer and the departing Barbara Rooney seemed a parable on the different ways in which age makes itself known. Amos had become the sublimation of his earlier selves, more perfectly now what he had professionally always been. But the look of concern suggested that he, like Barbara and the rest of us, dwelled in the valley of tears.

Inside, Amos was courteous to Marie, as always, eliciting a girlish delight from her, and the pastor hoped that his housekeeper would not misread ardor in these exquisite manners. But Marie kept her feet on the ground. She offered tea and Amos reacted with a delight that suggested she had introduced the beverage to a grateful public. They waited until she had served it—this took no time at all; she had, of course, known that Amos was coming—and soon Father Dowling and the lawyer were behind the closed door of the study.

"You may remember our conversation of some weeks ago about Kate Striker, Father."

"Yes, I do."

"She has come to see me."

"I see."

"Perhaps you do. I myself was quite surprised. She has asked me to check the local records as to Jerome Winegar's birth."

"Winegar!"

"You too are surprised. I was equally surprised to learn that she had visited the man while he was in jail. Given the charge he was under, that seemed an odd thing for her to do. She said that they discussed the fact that they are both orphans."

"That's a dramatic way to put it."

Father Dowling was aware that he and Amos were discussing matters about which they both had privileged information. He now thought he understood why Amos had felt it necessary to break off that earlier meeting in his office. Kate's interest in Winegar's origins seemed a metaphor for her concern about her own. Clearly Amos wondered what he might be getting into with respect to the latter if he did something about the former.

"At the risk of impropriety, I am asking if you know any reason why I should or should not take on this task."

"Am I mistaken in thinking that it is something she could easily found out herself?"

"Father, almost all the things we lawyers do can be done by a layman. You can defend yourself in court; you can demand access to public records; you can write your own will. There are books instructing people on these and other things."

Amos's tone did not convey the profound disapproval he felt toward this trend. As for lawyers' advertising, a topic on which Amos held a stern but minority view, this had now evolved into televised appeals to injury victims to avail themselves of the litigious services of the advertiser. Where would it all end?

"Can you tell me why she wants this information about Winegar?"

"She isn't sure. Apparently he expressed indifference about the matter, and she hopes to change his attitude. The knowledge would be a little gift for him."

"Out of Pandora's box?"

"Perhaps, perhaps."

"Amos, I would not be surprised if that information isn't included in the papers that were taken from St. Peter's School. Papers that were found in Winegar's possession. He may already know what she wants him to learn."

Amos lifted his long-fingered hands, then dropped them in his lap.

"It seems, then, that I can do no harm in helping her."

"I have a somewhat more delicate problem. As you know, Kate has come into a considerable amount of money."

"In the millions, I believe."

"There was so much to leave because of Mitchell Striker's great talent as a nurturer of money. Money, I'm told, cannot bear neglect. Six million dollars can't just be put into a savings account and forgotten. It seems that James Walsh has undertaken to be the interim manager."

"The dentist?" Amos barely mastered his surprise.

"Nancy's husband. She would very much like to have Bob Frankman manage Kate's money. He is willing. Now I have to get Kate to agree."

"That sounds like a straightforward matter, Father Dowling."

Roger Dowling made arrangements to have a retired Franciscan, Father Placidus, come say mass on the day he arranged to be in Milwaukee talking with Kate.

"That's very shrewd," Marie said.

"Having a noon mass?"

"Having a friar substitute. There are those who will remember what it was like in those days and be all the more appreciative of the present."

"Father Placidus is a saint."

"He may well be. But he will look like those that weren't."

"I am delighted to have him. There is no longer a large pool of priests one can ask in like this."

"I pray for vocations every day."

"Just so you don't get one."

Marie glared at him. He knew her opinion of all the agitation for women's ordination.

Influenced by Amos Cadbury's suggestion that it was no problem, Father Dowling came straight to the point with Kate after they had ordered. The restaurant was filled with the smell of boiled food and beer and the distinctive voices of students.

"There's no rush, Father."

"I suppose not."

"I mean Jim has got me tied up in something very fancy."

"How fancy?" He remembered Bob Frankman's remark, and it occurred to him that Nancy's reasons for wanting someone other than Jim looking out for Kate might not be exhausted by the fact that he had a busy practice.

"I didn't want to hear the details, Father. He needed my okay and I gave it."

"That would be a written okay, I suppose."

She nodded. His mission seemed, if not pointless, then less pressing.

"There's a man named Bob Frankman who is very good with money."

Kate made a face. "Jim can't stand him."

"Is that so?"

"Called him a buccaneer who had lost scads of money for him."

"I think he may have meant the St. Peter's endowment."

"That too."

When would Bob Frankman have had anything to do with Jim's money? It had been Father Dowling's understanding that Mitchell Striker took care of Nancy and Jim's money.

"We're not going to talk about money, are we?" Kate asked.

"Not until the bill comes."

70

"The seafood bisque is marvelous, Amos."

Amos said that he was becoming once more familiar with the menu of the Cliffdwellers, dining more frequently at the club as a show of solidarity in their effort not to be evicted from the quarters they had occupied since the club's founding. Bob Frankman had adopted a very proprietary attitude toward the club. He was frankly cultivating Amos, a truly distinguished citizen but one in whom Frankman detected, beneath the veneer of politeness, a distaste for the various stations of Frankman's career.

They began with the bisque. Amos seemed content to let him lead the conversation as if he wondered what would be the small talk of a man who had left the priesthood, divorced his first wife, and had the marriage that had produced two children declared null and void. Amos had no interest in sports, whether as a participant or a spectator, and this closed a vast area of male camaraderie. Somewhat to Amos's consternation, Frankman spoke of his class reunion.

"At St. Mary's?"

He became quite voluble, veering toward the sentimental, as he talked of getting together in that place with men he had known so well.

"Of course, I've kept in touch with many of them. Roger Dowling was there."

"You were classmates?"

"Yes."

The expression on Amos Cadbury's face posed the question: Was it progress to blur the distinction between those who fulfilled their promises and those who did not? It is one thing not to make the former priest a pariah but quite another to pretend that he has not abandoned his vocation. Soon it would be as it was with divorce, which since it no longer carried any stigma, became ever more frequent.

294

"I applied just in time, Amos."

"Is there a statute of limitations?"

"This pope slammed the door. It was one of the first things he did. It is no longer an easy matter to obtain laicization. It has become rare."

Amos seemed cheered by this and changed the topic. "I understand that you will be looking out for Kate Striker's money."

"If there's any left when Jim Walsh gets done with it."

"Aren't there millions involved?"

Frankman hunched forward. "I speak from bitter experience, Amos. You must have heard of the drubbing I took right after I assumed responsibility for the St. Peter's endowment from Mitchell Striker. There is a scheme involving international markets whereby one in effect bets on percentage rises. . . ."

Amos held up his hand. "Such details are lost on me, Robert."

"All right. Suffice it to say that some made unbelievable amounts overnight. But there were losers too. A whole British financial institution went under. I lost what I risked for the school. Earlier I had made money, for myself and for Jim Walsh. He was eager to try again. He lost at the same time as St. Peter's."

"It sounds like gambling."

"Investing is a species of gambling. Naturally, we avoid the word. There is a famous essay called 'On the Vice of Gambling and the Virtue of Insurance.' Same idea."

"I thought Mitchell managed the Walsh money."

"He did, he did. This was very hush-hush. Jim wanted to get out from under his father-in-law's thumb. Afterward, he went crying to Mitchell Striker. That is what really lay behind Mitchell's public rebuke of what I had done. Well, once burned, twice shy."

"That sounds wise."

"I wish Jim would see that. I'm afraid he wants to recover as quickly as he lost."

"With Kate Striker's money?"

Frankman lifted his brows in assent. Amos pondered this. He could imagine what Mitchell would have said to his son-in-law. His public rebuke of Bob Frankman would be mild indeed by comparison. He had treated James like a boy, and he himself ran his daughter's life for her. Just imagine his reaction to young Walsh's going to a rival investment adviser.

"Kate Striker is an amazing young lady," Amos observed.

"Perhaps I will come to know her better if I get the chance to restore her fortune."

"She has given me an astonishing assignment."

"You mean she is your client?"

Amos nodded. "I think it is more or less public knowledge that she became curious about her own origins after the death of Mitchell Striker. She confronted a brick wall. What she imagined to be their similar situations, led her to visit Winegar in prison."

"Good God."

"Fellow orphans, you see. Winegar told her he had no interest in finding out who his parents were."

"What difference could it make?"

"Kate found it difficult to believe his indifference. Hence my assignment." Anxiety had been rising in Frankman since this turn in the conversation. "She wants me to discover Winegar's origins."

"Are you going to do it?"

"I am hoping that you will do it."

"Me!"

"However indirectly the public record is consulted, it is possible that a rumor will be started. Any connection of such an inquiry with Kate Striker—or, I might add, with me—could have unsavory consequences."

"Absolutely."

"But there is another way."

"How is that?"

"The papers that were stolen from St. Peter's will be returned quite soon. Perhaps they already have been. It is my hunch that information about Winegar's parents will be found in his application papers at the school. You are on the board. . . ." Amos opened his hands.

"Leave it to me."

"I knew I could count on you."

His first feeling was of relief. What if Amos had simply checked the county record of births? Perhaps no one would immediately match the name on Winegar's birth certificate with the housekeeper Father Frankman had run off with, marrying her before a justice of the peace. Amos thought gossip about Winegar and Kate Striker might harm the girl. But what would the sensationalist media make of the fact that Bob Frankman had married and divorced the mother of Jerome Winegar? That had to be prevented at any cost. But how?

The papers at St. Peter's he could take care of. He would take care of them.

"If the information is not in the St. Peter's archives, I suppose there is no way the name could have been kept out of the public record."

296

"The mother's?"

"Yes."

Amos looked thoughtfully at him and then said, "I don't imagine she could have afforded to bribe an official. Assuming that she cared."

Some semblance of peace descended on Frankman's soul. What might have been done years ago, might be done in retrospect, by getting to the right person. A little alteration of the database and Elena Winegar would cease to exist, so far as the public record was concerned.

As an officer of the court, Tuttle could scarcely be indifferent to what Winegar had told him about seeing a man get out of the car in which Mitchell Striker's body was found. This put another killer—well, a killer— in the real world, no longer merely a theoretical requirement to account for the body. He had been seen.

He could easily imagine Winegar denying having said any such thing. Everything he knew about the man was contradictory. The obvious reason for his coming back to Fox River was to settle that old score, but he said he had come back out of nostalgia. Just being cute? Maybe. Tuttle realized that he had a far deeper and more disinterested desire to know what had happened than he did when he was Winegar's attorney. And the reason was Lucy Sommers. Tuttle felt responsible for her death.

More responsible than Winegar, who had arguably been at least an indirect cause, feeding her the description of the bearded man who had claimed to be the former tenant of her apartment. She had been killed because she could recognize him, but what difference did that make? Who was he, and what had he done, and how could Lucy Sommers know these things and thereby pose a threat?

Tuttle wanted to pose these questions to Winegar, but he could not find him. He stopped by Jude Thaddeus House at feeding time, and the derelicts were lined up to go through the line.

"Get in the back," someone growled. A young man with a dedicated expression came up to him. "Go to the end of the line and take a tray."

"I'm Tuttle the lawyer."

"I don't care if you're Sinbad the sailor, you've got to get in line."

"Is Winegar here?"

"The salad dressing is on the table."

Tuttle got out of there, indignant. Maybe he did need a new hat. But his tweed was a gift from his father, and to give it up would be to give up his good luck charm.

Actually the food had smelled pretty good, and he realized he was hungry. He found Peanuts asleep in the squad room. He bent over and whispered in his ear, "Shrimp fried rice, shrimp fried rice."

An eye opened. "You buying?"

From Peanuts he learned that the police investigation had not been closed down after the prosecutor's decision. That decision, the assumption was, had been made on the basis of the available evidence. Maybe more convincing evidence could be gathered.

"Step one is to solve the girl's murder."

"Exactly. Who's on it?"

"Horvath."

"Alone?"

Any allusion, however oblique, to Agnes Lamb could have a volcanic effect on the otherwise even-tempered Peanuts Pianone.

"Alone!"

After they finished eating, Peanuts wanted to go to Tuttle's office for a siesta.

"You go ahead; I have something to do."

"Is that woman there?"

The secretary. He had let her go. The place was so clean and neat, a man could hardly work there anymore. And she had objected to the accumulation of fast-food detritus.

"What the hell is detritus?" Peanuts wanted to know.

"What de treat is."

Peanuts accepted that. Tuttle told himself he would look it up. It was a pleasure to tell the woman that he was scaling back and had to let her go.

"That saves me the trouble of giving notice."

Horvath was not in his office. Agnes Lamb said he was on a job, so Tuttle went down to the dispatcher and had her contact Horvath's car.

"Can we talk, Horvath?"

"Talk."

"I mean get together."

"You going to be at your office?"

"I can be in front of the courthouse."

"In ten minutes?"

"Yup."

After the lawyer got into the passenger seat, Horvath drove around and listened impassively while Tuttle told him what he had been thinking.

"Everyone figures the bearded guy in the picture killed her."

"Yeah."

"Why?"

Horvath nodded. He obviously found this line of thinking familiar. "What did he think she knew?"

"She didn't know anything."

"He must have thought she did."

Horvath had sunk into a deep Hungarian pensiveness. When he came out of it, he said to Tuttle, "Know what it sounds like? It sounds like Winegar's got an accomplice. The girl is the ace in the hole. There doesn't have to be a bearded man at all. If there is and he's killing people who knew he was at that apartment, then he ought to kill Winegar too."

"Maybe he will."

"Where's Winegar?"

"I've been trying to find out."

Horvath remembered Keegan mentioning that Winegar had been back to St. Hilary's since he had been set free—when the pastor wasn't there, Marie had told Phil. So they stopped to talk with Willie.

"I understand you're our undercover agent, Willie."

"It was a line, Lieutenant, just a line. Telling a woman you're an ex-con tends to cool them off."

"I'm reactivating you. Why did Winegar come by here?"

"Geez, I don't know."

Horvath sat down and unbuttoned his jacket. He tipped his felt hat back. He looked like he was settling in. Willie began babbling, telling them everything he could remember about Winegar's visit.

"He said he came to see Marie Murkin, but that's bunk. He knew Dowling wasn't here, so it wasn't to see him."

"He came to see you, Willie."

"Why? We ain't friends. I don't know the guy."

Suddenly he shut up and the effort of thinking showed on his narrow face.

"He asked me about some people—did I know them."

"The name, Willie."

"I'm thinking."

And he visibly was. His face was screwed up with the effort. And then the wrinkles dissolved.

"Walsh. He asked me did I know the Walshes."

The arrest and indictment of Jerome Winegar had come as a tremendous relief to Nancy Walsh. That he had come back, after all these years, had filled her with disgust and then with fear when she considered the trouble he could cause. His cold rejection of her when she had told him what she supposed was their unexpected yet happy news had burned itself into her memory, and nothing could ever eradicate it. It had blotted out all the things about him she had loved. Her father's stubbornness, and his, had collided. He had suffered, and through the years she had imagined him as malevolent, hating her father, hating her.

Had he ever wondered about the baby they had made?

When her father was killed, she had known immediately it must be Jerome. That was why he had come back. Not to see her. Not to find out at last what had happened to her and the baby. But to get his revenge on the man who had exacted the greatest punishment for what he had done to his daughter.

His arrest, the continuing inquiries, the fact that at any time he could say what he chose about his motivation, about the circumstances of his hatred for Mitchell Striker, had made her feel more vulnerable to his cruelty than she had all those years ago. She had lived in the daily dread that her long-kept secret might become a matter of news and public gossip.

And now he was free. He was free and her father was gone. She prayed that he would go away into the obscurity from which he had returned. Her indignation that he could do this dreadful thing and then be allowed to go went hand in hand with her renewed dread that now he would turn his malevolent attention to her.

Jim had been deeply affected by the death of her father; she sensed this, but he also had the continuing duties of his practice as well as the additional duty of looking after their finances. Dad had always done that, and Nancy wished they would find someone else—Jason Broderick, Bob Frankman—to do it because along with everything else, it obviously weighed heavily upon Jim.

"Bob Frankman," he repeated.

"Well, Jason then. Someone."

He laughed in an unamused way. "Part of their mystique is to get us to believe they know something we don't. The fact of the matter is they devote all their time to it. That's the difference."

And Dad? She didn't ask that question; she didn't want to quarrel about something as stupid as money. When Kate reacted to her good fortune by suggesting she would just give it away, something in Nan responded to that impulse. What freedom it would be, not to have investments and holdings and possessions, to have only what they needed to live on. But then she thought of such extras as the lake place.

It was where she and Jerome Winegar had gone so long ago, to the original cottage. That was something the years had smoothed over, otherwise she could never have gone back there. When she and Kate were there a few weeks ago, when she had told her everything, almost everything, that visit to the cabin with Jerome came back into her memory, but it had been purged by at last telling someone of the torture she had endured all those years ago.

Jim had been saying something sarcastic about Bob Frankman's astuteness, apparently referring to the mistake he had made with the endowment at St. Peter's.

"I remember what Dad said about that."

He looked at her, then turned away. Had she missed the point of what he'd said? She went up to him and lay her hand flat on his back, gently, but he seemed almost to cringe at her touch. Then, abruptly, he turned and took her in his arms, gathering her to him as if he would crush her in his embrace.

"Everything will be all right."

Did she seem so mopey that she still needed reassurance? She was surprised at how quickly she had adjusted to the absence of her father. That was partly explained by the illusion created by the unchanged look of his apartment. But the place had begun to lose some of its power; she had used it too often.

"Let's go to the lake, Jim."

"Next weekend?"

"Now."

He stepped back and smiled down at her. "And what about my patients?"

"Oh, damn your patients."

"I often feel the same way."

"Can't you just cancel and reschedule?"

"Two and a half days' worth of appointments? It would take me months to straighten it out. We'll go up this weekend."

"This weekend."

"Nan, why don't you go up there now, have a few days by yourself first, and then we'll have the weekend together."

"You'll have the boys with you."

"That's all right. I'll bring them with me when I come on Saturday. Maybe Friday night."

It seemed self-indulgent and a little deceptive to act as if she were in a fragile condition and needed to recover, but the prospect of the lake, as always, appealed to her. And perhaps she did need a time of quiet and solitude after the events of recent weeks. There was, as well, her recent stay with Kate there that added to her sense of the lake as a place of reconciliation and peace.

The traffic on I-94 was heavy, and it was good to get into Wisconsin and leave it for lesser roads. Southern Wisconsin is one of the most beautiful places in the world, or so Nancy thought, and to be driving through the gently rolling hills where fields and pastures alternated was to return to the landscape of her youth. In an hour the terrain became wilder, less cultivated, and then she turned off onto the country road that led to the lake and their driveway. After she turned in and parked, she shut off the motor and sat for a time, letting the soothing sounds of the lake wash over her. What a wonderful suggestion that she come up early and alone.

Shadows were lengthening and the surface of the lake changed colors as the sun went slowly down. Nancy decided against preparing a meal and took some yogurt from the freezer and was about to turn on the television when she decided not to. This would be a kind of retreat, a shutting out of the world for a time while she restored her inner resources.

There was a paperback copy of Henry James's *The Wings of the Dove* that Kate had left. Nancy picked it up. It was the kind of novel one always intended to read and didn't, and this seemed a good time. The dense obliquity of the prose often made it necessary to read passages over to understand what they meant. After five pages, she gave up. James might be the master of the novel, as the copy on the back cover said, but the glacial pace, the overanalysis, and the precious style made for a punishing experience for the reader. Maybe some other time.

After she put down the novel, she closed her eyes and almost immediately fell asleep. When she awoke, it was dark and the cottage had grown cold with the coming of night. She checked the doors and stumbled into her bedroom, not wanting to become fully awake, and within moments was again asleep.

The clock read nine-thirty when she awoke. The sun was at the windows; there was the sound of a motor out on the lake and the soft whisper of the wind in the willow outside. She lay on her back, wondering how long she had slept, and the silly thing was that she was sure she could fall asleep again. This confirmed her sense that the last several weeks had taken more of a toll on her than she had realized.

Everything about the cottage reminded her of her father. But then her whole life had been dominated by him, ever since those events of long ago. When he could not bring about the result he wanted, he continued to preside over the unfolding of events. No wonder she had acquired the sense that nothing could go seriously wrong while she had her father to rely on. And so it had proved to be. It occurred to her how much Jim had married into her family, reversing the biblical passage, so that it was her people who became his. And her father had overseen their affairs, helped them in the purchase of the house, managed their finances, and finally, moved into the apartment that had been prepared for him in their home. These thoughts made her realize what a loss she had suffered. She had so little practice in relying on Jim.

What a patient man her husband was, self-effacing, happy to let her father make decisions. A lesser man might have resented that, but Jim had never shown any reluctance to accept Mitchell Striker's preeminence in their family. Almost never.

Some months ago, raised voices had reached her from the apartment, and she realized it was her father and Jim, apparently arguing. This was so unusual, she scarcely believed it. Whatever had been the cause, she did not want to know it. She felt a sense of vertigo at the thought of anyone rebelling against her father. When Jim came back to the house, he disappeared into the den, and by the time they went to bed, there was no trace of anger. It was almost possible to think that she had dreamed it.

After breakfast, call it brunch, she took Jane Austen out to the gazebo and found it far more to her taste. If Jane Austen was a great psychologist, James by contrast seemed paranoid. The familiar story, the simple wisdom, combined with the sounds of summer to take her back to her girlhood when she had read like this by the hour. She sighed and looked across the yard to the original cottage and the unbidden memory came. It was there that she and Jerome Winegar . . .

But she refused to think of it. From the house came the sound of the telephone, and Nancy groaned, realizing that she had forgotten to bring the portable phone with her. She ran across the yard and into the house and snatched up the receiver.

"Hello!" she cried, relieved that the line was not dead.

But no one replied.

"Hello?"

And then someone put down the phone.

She hated people who did that. It is one thing to dial a wrong number, but not to say anything when a stranger answers is far worse. When she went back to the gazebo, she took the portable phone with her, not wanting to have to repeat that twenty-yard dash.

She actually took a nap after lunch and then went swimming to stir up her blood, to wake up. Relaxation was a good thing, but she had not come up here to sleep the time away. Back in the house she showered and decided she would prepare the same meal she and Kate had had. Outside, she lit the grill and put the patties on, then stopped. She had heard something behind her. Her eyes lifted over the lake but there was not a boat on it.

"Hello."

She turned, her heart in her throat. Jerome Winegar stood next to the willow, smiling at her from twenty years ago.

"The place has changed," he said. "You haven't much."

She stared at him, her fright draining away, even her surprise. This was what she had expected ever since his return; she had always been certain that he had come back to see her. The imagined, rehearsed, exalted confrontations in which she had once triumphed over him seemed silly now that he stood before her, smiling, assuming a nonchalance she doubted he felt.

"What do you want?"

"To talk."

She shook her head. "There is nothing to talk about."

"May I?" He slumped into a wicker chair that stood upon the lawn and allowed his gaze to travel over the lake. He is showing me his profile, she thought. He thinks he still has power over me. He looked up at her suddenly. "Tell me about our child."

"How dare you."

"That's right. It is a dare. You owe me no account. I've gotten to know Kate."

Nancy sat some ten feet from him, in a matching wicker chair, and looked at him with horror.

"You leave Kate alone."

He held up a hand and shook his head slowly. "It isn't like that at all."

My God, she had never dreamed it was. But then she began to talk and could not stop, talking about that young journalist he had taken advantage of who was now dead and was not much older than Kate.

"We were much younger than she was."

"I forbid you to talk about anything having to do with you and me."

"You sound like your father, the Torquemada of St. Peter's School."

"And don't mention my father."

"I am sorry about what happened to him."

This was too much. Nancy accepted the common wisdom that this was her father's assassin. That was part of the horror of his coming here. But far more horrible was his assumption that she would sit down and chat with him about the consequences of his treachery.

"That's the place I remember." He had turned in his chair and was looking at the original cottage. It was painful to her that he had carried about with him all these years memories of when they had been close. In love. But that was what she found difficult to believe.

Had he ever grown up, she wondered. Apparently he had lived his life without taking on the responsibilities of a man. No duties, no obligation, no one dependent on him. His only goal had been to please himself. She saw all that, or thought she saw it, and wholeheartedly endorsed her father's decision to send him packing when he had rejected her. Thank God he had. At the time it had seemed horrible beyond belief. Even when she had given Kate a laundered version of those past events, the sadness and anguish had come flooding back, and she remembered how her heart had been broken.

But what if he had agreed to marry her, what if through all the intervening years she had been tied to this posturing pathetic Don Juan. That was written all over him. He had become a lady's man. He had diminished. Most pathetic of all was his assumption that he could once again charm her. He was looking at her now with sad eyes.

"I am sorry for what I did, Nan."

"You did me a great favor."

"Then I deserve no credit for it."

"No, you don't."

"And the child?"

"Don't."

"Please bear with me just this once. I'll go soon and it will be over. Kate regards me as an orphan, and she considers that a bad thing. I mean, who am I? I don't know and I don't care. I've always felt a bit like Adam. He has a belly button in all the pictures and so do I, but neither of us has a mother. But what if our child should feel the way Kate does?"

"I want you to go. I will not discuss these matters with you."

He leaned back in his chair, gripped its arms, and looked at her coldly, a look that seemed to be directed at her from decades ago. "We're alone here, aren't we?"

She said nothing. They were alone. The cabin was isolated; that was the point of it. There was only one other property abutting the lake, and that was in a cove on the southern shore, out of sight of the Striker cabin. Her anger gave way and fear began to return.

"Don't be an ass, Jerry."

"Jerry?"

There was an insolence about him, she felt, an indifference to what she might feel or think. It made her want to strike out at him. She half turned away. "You can sit here if you want. But it is against my will. I am asking you to go. You are trespassing."

"Forgive us our trespasses, as we forgive those . . ."

"Is nothing sacred to you?"

She started toward the house, walking deliberately. It seemed like a very long distance to the door, but she had to get away from him. She heard the squeak of the wicker chair, and then she began to run. Once she got into the house, she would lock the door; she would telephone Jim, someone, to force him out of here.

He grabbed her by the arm and made her stop, turning her as he did, so that she nearly fell. She tried to jerk her arm free, but he held fast, grinning into her face. They stood there on the patio, seemingly locked in one another's arms, as she struggled to free herself.

He stepped back at the sound of a car door, and they stood in silence, listening. And then someone began to call out. Kate!

When Jim told her that Nan was at the lake, he suggested that Kate might want to join her sister there.

"I can't make it till the weekend. She just had to get away."

"Maybe she'd rather be alone."

"I think she'd like to have you there."

"I'll give her a call. Are you making me richer?"

"Are you asking for an accounting?" His tone was suddenly distant.

"Don't be silly."

She phoned the lake place and let the phone ring and ring, imagining Nan racing toward the house to answer it. Why didn't she get into the habit of taking the portable phone with her when she left the house? After a zillion rings she hung up. She would wait a while and call again. But she looked at her watch. If she went, she didn't intend to spend the night, but if she waited around, it would be too late to make the round trip at a reasonable hour. What the heck. She knew Nan was there. Jim was right; she would be glad to see her. So she started off.

When she turned off the road and started up the long driveway, she saw an unfamiliar car parked off the drive just below the knoll on which the house stood. Nan must have asked a guest to stay with her until Jim came up, and Kate had the feeling she might not be as welcome as Jim had thought. She should have been more patient and waited until she got through by phone.

When she came to where the car was parked, it occurred to her that it was an odd place to leave it, almost as if the driver hadn't wanted to be seen from the house. She stopped and cut her motor and pushed open the door. The reassuring sounds of the place made her apprehension seem silly. The car had dealer's plates, Illinois plates. And then she had it. Clara Ponader!

Kate left her car there too and went striding up the knoll and into sight of the house. She half expected to see Nan and Clara out under the trees, but there was no one in view. And then she heard voices from the patio on the far side of the house.

"Hello, hello, hello," she cried, coming around the house.

She stopped in her tracks. There on the patio, sitting in facing chairs, looking for all the world like old friends, were Nan and Jerry Winegar.

"What are you doing here?" she asked delightedly. "I've been wanting to see you ever since . . ."

"My great vindication? An amazing turn of events. I am here to say to Mrs. Walsh what an experience it has been to be accused of killing a man for whom I had such respect and admiration."

Kate pulled a chair toward the two of them, but before sitting down said, "Anyone want a beer? I'm having one."

"I'm a teetotaler, kiddo. Bring me a Coke."

"Nan?"

Nan sat there with the strangest smile on her face as if a film she was in had been frozen on one frame. She fluttered her hand. "Anything."

"How about coffee?"

"I haven't made any."

"Then I'll do it. You two just loll on the patio, and I'll wait on you hand and foot."

She found herself grinning like a fool as she made the coffee. What a surprise. And wasn't that nice of him to drive all the way up here to say those nice things to Nancy? All that stuff about admiration and respect was a bit thick, but then you talk that way to people who've had a loss, and losing her father was the biggest loss Nancy had ever experienced. From what she had heard of what Mitchell Striker had done to him long ago, Jerry's visit here was even more impressive.

She took a Coke out to Jerry and put her beer next to the chair she would sit in. "Coffee's on."

"You needn't have bothered, Kate."

"Bother? Coffee?" She headed back inside. It was in the kitchen that the thought hit her. Was it possible? The coffee seemed to be taking forever. She switched a cup for the pot and let it fill and then made the switch again and took the coffee out to Nan. The two of them seemed to have been sitting there in silence all this time.

"Say, did you by any chance know Jerry when he was at St. Peter's?"

"What a question!"

"Oh, I knew the families of all the board members," Jerry said, grinning at her.

"It was just an idea."

Nan was biting on her lip for some reason, and when their eyes met briefly, Nan's seemed full of tears. What the heck? And then Kate felt like a real fool. She got up, holding her beer.

"I came up here for a book I left. I'll go see if it's in the house."

"Book?" Nan cried. "What book?"

"The Wings of the Dove. Wait'll I see if it's here."

She got inside and out of their sight, and her face was on fire with a blush. Of course the two of them could have known each other before. When they were kids. Jerry hadn't mentioned it and neither had Nan, yet here they were all alone at the lake, and Jim didn't know about it either. Kate was sure there was no hanky-panky going on, but it was pretty clear she had broken into some kind of reunion. What a dope. She could just see herself, coming around the house to the patio, crying out, "Hello, hello, hello." She had heard their voices before she saw them, and neither one of them had said much since she showed up. She had to figure out a way to make a quick departure.

She went upstairs to the boys' room, the room she and Nan had used a few weeks ago. Driving from Milwaukee, she had imagined a few more hours like that with Nan, and it made the trip worthwhile. Nan obviously wasn't answering the phone; this had been a chance for the two of them to sit out on the patio and talk. She had a pretty good idea herself what fun it was to talk to him. No wonder Nan had wanted him all to herself.

Kate repeated to herself that it was nothing else. I mean, Jim knew Nan was here. He was due on the weekend, if not before. Still, Nan and Jerry had looked like a couple, sitting there on the patio, turning in surprise when she burst upon them.

Bob Frankman would not have said that he was following Amos Cadbury's advice when he took Dolores Corcoran across the street to Figuerro's Tap & Grill and watched her eat the special while he sipped a tall cold glass of draft beer.

"I already ate," he explained.

"So did I."

She ate with the relish of a gourmand. She was a woman of great appetites. Particularly for money.

"Let me state an imaginary problem, Dolores."

"Sure."

"Say someone wanted a record removed from the courthouse. A marriage, a death, a birth, whatever. Am I right that you've transferred all that into a computer database for easier access?"

"I supervised the operation myself. Now new records go right into the computer."

He shook his head. "It's changed everything. Libraries. Restaurants. Income tax."

"Please. Not while I'm eating."

"I could put you on to some legitimate ways to pay less taxes."

"Legitimate?"

"Absolutely. Of course, the best way is to take cash."

"That's hard to do in records."

"Let's go back to my imaginary problem."

It was a ritual dance, and Frankman took pleasure in the slow circling of the proposal, which never had to be made in so many words.

"How much money do you think you could save, Mr. Frankman?"

"I was thinking five hundred."

She made a face. "A thou."

"Done."

He went back across the street with her, but not until she had had the lemon meringue pie and two cups of coffee. He himself had had three beers. She took him into her office.

"Close the door, Bob." He had told her to call him Bob. She pointed to the computer beside her desk. "You bring the money, and we can handle it right here."

"I've got the money."

"A thousand?"

He brought out an envelope. "Yes."

She looked at the envelope greedily, then had a thought. "You said five."

"I assumed you would up the ante."

"What if I had asked for more?"

"We would have put it off until another day."

She thought about that. "Okay, a thousand it is. What do you want removed?"

If she was surprised at his instructions, she gave no sign of it. Her fat index fingers stabbed at the keyboard.

"Want to see what you're paying for?"

He got behind her so he could read the monitor. The entry recording Jerome Winegar's birth. Mother: Elena Winegar. Dolores hit a key and the entry was deleted. He dropped the envelope on her desk. When he had the door open, she said in a loud voice, "Thanks for lunch."

"My pleasure."

As he went across the great marble-floored area under the courthouse rotunda, he told himself that all he needed to do now was remove the record from St. Peter's and Elena's connection with Jerome Winegar would be gone forever.

If 'twere done 'twere well 'twere done quickly, he reasoned, since there was nothing to be gained by delay. When Gloria had shown him around before, he had taken careful note of how one might gain entrance to her domain—particularly someone with access to the key. Cottage had a weak sense of security. His master keys hung inside the cabinet in the outer office of the headmaster's suite. Frankman drove to the school from the courthouse, paid his respects to Cottage, and, having bade the headmaster good-bye, went down the hall fifty feet, turned, stepped into the outer office, opened the cabinet, and then was on his way again, armed with the keys.

It was not yet seven-thirty that evening when he was back. The windows of the headmaster's office were dark. Cottage would be in his living quarters on the far side of the campus. Frankman let himself into the administration building and went swiftly down the hall to the wing that housed the archives. He had decided against furtiveness. He knew what he was after. He would go and get those Winegar records and be gone. Accordingly, after he let himself into the archives, he turned on the lights and passed through Gloria's office into the temperature-controlled inner sanctum. He closed his eyes and summoned his memories of her tour of the place. With his eyes still closed, he moved to the relevant cabinet. He opened the drawer, his fingers moved over the tabs, and there they were. He pulled out the papers and began to look through them. He would take only what linked Winegar to Elena.

The records evoked another time, decisions on which a life had depended. He set aside one item, Winegar's application for admission to St. Peter's. His impulse was to take that and go, but an incomplete eradication of the connection was no eradication at all. He would be patient, and thorough.

"What are you doing in here?"

He froze. It was the unmistakable voice of Gloria behind him. Instinctively he began to stuff the papers inside his jacket. That was stupid. He turned.

"Ah, Gloria. I was hoping to find you here."

"How did you get in?"

"I used the headmaster's key."

"Is that how you expected to find me here?"

This must be how she talked to the boys. He considered the wisdom of calling her attention to his position in this school. But sweetness first.

"Remember the other day when you showed me around?"

"You are not answering my question."

"Something in these papers fascinated me." He waved the papers he had removed from the box. "I wanted to check them again."

"You broke in here, didn't you?"

"Now see here, Gloria. I resent your tone of voice."

"And I resent you breaking into the archives."

"What are you doing here at this hour, anyway?"

"Weren't you expecting to see me?"

"This is ridiculous."

She turned and left the cold inner room. Frankman stuffed the sheet on which he had found Elena's name into his pocket, put the rest back in the box, and returned it to its place. When he came into the outer office, Gloria was on the phone.

"Of course I will press charges," she said.

"Is that the headmaster?" Frankman held out his hand for the phone.

"It is the police."

He left. He had to get out of there and get rid of the paper he had removed and hope that there was nothing else in the Winegar papers about Elena.

"Just look at those headlines," Marie Murkin said with disgust. "When he was the financial genius nobody mentioned it, but as soon as he's arrested he's a former priest."

"St. Paul got arrested."

"St. Paul wasn't a former apostle."

Father Dowling laughed. "No, and I don't think he was a financial genius either."

Phil Keegan was there, glowering at the thought that anyone would rely on the newspaper for anything. "They've stolen every base on this up until now, and I don't suppose they're done yet. When we arrested Winegar, they painted him black as sin. When he was being tried, he was the underdog. Until we arrested Frankman, they were referring to Winegar as the man who got away with murder. Wait until tomorrow, Marie."

"I wish all readers of newspapers were as cynical as you."

"Philosophical, Marie," Father Dowling corrected.

"A man who's been married ten years doesn't talk like a bridegroom, but he's not a cynic." Phil was proud of his analogy.

"St. Paul didn't read the papers," Father Dowling said. "Phil, give us the straight, nonnewspaper account."

Bob Frankman had been surprised in the St. Peter's School archives by Gloria, once Father Gorman's secretary, now archivist. She found his explanation of how he had gotten into her locked domain and what he was doing there unsatisfactory and, in the light of recent events, called the police.

"She could call us but not arrest him. He left the school and went home, which is where we found him. I went myself, sending Cy to the school. Frankman tried to laugh the thing away, but since the original call mentioned the Winegar papers, I was as interested in the theft of those as I was in a charge of breaking and entering. Frankman was, after all, a member of the board, the school's financial adviser, and could have been doing things required by those functions. I didn't want us dragged into what might be some kind of intramural quarrel. You remember when Striker publicly criticized Frankman for the way he was handling the endowment."

Cy called to say that it was the Winegar papers that Frankman had been looking at and that at least one item was missing. Phil asked Frankman about that. He denied taking anything.

"If he had, he had also had plenty of time and opportunity to hide it, destroy it, or whatever since leaving the school."

Nothing had happened that night, but Dolores Corcoran from the courthouse came forward the next morning and said Bob Frankman had tried to bribe her into destroying an official record. It was a record involving Winegar.

"I pretended to delete it," she said.

"Did he pretend to pay you?"

"I turned in the money he gave me."

"What was the bribe?"

"Two hundred dollars."

Frankman was on his way to his office when arrested that morning. "He was madder than hell: Markets were opening, and he had the money of clients in his sacred trust. I told him the quicker we straightened things out, the quicker he would be back in his office," Phil said.

A warrant had been obtained to enter Frankman's apartment. What proved to be the ashes of a missing document were found in his fireplace. Gloria as a precaution had photocopied the Winegar documents when the judge returned them.

"The stolen and burned document had the name of Winegar's mother. That was the name he had bribed Dolly Corcoran to expunge from the county database," Phil said.

"What did he care about his mother for?" Marie asked.

"Right now that is the least of our worries."

What these developments suggested to the police, as they had to the newspapers, was that Frankman was deeply involved in the death of Mitchell Striker. The papers remembered, as Phil had, that Frankman had been publicly criticized by Striker.

"Up until a few weeks ago he wore a beard. He seems to have shaved it off about the time that composite picture was published by the Sommers girl."

Who had been brutally strangled. As previously with Winegar, the case against Frankman seemed to be building fast.

"What was the name of Winegar's mother, Phil?" Father Dowling asked.

"Elena."

Father Dowling went downtown to talk with Frankman, and his old classmate was pathetically pleased to see him. And going crazy being locked up.

"Roger, I've got a business that depends on me. I cannot delegate what I do. As we sit here, money is being lost, at least it could be. I don't know. They won't let me have a computer in here. If I had a modem connection to my office computer, I could keep abreast of things."

Father Dowling agreed that arrest must be more than an inconvenience.

"Amos Cadbury is not returning my calls, Roger."

"He may not be the lawyer for this sort of thing."

"What do you think of Tuttle?"

"More than I did. But I'd try for someone else."

"Advise me, Roger."

They talked about lawyers, and Father Dowling said he would ask Amos Cadbury's advice immediately.

"I don't think the police have figured out yet what you were interested in doing."

Frankman looked at the priest. "And you have?"

"She was your first wife, wasn't she?"

Frankman's sigh seemed to release a world of frustration. "I knew she'd had a child and given it up. Whatever trouble Winegar was in had nothing to do with her. It certainly had nothing to do with me. Well, the papers this morning show you what I feared could happen to me."

"And what else did you do to prevent that happening, Bob?" He added, "That is what the police will be asking."

"Talk with Cadbury, Roger. I want a lawyer."

Amos Cadbury was even more pained by the notoriety accorded Bob Frankman than Marie Murkin was. But he did not share her view that Frankman was being unfairly treated because he was a laicized priest. He was described variously as a retired, resigned, defrocked, ousted, and former priest. FROM GOD TO CAESAR was one headline and, more tendentious still, THE JUDAS FACTOR.

"He should have had a lawyer from the beginning, Father."

"I think he hoped that would be you."

Amos did not comment on this. "There is a young man here named Roper who may be just the man. I will send him over to speak with Frankman."

He made a call, and a moment later Roper appeared. He listened to Amos in a way that suggested that if the senior partner asked him to jump out the window he would do that. Of course, Amos had introduced Roper to Father Dowling before doing anything else.

"He went to Notre Dame," Amos said when Roper had gone.

"You do stick together, don't you?"

"He is an excellent lawyer."

"I never doubted it."

"What on earth is Frankman up to, Father?"

Amos listened to what seemed the explanation: possible embarrassment to Frankman and his firm if the media got hold of the fact that he had married and then divorced the woman who had given birth to Winegar and then put him in an orphanage.

"A man who has left the priesthood, married, divorced, married again, and left his family is worried about that?"

"It is a motive, Amos, if not a reason, if by reason you mean something logical."

"And of what is it the motive, Father Dowling?"

He left Amos to meditate on that. The suppression of that information would give an explanation for what Frankman had done at St. Peter's and at the courthouse. Dolores Corcoran reenacted for the television cameras what Frankman had tried to get her to do. The screen filled with the item

316

shown on her monitor, and the name Elena Winegar was clearly visible. Sooner or later the connection would be made.

But the brazenness with which Bob Frankman had gone about trying to remove even a remote link between himself and Winegar was striking.

And he had lied to Gloria and then to the police about not taking the document he had burned in his fireplace. This was the portrait of a man who would go to great extremes to keep secret the fact that Winegar's mother had been the housekeeper with whom Bob Frankman ran off and married before a justice of the peace.

"I wonder if she's still alive," Marie said.

"Are rectory housekeepers mortal?"

"And I wonder what Jerome Winegar makes of all this."

The recent turn of events had increased Phil Keegan's respect for Cy Horvath. After the disheartening outcome of the Winegar trial, rather than say that Plover had blown a good case, that they had done all they could have done, Cy had asked himself what the evidence would look like if they took seriously the thought that Winegar was innocent.

"It was not a declaration of innocence," Agnes Lamb had reminded him.

"If we are going to nail anyone with the Striker killing, we have to start over."

Agnes wanted to talk about the girl reporter, and that was important, but Cy asked for clearance to reopen the investigation, and Phil told him to go ahead. Cy's reports had taken him to the point of asking whether the theft of the Winegar papers had not been an inside job, and in a list of possibilities appeared the name of Bob Frankman. Gloria's call—of course, she had been on the list as well—had strengthened this line of inquiry.

"But what's it get us?" Cy asked, determined, it seemed, not to derive any satisfaction from this turn of events.

"The guy who stole the papers. Those papers have always been a big deal. Big enough to steal. Big enough to kill for." Agnes was being very patient. "To bribe for, to lie for, to burn."

"That's the mistake we made before."

"What's the mistake we made before?"

"Jumbling everything together. Look, if Frankman stole the papers before, we would never have known about it. Gloria says she might never have missed them. His interest was to destroy them, or at least one of them. Instead, the papers are used to nail Winegar."

"They're planted on him?"

"You think he stole them? He said he didn't. Why would he? What interest do they have for him?"

At the time it had been easy to say that Winegar took the papers because he had come back to destroy his past: That's why he killed Striker; that's why he removed any record of his stay at St. Peter's.

"That would have made sense if he came back anonymously, did these things, and then vamoosed."

"Vamoosed?"

"Left."

"Is that Hungarian?"

"Instead, he comes back and cuts a pretty big swath. It's no secret that Winegar's back in town. Striker is killed and he sticks around." Cy shook his head.

"So we have two thefts of the same papers?"

"And two thieves?"

This was not a welcome conclusion. It was more attractive to have a unified theory. But any way they tried it, it made no sense. Frankman definitely took the papers the second time, but no effort to identify him as the first thief made any sense.

Meanwhile, Roper had demanded that charges be filed or Frankman be released. What they had against him was not a capital crime, and with him on the streets, the media would cover their own excitement over his arrest by blaming the police for seeking a scapegoat for their unsolved murders.

"I thought we had Lucy Sommers's murderer."

"Maybe we do."

Keegan asked Cy to expand on the point.

"Frankman was a man desperate to get hold of those papers. Maybe his first visit to the girl's apartment was a failed attempt to get them. He fails, we find them in the apartment, along with the Demerol and needles. Later when the girl publishes that picture, he panics."

"The prosecutor will need more, Cy."

"There is more."

"What's that?"

"Winegar. I think he can identify Frankman as the man who posed as the former tenant."

Agnes said, "If he killed her, he would have killed Winegar too, wouldn't he?"

"Get hold of Winegar, Cy."

"He came by St. Hilary's and asked Willie what he knew of the Walshes."

"Where's he living?"

"Maybe down at Jude Thaddeus House."

Keegan sent Cy and Agnes to see. He himself undertook to talk to the Walshes.

"I'm just on my way to the office, Captain," James Walsh said when Phil called the house.

"Could I talk to Mrs. Walsh?"

"I'm sorry. She's not here."

"I'll meet you at your office then."

"My appointments start in forty-five minutes."

Some schedule—begin at ten, finish when? When Phil's girls were young and fluoride had made cavities a thing of the past, people had said that dentistry would go the way of phrenology. If Walsh was any indication, dentistry was thriving. At least dental surgery.

"I do open mouth surgery," Walsh said, and waited for a laugh.

He was already wearing his green operating outfit and what looked like white jogging shoes with two-inch soles. His setup was high-tech efficiency. He could have three patients in different chairs at different stages of a root canal.

"My patients are all referrals from other dentists."

The waiting room had been filling up; nurses were hustling about with clipboards; phones were ringing. Walsh's office was full of family pictures.

"What is it, Captain?"

"We're back on your father-in-law's death, Doctor. We arrested Robert Frankman last night."

"It's about time."

"How do you mean?"

"The man's incompetent. He lost money for the school; he lost money for me."

"Do you read the papers?"

"The *Wall Street Journal.*"

"This isn't about his business failings. He broke into St. Peter's school and removed some records. He also tried to bribe a county official to alter records."

"What records?"

"Jerome Winegar's."

Walsh's shoes made a complaining noise on the floor as he drew in his feet. "Winegar!"

"That's right."

"Were they in it together?"

"We're looking for Winegar so we can ask him."

"Why are you coming to me?"

"Winegar was making inquiries about your family."

Walsh became agitated. "He was! Why did they let him go? He shouldn't be running around free. Everyone knows he killed Mitch Striker."

"Did he get in contact with you or your wife?"

Walsh got to his feet, checking a watch that looked as if it told time on Mars. "You think he's after us too? Does he intend to wipe out the entire family? You better lock that man up, Captain."

"Where is your wife?"

"Safe, thank God."

"Where?"

He had come around the desk and was looking at the watch again. Then he looked at Keegan.

"I'm not going to tell you that. She's where he can't find her. I suggest that you concentrate on finding Winegar."

Cy Horvath had not yet found him either.

"Maybe Kate Striker would know where Mrs. Walsh is."

"Do you think it really matters where she is, Cy?"

"Probably not. You got anything better for me to do?"

"I guess not."

78

Father Dowling asked Phil Keegan to stay for lunch after the noon mass, but his old friend reluctantly turned him down.

"We're chasing a lot of false leads. We can't find Winegar. We can't find Mrs. Walsh."

"Are they connected?"

Phil shrugged. "Who knows? I said they were false leads."

For a moment Father Dowling wondered whether the big secret had been discovered and the old love affair between Winegar and Mitchell Striker's daughter recognized as the cause of the expulsion of Winegar from St. Peter's.

"Apparently he asked Willie about the Walshes."

"Willie!" Marie cried. "What would he know about the Walshes?"

Having lunch alone, his mood still half contemplative from celebrating the mass, Father Dowling thought of all the things that had happened since Jerome Winegar had come back to Fox River. The return of the exile had stirred up memories of events of two decades before, when he had been expelled from St. Peter's and the possibility of a brilliant future had been snatched from him.

Because he would not marry the girl he had got with child.

Because he repudiated the child and spurned the girl.

Terrible as those were in themselves, they had become high treason when committed against the daughter of Mitchell Striker. It was inconceivable that such a boy should continue as a student at St. Peter's. Nancy had her child; it was given up for adoption; she had never known it. All this had been arranged by her father. And all traces of the child, of its connection with Nancy and above all with Jerome Winegar, were absent from the public record.

But equally untraceable was the child that the Strikers then adopted, as if they could substitute one child for the other. But, it was the same child. Nancy had had to guess this; Mitchell Striker did not tell even her what he had done. It was the child's relation to him, rather than to Nancy, that weighed heaviest in his appraisal.

After the death of Striker, Kate became obsessed with finding out who she really was. To discover that would be to learn that she was the daughter of the man accused of killing her adoptive father, whom she would then know to have been her grandfather. Her maternal grandfather. And Nancy, the beloved sister, would be revealed as her mother.

Nancy had her father's pride and was determined that Kate should not learn that Winegar was her father. Father Dowling was sure that the freeing of Winegar by the judge had not altered Nancy's resolve to keep from Kate knowledge of her origins, even if that meant continuing to conceal that they were mother and daughter.

"If Jerome Winegar wanted to know about the Walshes, why on earth wouldn't he ask someone who knew?"

"Like yourself?"

Marie Murkin bobbed her head once. "I knew them from the time they were members of this parish."

"The Walshes?"

"The Walshes never amounted to much. The Strikers."

"And then they rose in the world."

"St. Hilary's was a far more fashionable parish in those days. And Mitchell Striker was worth plenty then too. Why, they had a lake place in Wisconsin."

"Is that right?"

"Of course it's right. The family spent most of the summer there, and the odd weekend."

In his study, the pastor tried to put these thoughts out of his mind. He took down the *Summa theologiae* and began to read the discussion of prudence. St. Thomas cited the Book of Wisdom in the Vulgate: *incertae sunt providentiae nostrae.* Our providences are uncertain? Better, our foresight is unsure. Our predictions chancy. We cannot see around the corner of time but can only guess from turning past corners what may lie ahead. It is on such a flimsy basis that we must act. He picked up the phone and called Manresa and asked to speak with Kate Striker.

"I just got back from there," she said, when he asked about the lake place in Wisconsin.

322

"Is your sister there?"

"Guess who else is there?"

"Jerome Winegar."

"How would you know a thing like that!"

"I don't know. Our foresight is unsure."

He asked her where precisely the lake cottage was located, and the directions got very complicated.

"Are you planning on going there?"

"I thought I would."

"You'll never find it, not the first time." She paused. "Come through Milwaukee and I'll take you there."

"But you just got back."

"And was wondering why I left. What was that you said?"

"Our foresight is unsure."

"Yeah. Do you need directions to Manresa?"

Finding Manresa was easier than following the campus directions he got from the guard at the gate. He was about to return to the entrance for clarification when he saw Kate sitting on the front steps of a resident building. She responded to his honking but came toward the car with an amazed look.

She stood next to the car, shaking her head. "I'm surprised you got this far."

"There are a lot of miles left in this car."

Kate got in. What the heck. It was better than driving all the way back to the lake herself.

"I didn't ask why it's so urgent that you see Nancy."

"Did I say it was urgent?"

"Driving this heap over twenty-five miles is my definition of urgency."

"Listen, it's paid for."

Maybe she would buy the parish a new car, if he would take it. She sensed in Father Dowling a preference for the car they were in.

"Is that gauge right? Ninety thousand miles!"

"It's gone around once already."

"Good grief." Her own jeepster had four thousand miles on it. "If we were in my car, we could phone ahead and tell them we're coming."

"Do you want to find a phone?"

And say she was coming back for *The Wings of the Dove?* No thanks. No matter what, Nan was going to think she was coming back to check up on her and Winegar.

"What beautiful country this is," Father Dowling said.

"Wait till we get off these main roads."

"This is a main road?"

The road that led to the lake was blacktopped, but that was only to hold down the dust. It followed the contours of the land, curved all over the place, and the curves were not banked, so you had to slow to a crawl.

"How did Winegar find this place?"

"I think he had been there before."

Cy called St. Hilary's to see if Phil Keegan was there.

"He didn't even stay for lunch," Marie said.

"Let me talk to Father Dowling."

"He's gone to Wisconsin."

"Wisconsin!"

"The Strikers have a lake place up there. He went to Milwaukee to pick up Kate, and they were going on to the lake."

"Where is it?"

"In Wisconsin!"

"That narrows it down. Do you know where in Wisconsin?"

"How would I know a thing like that?"

Agnes reported that she had had no luck tracing Mrs. Walsh.

"I think she's in Wisconsin."

"You going to take me across a state line?"

"You've been emancipated, haven't you?"

"Whoa. Do you mean in the slave sense or in the feminist sense?"

But Cy was thinking of Mitchell Striker's apartment at the Walsh residence. There had been a little stack of homemade maps on Striker's desk. Directions to the lake?

"What do you say to a little breaking and entering, Agnes?"

"Why not?"

"Remember the Striker apartment?"

"Why break and enter? I think we still have the key downtown."

She did. After pulling in the driveway and ringing the front bell several times, they went around to the back of the house and opened the outside door of the apartment. The maps were where Cy remembered them. Directions to the lake.

"You drive and I'll map-read."

"The Mann Act got you that worried?" Agnes said.

"This is verging on sexual harassment."

"Tell me where to go."

324

"Well, I'll tell you where to drive. Hey, know who that was?" A white sports car had just zinged by them. Cy turned and watched it enter the Walsh drive. "That's James Walsh, DDS. Pull over."

It wasn't ten minutes before the white car nosed down the driveway and started toward them. They bumped heads as they ducked out of sight.

"Follow that car."

"I thought we were going to the lake."

It turned out to be the same thing. Only they were no match for a sports car driven by someone who knew where he was going.

"Forget him," Cy said when Agnes was trying unsuccessfully to close the distance between them and the sports car on the crowded four-lane going north. "We can follow the map."

After Kate left, Nancy felt oddly relaxed. It had seemed impossible that the three of them should be together long, she and Kate and Jerry, without some intimation coming to the other two.

"Twenty years," Jerry said.

"You joined the army."

"I couldn't find the recruiting office for the foreign legion. The army was bad enough. I went to Vietnam. Twice."

"Was it horrible?"

"Not as bad as having a baby alone."

She thought of those long bleak days of waiting for something that, when it came, was as though it hadn't happened. Being with other girls in the same predicament was partly consoling but partly annoying, as if what she had done was not unique.

"I don't blame you for not answering my letters."

She looked at him. He was serious. "What letters?"

"My first stint in Vietnam, I began to write you these long long letters. I'd add to them until they were huge and then mail them off."

"Jerry, I never received any letters. Where did you send them?"

"To you."

"At home?"

"Where else?"

She looked at him and they both understood what had happened. All these years she had hated his cruelty, and he had been cruel, all the crueler for never writing.

"What did your letters say?"

"That I was sorry." He leaned back and looked up through the branches of the tree at the sky above. "I thought we could keep our baby and I would go to school the way I had planned. I had already taken the SATs." He looked at her. "I aced them."

"I'm sure you did." She didn't know what to say. He was suggesting that there was a life together they might have lived, the three of them. But that is what she had thought she could never have, so she had hated him and tried to forget him and married Jim and had her boys.

"When I got back that first time, I called."

"You telephoned!"

"Your father told me if I ever tried to reach you again he would have me arrested. He said you had recovered, you didn't want to see me. . . ."

"Jerry, I knew none of this."

"So I volunteered to go back."

"Oh my God." Her heart was pounding within her and her mind was spinning. She had to tell him now. "Jerry, you know Kate."

"Of course."

"Do you know who she is?"

They looked deeply into one another's eyes, watching the play of thought on the other's face, the flicker of recognition of what was and of what might have been and what could never be now, and he understood it all.

"Kate?" He said the name with reverent wonder.

"Kate."

He got up, came to her, and took her hand, and she too got to her feet and faced the man to whom she had given her first love, whose child she had borne, who had wanted to come back to her and their child. He was drawing her closer, across the decades, and she wanted so much to let him take her in his arms.

But no. She stepped back, shaking her head. He took her wrists and again pulled her toward him. She tried to pull free, but he hung on to her wrists, trying desperately now to fill the void of the last two decades, but other things had happened; she was not free. She began to sob. "Please. Don't. Don't!"

"Let her go!"

They turned and there was Jim, his face twisted with rage. He was carrying a gun. Winegar let go of her and she stumbled toward the house, toward Jim. He didn't understand. She was nearly to him when the shot rang out.

She turned. Jim was holding the butt of the gun against his shoulder and sighting along the barrel as if he were at the rifle range. Jerry faced him, a startled expression on his face. His shirt front was beginning to discolor. He looked down; he put his hands to his chest; he looked at Jim.

"Jim!" Nan screamed, and lunged at her husband. And a second shot sounded, slapping off the trees. Nan spun from the impact of the bullet, crashing into a patio chair. Winegar started forward, arms outstretched, as if to welcome the third blast from the rifle. He stopped, his face horribly full of blood, and then he stumbled and fell forward.

From far across the lake the echo of the three shots returned.

During the days that followed, Marie Murkin sought in vain for an appropriate attitude toward what had happened, and Father Dowling found himself reluctant to offer her the usual sort of explanation. Well, not explanation, but a reason to accept what had happened as part of a benevolent plan. He heard the housekeeper engage herself in dialogue in the kitchen, and more than once, after she had set dishes on the dining room table, she would pause as if she had finally hit on what she wanted to say. But after a moment she would push through the swinging door into her kitchen. Phil Keegan was equally affected.

"A hell of a thing, Roger."

What stuck in his own mind was how so many of them had converged on that lake cottage almost simultaneously. When he had turned off the road onto the non-Euclidean tracks that led to the cabin, Kate had sat forward.

"Jim's here. That's his car."

There was an anxious edge to her voice that he had not understood until later. "He must have been in a rush."

The driver's door of the sports car was ajar, and Kate shoved it shut when she went past it toward the cottage. She moved as if drawn forward against her will now, and Father Dowling followed. He had just come around the corner of the cottage and in view of the patio when the first shot rang out.

He had described that scene again and again. The local sheriff reacted ambiguously to the presence of a captain, lieutenant, and detective from the Fox River, Illinois, police department apparently pursuing their business in his jurisdiction. "Hot pursuit," Phil told him. "We're at your disposal, Sheriff."

Such courtesy placated the sheriff, and Phil and his colleagues carried on.

"What did you see when you came round the corner, Roger?"

"The lake."

"Didn't you say you heard a shot?"

He would never again be critical of the testimony of others to important events. He was called an eyewitness of what had happened, but it had taken him at least a full minute to put together what his senses reported. He had been conscious of the great blue expanse of the lake and the edging of pine trees on the far shore. Jim Walsh was pointing his rifle at Winegar, whose expression was the pained surprise of the combat veteran when the shot meant for him has finally been fired. Winegar put his hand to his shirt front as if in slow motion and then took it away. He looked at Jim Walsh. He shook his head, but then his expression changed and he charged desperately at Walsh. Nancy Walsh's scream faded into the second shot as she leaped between her husband and Winegar. She was sent spinning across the patio when the cartridge meant for Winegar tore through her chest.

"And then he fired again?"

"He must have."

"You were there. Didn't you see it?"

What he had seen was Nancy falling and the patio chair she reached for toppling too. The third shot roared above his head as he knelt beside Nancy, his lips forming the words of absolution. Her eyes found his as he prayed over her, and then seemed to turn off, their inner light gone. He stood, pushing Walsh aside, and went to Winegar.

"He was forcing himself on my wife!" Walsh cried. And then, "Oh, my God!"

Winegar was still conscious when Father Dowling traced the sign of the cross over him. The dying man nodded as if in assent.

Only later did Roger come to know what had happened, what he had been eyewitness of, the larger story pieced together from such pieces as he had provided. Kate had wrestled the rifle from Jim Walsh's hands and was holding it when Cy Horvath came barreling around the corner of the cottage, followed by Agnes Lamb. The poor girl was wrestled to the ground and her wrists manacled behind her back. She went into shock then, so it was minutes before Cy found out who had done the shooting.

"He was forcing my wife!"

Walsh repeated this statement again and again to whomever would listen and then to the world at large. When Phil Keegan arrived, Walsh gave his explanation to Phil and then to the sheriff when he got there. The sheriff's daughter edited the local weekly, but her father's account of the crime of passion at the Striker place prompted her to put through a call to Milwaukee and then to Chicago. For two full days the story was treated as a wronged husband's invocation of the unwritten law in the wilds of Wisconsin. Only Kate's insistence that the two victims had been renewing an old acquaintance, that it was nothing like what Jim thought at all, finally made it clear that the supposed danger to his wife existed only in Jim Walsh's mind and not in the real world.

"Nan tried to stop him," Kate pointed out, her voice breaking. "She tried to shield Winegar from the second shot."

And she had succeeded. It was the third shot that placed Winegar beyond hope. Still, there remained a disposition to excuse what Walsh had done. A tragic misconception became the recurrent phrase in accounts of the episode. Media interest lasted almost a week, then faded before fresher fare for the jaded reader and viewer.

In prosecutor Plover's office the preferred explanation was money, with Kate the true target of Jim Walsh's rifle.

"Old man Striker left that girl millions, while Walsh was losing big in an effort to recoup earlier losses."

"He was using the girl's money," Pep Ardmore added.

Frankman, out on bail, had justified his own strange behavior as an effort to wrest control of Kate Striker's money from Jim Walsh.

"You have to bear me out on this, Roger," he pleaded, sitting on the edge of a straight-backed chair in Father Dowling's study, hands cupping his knees, leaning toward his old classmate.

"Is it relevant?"

Frankman sat back, his shoulders slumped. "You sound like Amos Cadbury."

Amos Cadbury was the only one with whom Father Dowling felt fully at ease discussing the drama that had played itself out in the Striker family. They consulted each other on their problems of conscience.

"Am I absolved of my promise to Mitchell Striker, Father?"

"You want to tell Kate who she really is?"

"Should it matter anymore? Perhaps not to you and me, but it does to her."

Father Dowling had concelebrated the funeral mass for Nancy Walsh with Panzica, her pastor.

"You preach, Roger. I think you knew the family better than I did."

He agreed to preach but inwardly rejected the suggestion that he had really known any of them. The Mitchell Striker he had known was a slightly comic bore who wished to discuss financial futures with a group of people nearing the end of their lives. He had been oblivious of the infatuation Barbara Rooney had felt for him, another comic note. But the past of the man revealed a moral monster who had come to his daughter's defense by ruining the life of Jerome Winegar and raising Nancy's daughter as her adopted sister. When Nancy ultimately guessed the truth, she had been afraid to talk about it with her father, preferring the long pretense he had engineered.

His sermon was made up of the thoughts he had been unwilling to formulate for Marie Murkin. Providence is not always a cheerful truth when we are made conscious of it, since it is usually undeserved evil that raises the question. Few wonder why good things happen to us, good things we do not deserve and did not expect. Finally, it is the Book of Job that provides such consolation as there is. The Lord gives and the Lord takes away. Blessed be the name of the Lord.

A problem of etiquette arose with respect to Jim Walsh's attendance at his wife's funeral. He had, after all, killed her, and the fact that it was accidental did little to lessen the horror. Kate, God bless her, solved the problem by insisting that they sit side by side in the front pew. It was Walsh who began to sob and had to be comforted by Kate. The reaction to Walsh's grief was ambiguous.

"Painless dentistry," Panzica growled in the sacristy.

"You going to the cemetery?" Dowling asked.

"It would be a great help if I didn't have to."

Those who came on to the burial took their cue from Kate and offered comfort to the weeping husband.

"He was forcing himself on her," Walsh was saying when McDivitt led him back to one of his limousines. "That's why I did it."

"It's ironic, Father," Kate said when she had come to thank him. "The only blood relatives now are the boys, and they weren't here."

Nancy's children had been whisked away from the awfulness, taken to Florida by Clara Ponader.

Kate came to the funeral mass Father Dowling offered for Jerome Winegar the following day. The few words he said by way of homily returned to the baffling subject of the meaning of life. Tracing the line of Winegar's life, it was difficult to see what it added up to. But Nancy Walsh's life, when scrutinized, was equally odd, a mishmash of the understandable and the absurd. And her father's life as well. Everyone's, when you stop to think of it. What seems to sap life of meaning is the inescapable fact that it must end in death.

"That, my dear friends, is a mystery deeper than life. If death is the ultimate victor, all life's battles are lost, no matter the short-term gains. But you and I are here in the confidence that death is not the end. We are destined for a life beyond this one, a life that shall never end."

At the graveside Marie Murkin wept, and Barbara Rooney too. Edna had a far-off look in her eye. Willie stood next to Marjorie White, head down, the toes of his loafers lifting and falling. Tuttle clutched his tweed hat in both hands and frowned at the casket. Father Dowling remembered the little lawyer's gracious actions when Lucy Sommers was buried in this same cemetery.

"Why did Winegar go up to Wisconsin in the first place?" Phil asked some days later. He had come to dinner, and they were finished but still at table, having been joined by Marie.

"To see the daughter," Marie said.

"Daughter?"

"Of Mitchell Striker. The man who had ruined his life."

Phil looked at Roger Dowling. "Do you know Dr. Pippen's new theory about Striker's death?"

"What?"

"Actually it's a new version of an old one. Frankman did it."

"Frankman!"

"That's right. He killed Striker because he publicly questioned his professional competence. He also killed that reporter, Lucy Sommers."

"Why?"

"She surprised him when he was planting evidence to strengthen the case against Winegar."

"Well, Frankman did wear a beard that he shaved off after that picture appeared."

Phil recalled that he had gone in pursuit of Winegar to see if he could

331

identify Frankman as the bearded stranger who had claimed to be the former tenant of Lucy Sommers's apartment.

"Wasn't there a building manager there, Phil?"

Phil stared at the priest for a moment. "Let me use your phone."

Thus it was that Hilda Lilienthal was brought face-to-face with Robert Frankman and identified him as the man who had visited Lucy.

"He had a beard then. But he was never a tenant."

Plover indicted Frankman with a maximum of public posturing, eager to make up for his loss to Tuttle.

Amos Cadbury understandably wondered what further secrets the client he had reluctantly accepted for the firm might have. Roger Dowling visited his old classmate.

"Did you go to that apartment, Bob?"

"Yes. And I put the papers there. I was certain Winegar had killed Mitchell Striker and I wanted the trial over. You know why. I was fearful my connection with his mother would become public. My God." His eyes filled with wonder at what he had once feared might cloud his name. Now he had been indicted for murder. "That's nonsense, I killed no one."

Plover was bringing him to trial for the murder of Lucy Sommers, but the grand jury was ready to indict Frankman for the murders of Gerry Major and Mitchell Striker. Motive? Frankman wanted revenge on Striker. The planted records were meant to divert suspicion to Winegar as well as tarnish Striker's name. The fact that Bob admitted planting the papers in Lucy's apartment was taken to be a first installment on a full confession.

In the rectory study, Roger Dowling and Phil Keegan went through it all again and again, from the rainy night when Mitchell Striker's body was found in his car in the parish parking lot through the arrest of Winegar and the gathering of evidence that had seemed to insure his conviction. Phil resisted the cogency of the case Plover would bring against Frankman but increasingly came to accept it.

The secrets to which Roger was privy had seemed to strengthen the case for Winegar's guilt, but they had remained secret. No one had asked why Mitchell Striker had proved to be such a relentless enforcer of the rules of St. Peter's School, but it was the blighting of Winegar's prospects by Striker that had seemed motive enough.

"If that girl hadn't been killed, Winegar would be serving a life sentence right now."

"And still alive."

Mitchell Striker's vendetta against Winegar could cast doubt on Frankman's supposed responsibility for Striker's death, but in this matter Amos Cadbury was in an unenviable position.

"It was shrewd of Plover to bring him to trial for the death of the girl," Amos said. Roger Dowling took the lawyer to be saying that this relieved him of a good deal of pressure to save his firm's client by revealing what he and Mitchell Striker had done so many years ago. Those secrets would show that Winegar had far stronger reason to kill his old nemesis than Bob Frankman. Plover looked to have smooth sailing in gaining a conviction on the charge of the garroting of Lucy Sommers.

The prosecutor might want only the conviction he could get, but Phil Keegan had two deaths to account for: Striker's and Gerry Major's. And Plover's scenario assigned Frankman conflicting roles. On the one hand, he planted evidence to insure Winegar's conviction and to divert attention from the fact that it was he who had killed Striker. But by killing the girl he had effectively freed Winegar.

Of course, he need not have intended that. In any case, it was no part of Plover's plan to convict him of anything other than the murder of Lucy Sommers. Faced with the prospect of two unsolved murders, Phil took little comfort from Roger Dowling's reminder that there was a file full of unsolved murders downtown. Father Dowling's own speculations on what had really happened seemed as wild as anything Dr. Pippen had dreamed up. That is why he kept it to himself for so long.

Two weeks later Kate telephoned, her voice oddly remote.

"I've got to see you."

"What is it?"

"There's no one else I can turn to."

"Are you at school?"

"No. I'm home. I'm calling you from Dad's apartment. Could you possibly come over here?"

"What did she want?" Marie asked when he went through the kitchen.

"Who?"

"Kate Striker."

"Didn't you take notes?"

"Father Dowling, I answered the phone and switched it on to you. She told me who she was. If it is a big secret that you cannot entrust to a housekeeper who has . . ."

"She asked me to come over."

"Why?"

"I have to go to find out."

"She sounded so . . ." Marie stopped, visibly searching for a word. "What did you think she sounded like?"

"Maybe it's your extension."

Kate welcomed him in an almost distracted manner and led him through the Walsh home to the apartment over the three-stall garage that had been Mitchell Striker's retirement home. The door that led to the garages below was ajar, and Kate pushed it shut as she went by it. The shelves had been emptied, and piles of books formed a box graph on the worktable Striker had used to hold the elements of his home office—computer, printer, fax, scanner.

"I was going to call you to see if you wanted any of these books."

"But that isn't why you called."

"Jim thinks it's past time we cleaned out this apartment and I agree. I've been at it a couple of days."

"Where are you taking things?"

"Those clothes are going to Jude Thaddeus." She nodded toward the full carton that had been placed on Mitch's wheeled chair and pushed next to the stairway leading to the garages. "It will be my second trip."

Father Dowling waited. Kate's manner now matched the quality of her voice on the phone: She seemed overwhelmed with wonder.

"I found these letters."

He realized that she had been carrying the packet of letters when she met him at the door.

"These are letters to Nancy, written by Jerome Winegar."

"I see. They were in your father's possession?"

"I don't think Nancy ever saw them."

"You've been reading them?"

She studied him closely. "Do you know what I've discovered?"

"I think so. Yes."

"Do you know who I really am?"

He nodded.

"Why didn't you tell me!"

He did not answer. It was not his silence that mystified her. She would wonder how her grandparents, how her mother, could have carried on such a deception, one that had been compounded since Mitchell Striker's death. Nancy had known how desperately Kate wanted to discover her origins.

"Nancy was my mother."

"Yes."

"And my father was . . ."

"Jerome Winegar."

The words were spoken but still seemed detached from their meaning, as if they were meant to shape thought rather than express it. Kate said she had known there was something special about Jerome Winegar; she had sensed it when they talked. And as for Nancy, they had always been much closer than sisters.

"She *tried* to tell me, Father. When we were at the lake together. But she couldn't do it, not then. But she would have."

"I think you're right. You have to remember that she herself didn't *know.*"

"What do you mean?"

"Mitchell Striker never discussed it with her. She guessed, but she was afraid to ask him outright."

"He must have kept these letters secret from her, Father. They go way back. Before she married Jim. If she had read them . . ."

He stayed with her for an hour, listening as she recounted events in her life that had now taken on an entirely different meaning. Was she happy to have made the discovery she had longed for? Happiness was not the word for what she felt, perhaps, but there was a firmer sense of her own worth, of the uniqueness that both set her off from and related her to others. Now she knew the bloodlines that made her the true daughter of the Striker household and rightful heir of Mitchell's millions.

"I'll help you with that," he said before he went, taking the carton of clothes from the chair beside the stairway door. Kate went before him down into the garage where her car awaited. Father Dowling was startled to see the yellow car in which the body of Mitchell Striker had been found.

Tuttle came and sat twirling his tweed hat, not getting comfortable in his chair, as if he sensed that Marie had admitted him only on sufferance. Nothing Father Dowling said could put the little lawyer at ease. There was something he had to say to the pastor of St. Hilary's.

"I never knew when Winegar was spoofing me and when he was telling the truth, but I think he was telling the truth this time. He was here that night, Father, the night Mitchell Striker was killed."

Father Dowling stopped drawing on his pipe. Had Winegar admitted guilt to his lawyer?

"He was here, and he saw the car drive in, and he saw someone get out of it."

"Someone other than Mitchell?"

"Another man."

Father Dowling sat back. "Did he say whether he got out of the back or the front of the car?"

Tuttle gave that serious thought, his hands moving over the rim of his hat as if it were a rosary. He shook his head. "No. But what he meant to tell me was that he had seen the man who must have killed Striker."

"Do you suppose he recognized him?"

Tuttle thought for a moment. "I didn't get that impression."

The little lawyer thought Father Dowling ought to know that there might be a killer still prowling about his parish. The pastor thanked him, but he did not share Tuttle's concern. Jerome Winegar might not have recognized the man who got out of Mitchell Striker's car that rainy night, but he was destined to see him again. Had he recognized him at the end?

After Tuttle left, Father Dowling telephoned Cy Horvath and asked if James Walsh had reported the theft of items from his clinic.

"Give me a minute, Father, and I'll bring it up." This apparently emetic remark referred to the computer on which Father Dowling could now hear Cy tapping. "Here it is."

"He reported it?"

"Yes."

"When?"

The date Cy gave him brought a Hungarian hum along the wire. It was two days after the death of Mitchell Striker.

"Did anyone ever check out the clinic, Cy?"

It was several hours later when Cy called back. He himself had gone to the clinic and talked with the staff. No one there knew anything about the theft of drugs and paraphernalia until Dr. Walsh reported it.

"Have you talked with Walsh?"

"It's Wednesday. He's at home. His day off. I'm going to the house."

"Let me talk to him first, Cy."

A long pause. "I'll give you an hour."

Jim Walsh was at the computer in the apartment over the garage, work-ing on his investments. The expression of baffled worry remained on his face when he turned to look at Father Dowling.

"This is a more powerful computer than mine," he said. "Luck-ier too."

Father Dowling sat on the arm of a couch. "Where's Kate?"

"You should have called first. She's gone back to school."

"I came to see you."

Walsh glanced at the monitor. Obviously he would have preferred brooding over the array of figures on the screen. Is that what wealth is, numbers that come and go like dust in the sun?

"Father, I want to thank you . . ."

The priest stopped him. "The police will be here within the hour."

"The police?"

"Yes."

"What is it?"

"A number of things. The alleged theft at your clinic, for one. That, for another." Father Dowling nodded at the screen. "You have been un-lucky, haven't you?"

"Do you really mean that about the police?"

"What did your father-in-law think when he found out you had given Bob Frankman control of your money?"

"Frankman! That man's office should be shut down."

"It is, more or less. He will be tried for the murder of Lucy Sommers."

"That brainless scheme of his nearly wiped me out."

"How much of Kate's money have you lost?"

"The market fluctuates."

"When did Mitchell Striker find out what Frankman had lost?"

Walsh turned his chair more directly toward Father Dowling as if this was a topic worth discussing.

"It's ironic. That's how he discovered what Frankman had done to the St. Peter's endowment."

"When you told him how much you had lost?"

"I didn't tell him! The window had to stay open for only two more days; that was the idea. The money would have trebled, and I would tell Mitchell what a brilliant thing I had done. Then he found out about it, he had ways, and tried to get me out. But it was too late."

"What did he do when the window closed?"

"He went immediately to St. Peter's and asked Cottage about the endowment."

"And publicly criticized Frankman."

"Yes."

"What did he say to you?"

Walsh's eyes darted about the room as if in search of some scenario different from the one his memory gave him. He looked intently at Father Dowling, and then his shoulders slumped.

"He treated me like a kid. He always had, but this was worse. I had undone all his work to provide for his children. I . . . ." But Walsh did not want to go on.

"Was that here in this room?"

"Every time."

"What do you mean?"

"It was going to be our secret; the girls were not to be told. Publicly he could take it out on Frankman. But I was to be his own private doll. He could stick pins in me whenever he felt like it, and there was nothing I could do about it. He insisted that I go with him to St. Hilary's and listen to his speech. I might learn something, though he doubted it. I had no choice."

"You went with him?"

"Father, you were there when I fired those shots at the lake. I knew what I was doing then. I *did* that and I had a reason. That reason has been accepted. He was forcing himself on Nancy. I had every right . . . ."

"What happened to Mitchell?"

Walsh hesitated and then went briskly on. "He was here, at the computer. I was there. I had made up my mind that I would not put up with any more of his sadistic condescension. He was looking at the monitor, prattling away. He must have thought that I had come up behind him so I could follow better what he was saying."

"And you injected Demerol."

"He wouldn't have felt a thing."

"And then?"

Walsh stood and put his hands on the back of the chair. He rolled it toward the stairs leading down to the garage. Father Dowling recalled his surprise at seeing the yellow car in its stall a few days ago.

"I rolled him here." Walsh had reached the door to the stairs. He opened it and his expression changed. "Good-bye, Father."

He turned, pulling the door shut behind him, and there was the sound of him clattering down the stairs. A sound that stopped abruptly. Father Dowling opened the door and looked down at James Walsh, struggling in the restraining embrace of Cy Horvath.

❧ **Epilogue** ❧

"He's as sane as I am," Marie Murkin harrumphed when James Walsh's lawyer pleaded him innocent for reasons of insanity.

"That's his plea."

She ignored this. Father Dowling had been surprised too. When he visited Walsh, the dentist had said that he was eager to pay for what he had done.

"It's worse than Mitchell's incessant nagging." He patted his chest. "My conscience will give me no rest."

Roger Dowling tried to speak of God's forgiveness, but Walsh was caught up in the drama of his own guilt. After murdering Striker, he had gone on a veritable rampage. Gerry Major was a busybody who had noticed too much about the murder. Then came Lucy, an innocent bystander, in the apartment when Walsh first came looking for Winegar. Finally Winegar himself, and Nancy. He seemed astonished, almost proud, of what he had done. And insistently ashamed.

"I would have let Winegar be punished for what I had done."

Why mention that Winegar had suffered twice because of Walsh, the second time fatally? Walsh had the volubility of a reformed drunk, wanting to wallow in the memories of his misdeeds. They ceased to be crimes for him, so how could he see them as sins?

Bob Frankman was a chastened man. He got St. Peter's into the black and then resigned from the board. In a marathon session in Father Dowling's study he had reviewed his life.

"What a mess I've made of it, Roger."

" 'The best of a bad job.' "

Frankman smiled ruefully. He had acted in that Eliot play at Mundelein.

"I'm closing my office."

"You must have more than you need."

Frankman shook his head. "I don't even want to think about investments." He peered at Roger Dowling. "It's out of the question, but you know what I would really like to do?"

Father Dowling was not surprised. Bob would want to go back to some point before which he felt things had gone wrong in his life. And that was the priesthood. But that, as he realized, was out of the question.

Kate had acquired a difficult wisdom from her ordeal. "It's selfish, but I just wish it was all over."

She meant the trial of Jim Walsh. Amos Cadbury was proceeding with arrangements that would make Kate the legal guardian of Nancy's boys.

"My half brothers," she said, wonder in her voice. "I even like them better now."

"Are they still in Florida?"

"I'll join them there, right after graduation."

Florida seemed anything but a haven at that time of year, but it would be what wasn't there that made it attractive. Kate wanted to be alone with the boys and establish the life the three of them would have together.

"Walsh tried to hire me," Tuttle said, unable to suppress his pride. "I told him I had a conflict of interest."

"What is that?"

"Lucy."

Father Dowling understood, but he did not pursue it. What a bottomless mystery is the human heart.

When Marjorie White and Willie came to the rectory to make arrangements for their wedding, Marie said she did not know whether to laugh or cry.

"Oh, be a good sport," Father Dowling advised.

"What do you mean!"

"There are lots of fish in the sea, Marie. Not many Willies, of course, but you should be able to find a substitute for him."

He dined that night with Phil Keegan at a steak house in Naperville.

"What's wrong with Marie?"

"She's indisposed."

"I was going to suggest bringing her along," Phil said.

"I'll tell her that."

If he could find a way to say it that did not sound like teasing. He did not want Marie Murkin indisposed for long.